SUNCATCHER

JOSE PIMIENTA

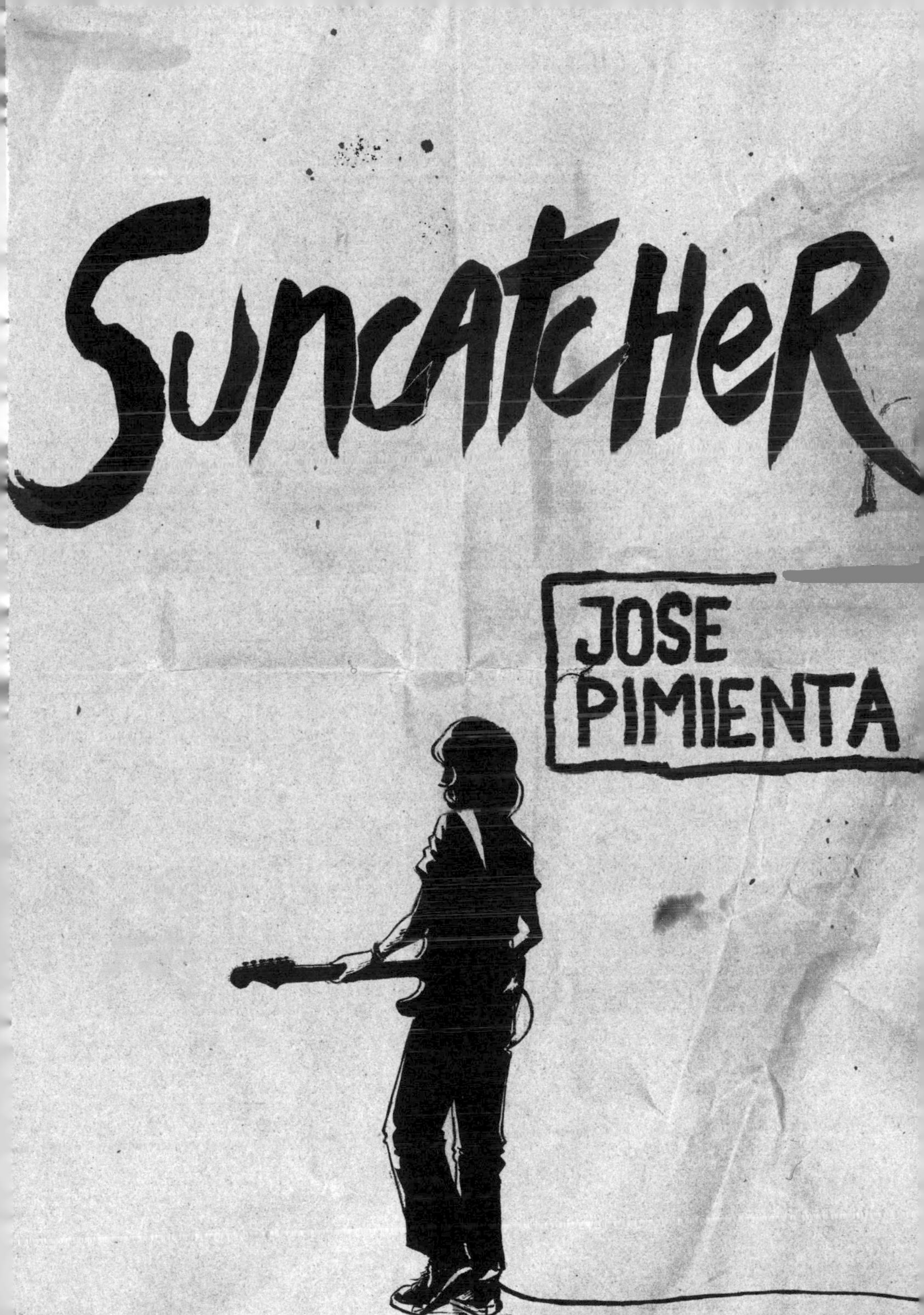

Also by Jose Pimienta
Soupy Leaves Home
The Leg

. . . .

This is a work of fiction. Names, characters, places, and incidents either are the product of the author's imagination or are used fictitiously. Any resemblance to actual persons, living or dead, events, or locales is entirely coincidental.

Cover art, text, and interior illustrations copyright © 2020 by Jose Pimienta

All rights reserved. Published in the United States by RH Graphic,
an imprint of Random House Children's Books, a division of Penguin Random House LLC, New York.
Originally published through Kickstarter in 2019.

RH Graphic with the book design is a trademark of Penguin Random House LLC.

Visit us on the Web! RHKidsGraphic.com • @RHKidsGraphic

Educators and librarians, for a variety of teaching tools, visit us at RHTeachersLibrarians.com

Library of Congress Cataloging-in-Publication Data
Name: Pimienta, Jose, author, artist.
Title: Suncatcher / Jose Pimienta.
Description: First RH Graphic edition. | New York : RH Graphic, [2020] | Audience: Ages 14–18 | Audience: Grades 10–12 | Summary: "Beatriz must play the perfect song in order to free her grandfather's soul from his guitar after he passes away"—Provided by publisher.
Identifiers: LCCN 2019026149 | ISBN 978-0-593-12481-9 (paperback) | ISBN 978-0-593-12482-6 (hardcover) ISBN 978-0-593-12525-0 (library binding) | ISBN 978-0-593-12483-3 (ebook)
Subjects: LCSH: Graphic novels. | CYAC: Graphic novels. | Music—Fiction. |
Death—Fiction. | Grandfathers—Fiction.
Classification: LCC PZ7.7.P5316 Sun 2020 | DDC 741.5/973—dc23

Designed by Patrick Crotty

MANUFACTURED IN CHINA
10 9 8 7 6 5 4 3 2 1
First RH Graphic Edition

Random House Children's Books supports the First Amendment and celebrates the right to read.

Penguin Random House LLC supports copyright. Copyright fuels creativity, encourages diverse voices, promotes free speech, and creates a vibrant culture. Thank you for buying an authorized edition of this book and for complying with copyright laws by not reproducing, scanning, or distributing any part in any form without permission. You are supporting writers and allowing Penguin Random House to publish books for every reader.

A comic on every bookshelf.

FOR THE MEXICALI BANDS
AND THEIR FANS

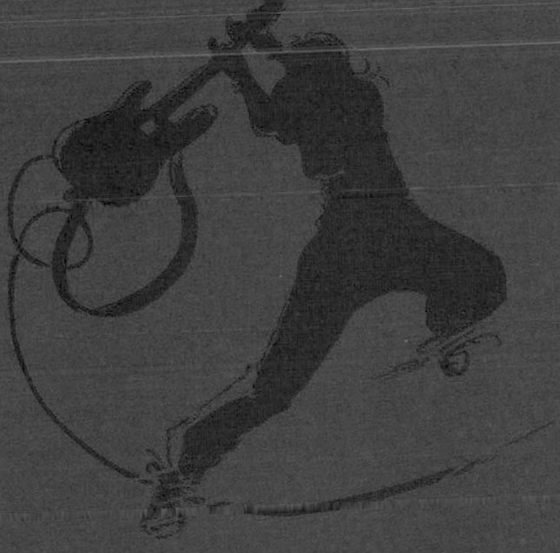

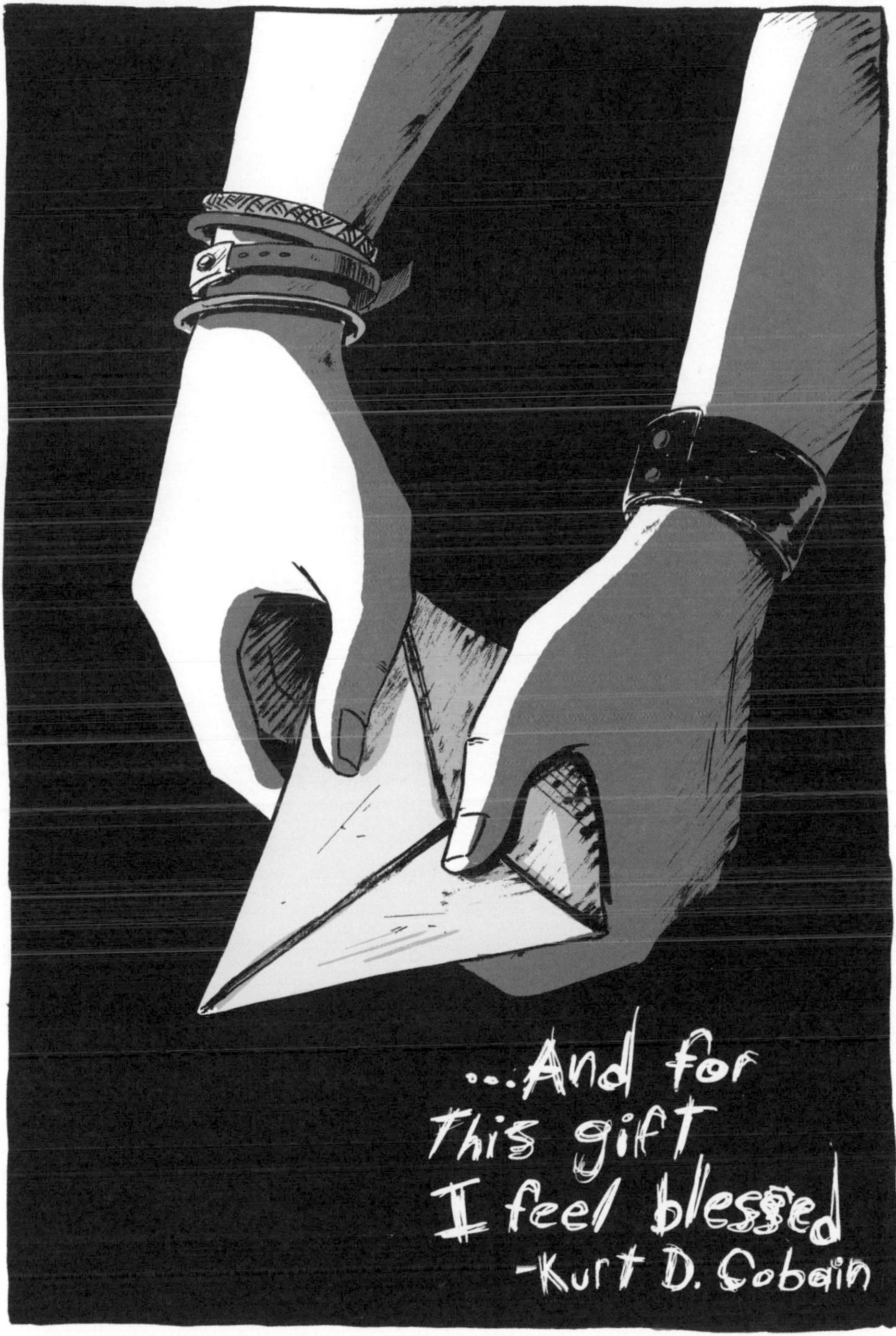
...And for
This gift
I feel blessed
-Kurt D. Cobain

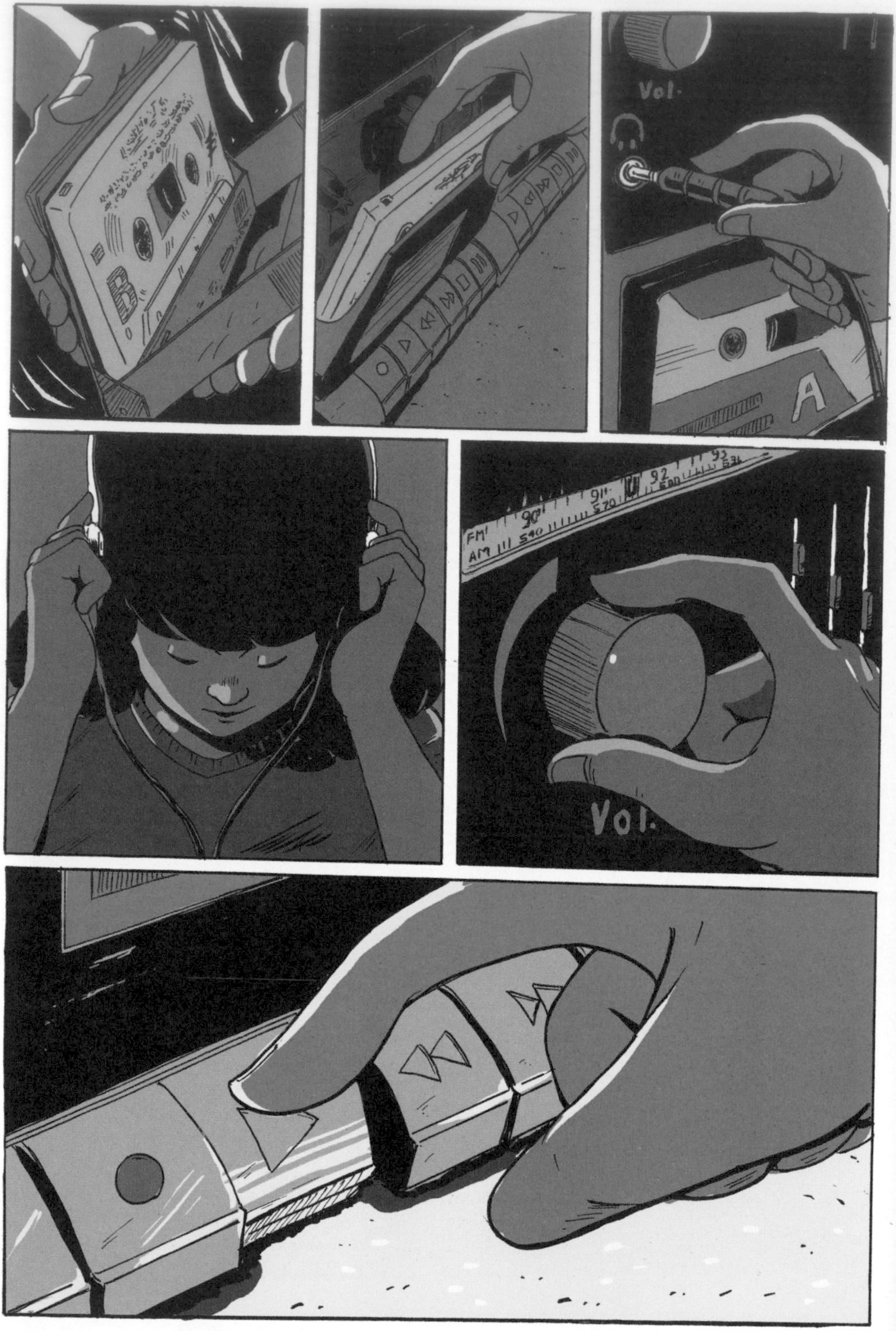
B
Vol.
A
FM
AM
90
91
92
540
570
600
Vol.

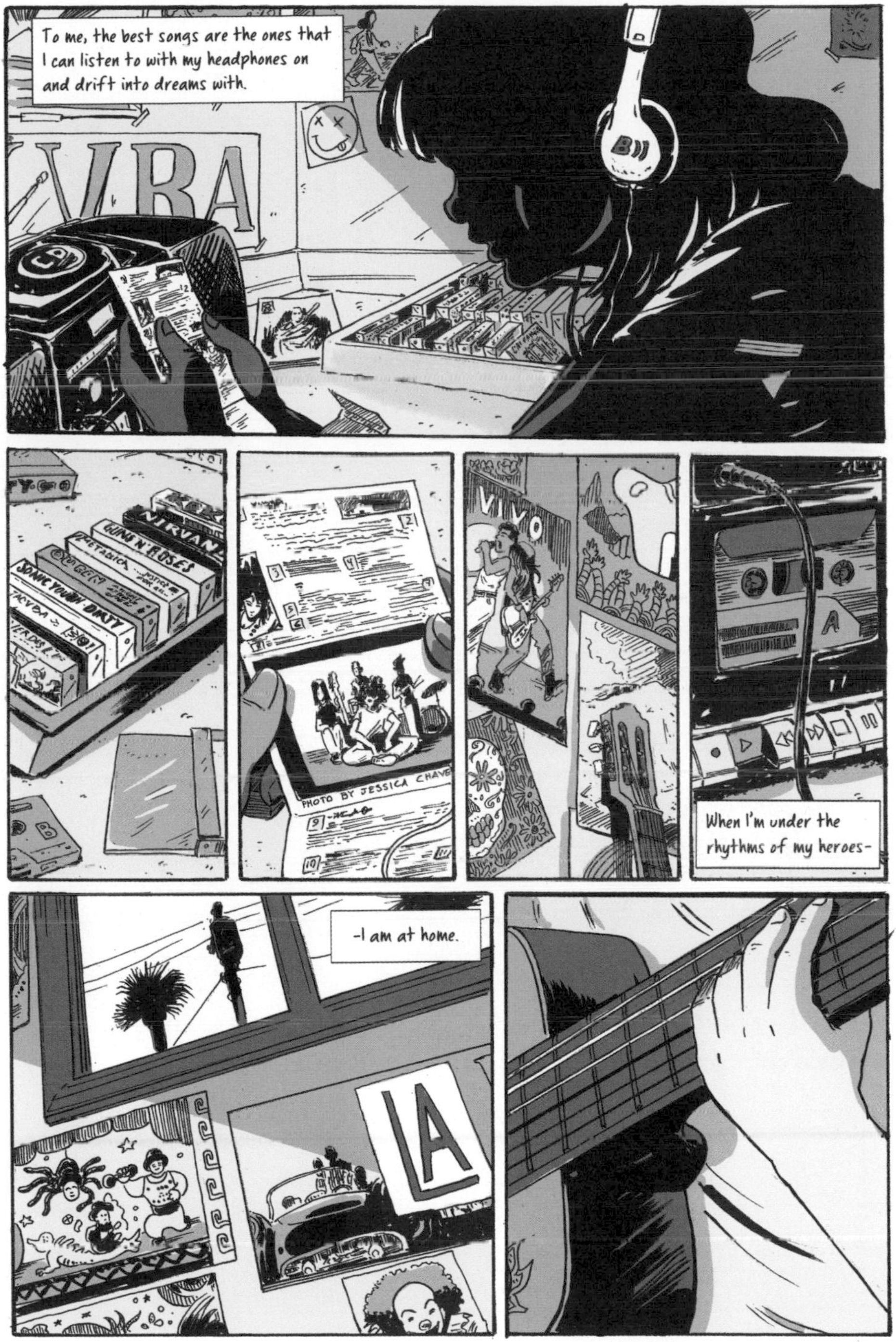
To me, the best songs are the ones that I can listen to with my headphones on and drift into dreams with.
GUNS N' ROSES
SONIC YOUTH · DIRTY
VIVO
When I'm under the rhythms of my heroes-
-I am at home.
LA

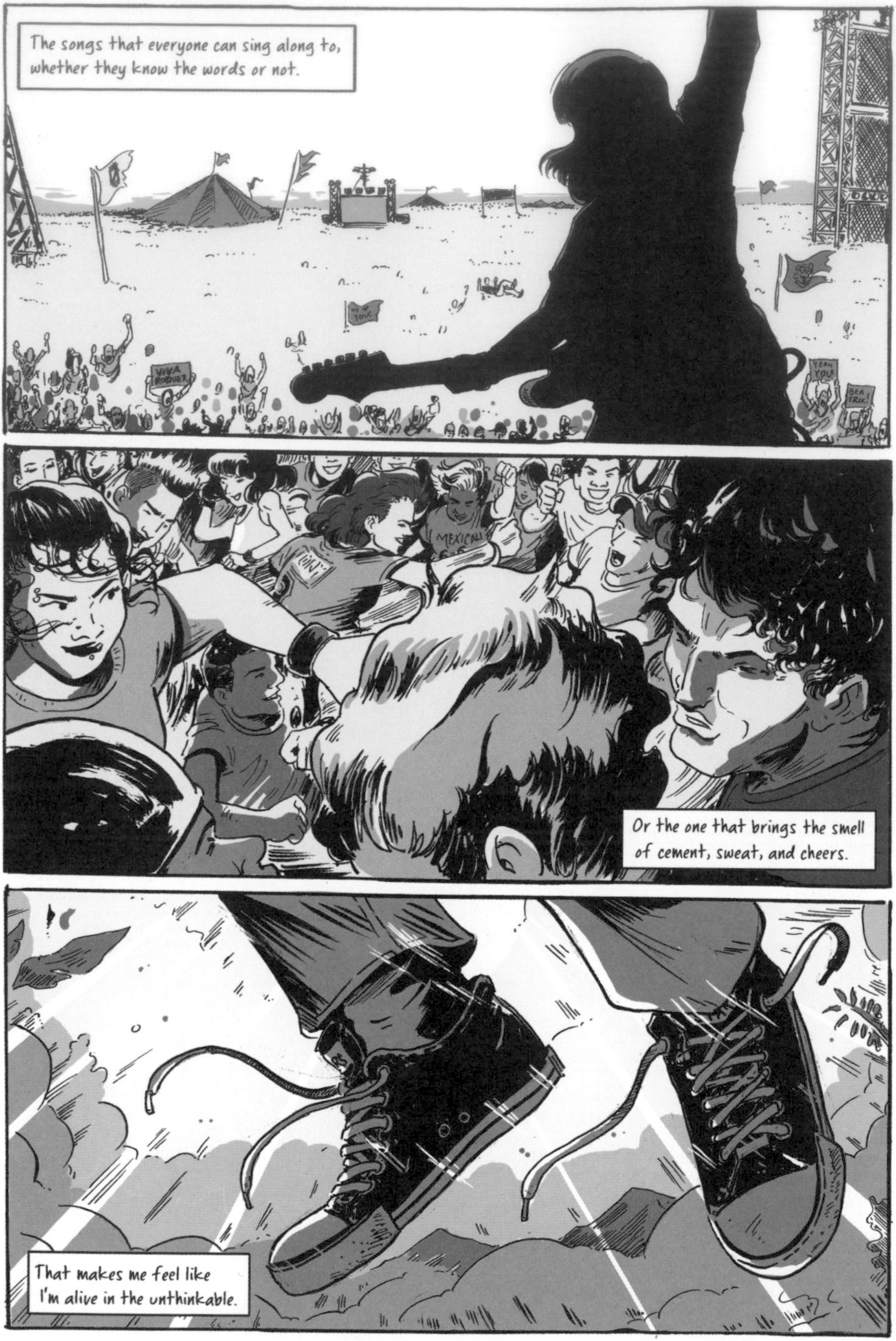
The songs that everyone can sing along to, whether they know the words or not.
Or the one that brings the smell of cement, sweat, and cheers.
That makes me feel like I'm alive in the unthinkable.

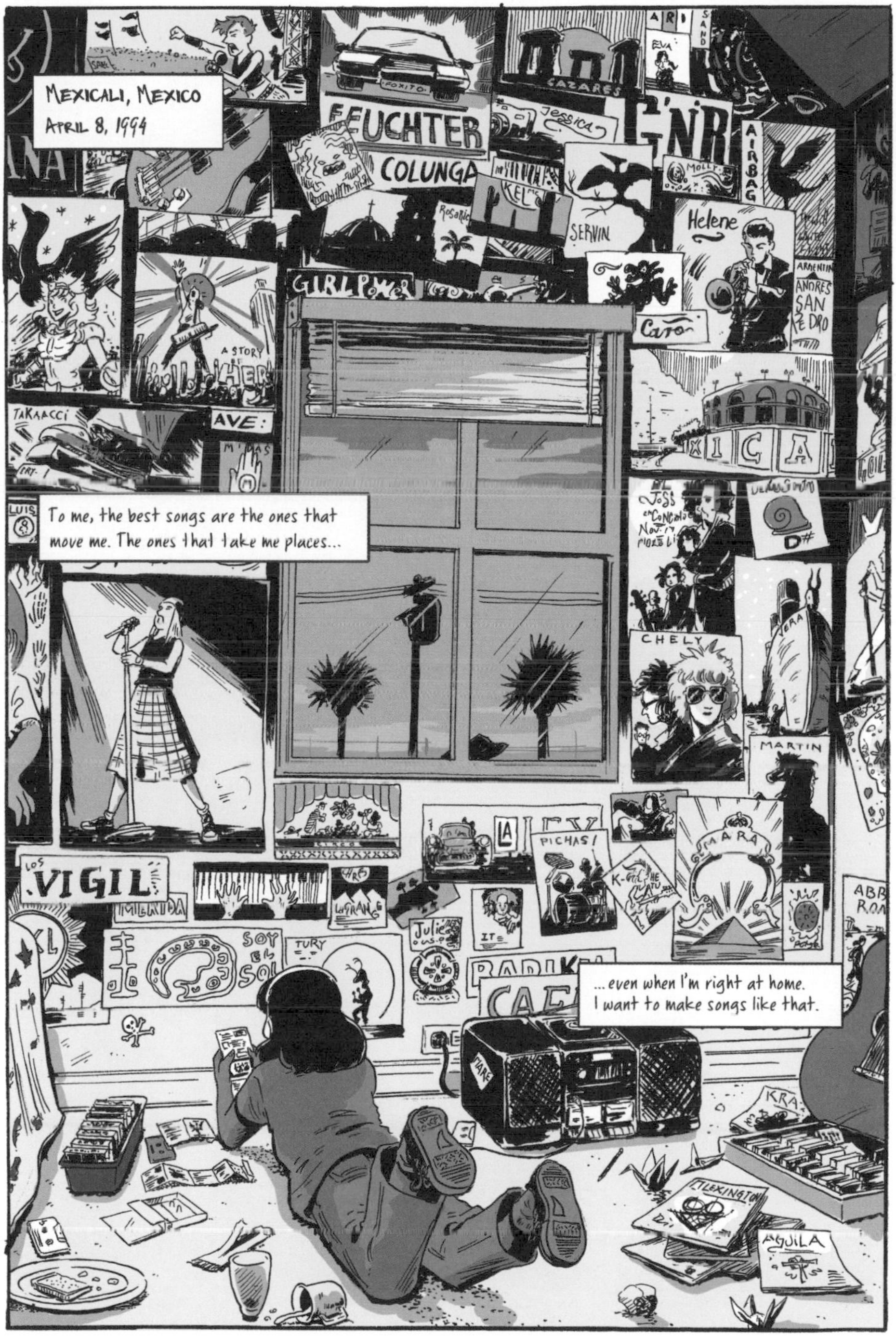
MEXICALI, MEXICO
APRIL 8, 1994
To me, the best songs are the ones that move me. The ones that take me places...
...even when I'm right at home. I want to make songs like that.
FEUCHTER
COLUNGA
GNR
AIRBAG
Helene
SERVIN
GIRLPOWER
Caro
CHELY
MARTIN
VIGIL
PICHAS!
SOY EL SOL
TURY
LEXINGTON
AGUILA

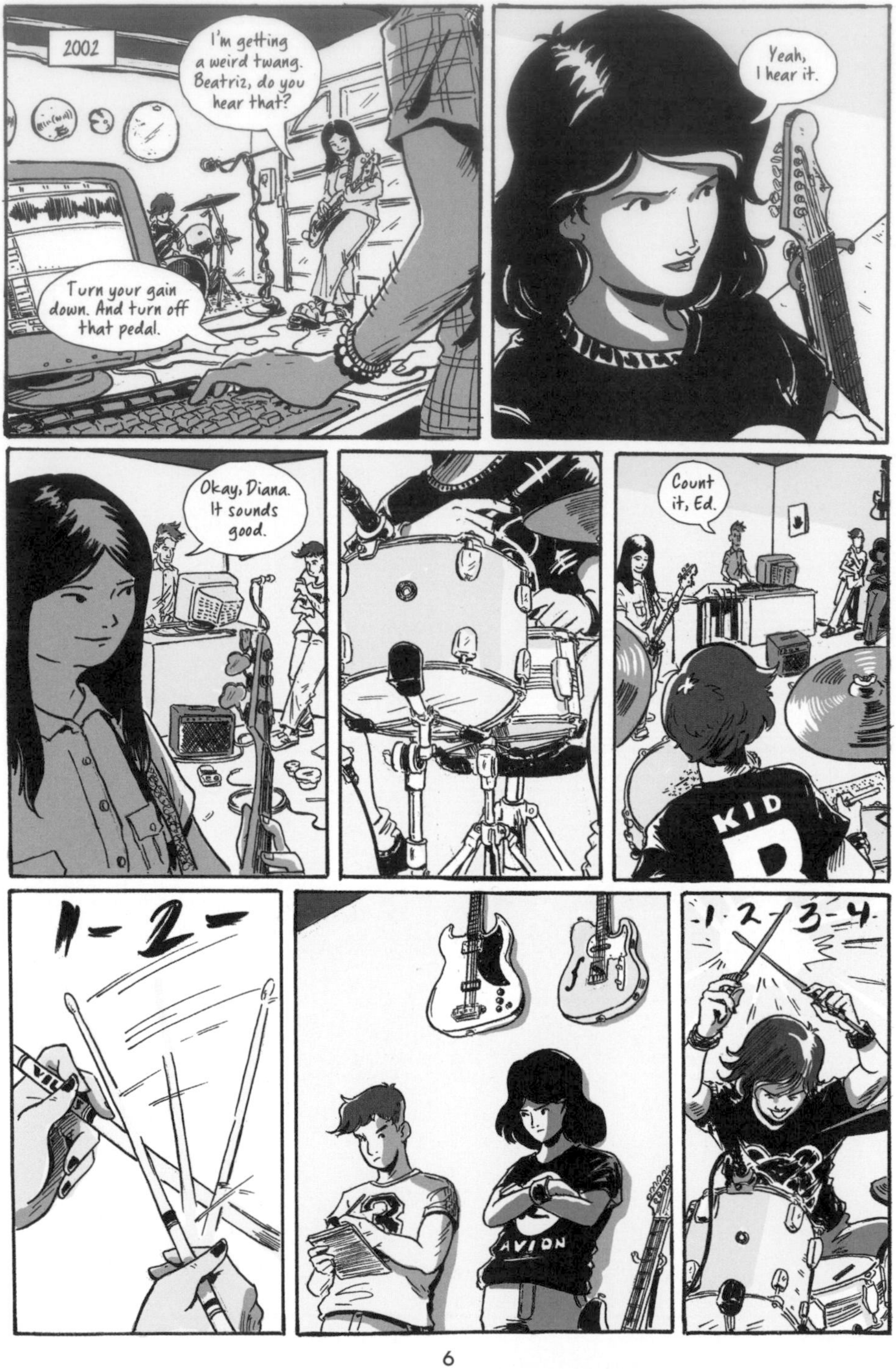
2002
I'm getting a weird twang. Beatriz, do you hear that?
Turn your gain down. And turn off that pedal.
Yeah, I hear it.
Okay, Diana. It sounds good.
Count it, Ed.
KID
1- 2-
AVION
-1-2-3-4-

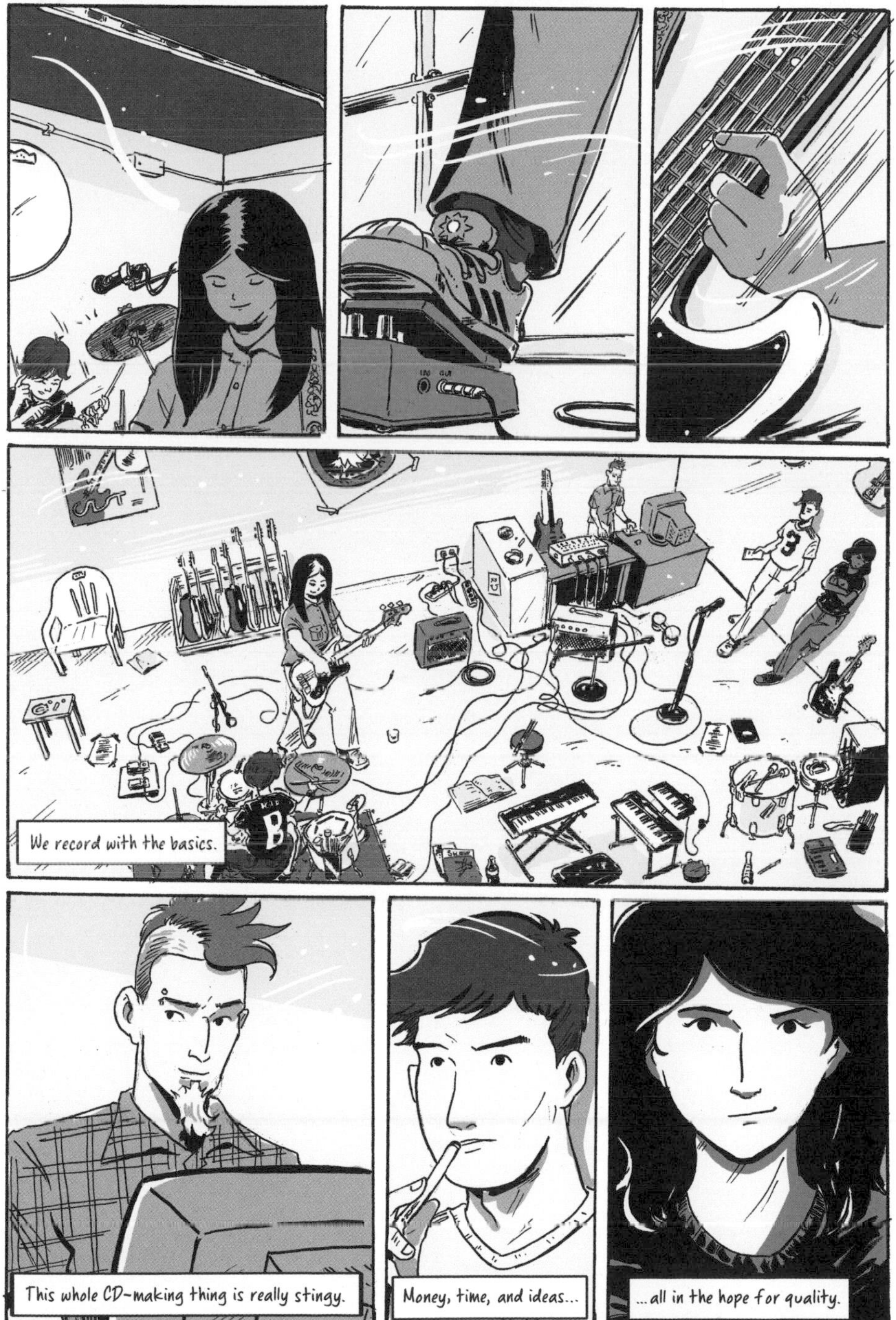

We record with the basics.
This whole CD-making thing is really stingy.
Money, time, and ideas...
...all in the hope for quality.

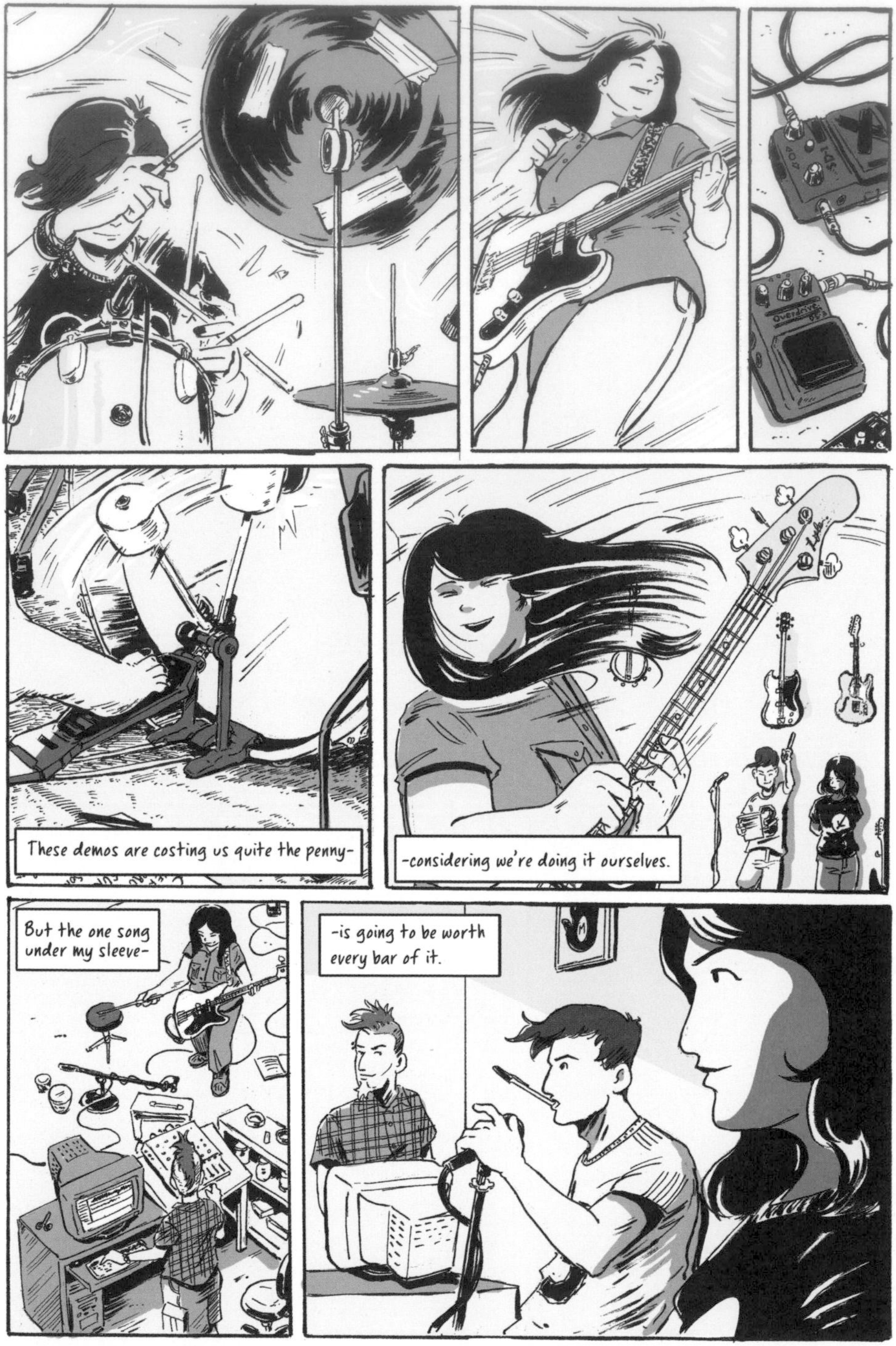
SD-1
Overdrive
These demos are costing us quite the penny-
-considering we're doing it ourselves.
But the one song under my sleeve-
-is going to be worth every bar of it.

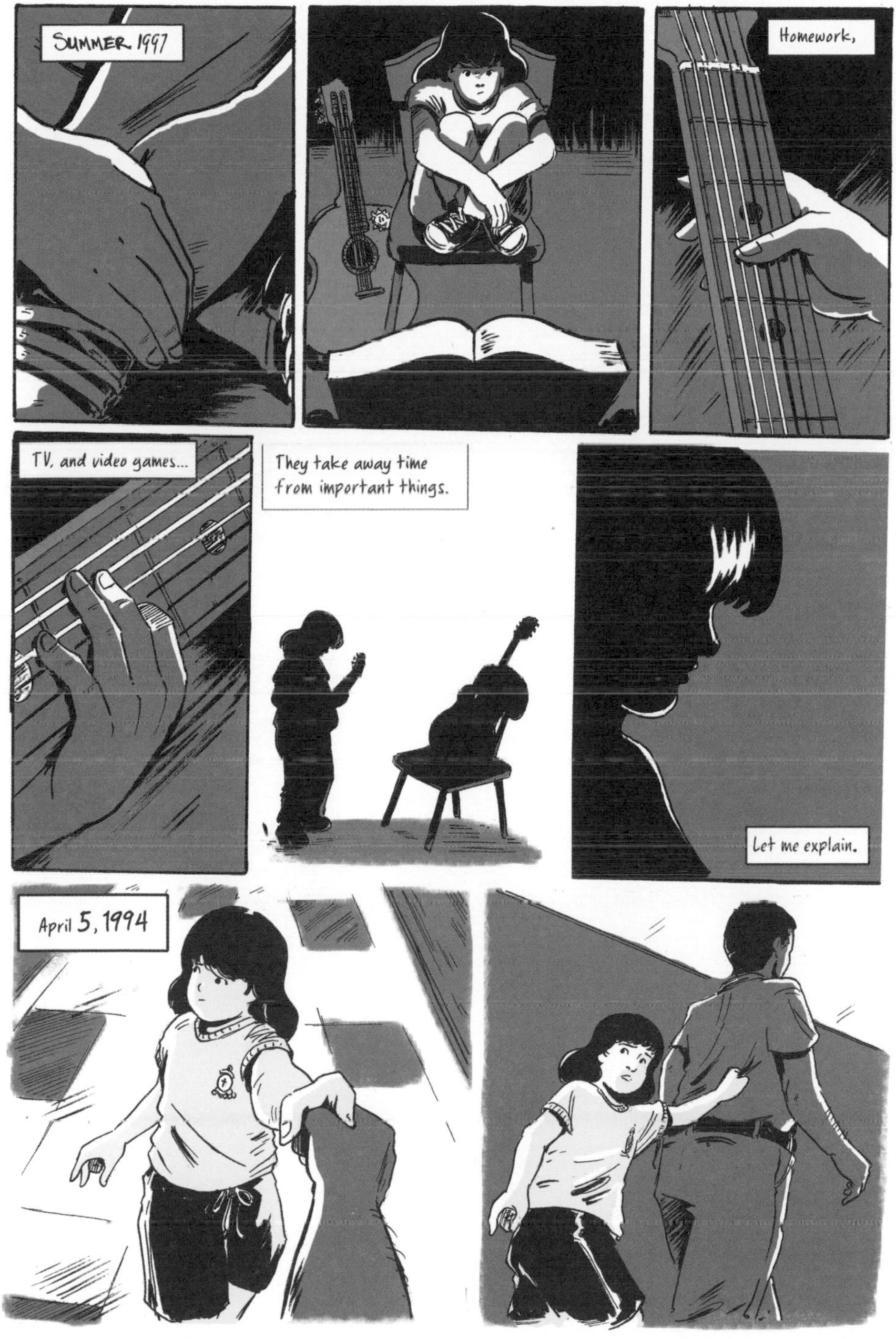

SUMMER 1997
Homework,
TV, and video games...
They take away time from important things.
Let me explain.
April 5, 1994

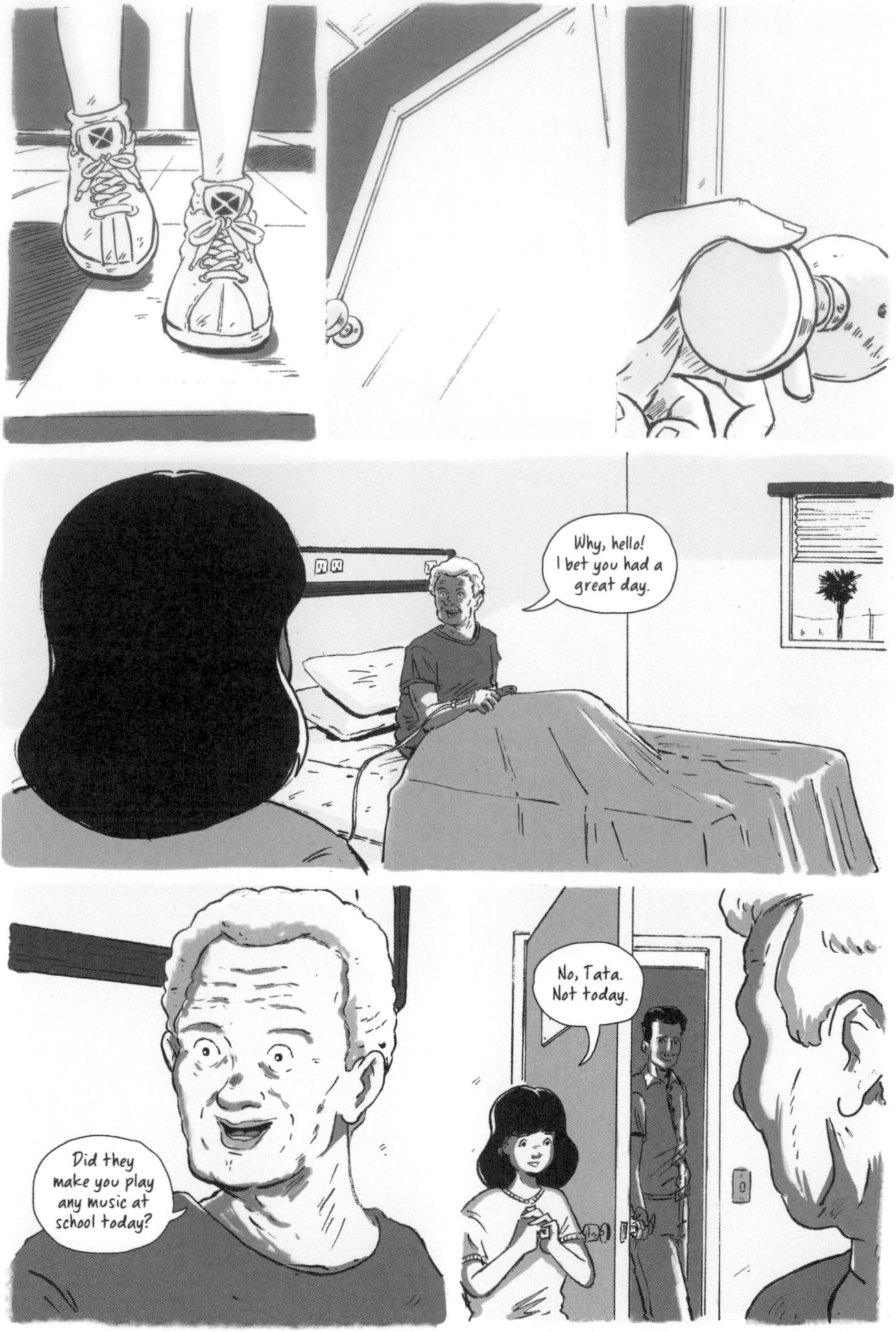
Why, hello! I bet you had a great day.
Did they make you play any music at school today?
No, Tata. Not today.

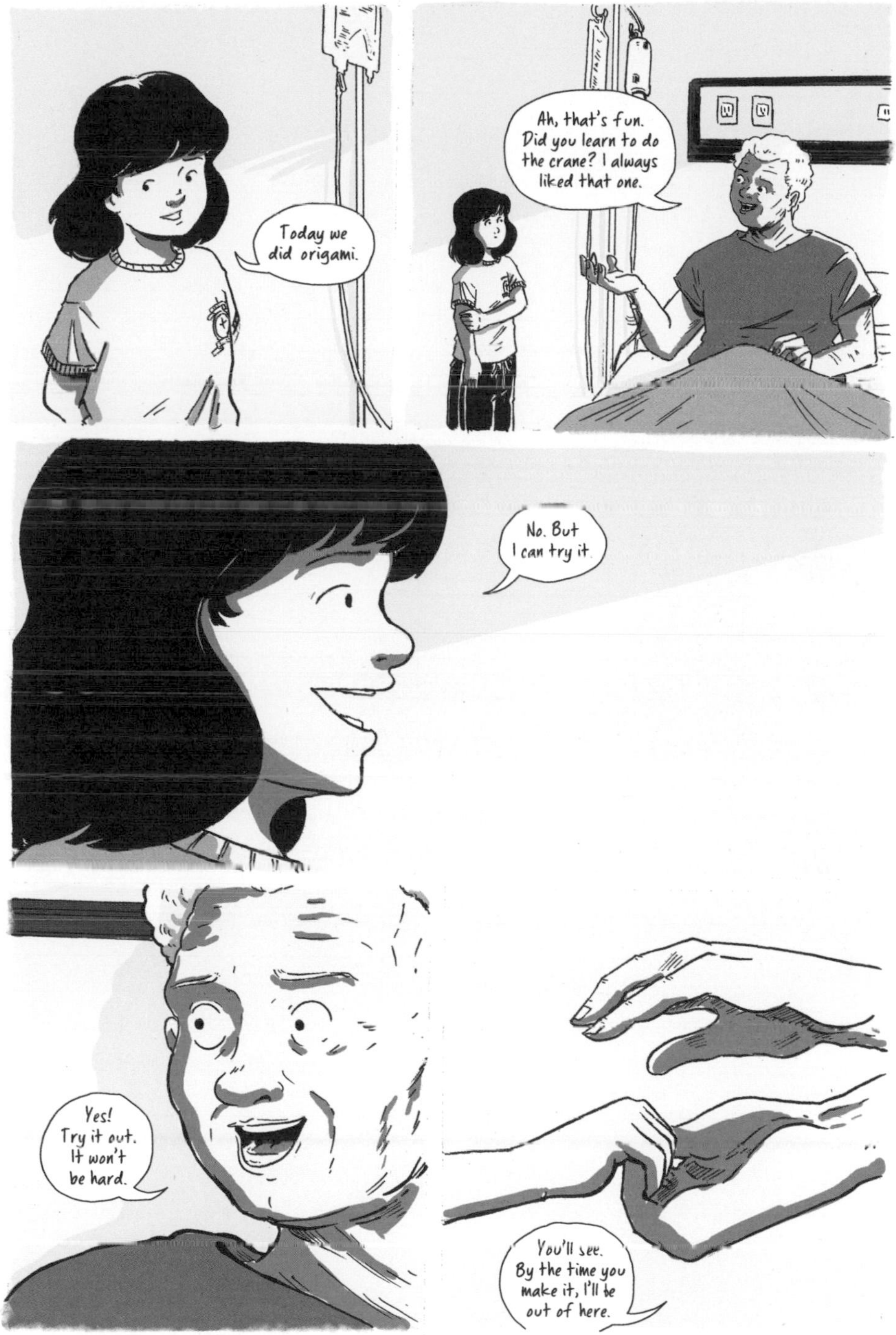
Today we did origami.
Ah, that's fun. Did you learn to do the crane? I always liked that one.
No. But I can try it.
Yes! Try it out. It won't be hard.
You'll see. By the time you make it, I'll be out of here.

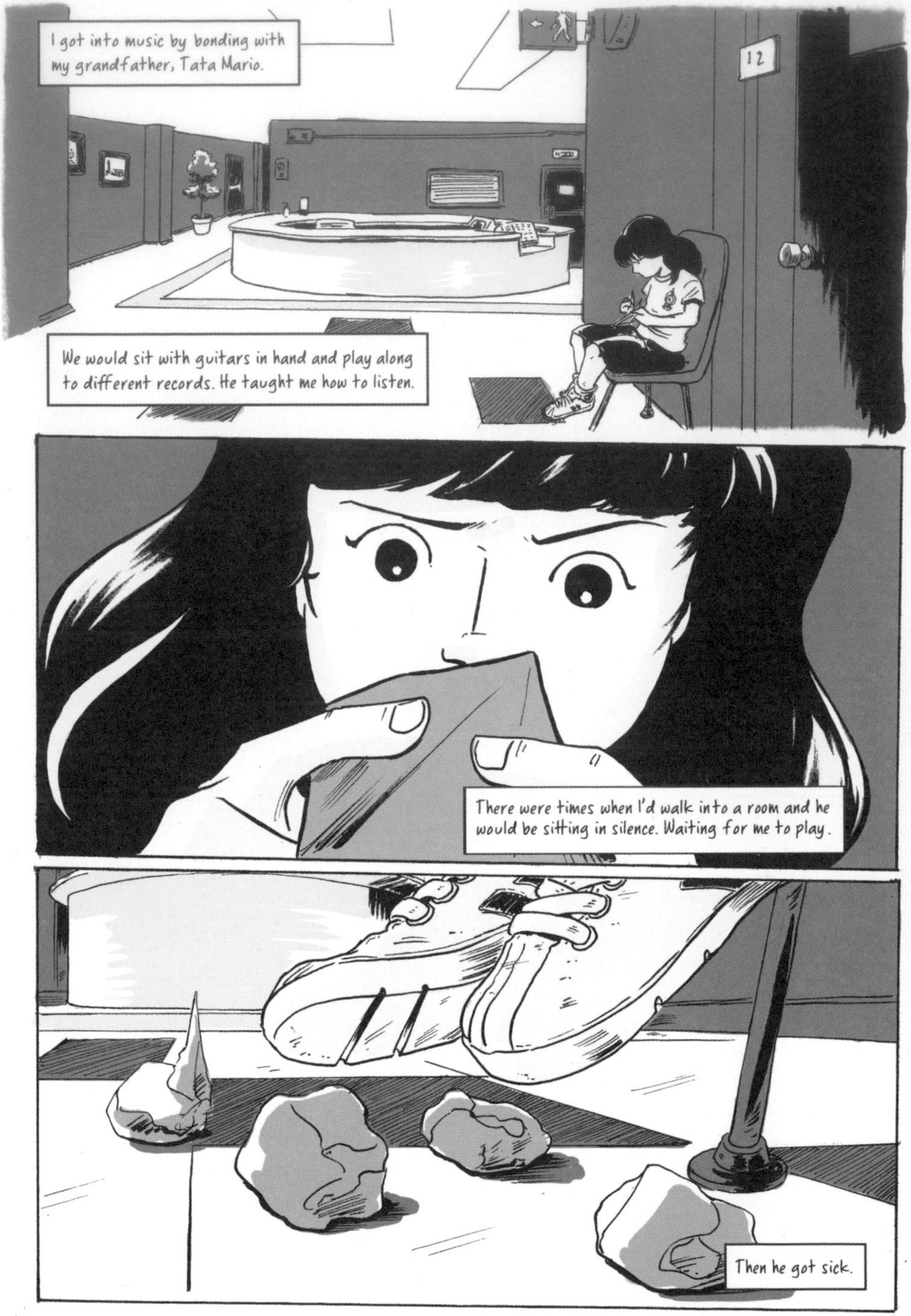
I got into music by bonding with my grandfather, Tata Mario.
12
We would sit with guitars in hand and play along to different records. He taught me how to listen.
There were times when I'd walk into a room and he would be sitting in silence. Waiting for me to play.
Then he got sick.

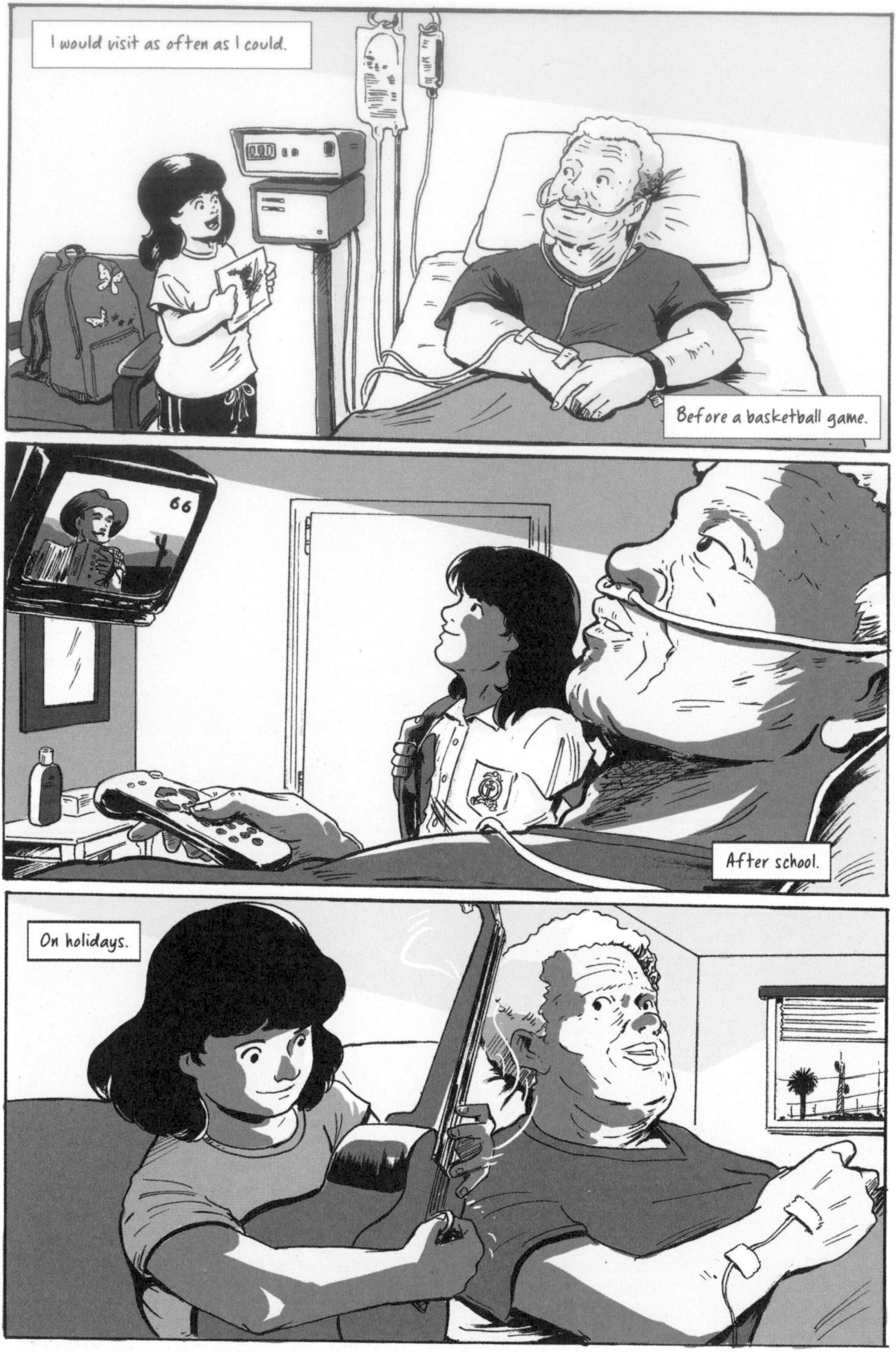
I would visit as often as I could.
Before a basketball game.
66
After school.
On holidays.

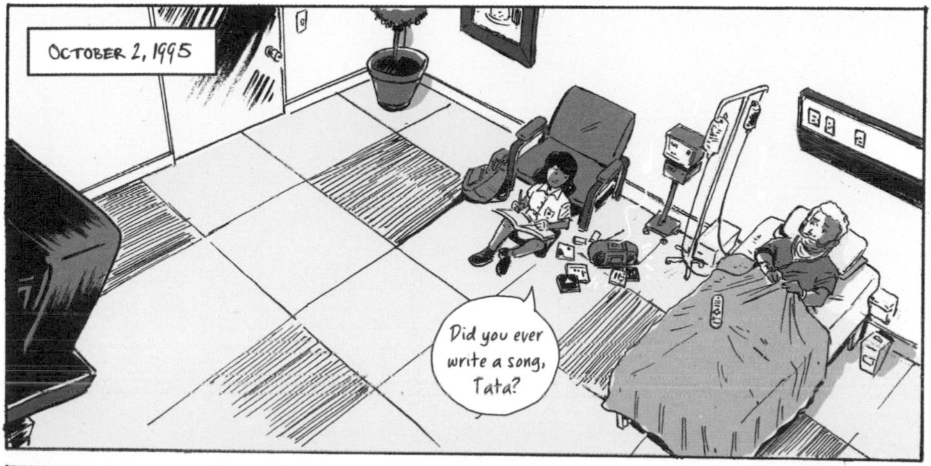
October 2, 1995
Did you ever write a song, Tata?

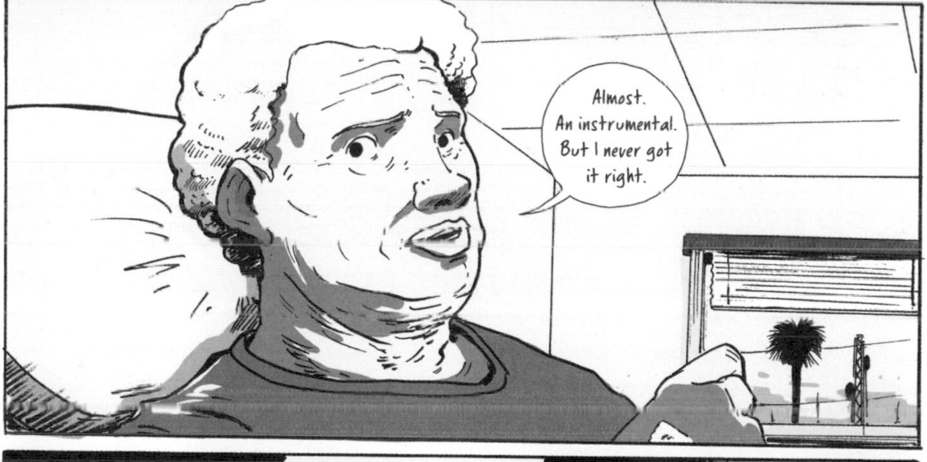
Almost. An instrumental. But I never got it right.

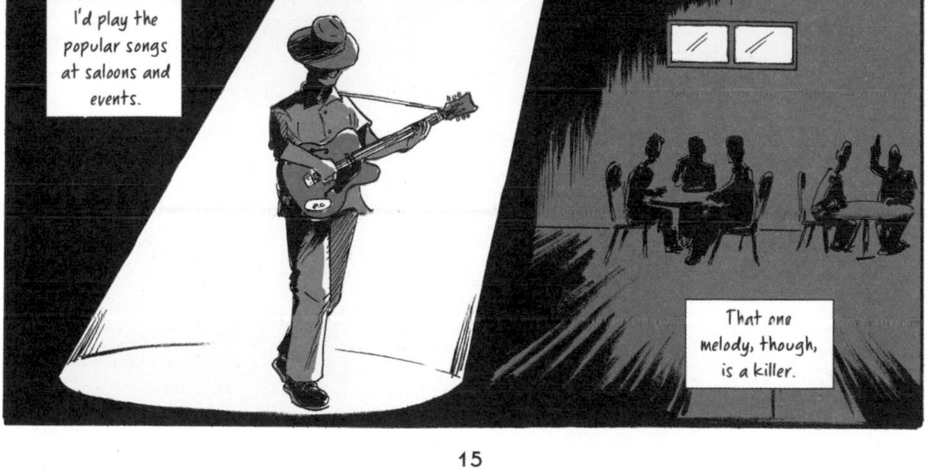
I'd play the popular songs at saloons and events.
That one melody, though, is a killer.

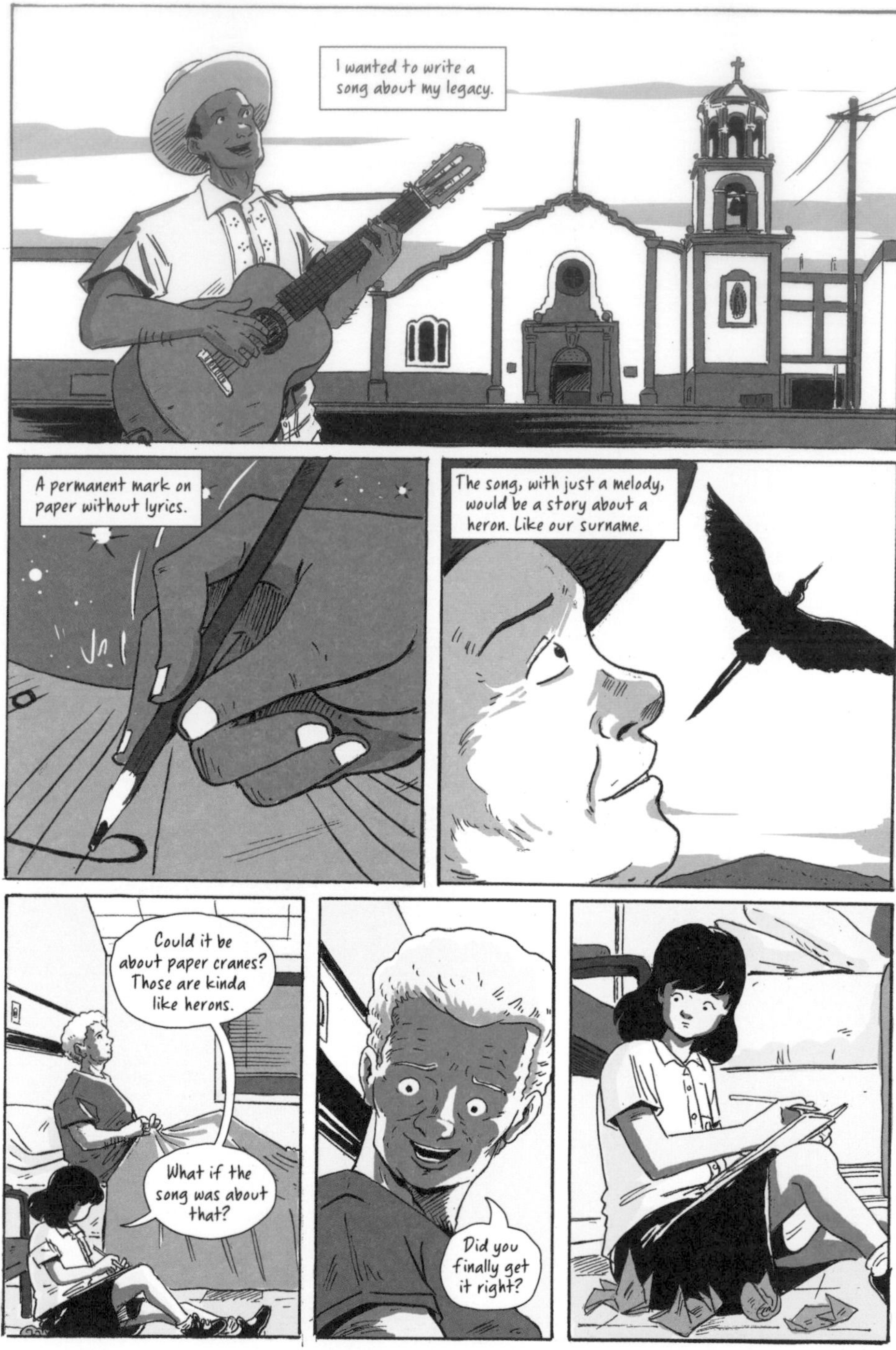
I wanted to write a song about my legacy.
A permanent mark on paper without lyrics.
The song, with just a melody, would be a story about a heron. Like our surname.
Could it be about paper cranes? Those are kinda like herons.
What if the song was about that?
Did you finally get it right?

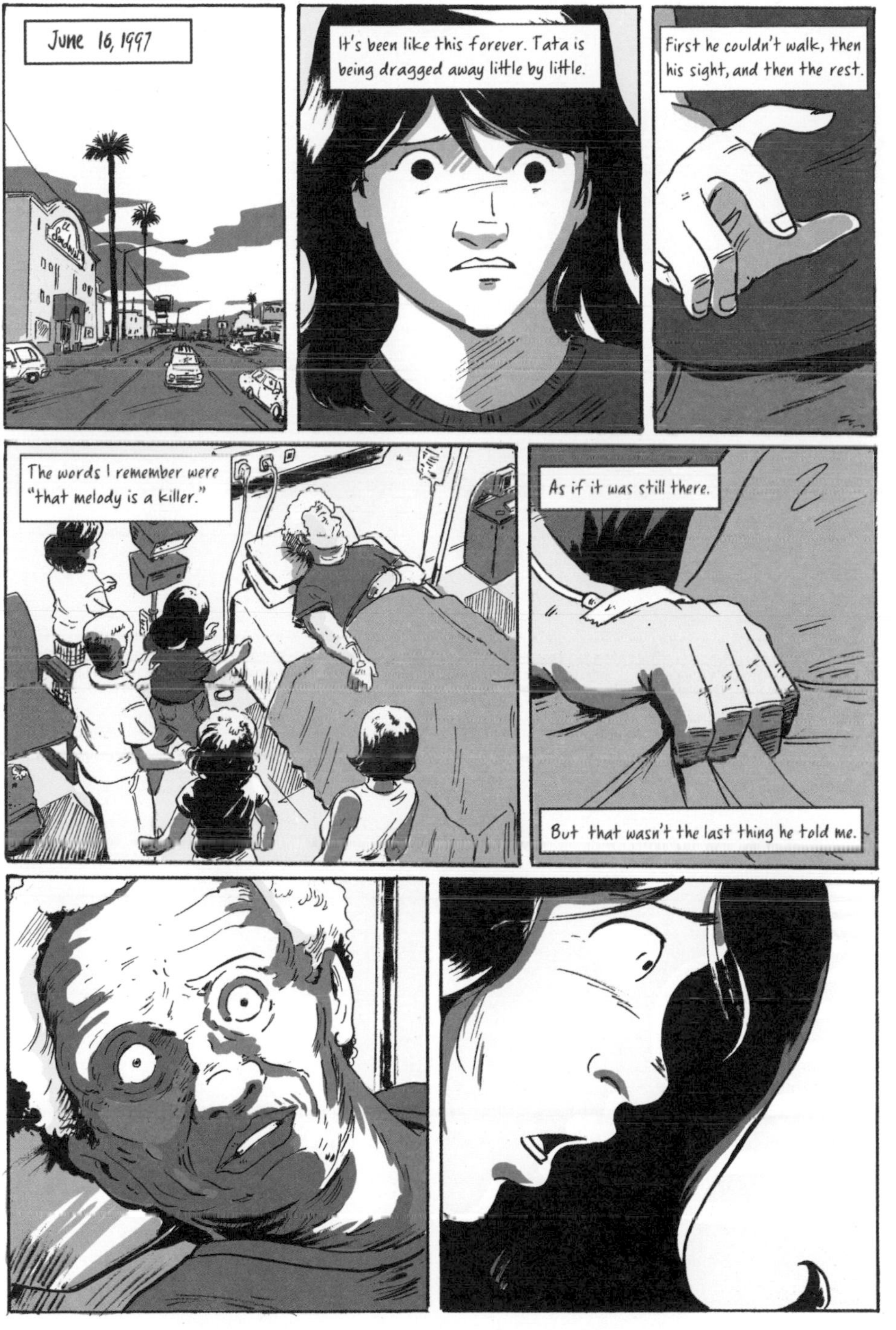
June 16, 1997
It's been like this forever. Tata is being dragged away little by little.
First he couldn't walk, then his sight, and then the rest.
The words I remember were "that melody is a killer."
As if it was still there.
But that wasn't the last thing he told me.

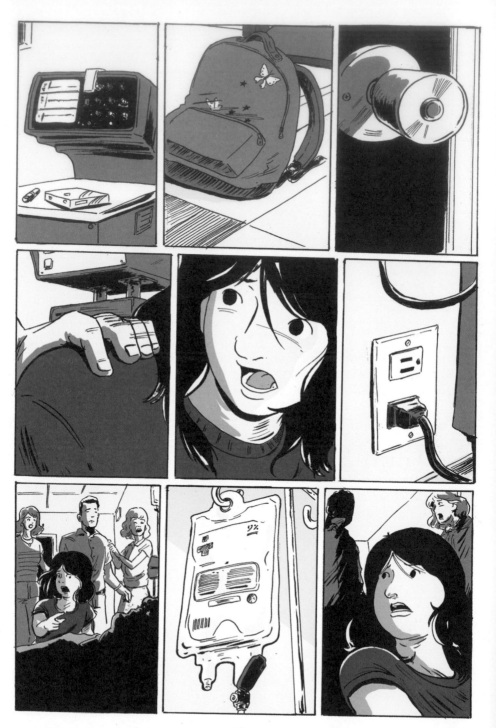

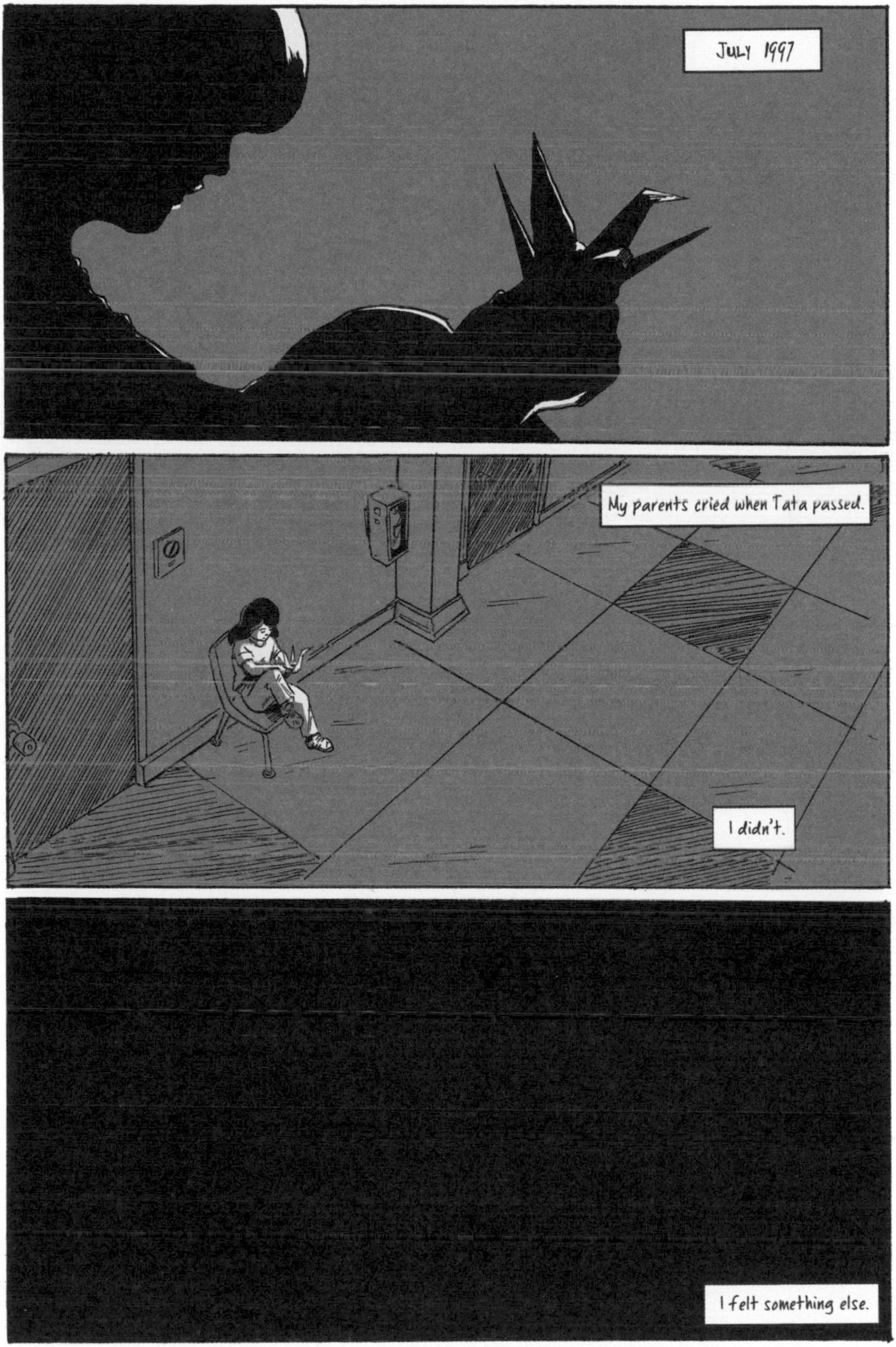
July 1997
My parents cried when Tata passed.
I didn't.
I felt something else.

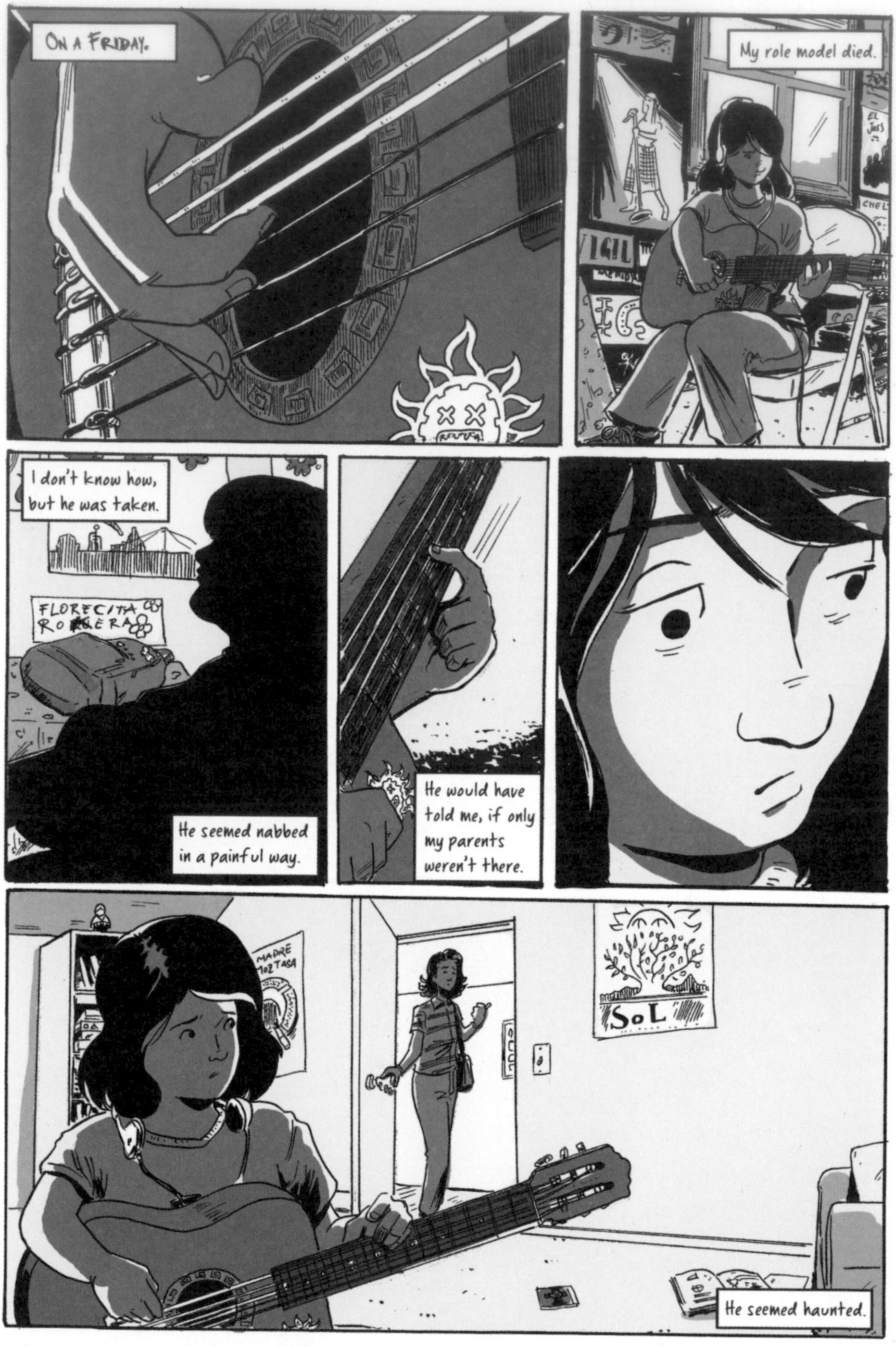
On a Friday.
My role model died.
I don't know how, but he was taken.
FLORECITA ROQUERA
He seemed nabbed in a painful way.
He would have told me, if only my parents weren't there.
MADRE TIERRA
SoL
He seemed haunted.

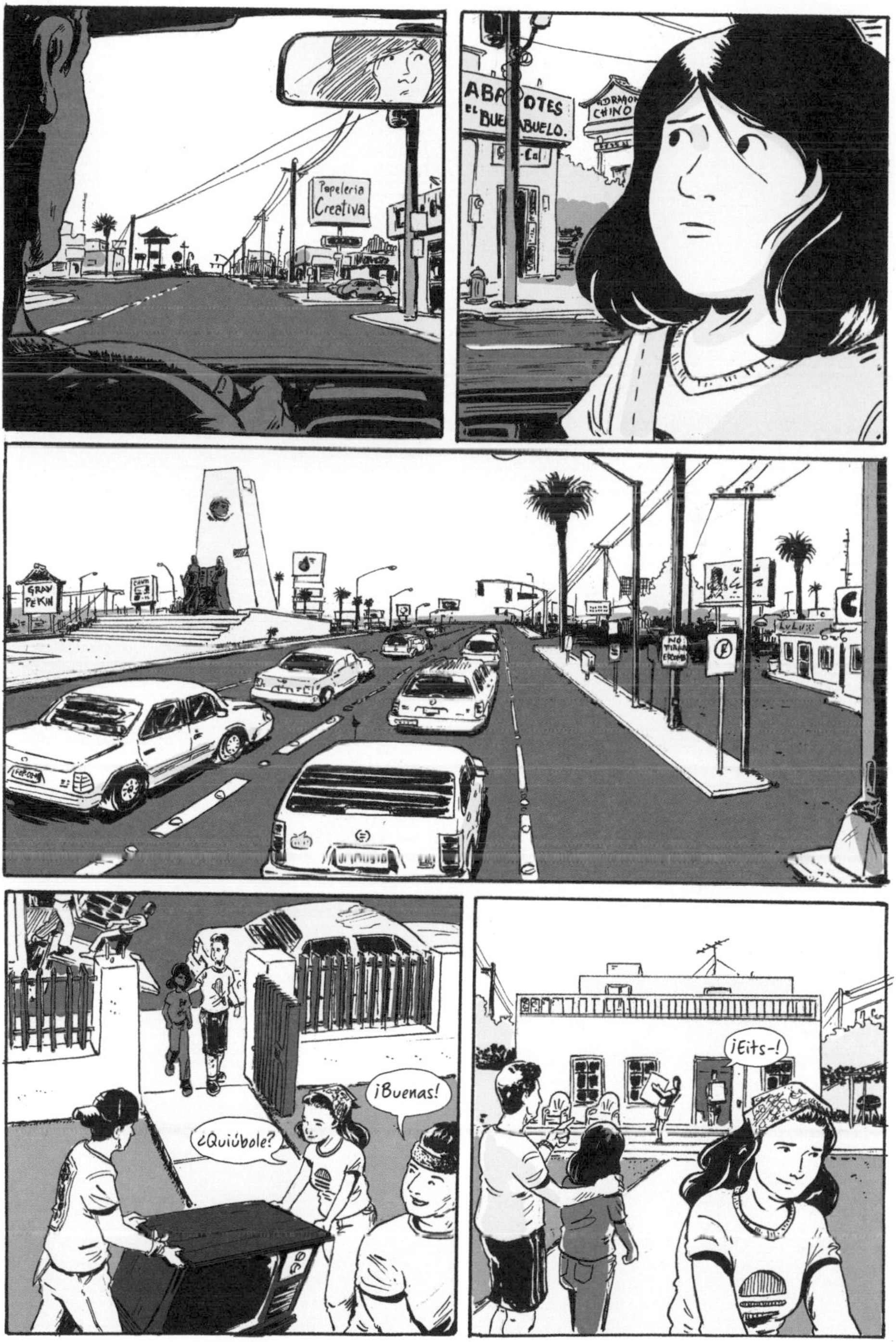
Papeleria
Creativa
GRAN
PEKIN
¿Quiúbole?
¡Buenas!
¡Eits-!

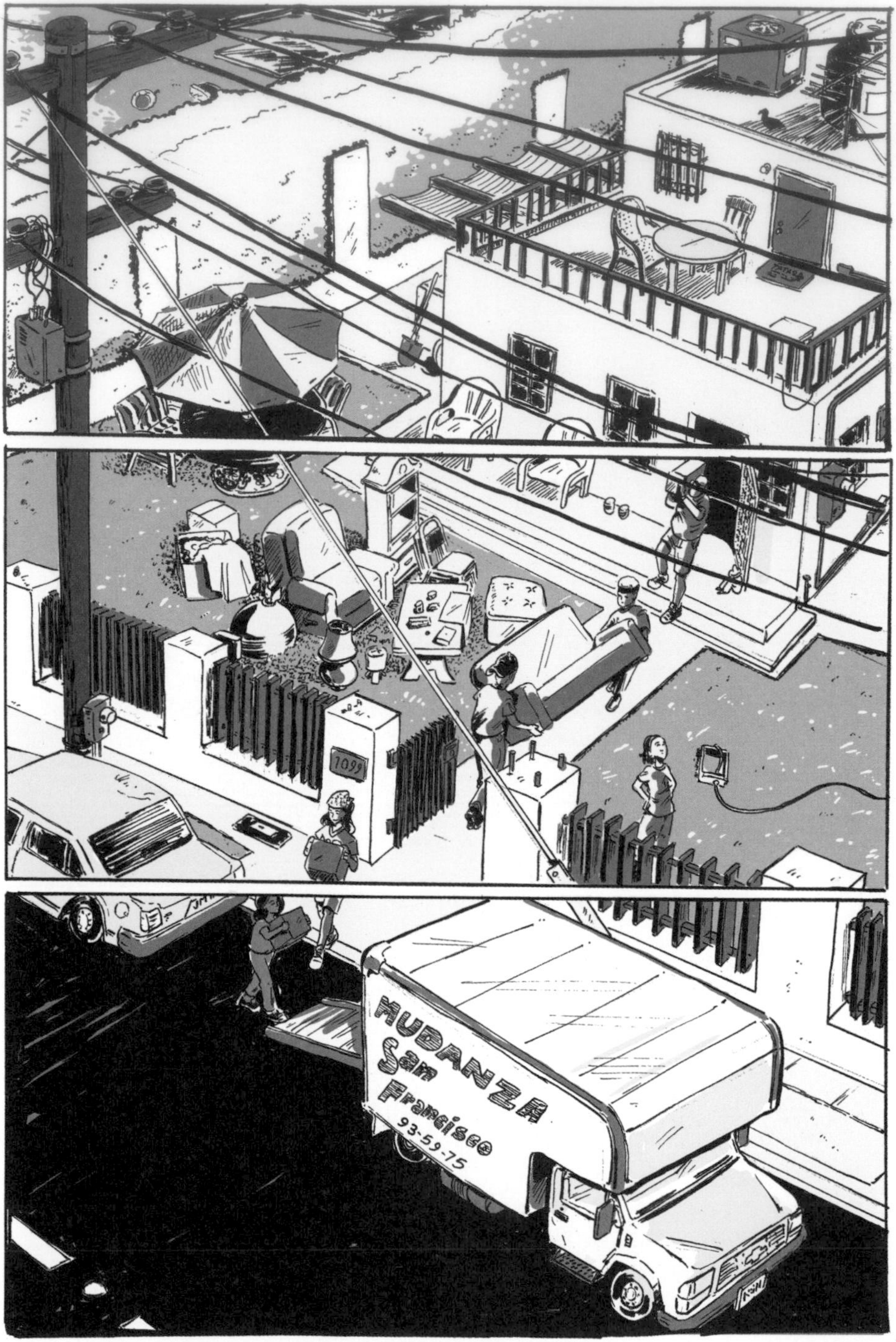
1099
MUDANZA
San
Francisco
93-59-75

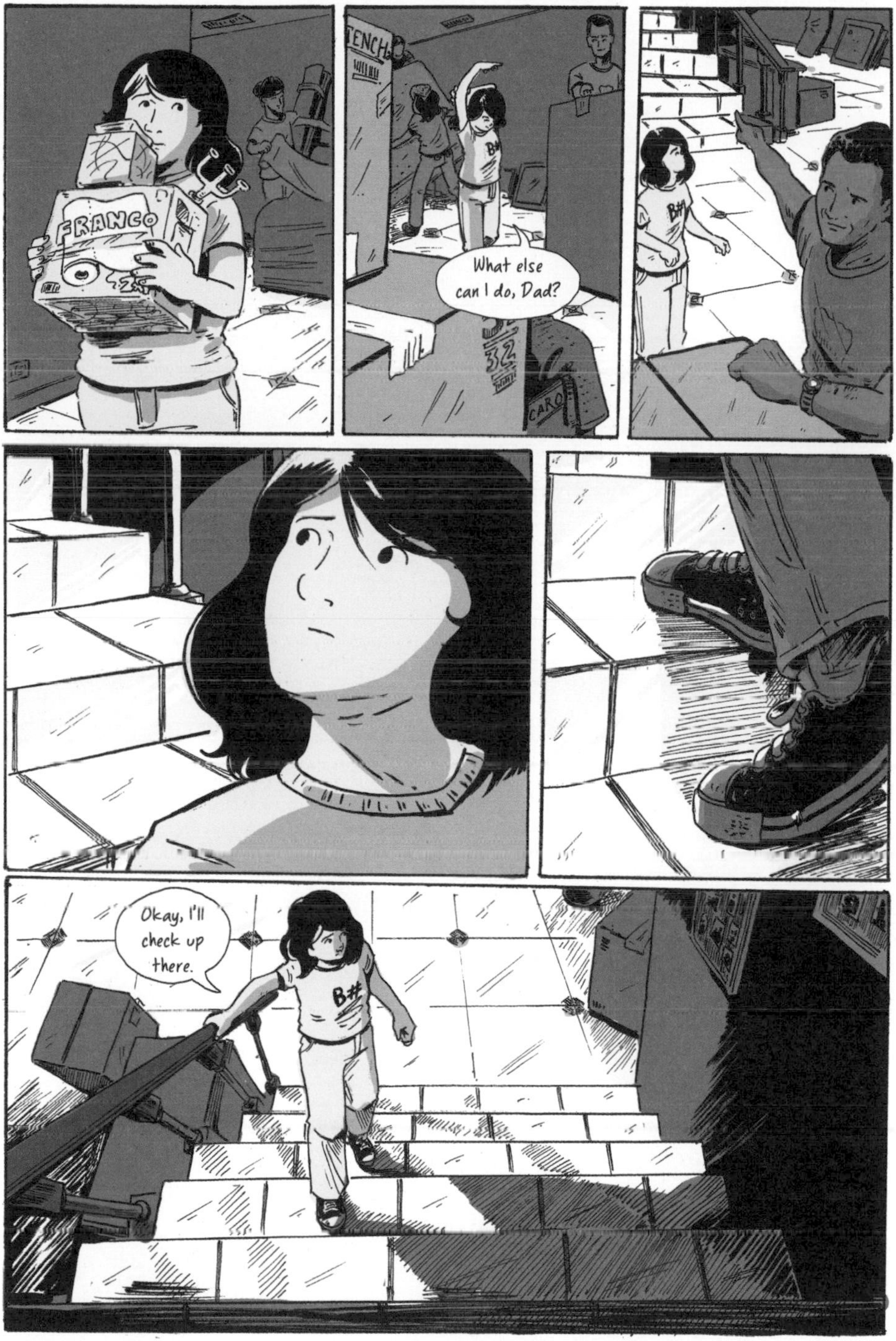
FRANCO
TENCH
What else can I do, Dad?
32
CARO
Okay, I'll check up there.

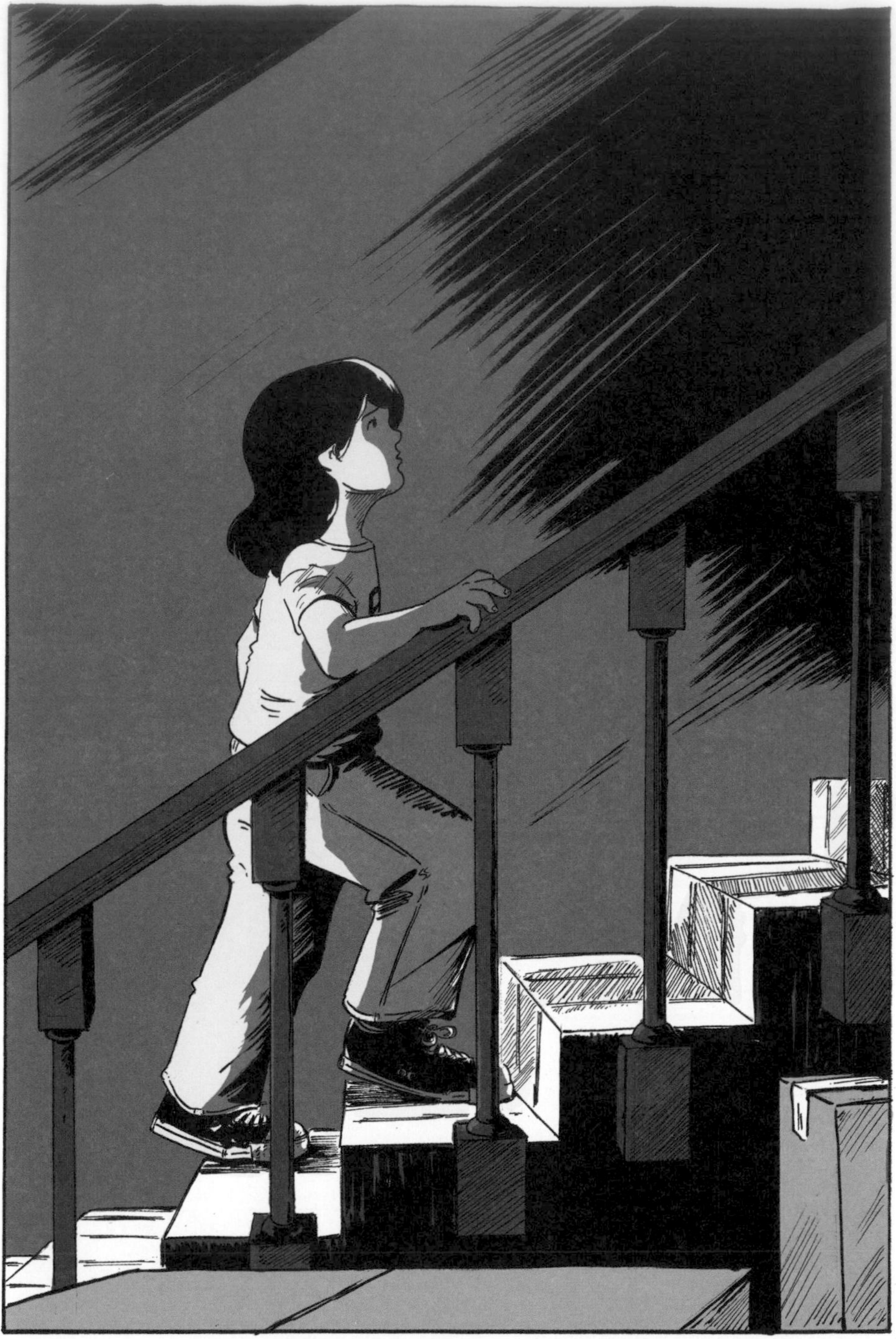

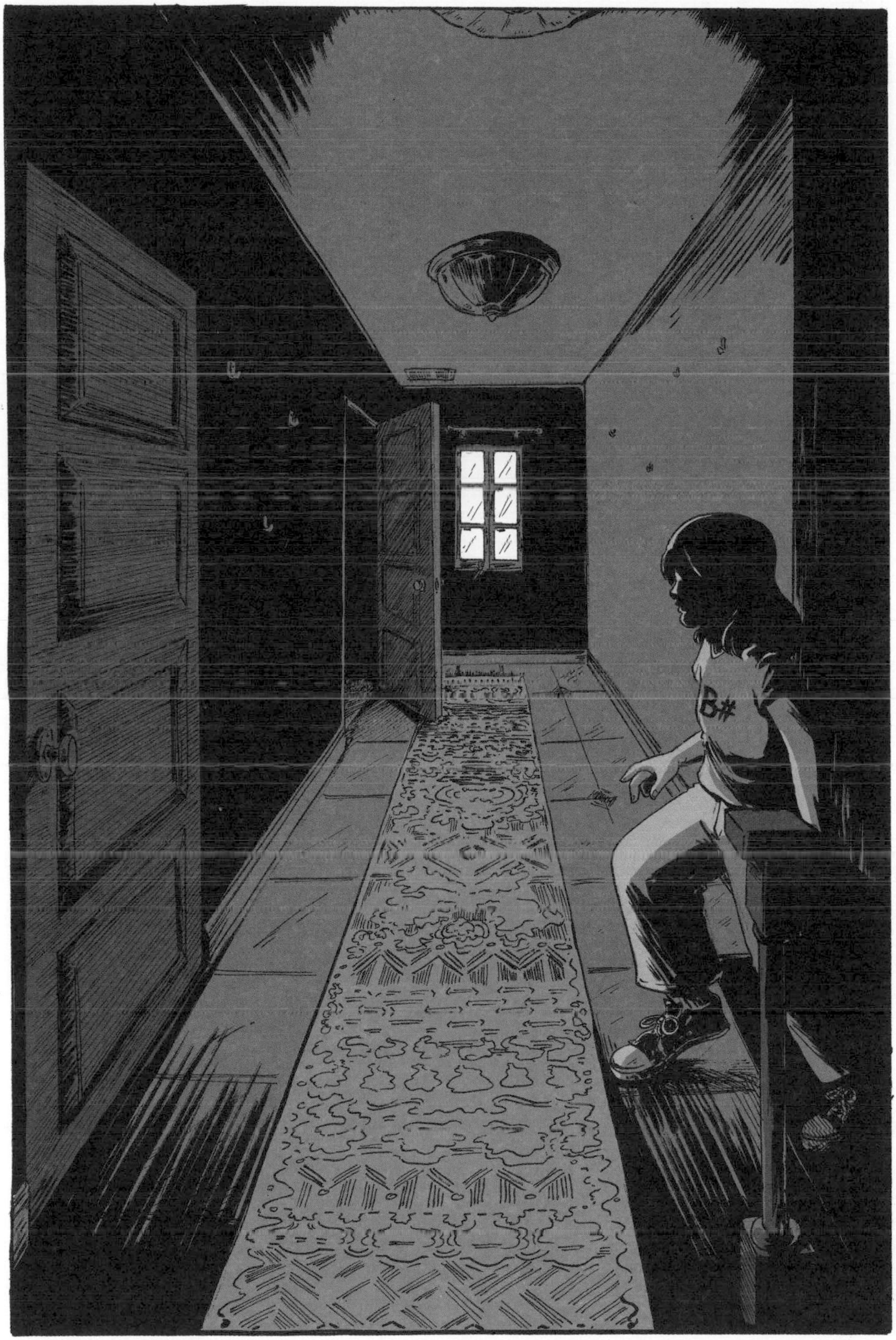
B#

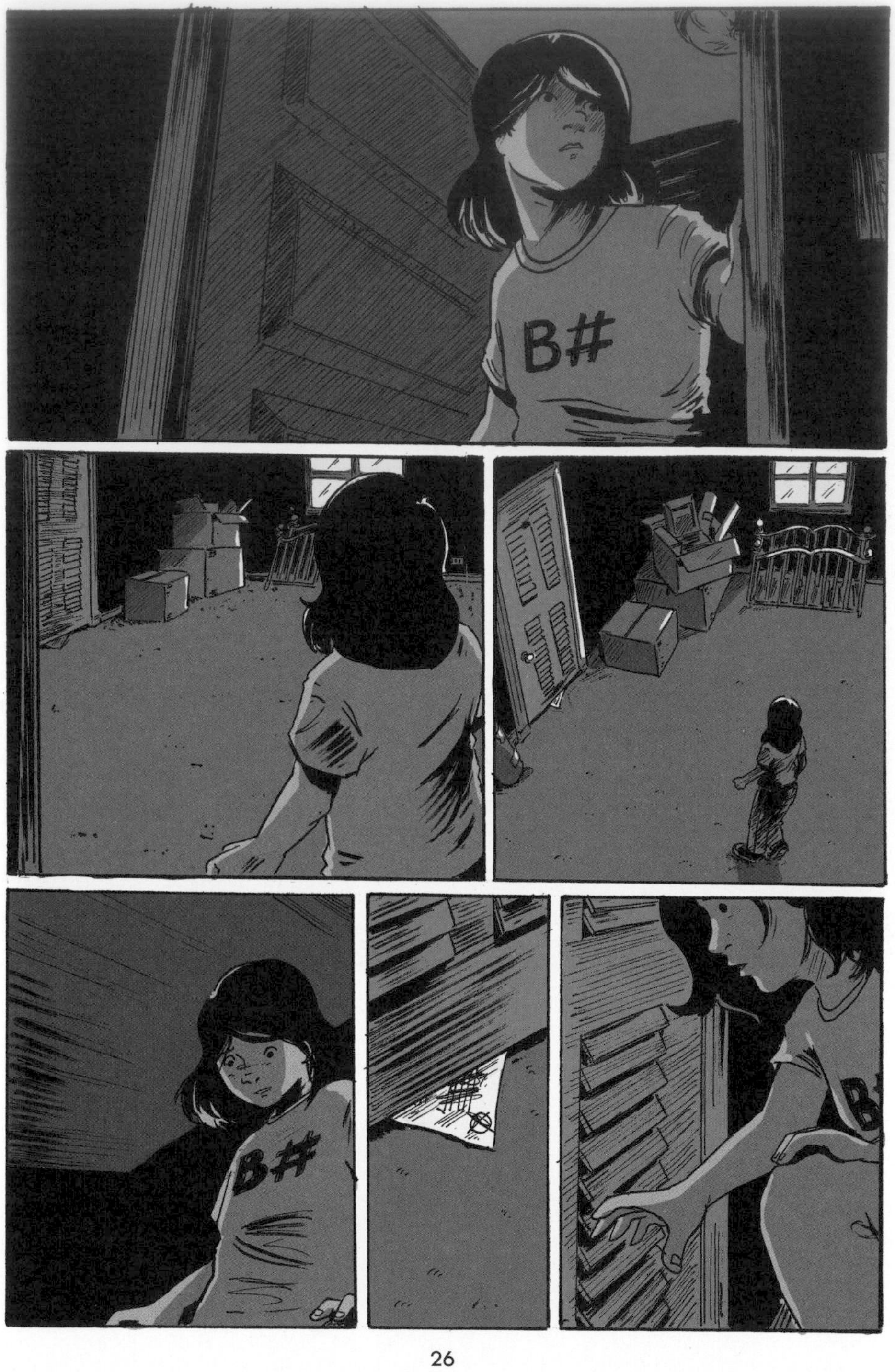
B#

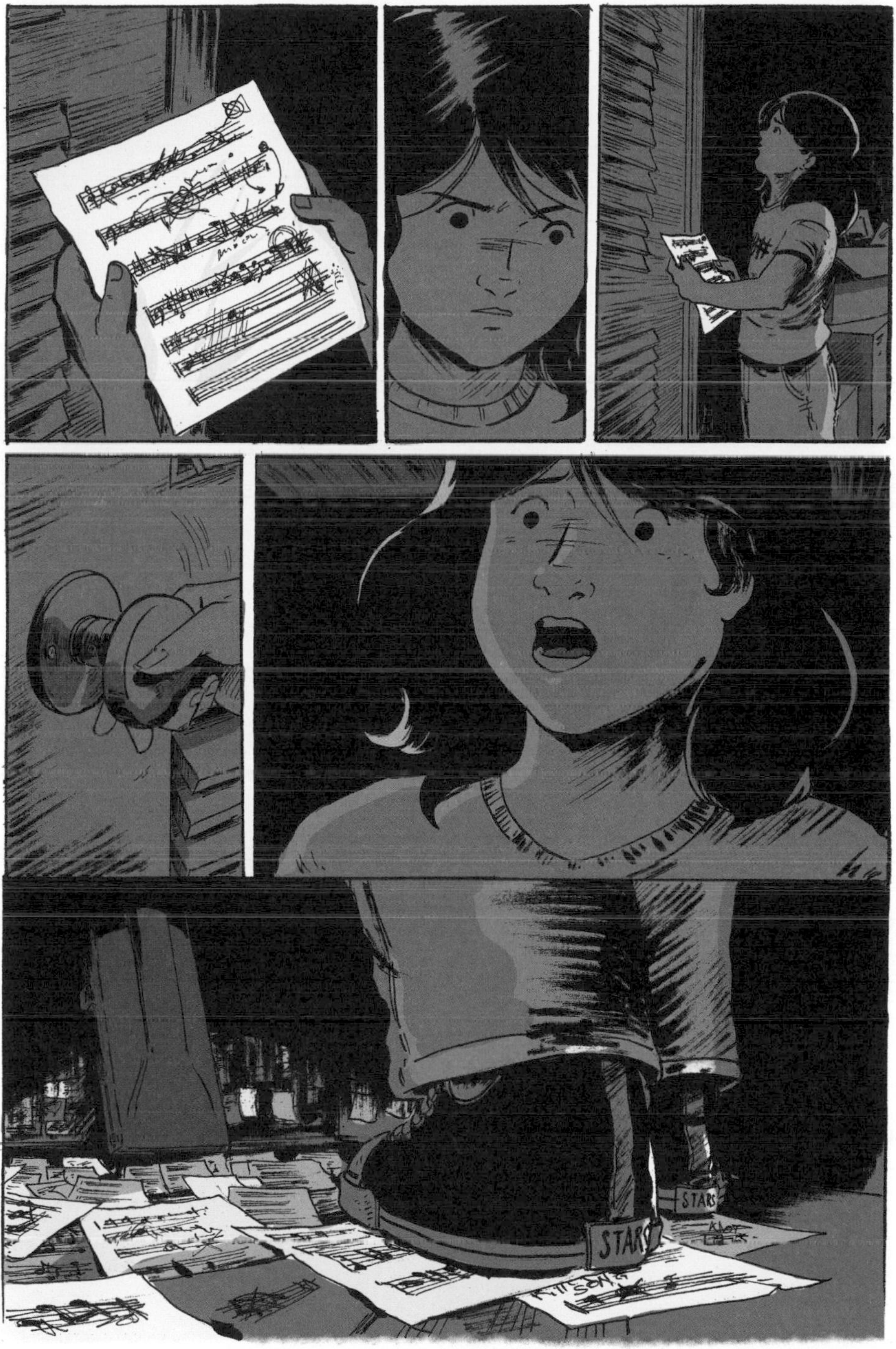
STARS
STARS

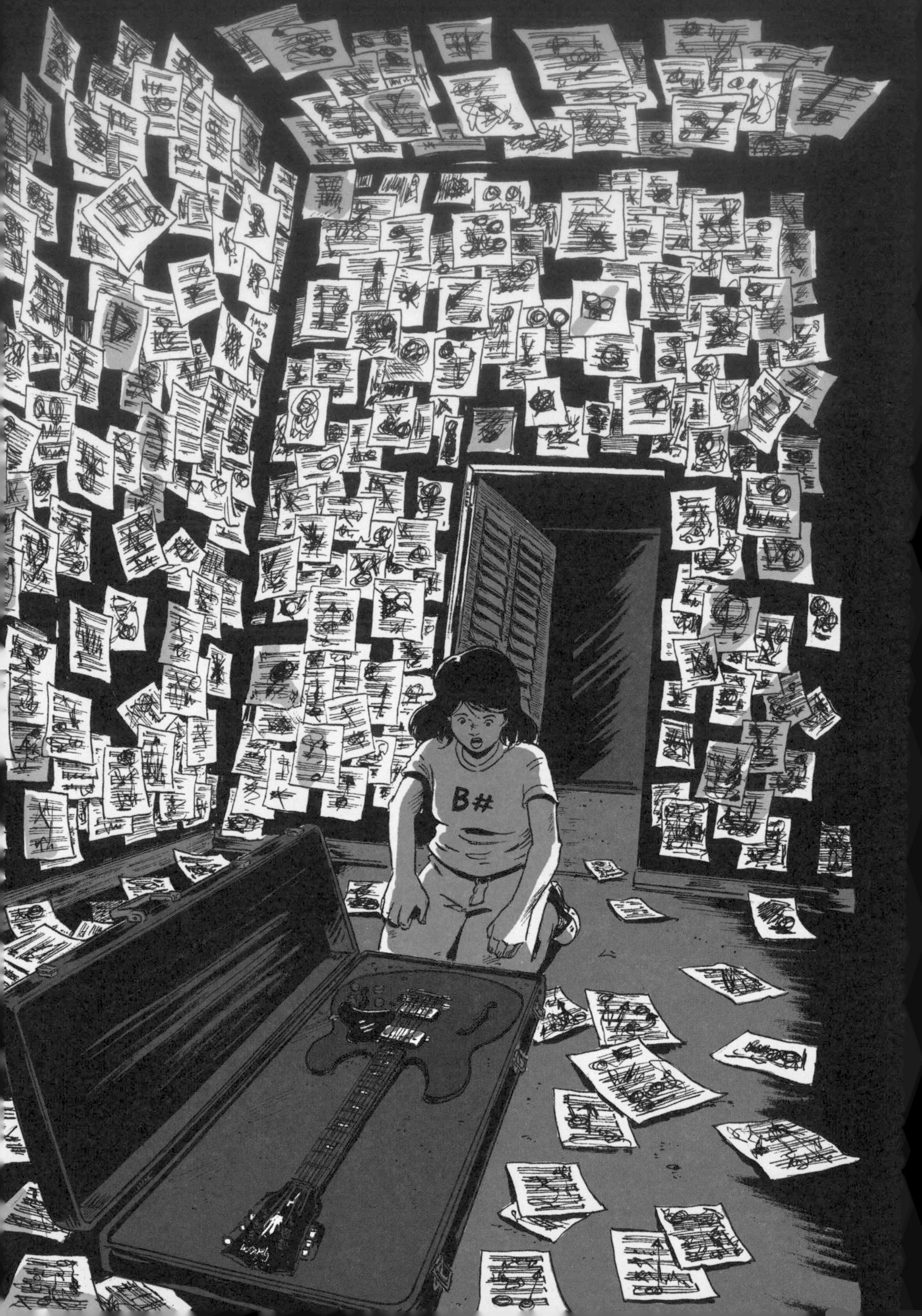
B#

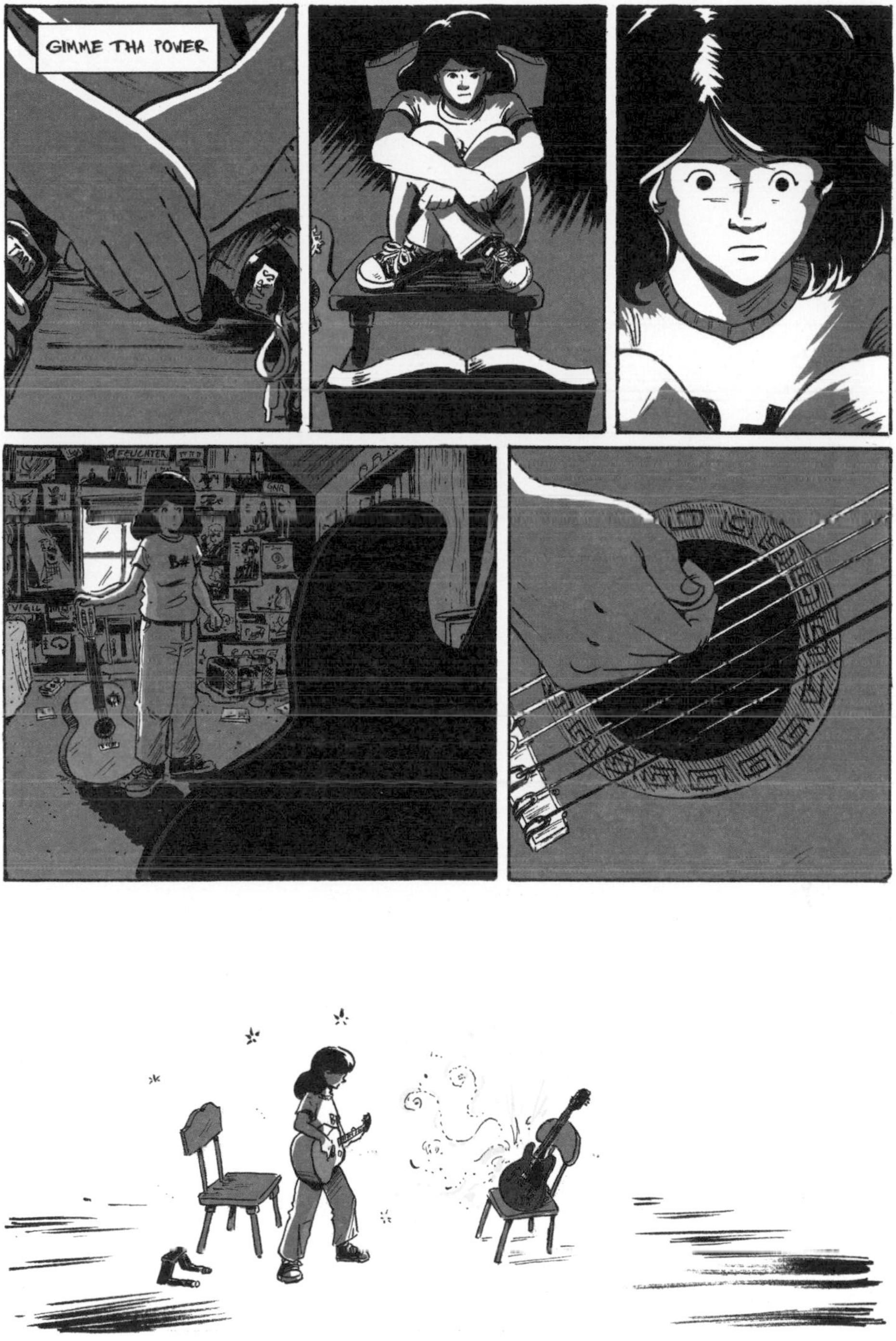
GIMME THA POWER

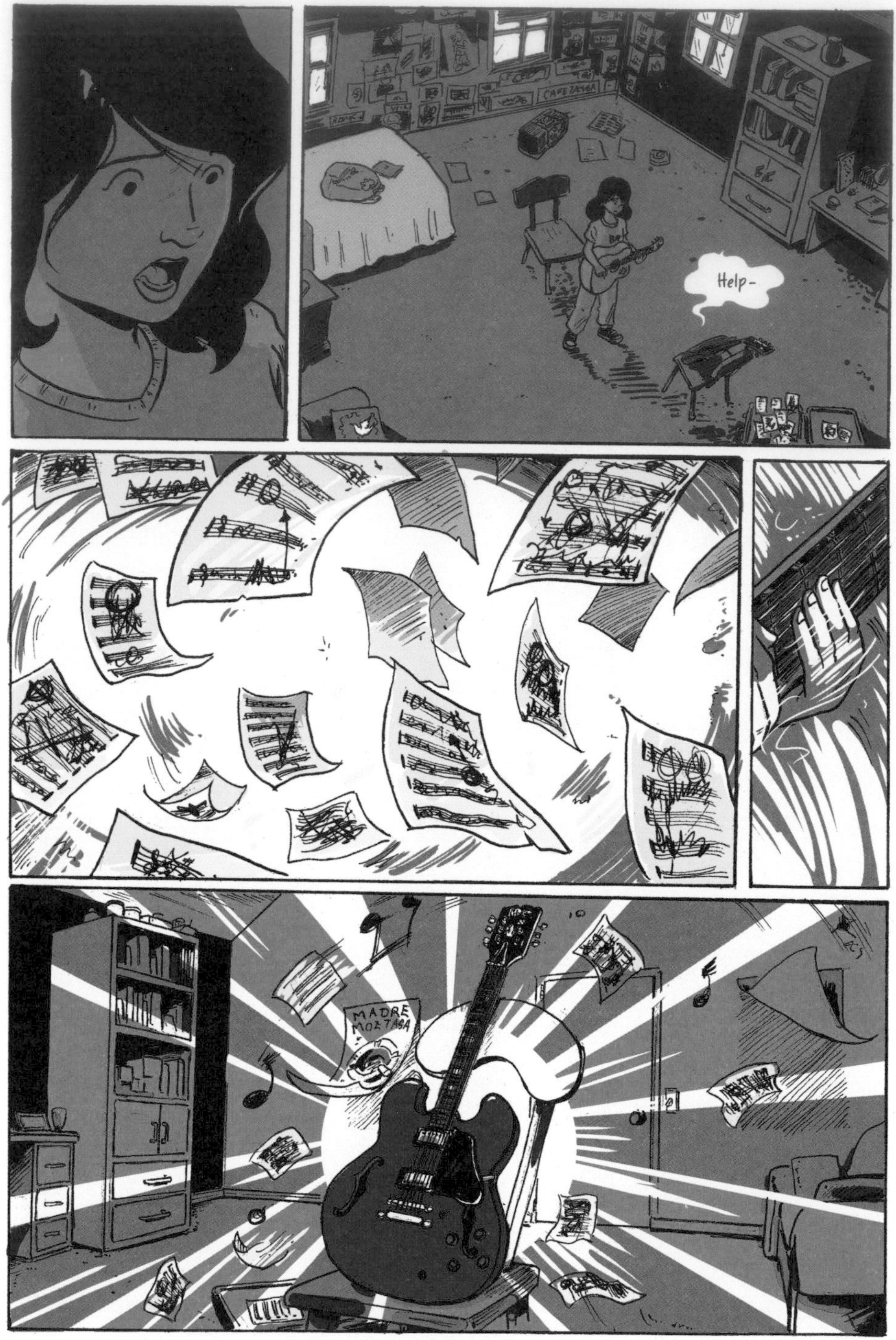

Help-
MADRE MOZTAZA

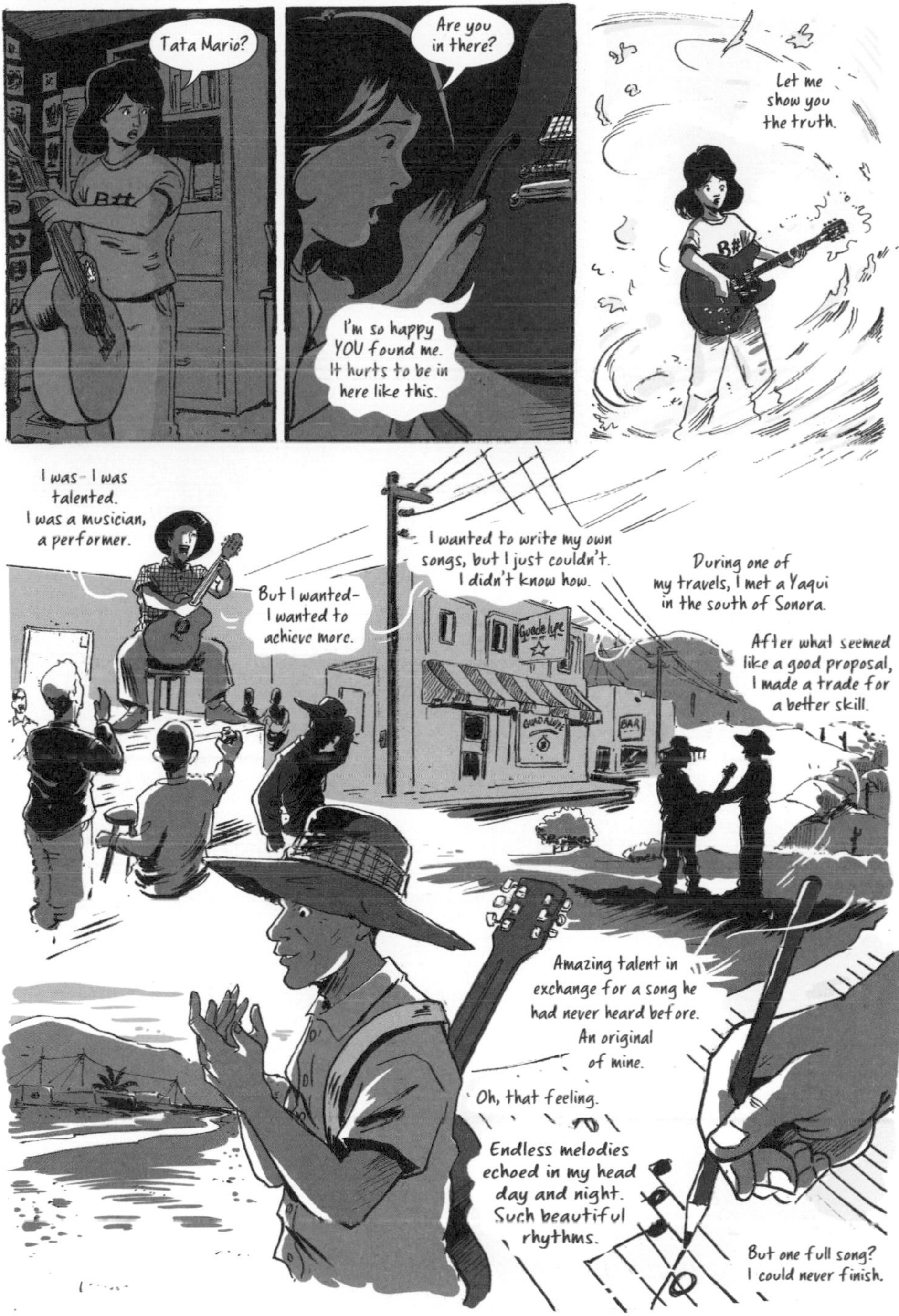
Tata Mario?
Are you in there?
I'm so happy YOU found me. It hurts to be in here like this.
Let me show you the truth.
B#
I was- I was talented. I was a musician, a performer.
But I wanted- I wanted to achieve more.
I wanted to write my own songs, but I just couldn't. I didn't know how.
During one of my travels, I met a Yaqui in the south of Sonora.
After what seemed like a good proposal, I made a trade for a better skill.
Guadalupe
BAR
Amazing talent in exchange for a song he had never heard before. An original of mine.
Oh, that feeling.
Endless melodies echoed in my head day and night. Such beautiful rhythms.
But one full song? I could never finish.

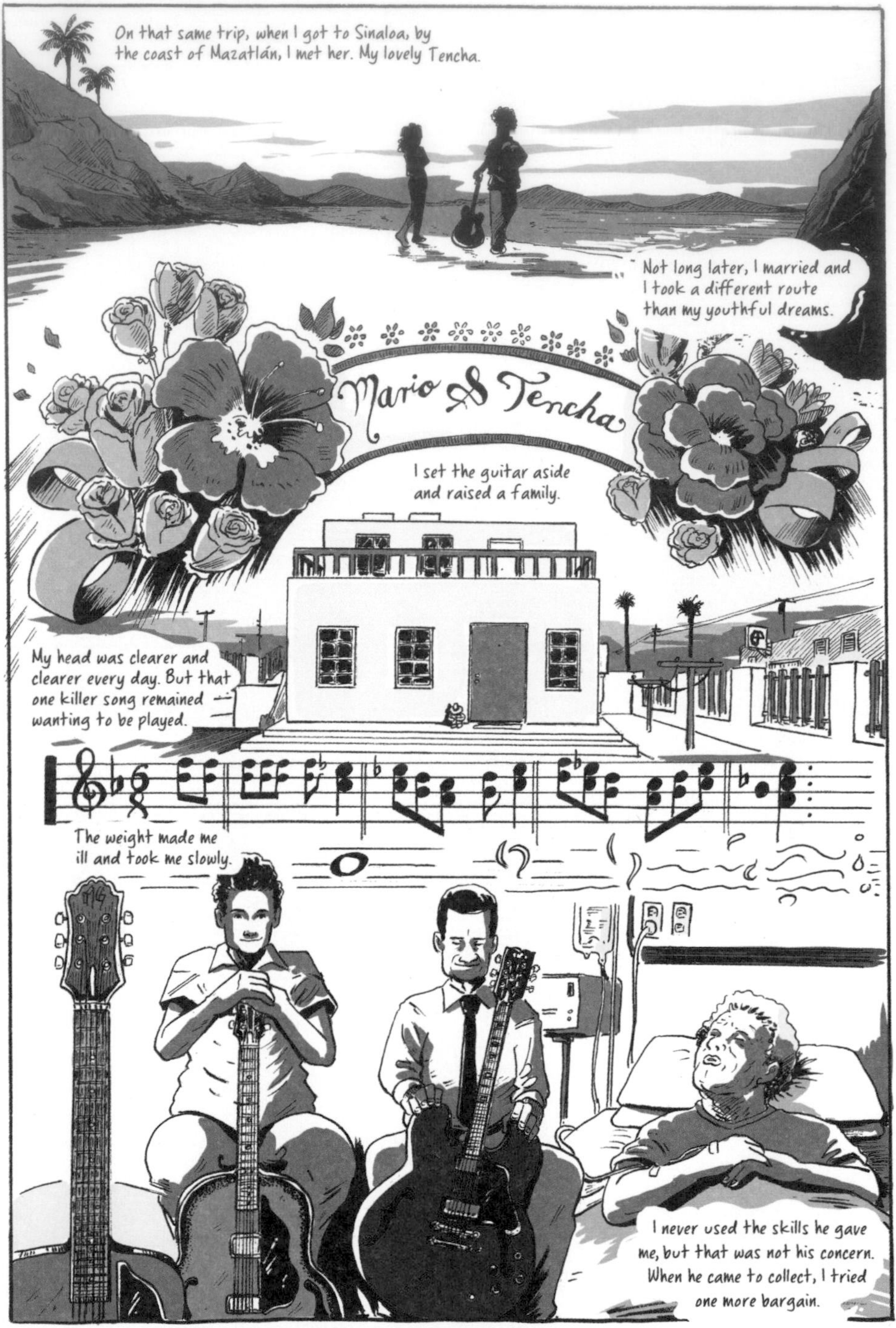
On that same trip, when I got to Sinaloa, by the coast of Mazatlán, I met her. My lovely Tencha.
Not long later, I married and I took a different route than my youthful dreams.
Mario & Tencha
I set the guitar aside and raised a family.
My head was clearer and clearer every day. But that one killer song remained wanting to be played.
The weight made me ill and took me slowly.
I never used the skills he gave me, but that was not his concern. When he came to collect, I tried one more bargain.

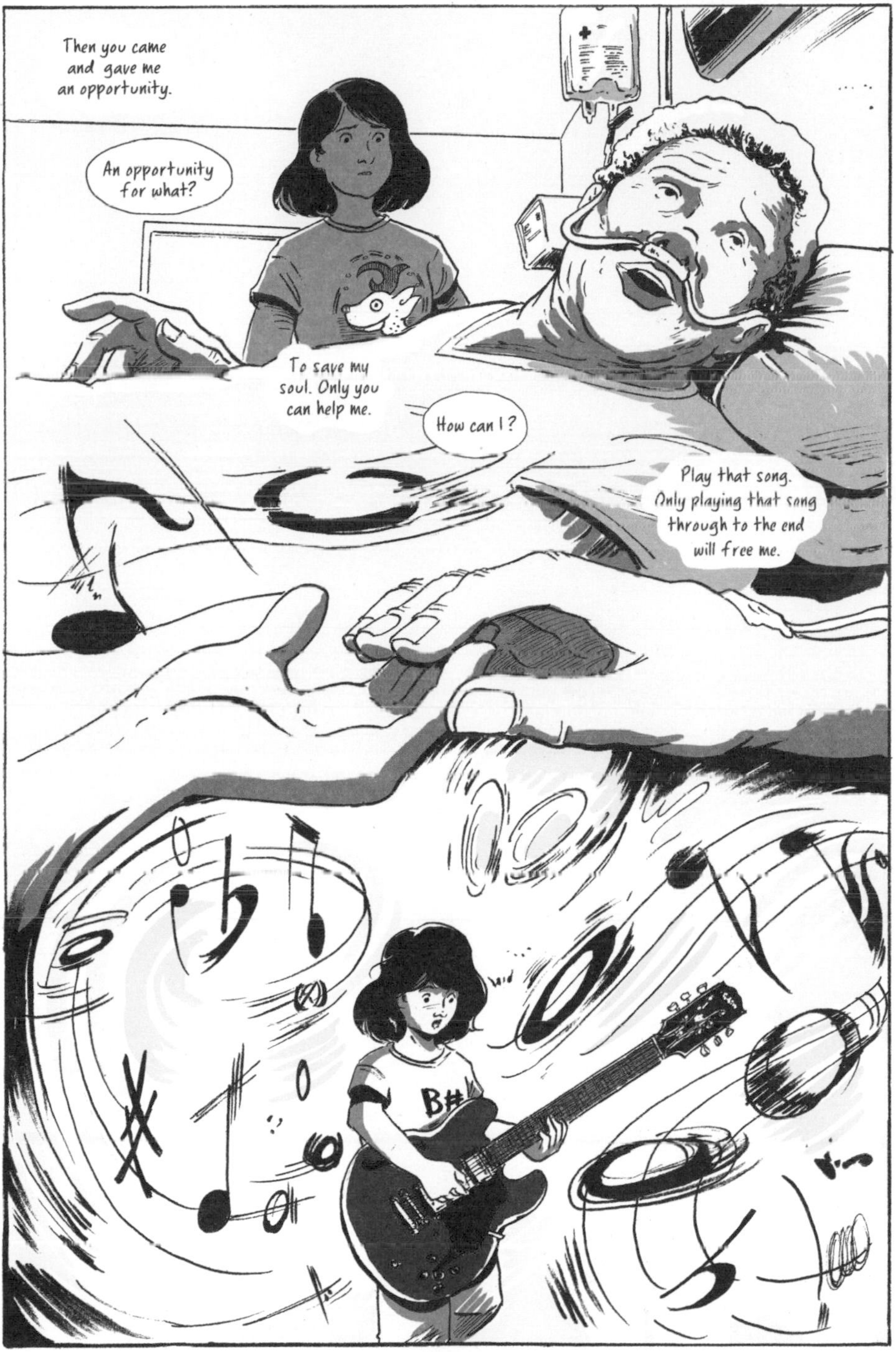

Then you came and gave me an opportunity.
An opportunity for what?
To save my soul. Only you can help me.
How can I?
Play that song. Only playing that song through to the end will free me.
B#

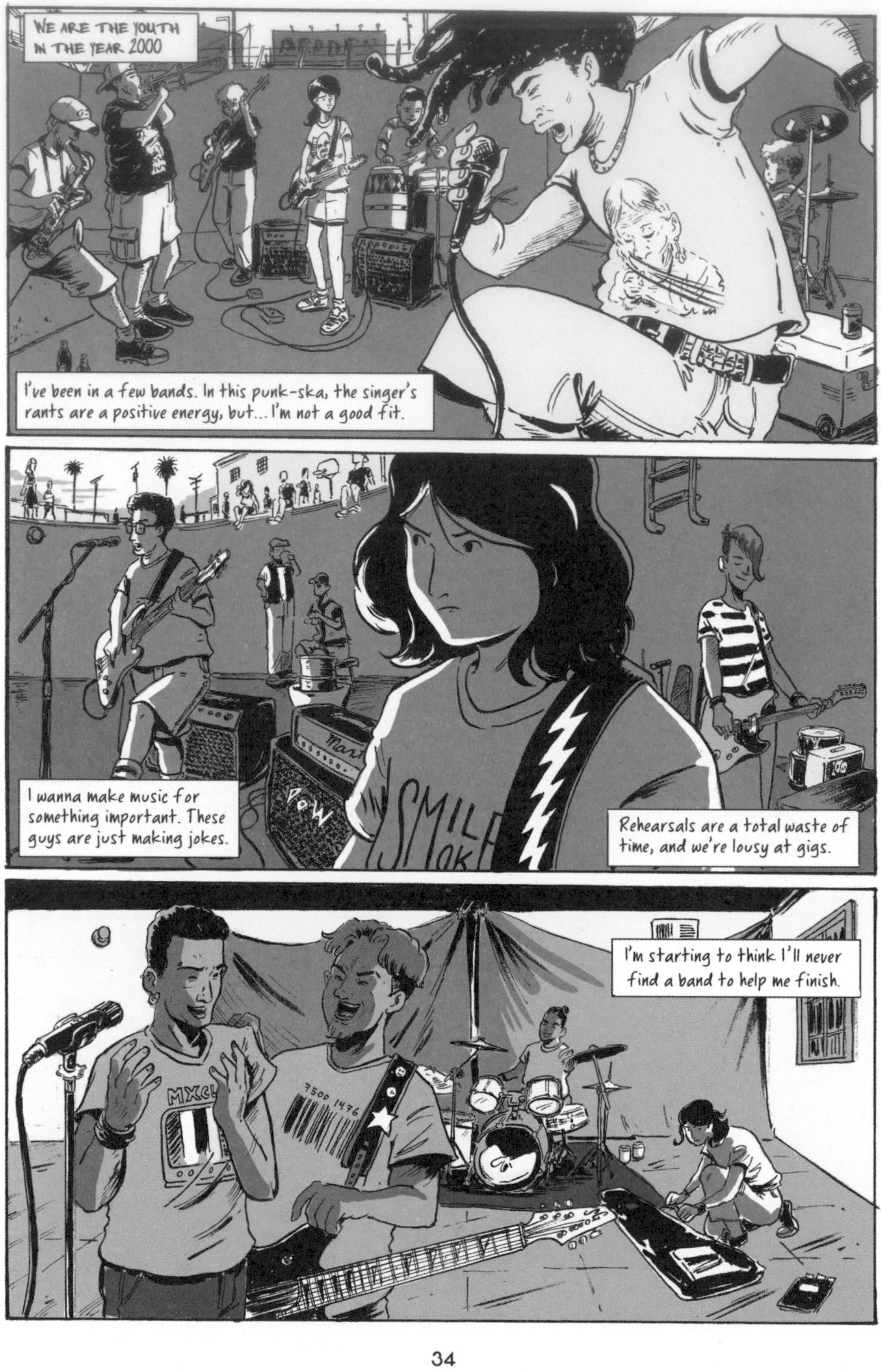
WE ARE THE YOUTH IN THE YEAR 2000
I've been in a few bands. In this punk-ska, the singer's rants are a positive energy, but... I'm not a good fit.
I wanna make music for something important. These guys are just making jokes.
Rehearsals are a total waste of time, and we're lousy at gigs.
I'm starting to think I'll never find a band to help me finish.

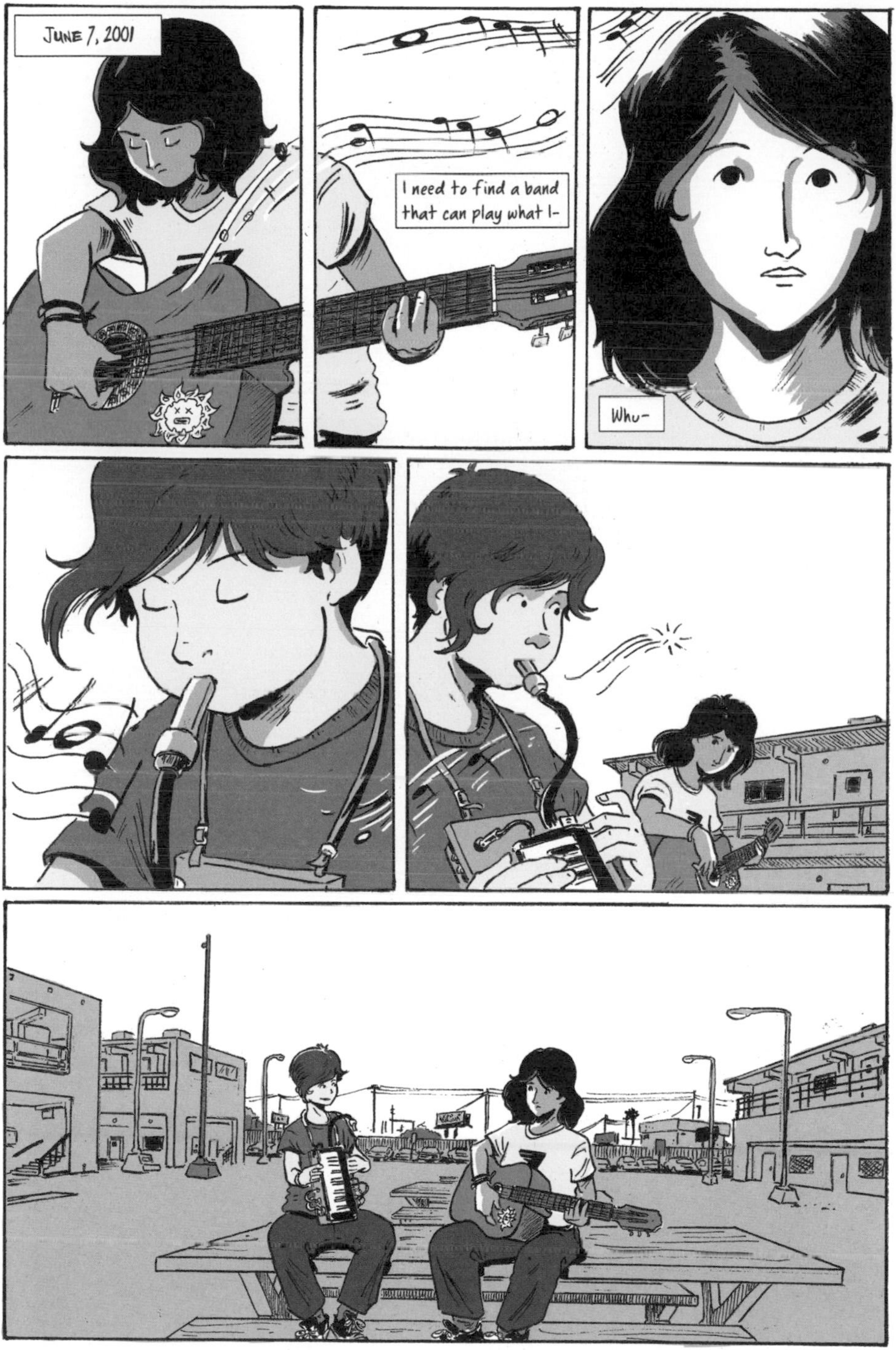

June 7, 2001
I need to find a band that can play what I-
Whu-

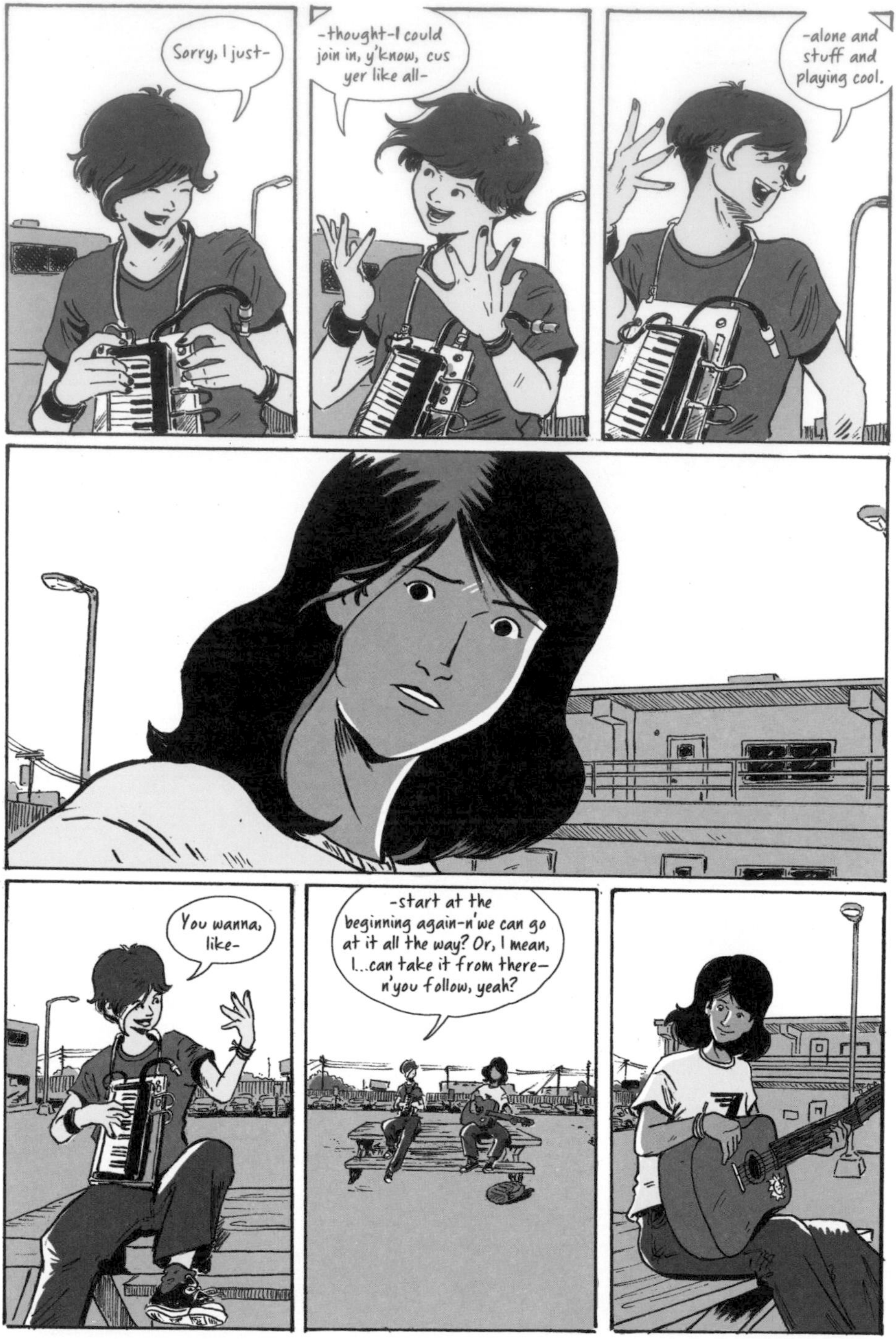
Sorry, I just-
-thought-I could join in, y'know, cus yer like all-
-alone and stuff and playing cool.
You wanna, like-
-start at the beginning again-n'we can go at it all the way? Or, I mean, I...can take it from there-n'you follow, yeah?

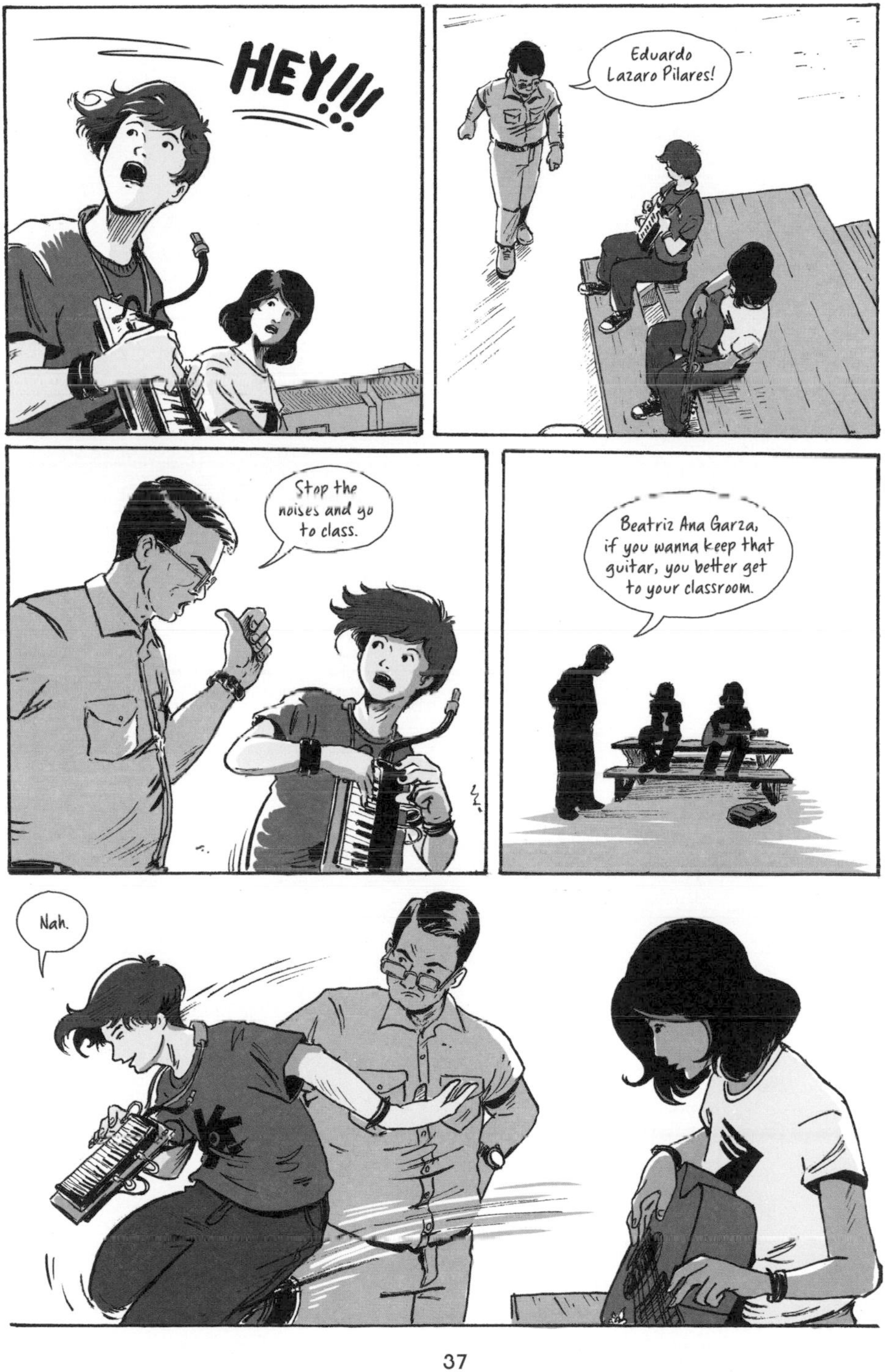
HEY!!!
Eduardo Lazaro Pilares!
Stop the noises and go to class.
Beatriz Ana Garza, if you wanna keep that guitar, you better get to your classroom.
Nah.

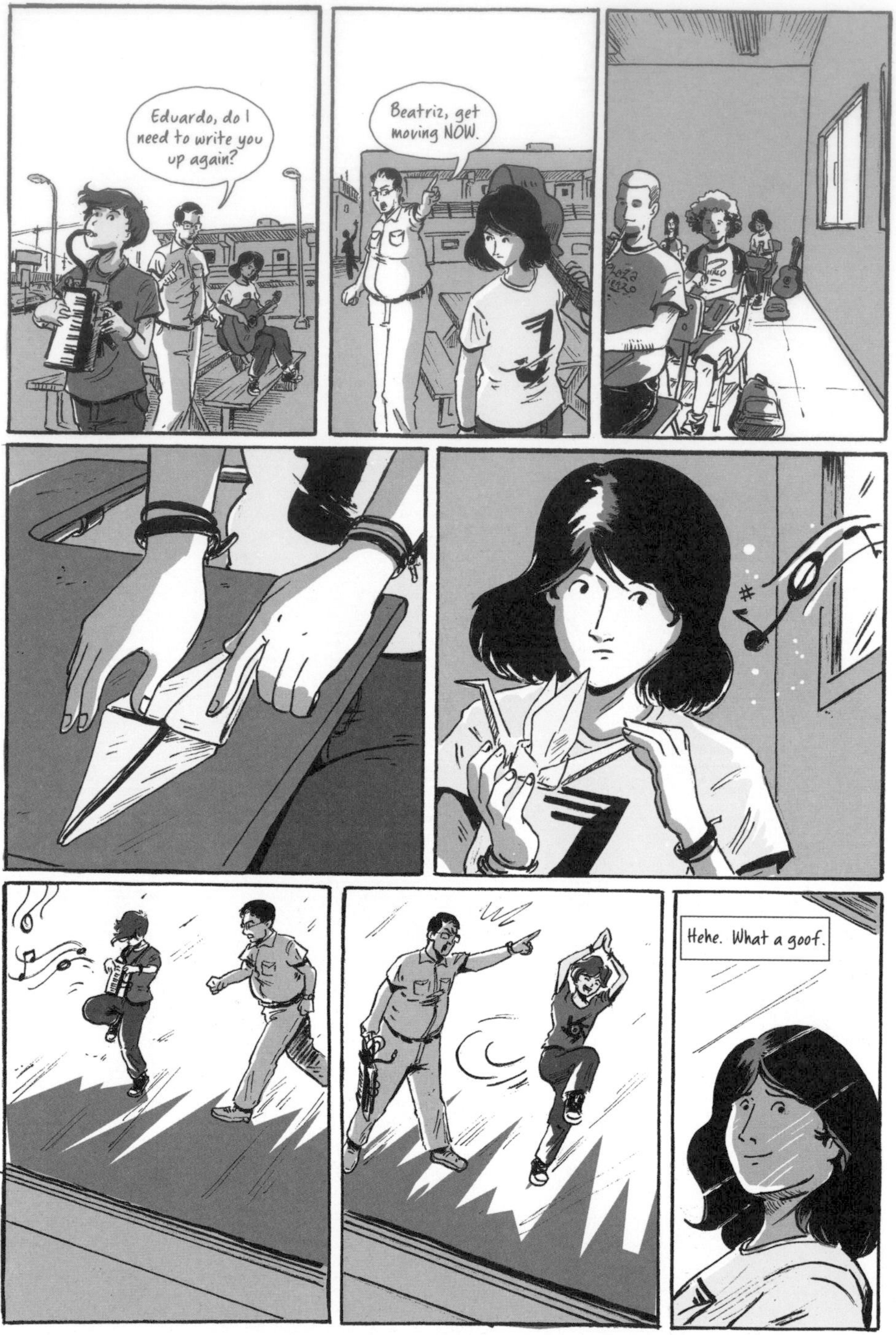
Eduardo, do I need to write you up again?
Beatriz, get moving NOW.
Hehe. What a goof.

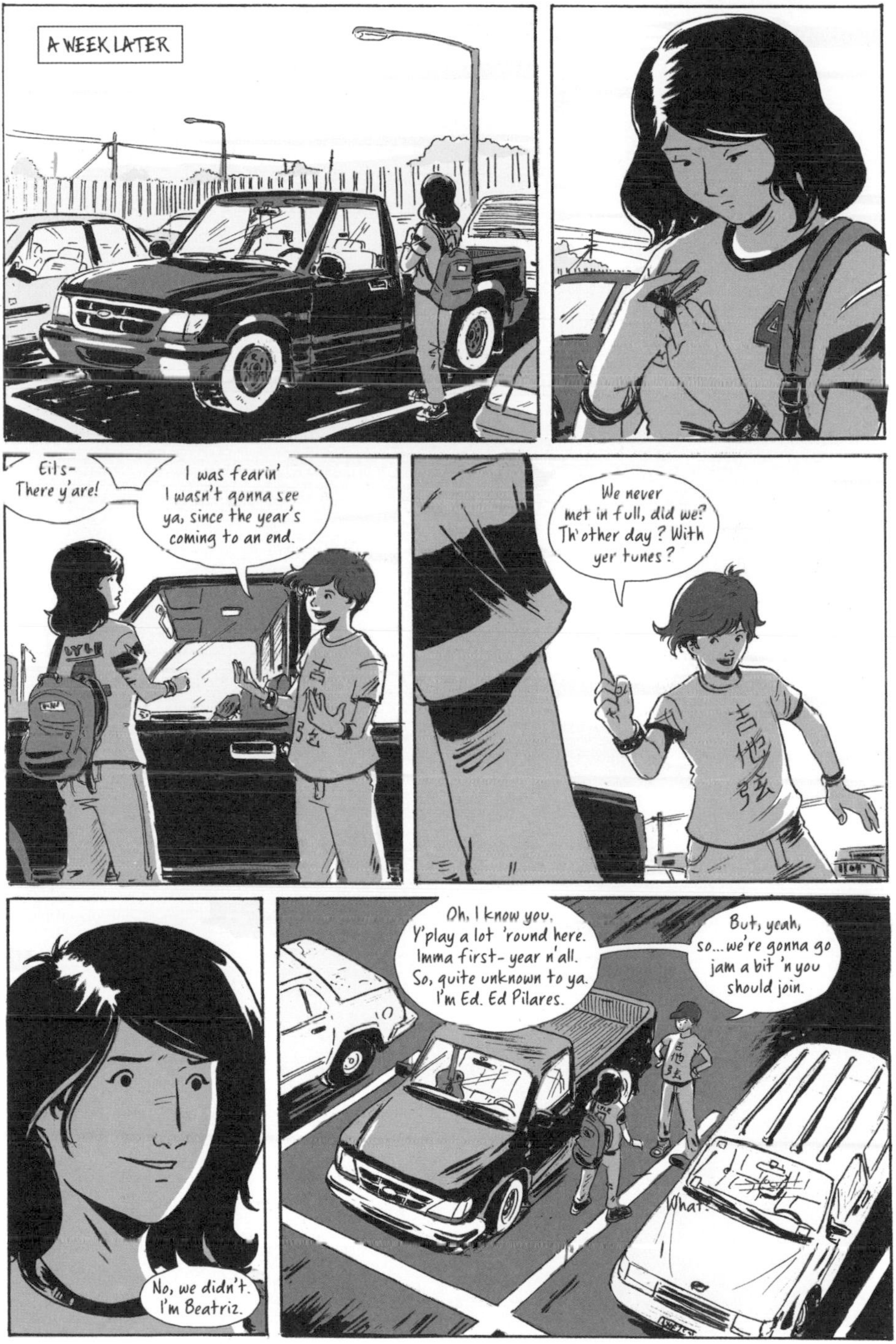
A WEEK LATER
Eils- There y'are!
I was fearin' I wasn't gonna see ya, since the year's coming to an end.
We never met in full, did we? Th'other day? With yer tunes?
No, we didn't. I'm Beatriz.
Oh, I know you. Y'play a lot 'round here. Imma first-year n'all. So, quite unknown to ya. I'm Ed. Ed Pilares.
But, yeah, so... we're gonna go jam a bit 'n you should join.
What?

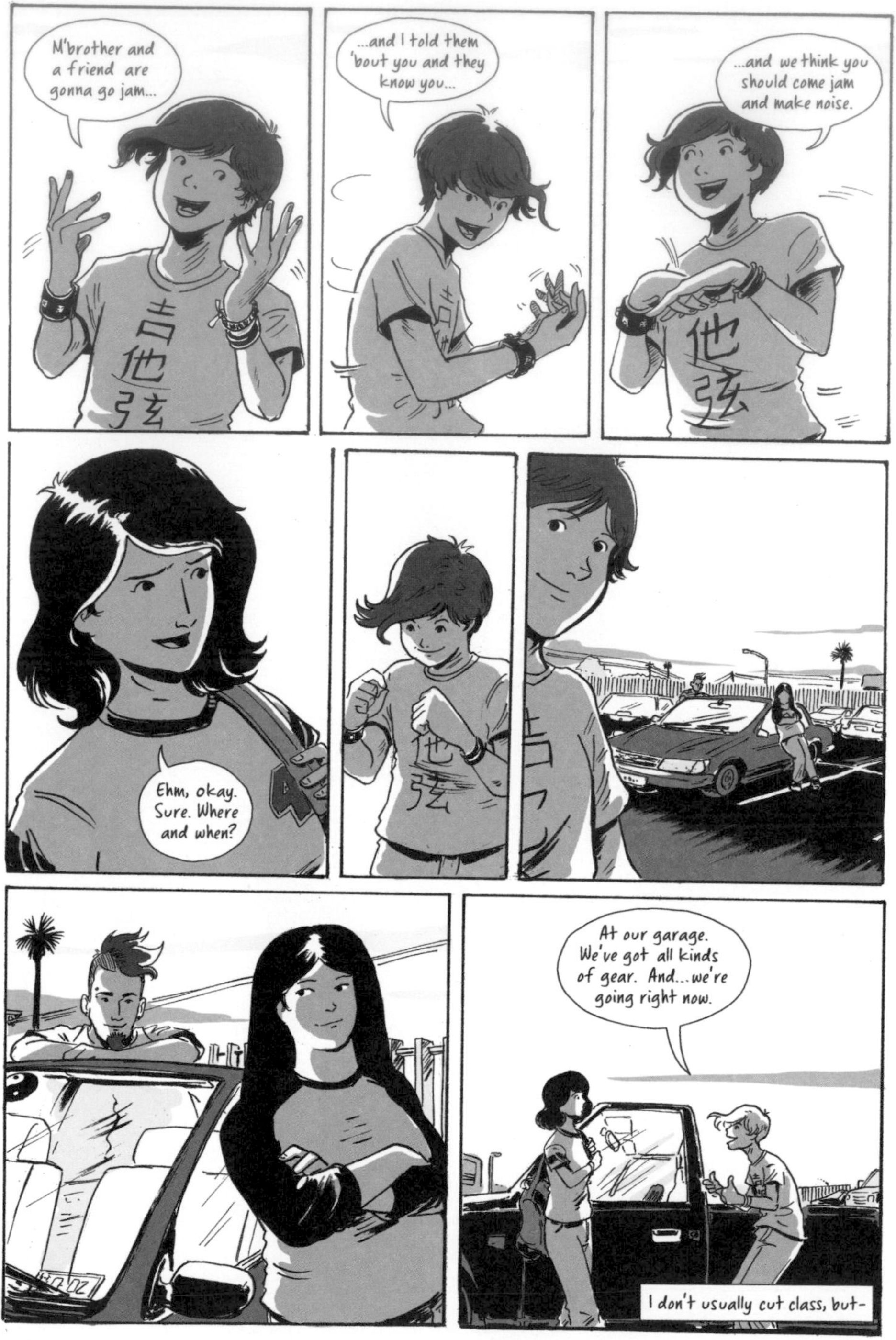
M'brother and a friend are gonna go jam...
...and I told them 'bout you and they know you...
...and we think you should come jam and make noise.
吉他弦
他弦
Ehm, okay. Sure. Where and when?
At our garage. We've got all kinds of gear. And...we're going right now.
I don't usually cut class, but-

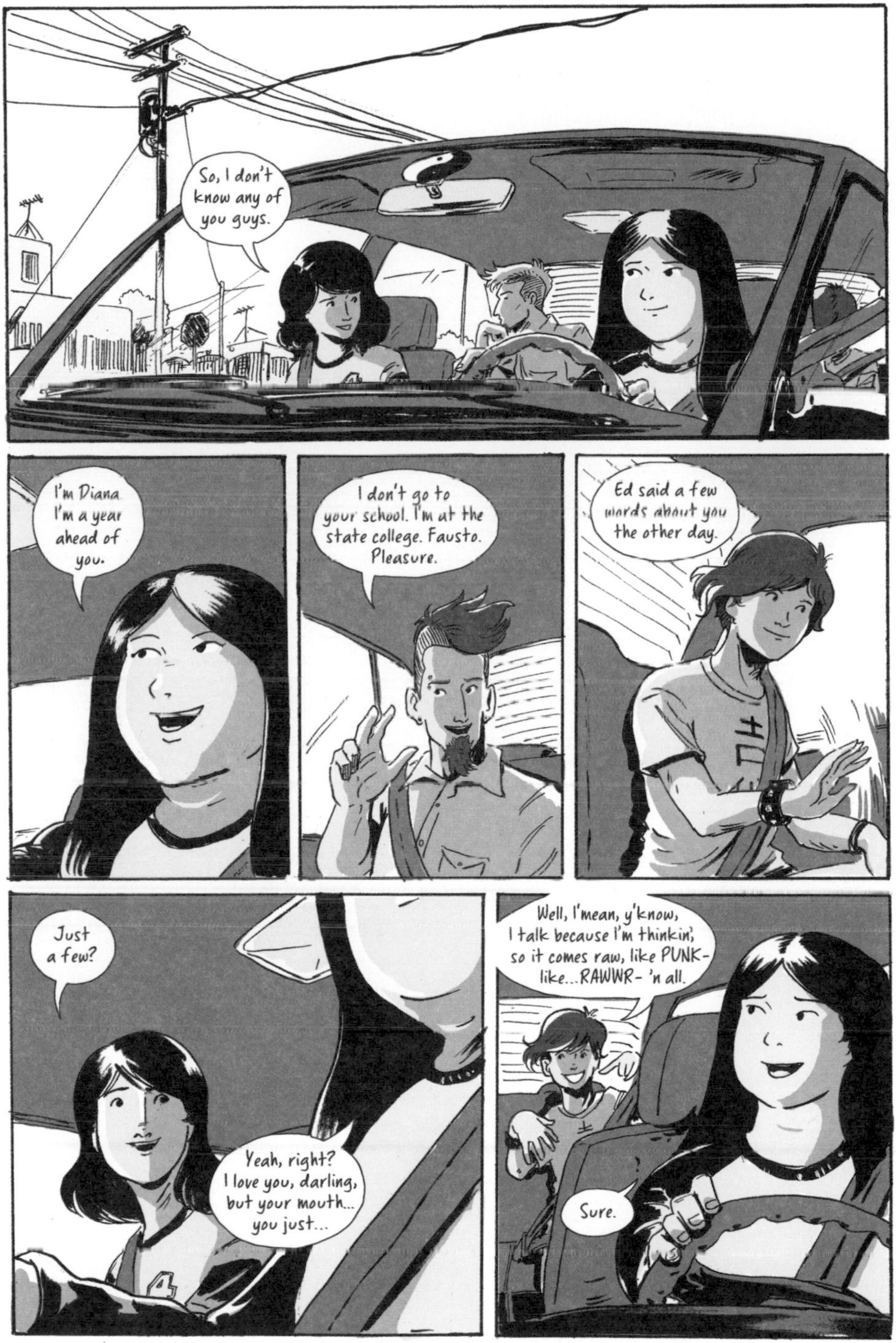

So, I don't know any of you guys.
I'm Diana. I'm a year ahead of you.
I don't go to your school. I'm at the state college. Fausto. Pleasure.
Ed said a few words about you the other day.
Just a few?
Yeah, right? I love you, darling, but your mouth... you just...
Well, I'mean, y'know, I talk because I'm thinkin', so it comes raw, like PUNK-like...RAWWR- 'n all.
Sure.

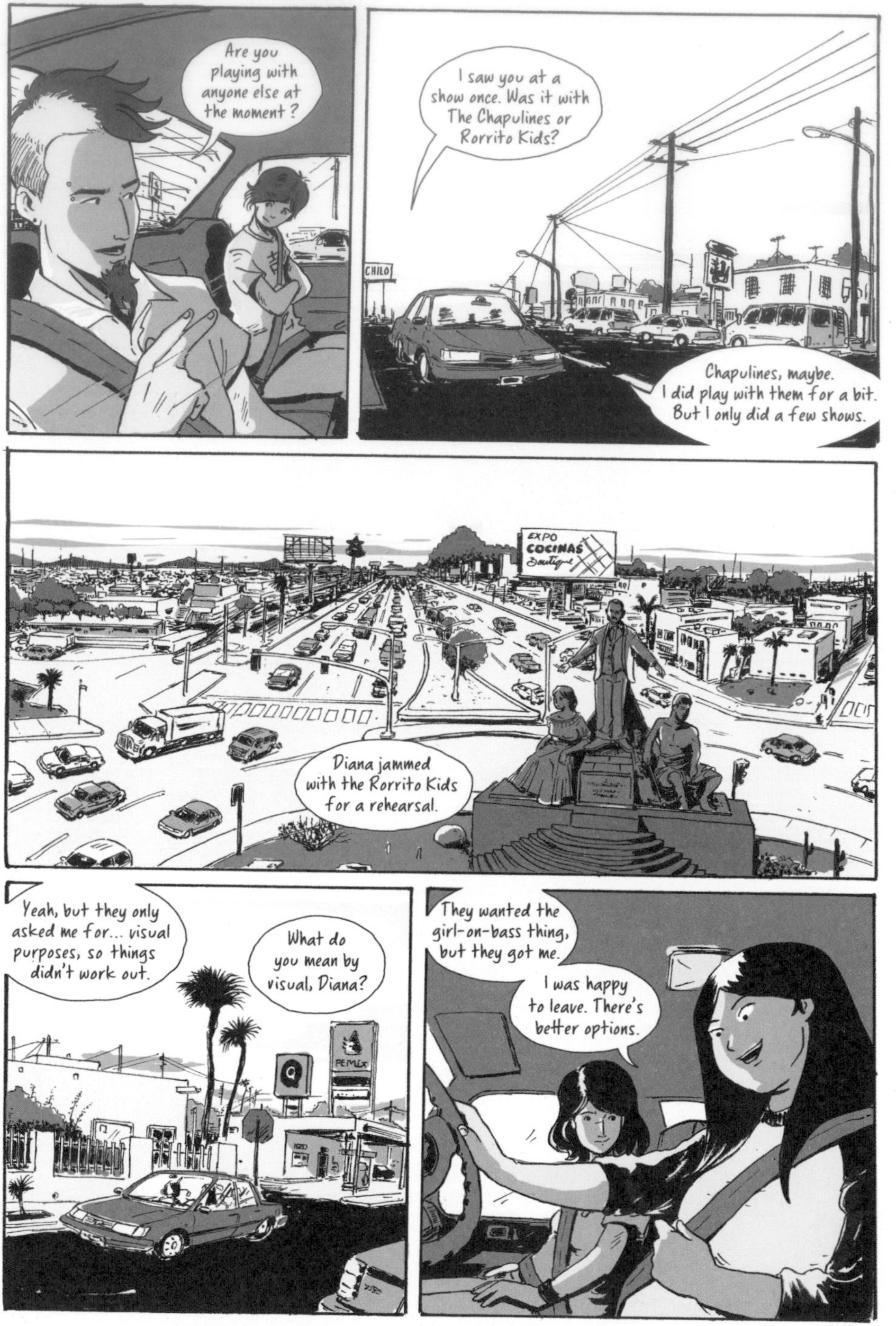
Are you playing with anyone else at the moment?
I saw you at a show once. Was it with The Chapulines or Rorrito Kids?
CHILO
Chapulines, maybe. I did play with them for a bit. But I only did a few shows.
EXPO COCINAS Boutique
Diana jammed with the Rorrito Kids for a rehearsal.
Yeah, but they only asked me for... visual purposes, so things didn't work out.
What do you mean by visual, Diana?
PEMEX
They wanted the girl-on-bass thing, but they got me.
I was happy to leave. There's better options.

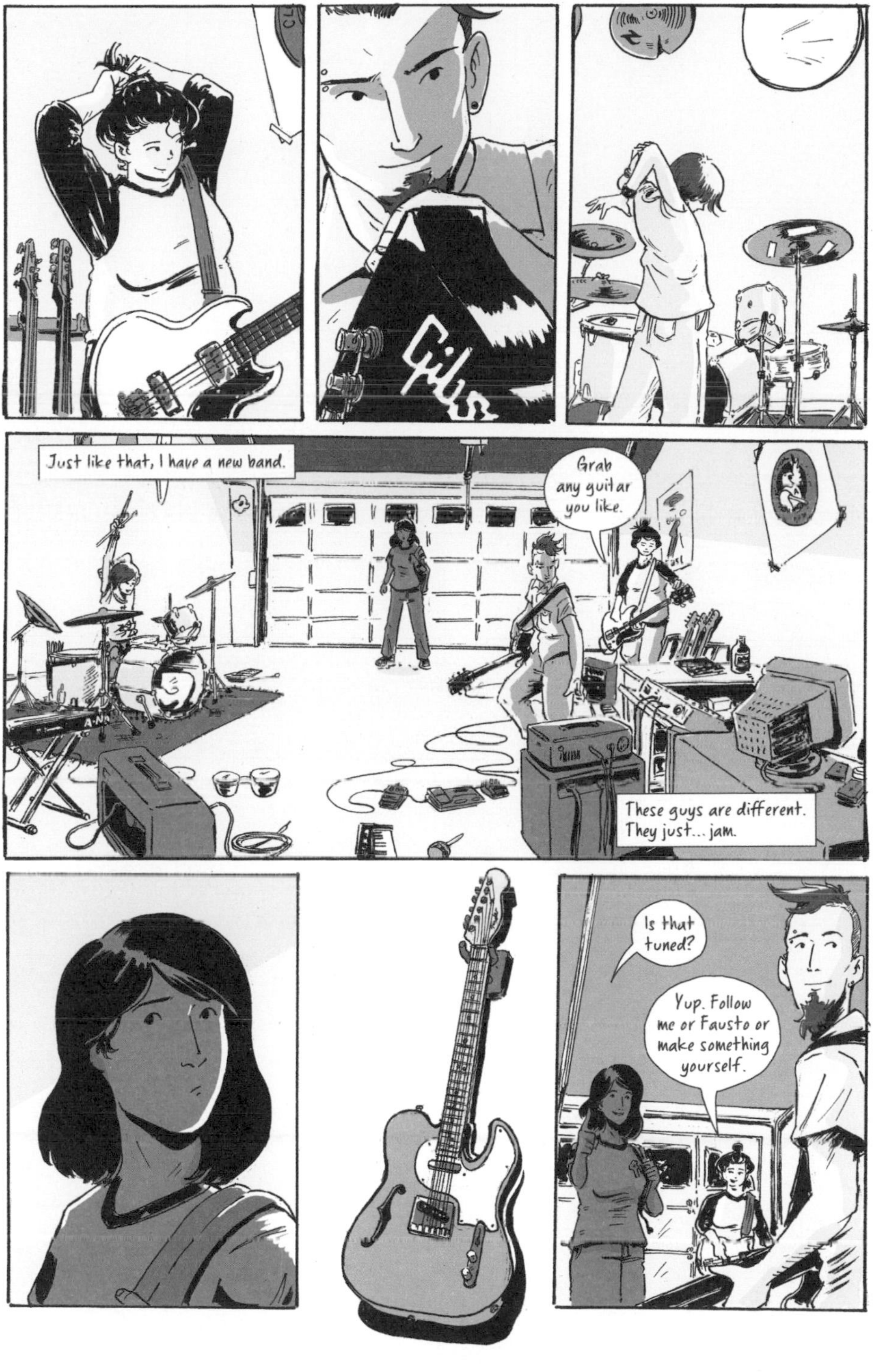

Just like that, I have a new band.
Grab any guitar you like.
These guys are different. They just... jam.
Is that tuned?
Yup. Follow me or Fausto or make something yourself.

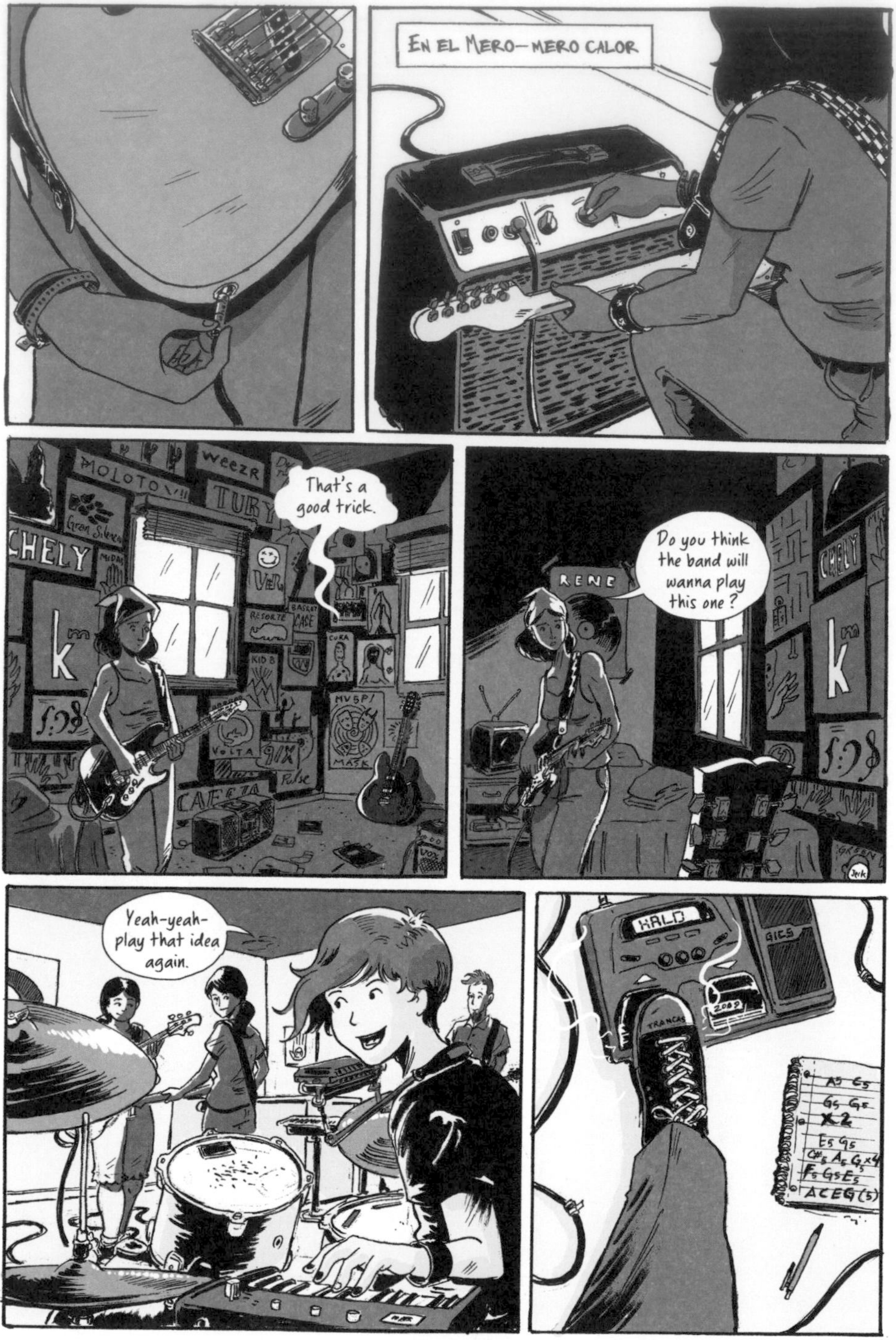
En el Mero—mero calor
That's a good trick.
Do you think the band will wanna play this one?
Yeah-yeah-play that idea again.

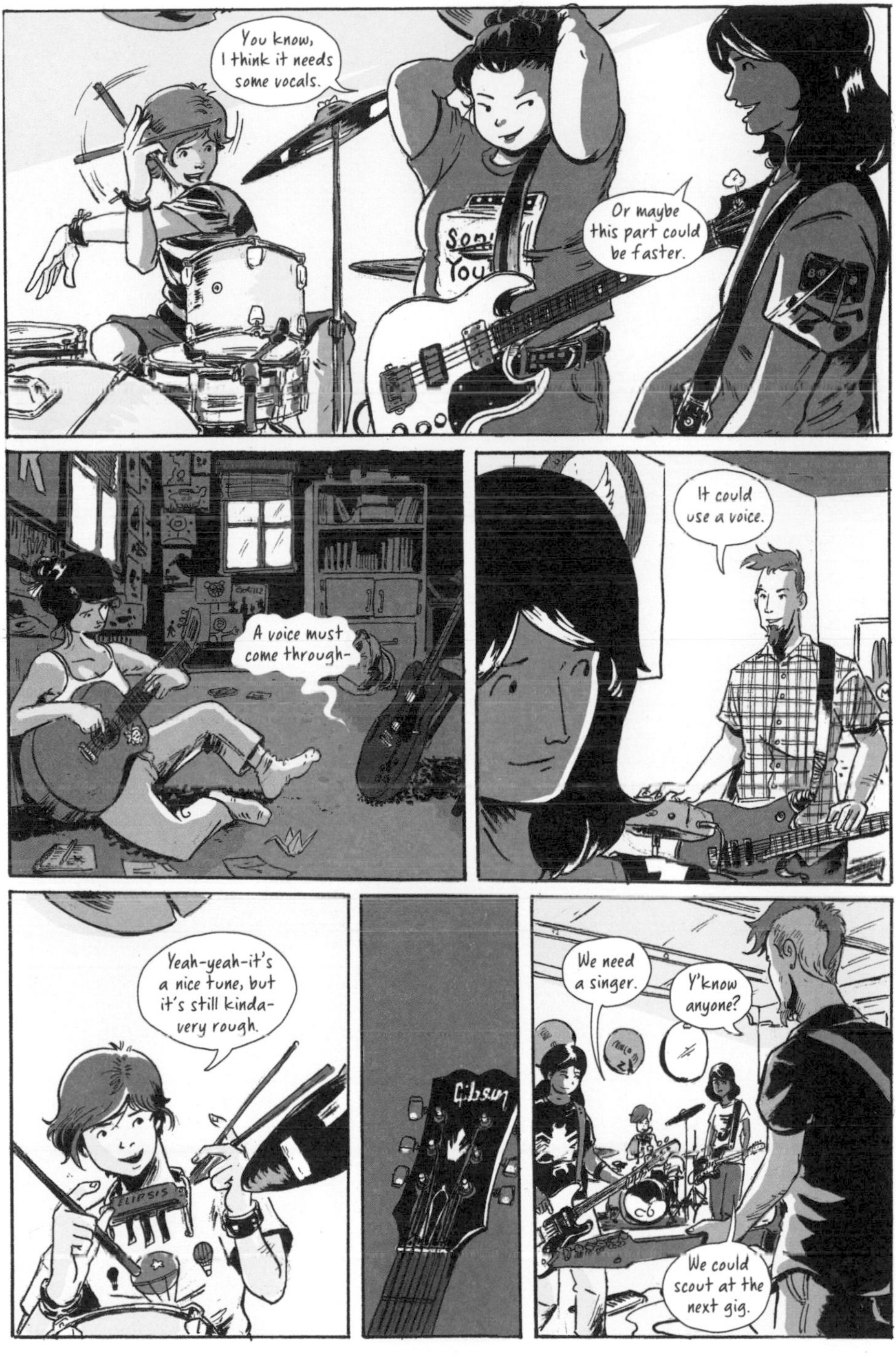

You know, I think it needs some vocals.
Or maybe this part could be faster.
A voice must come through-
It could use a voice.
Yeah-yeah-it's a nice tune, but it's still kinda-very rough.
ELIPSIS
Gibson
We need a singer.
Y'know anyone?
We could scout at the next gig.

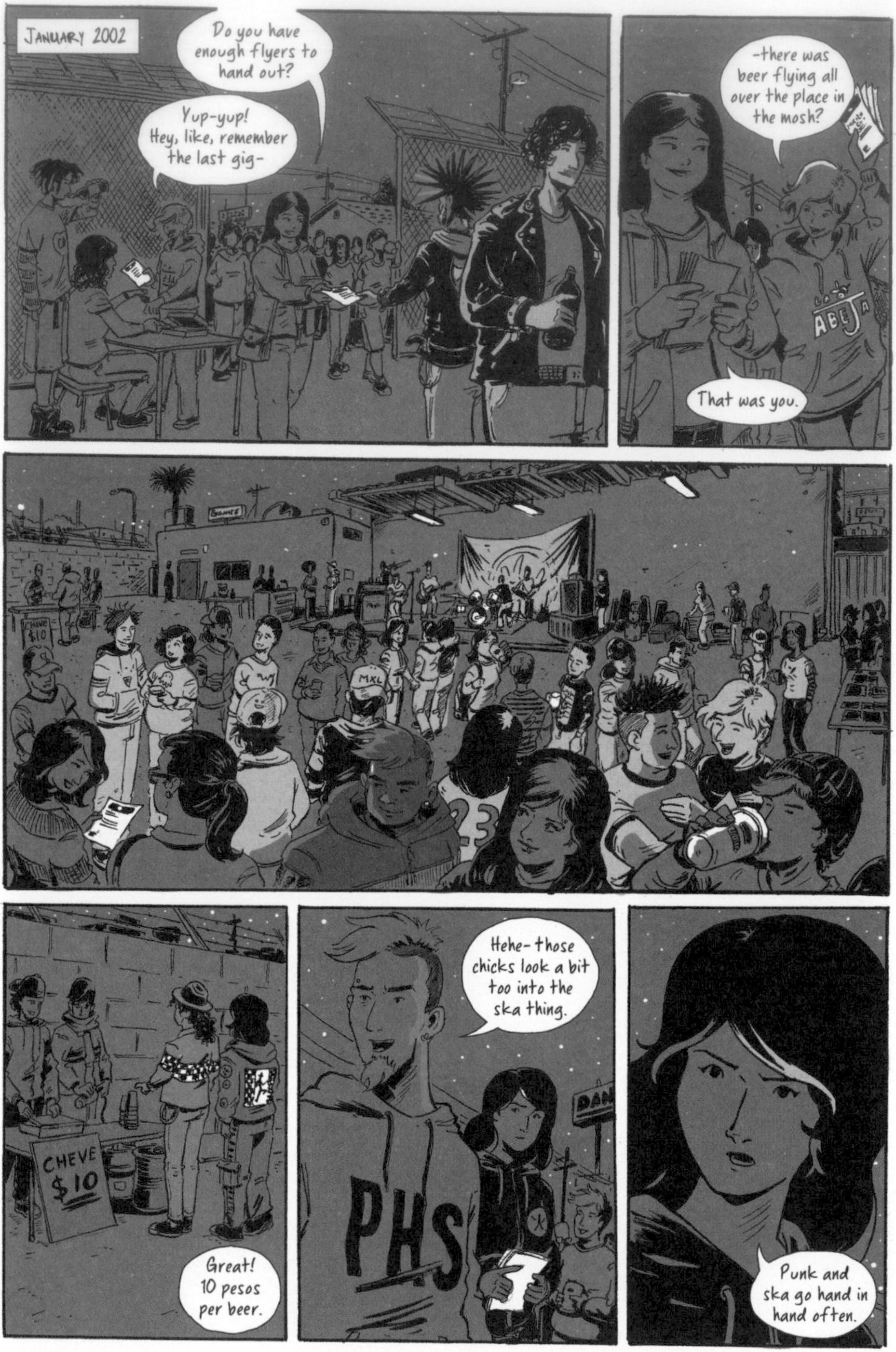
January 2002
Do you have enough flyers to hand out?
Yup-yup! Hey, like, remember the last gig-
-there was beer flying all over the place in the mosh?
That was you.
CHEVE $10
Great! 10 pesos per beer.
Hehe- those chicks look a bit too into the ska thing.
PHS
Punk and ska go hand in hand often.

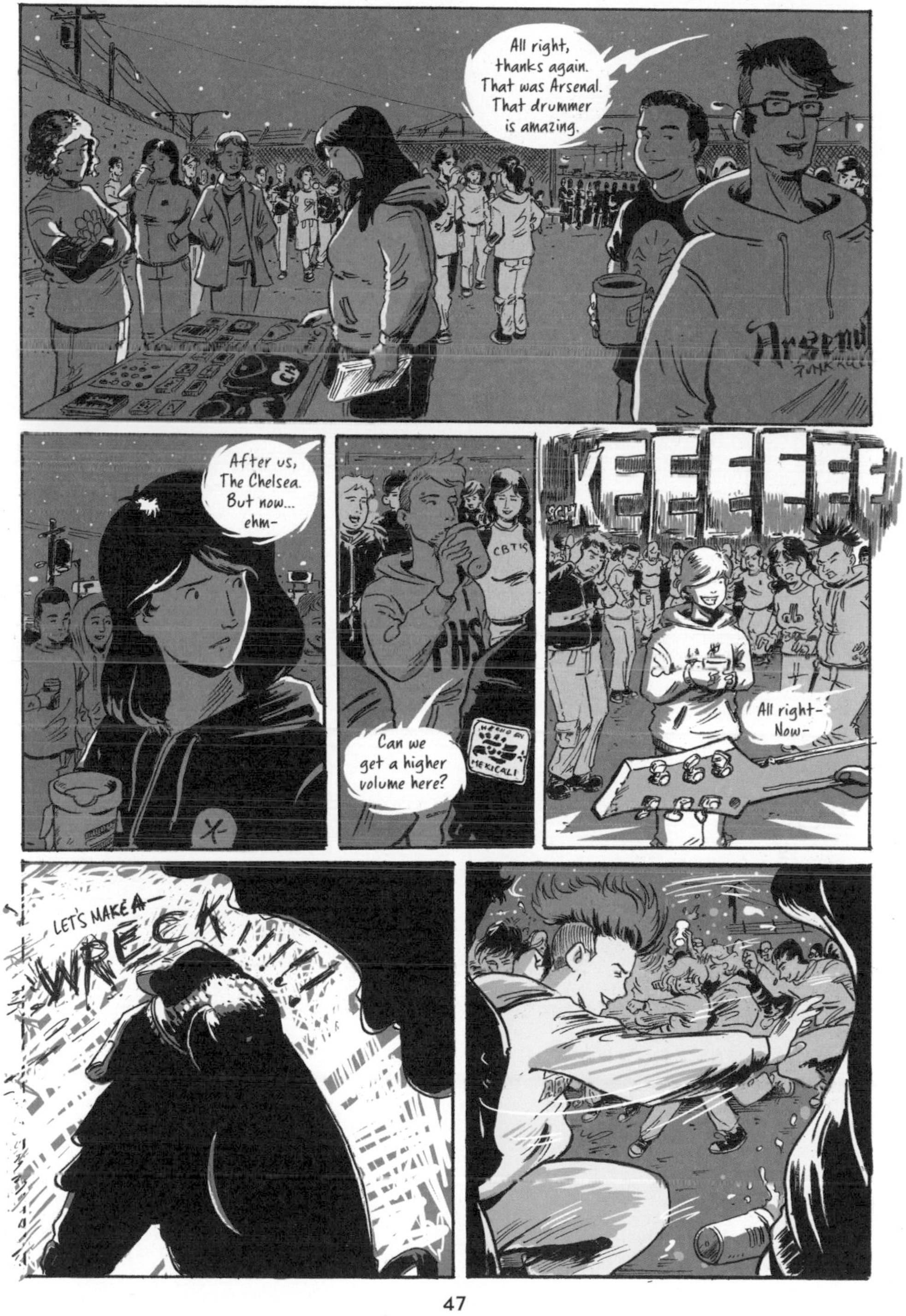
All right, thanks again. That was Arsenal. That drummer is amazing.
Arsenal
After us, The Chelsea. But now... ehm-
CBTIS
Can we get a higher volume here?
SCH
KEEEEEE
All right- Now-
LET'S MAKE A- WRECK!!!!

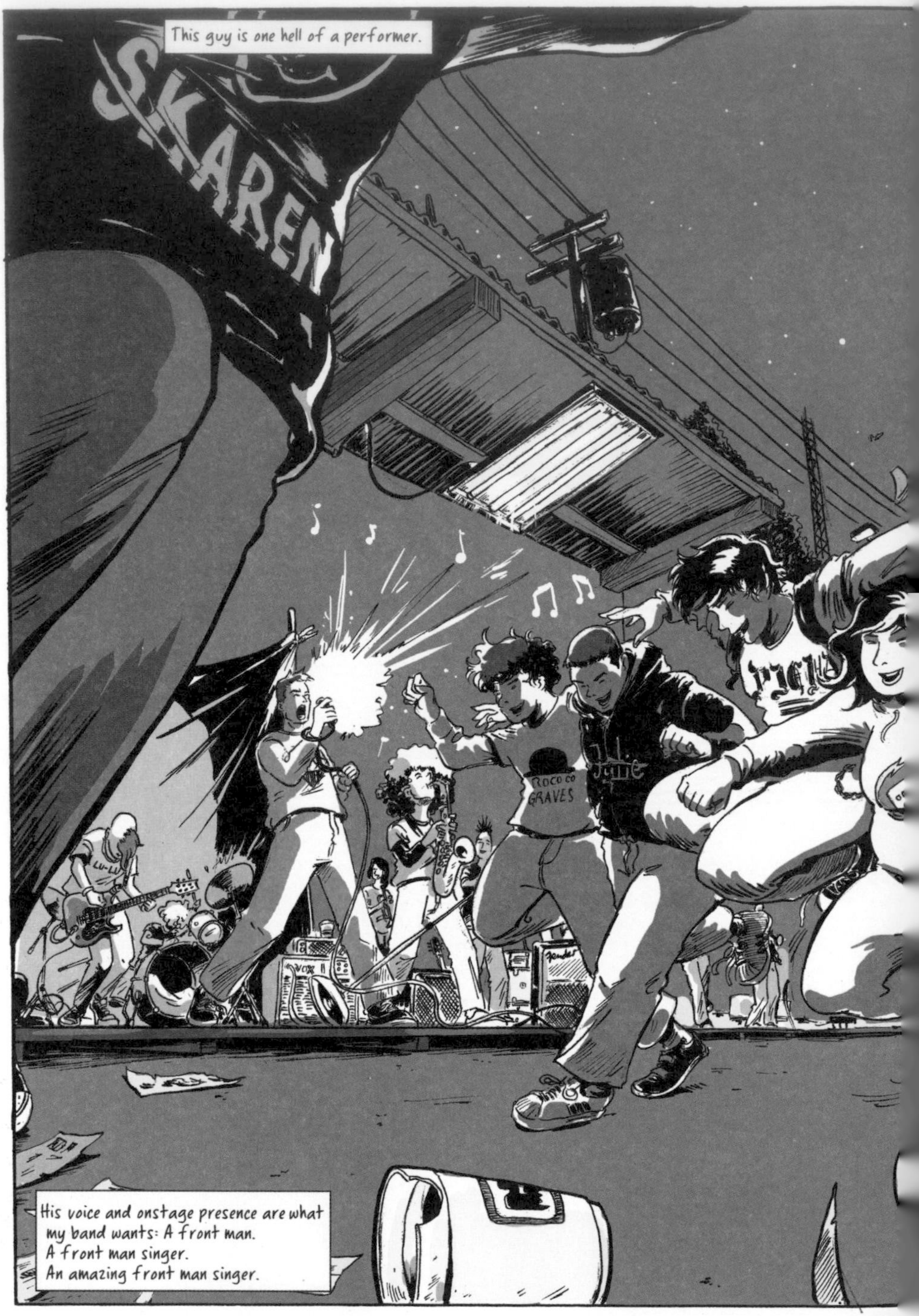
This guy is one hell of a performer.
SKAREN
ROCOCO GRAVES
His voice and onstage presence are what my band wants: A front man.
A front man singer.
An amazing front man singer.

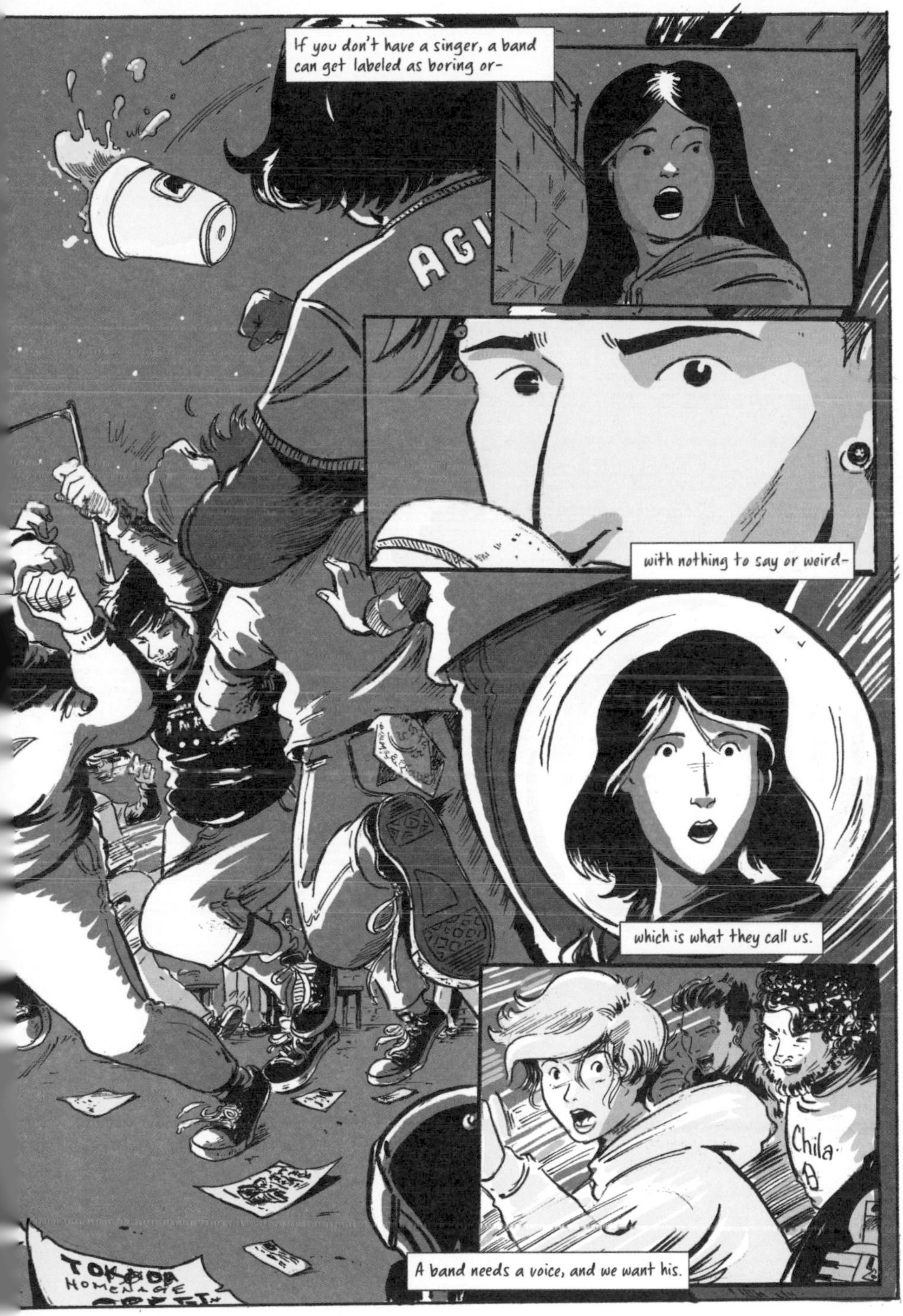
If you don't have a singer, a band can get labeled as boring or-
AGI
with nothing to say or weird-
which is what they call us.
Chila
A band needs a voice, and we want his.
TOKBOA
HOMENAGE

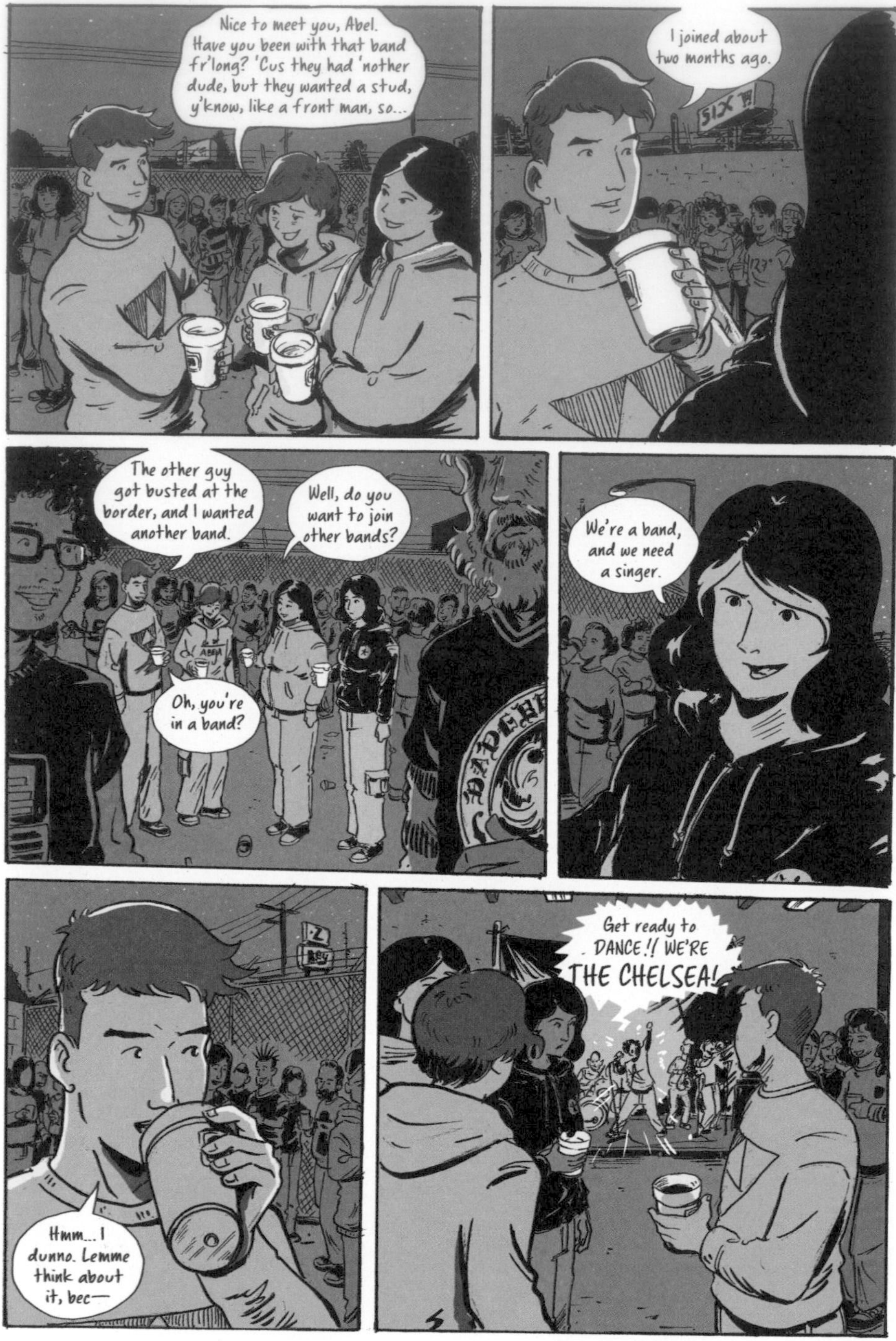
Nice to meet you, Abel. Have you been with that band fr'long? 'Cus they had 'nother dude, but they wanted a stud, y'know, like a front man, so...
I joined about two months ago.
The other guy got busted at the border, and I wanted another band.
Oh, you're in a band?
Well, do you want to join other bands?
We're a band, and we need a singer.
Hmm... I dunno. Lemme think about it, bec—
Get ready to DANCE!! WE'RE THE CHELSEA!

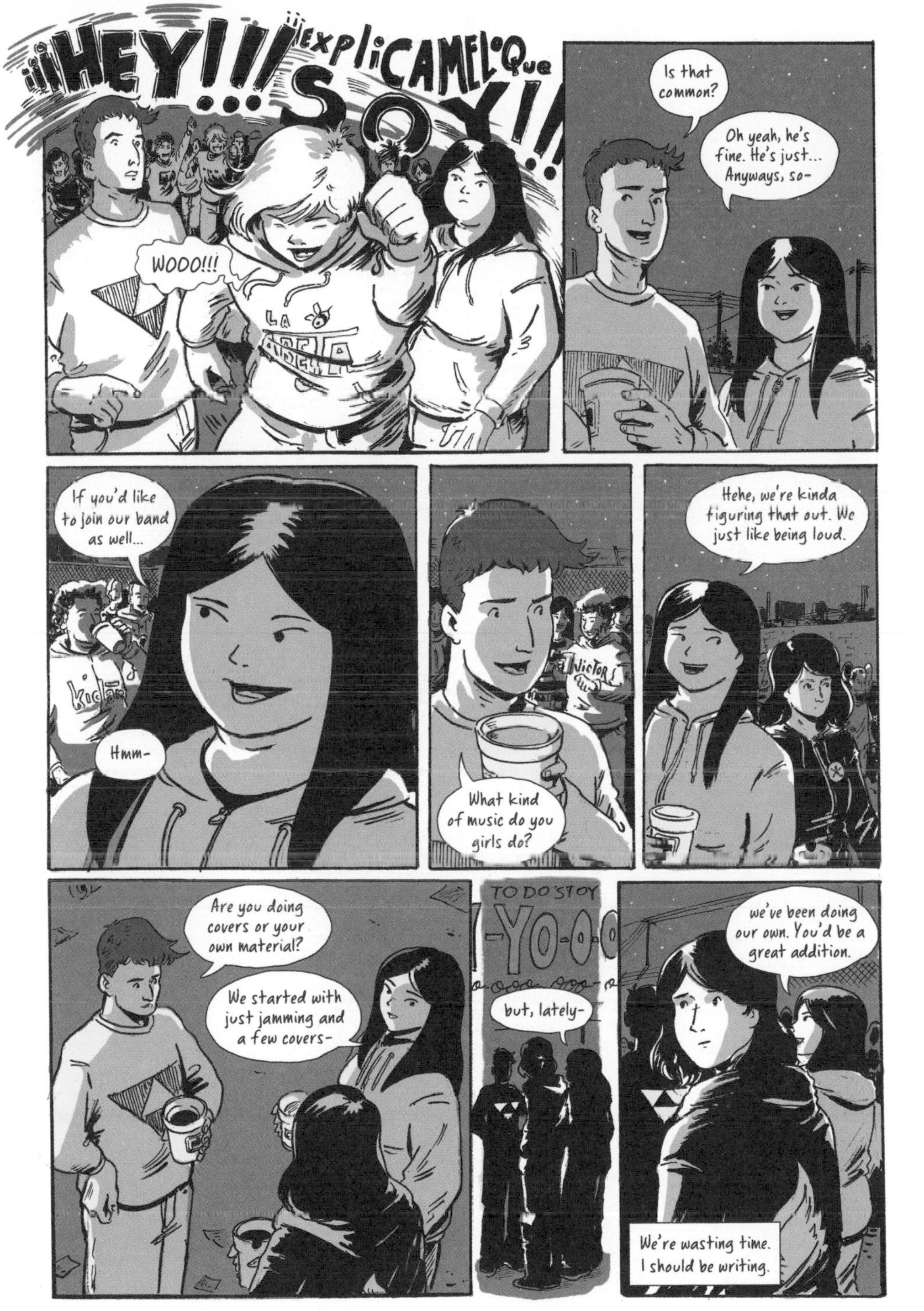
¡¡¡HEY!!!...
¡¡¡Explicamelo que SOY!!!
WOOO!!!
Is that common?
Oh yeah, he's fine. He's just... Anyways, so-
If you'd like to join our band as well...
Hmm-
What kind of music do you girls do?
Hehe, we're kinda figuring that out. We just like being loud.
Are you doing covers or your own material?
We started with just jamming and a few covers-
but, lately-
we've been doing our own. You'd be a great addition.
We're wasting time. I should be writing.

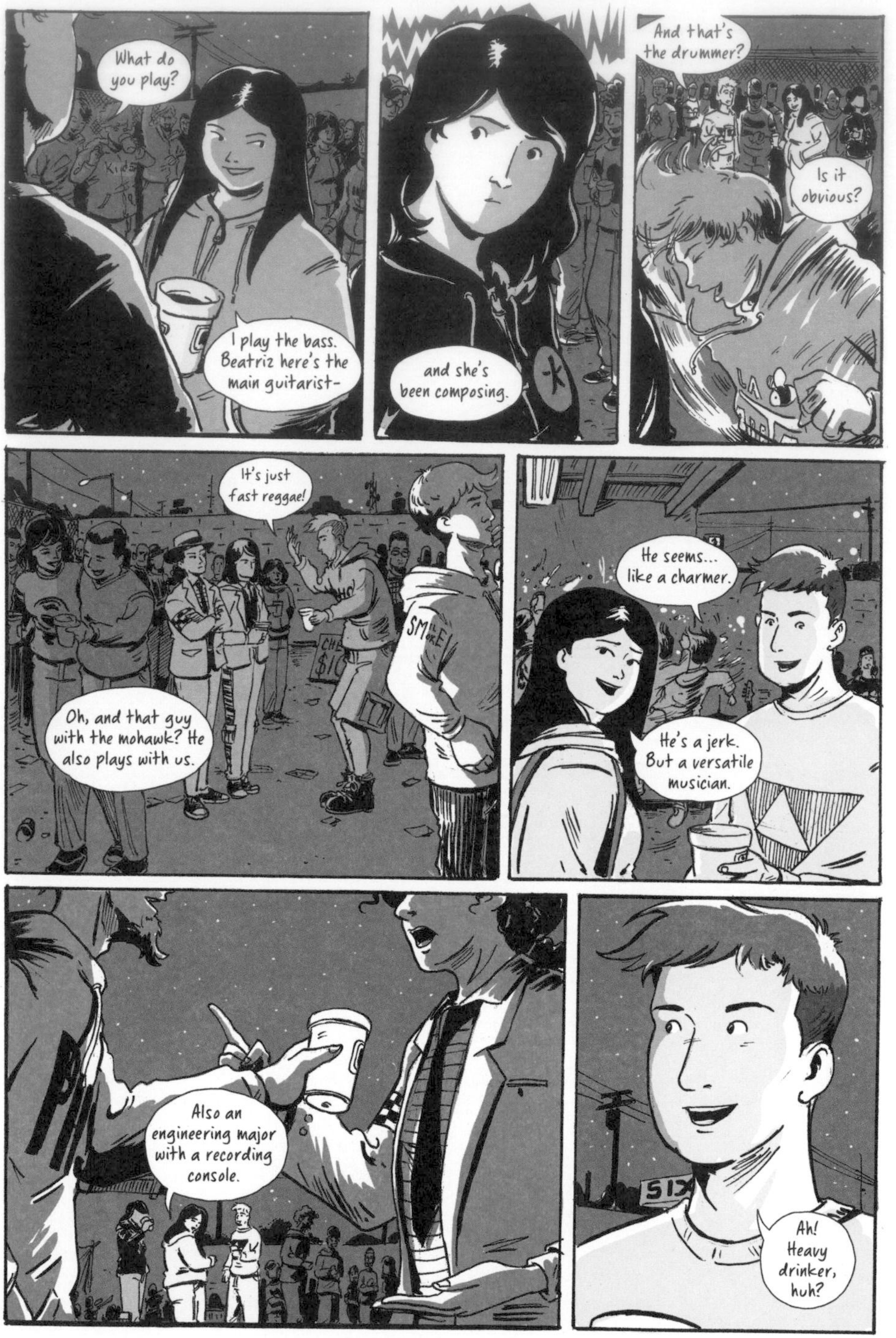
What do you play?
I play the bass. Beatriz here's the main guitarist-
and she's been composing.
And that's the drummer?
Is it obvious?
It's just fast reggae!
Oh, and that guy with the mohawk? He also plays with us.
He seems... like a charmer.
He's a jerk. But a versatile musician.
Also an engineering major with a recording console.
Ah! Heavy drinker, huh?

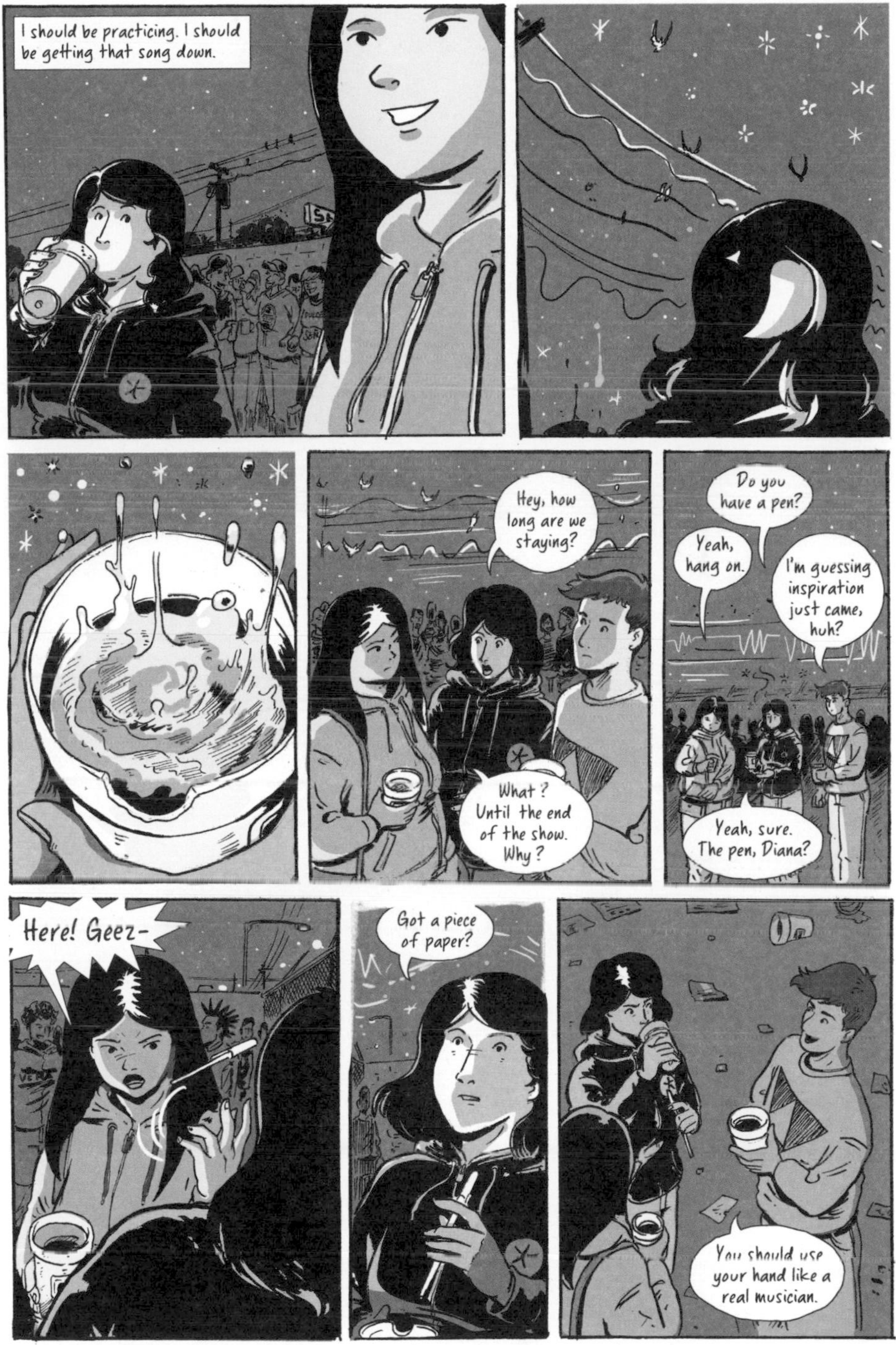
I should be practicing. I should be getting that song down.
Hey, how long are we staying?
What? Until the end of the show. Why?
Do you have a pen?
Yeah, hang on.
I'm guessing inspiration just came, huh?
Yeah, sure. The pen, Diana?
Here! Geez-
Got a piece of paper?
You should use your hand like a real musician.

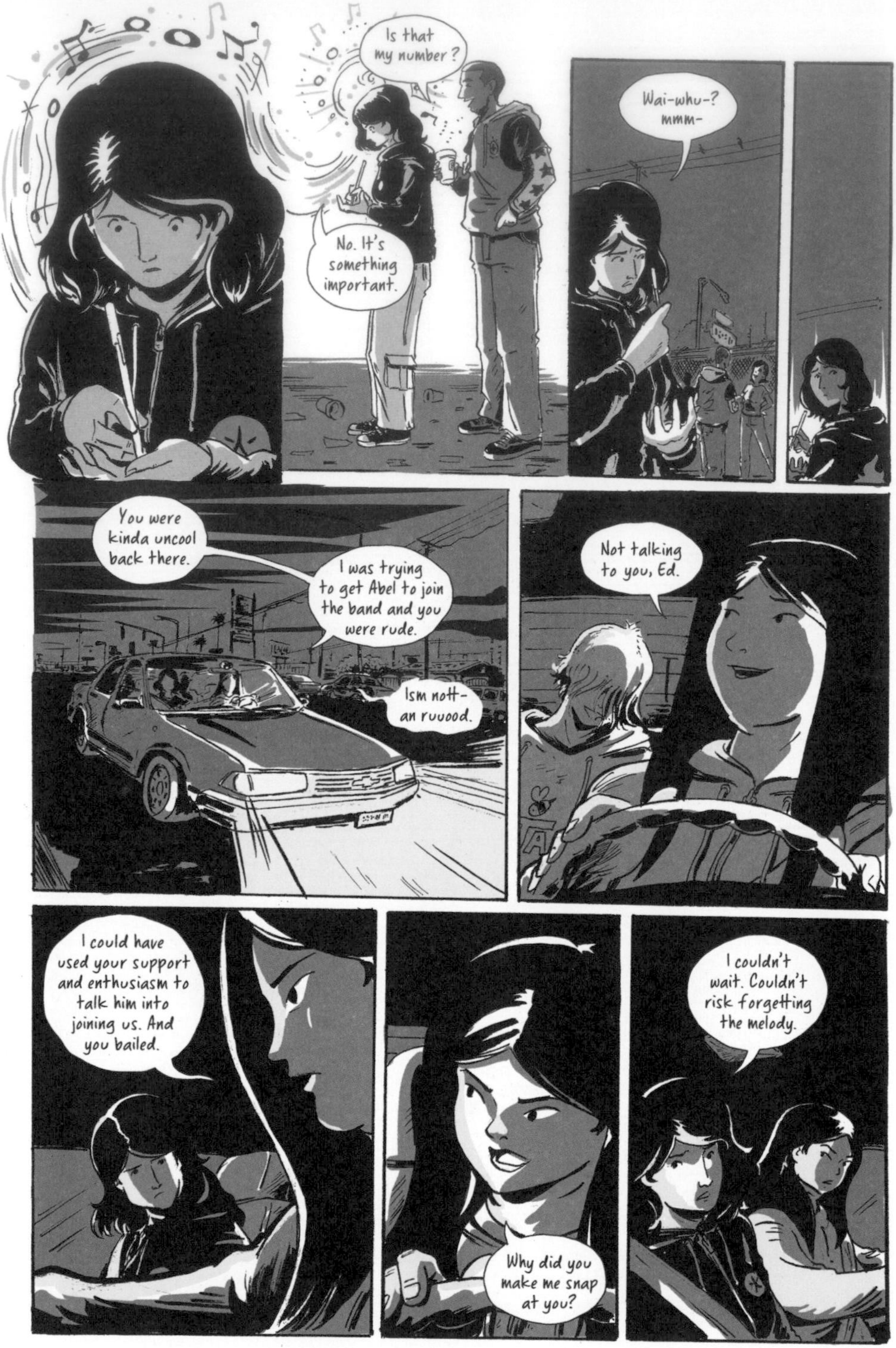
Is that my number?
No. It's something important.
Wai-whu-? mmm-
You were kinda uncool back there.
I was trying to get Abel to join the band and you were rude.
Ism nott-an ruuood.
Not talking to you, Ed.
I could have used your support and enthusiasm to talk him into joining us. And you bailed.
Why did you make me snap at you?
I couldn't wait. Couldn't risk forgetting the melody.

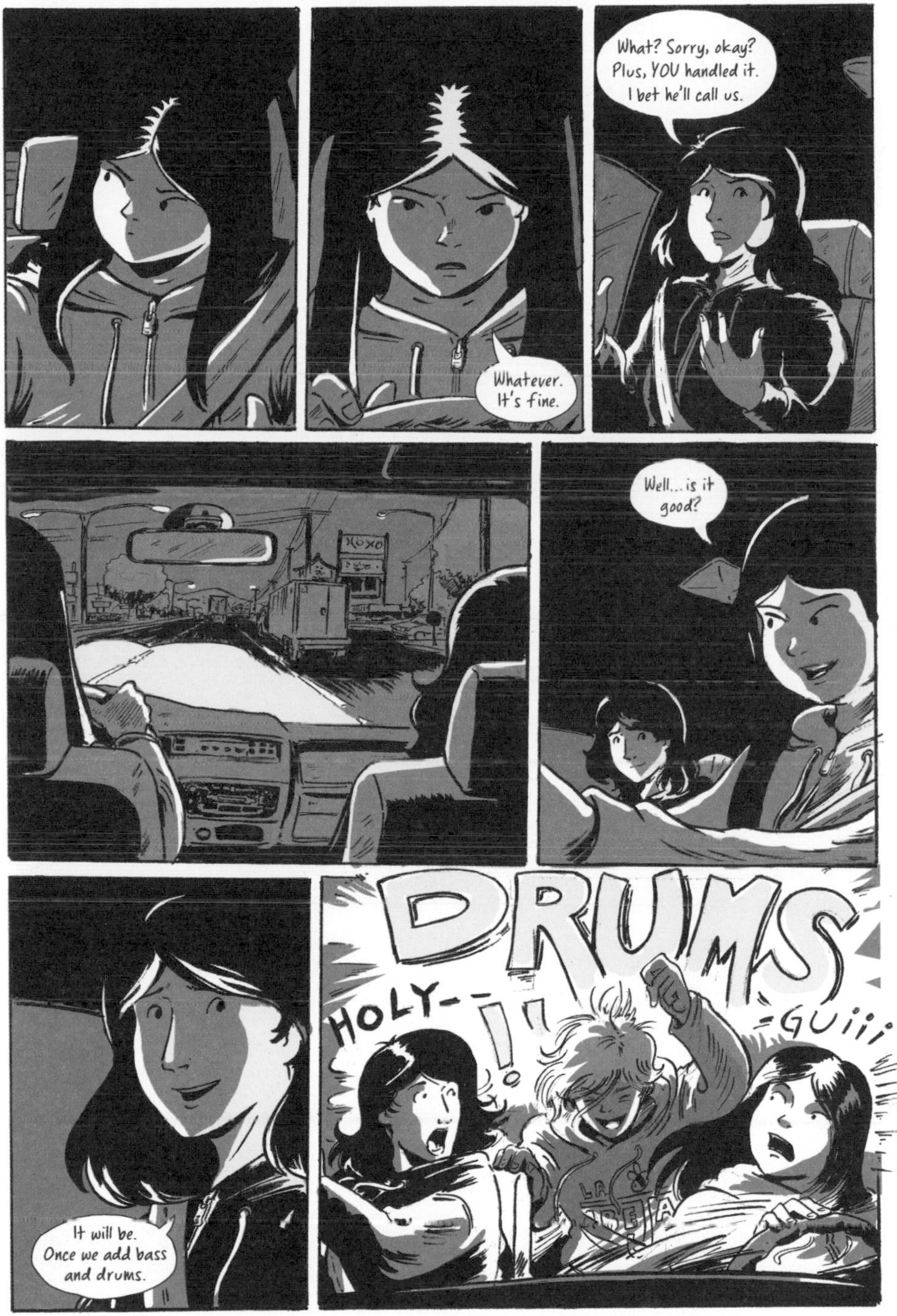
Whatever. It's fine.
What? Sorry, okay? Plus, YOU handled it. I bet he'll call us.
Well... is it good?
It will be. Once we add bass and drums.
DRUMS
HOLY--
-GUiii

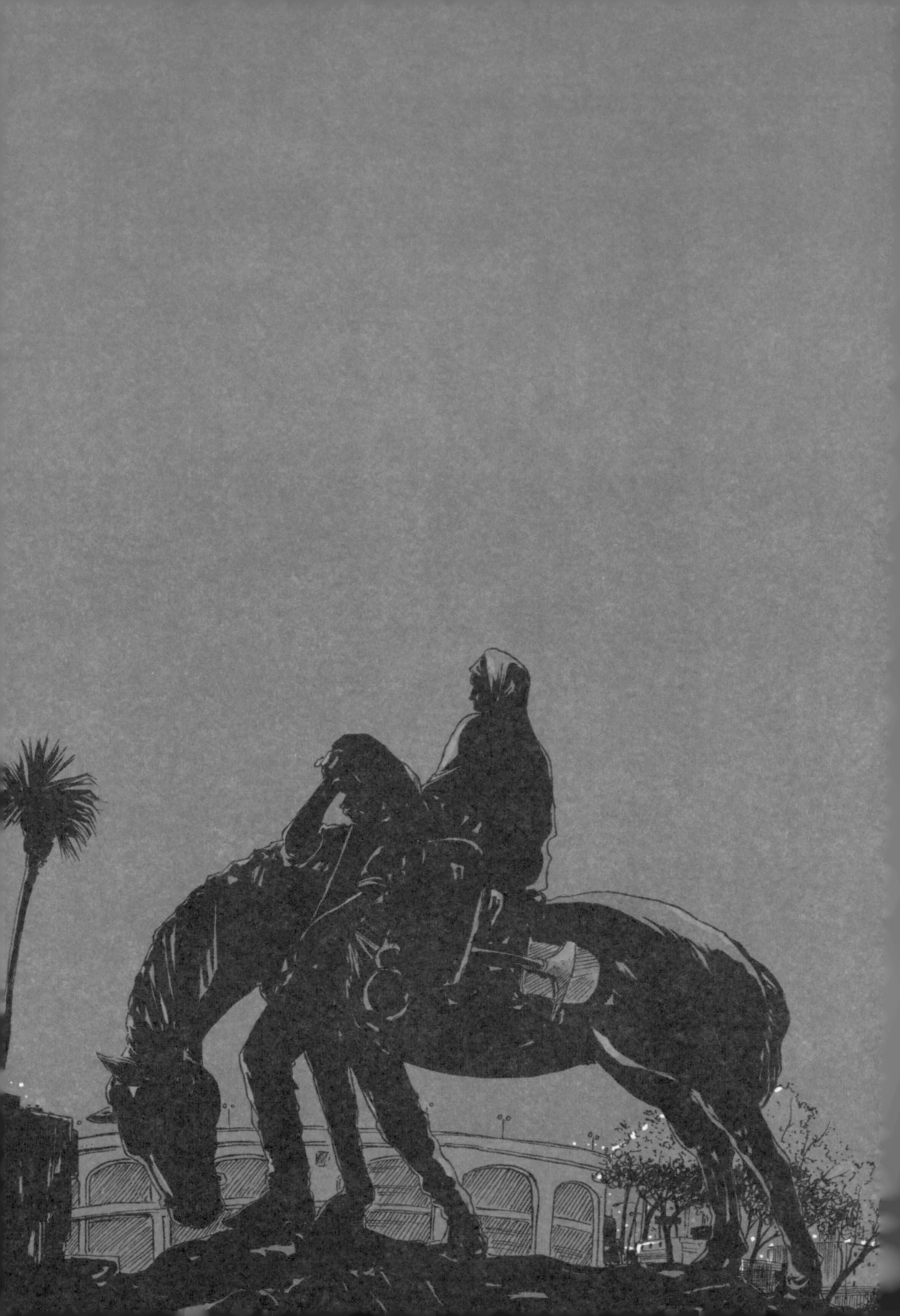

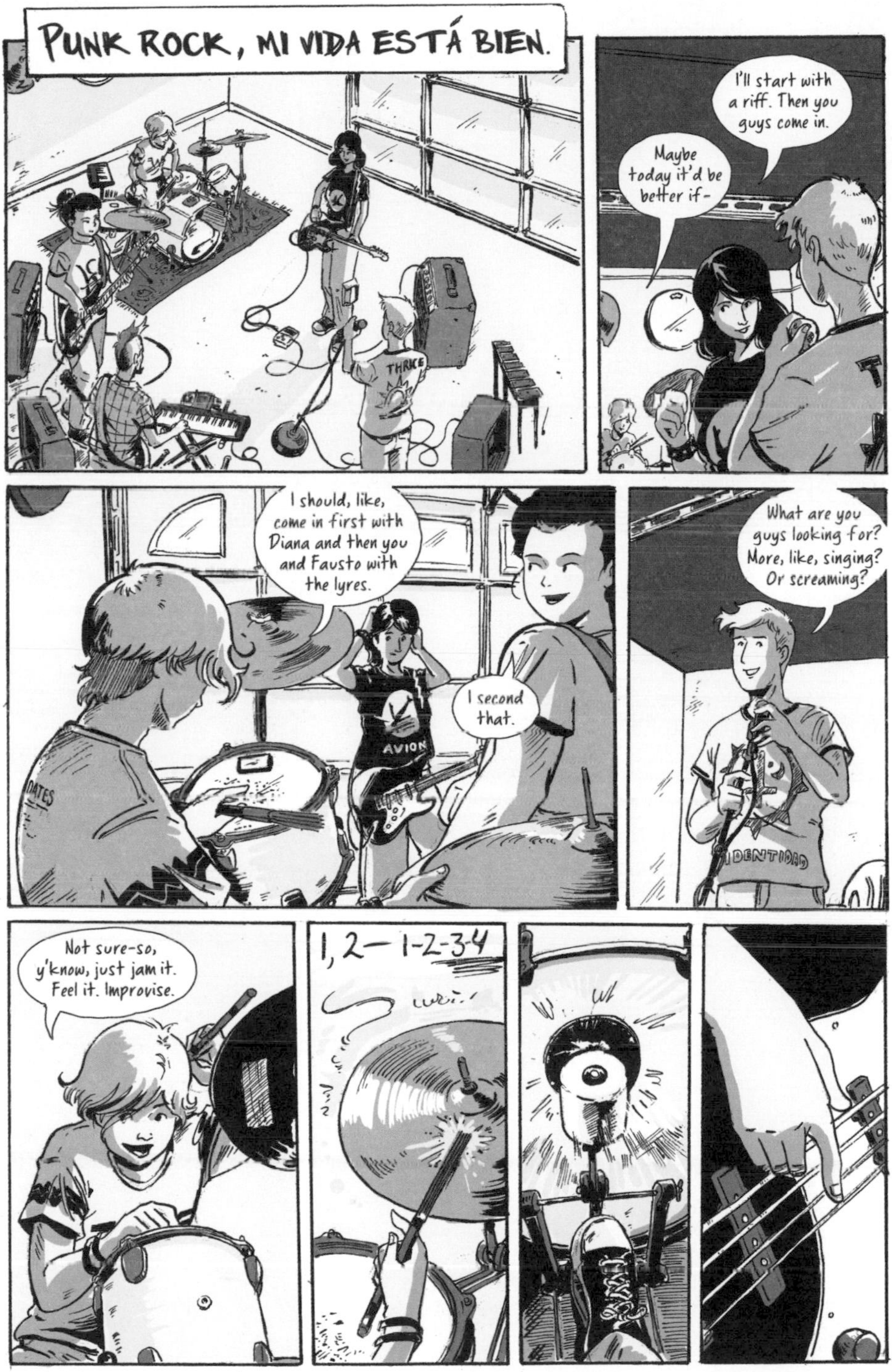
PUNK ROCK, MI VIDA ESTÁ BIEN.
THRICE
I'll start with a riff. Then you guys come in.
Maybe today it'd be better if-
I should, like, come in first with Diana and then you and Fausto with the lyres.
AVION
I second that.
What are you guys looking for? More, like, singing? Or screaming?
IDENTIDAD
Not sure-so, y'know, just jam it. Feel it. Improvise.
1, 2— 1-2-3-4

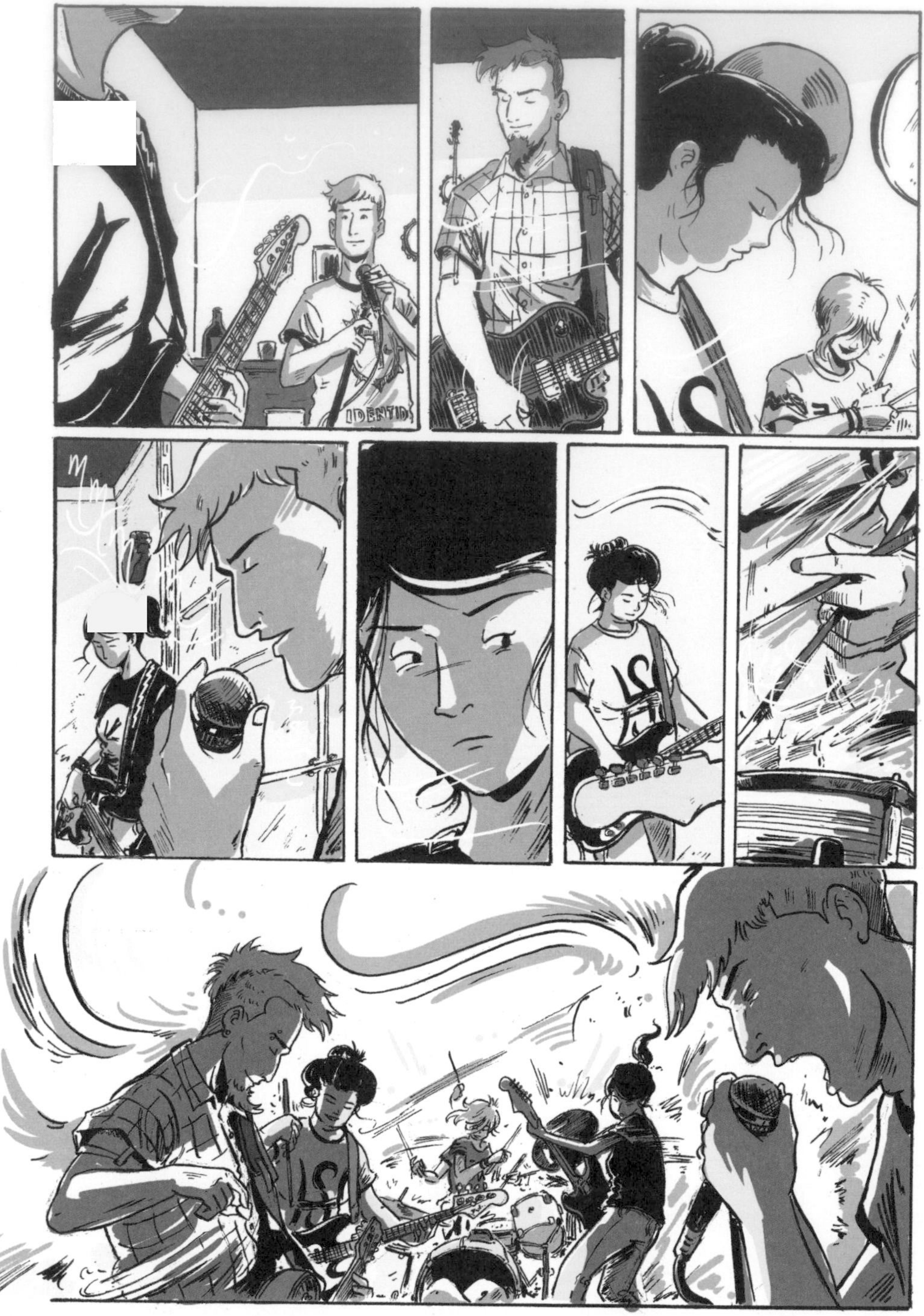

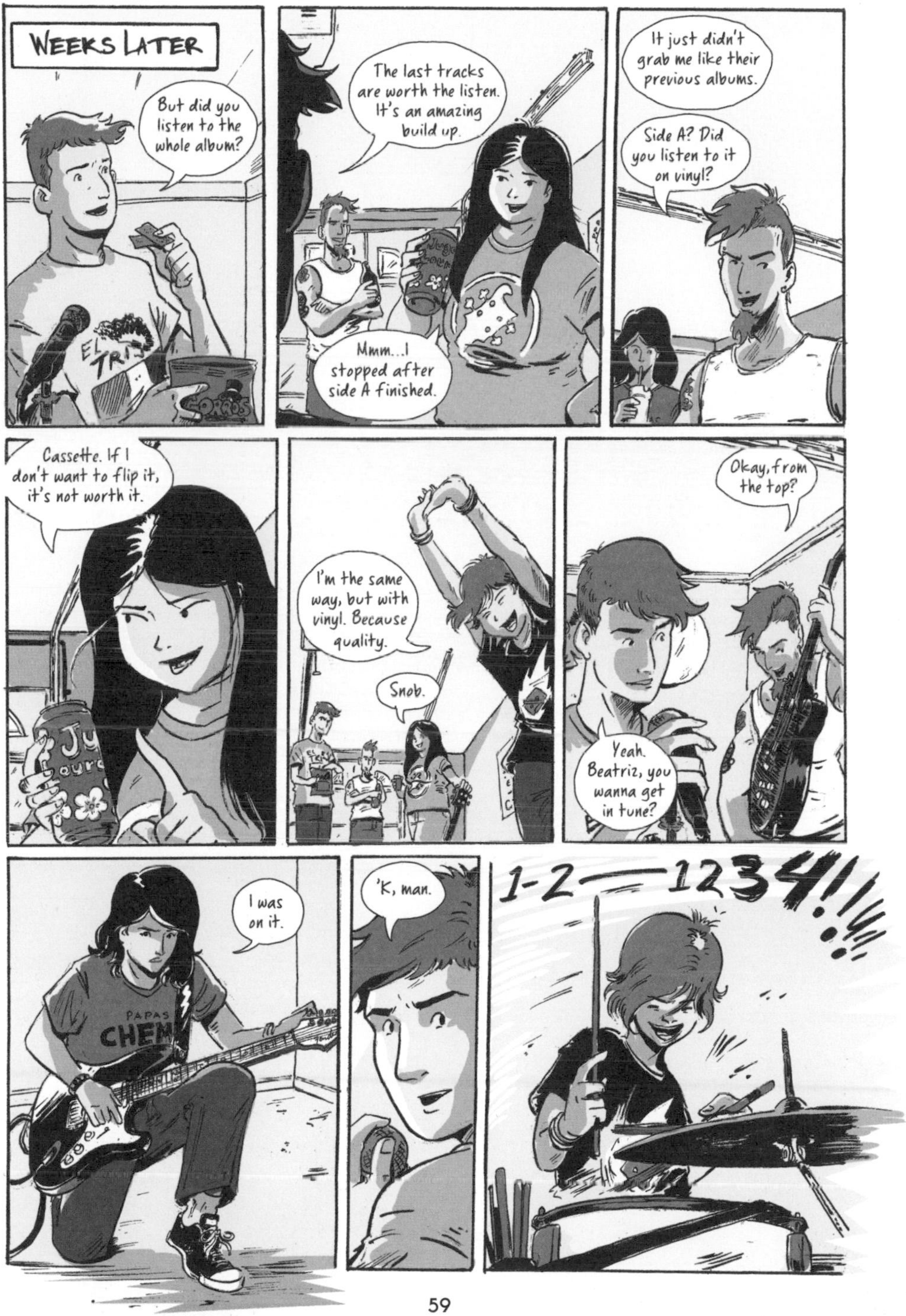
WEEKS LATER
But did you listen to the whole album?
The last tracks are worth the listen. It's an amazing build up.
Mmm...I stopped after side A finished.
It just didn't grab me like their previous albums.
Side A? Did you listen to it on vinyl?
Cassette. If I don't want to flip it, it's not worth it.
I'm the same way, but with vinyl. Because quality.
Snob.
Okay, from the top?
Yeah. Beatriz, you wanna get in tune?
I was on it.
'K, man.
1-2—1234!!

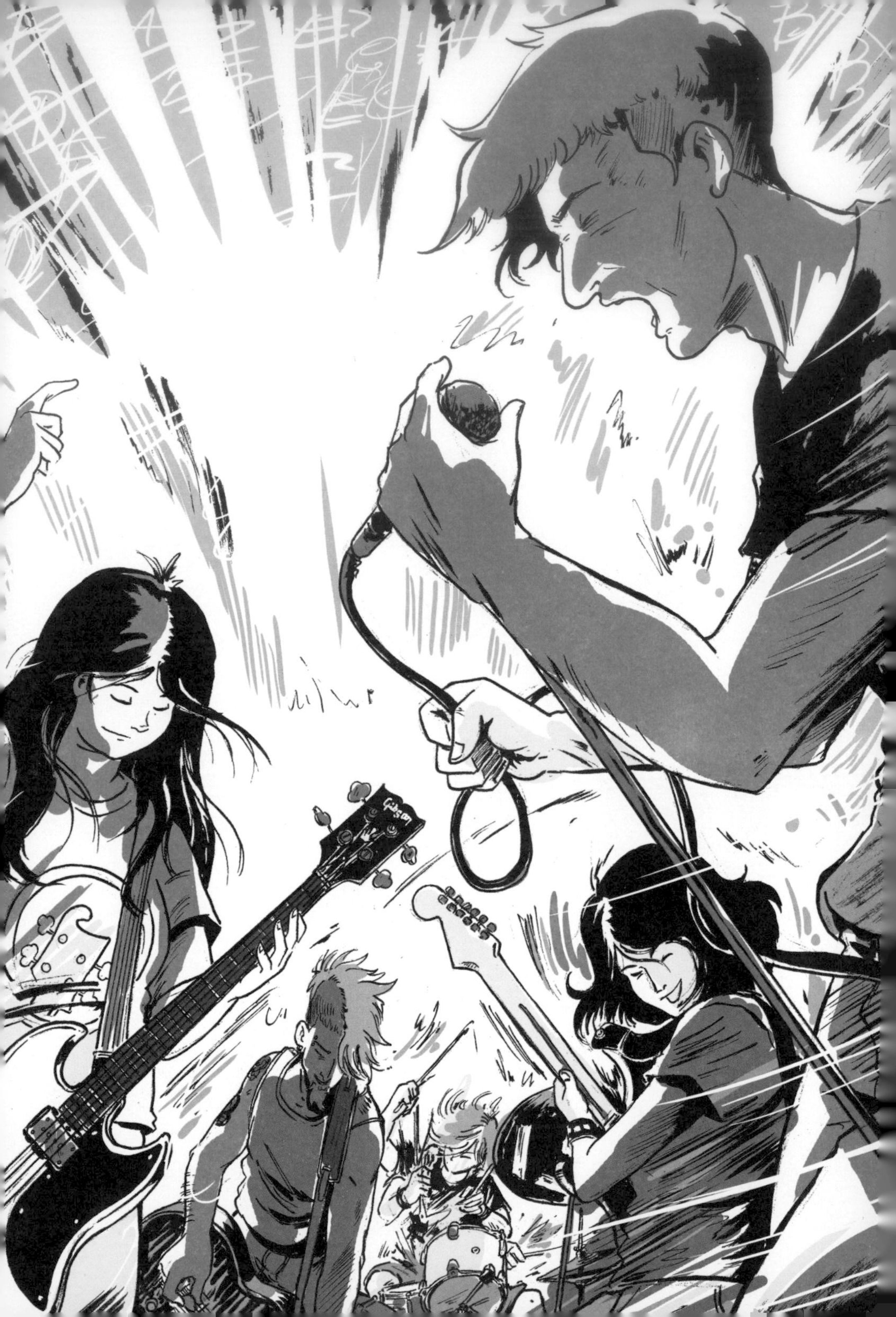
Gibson

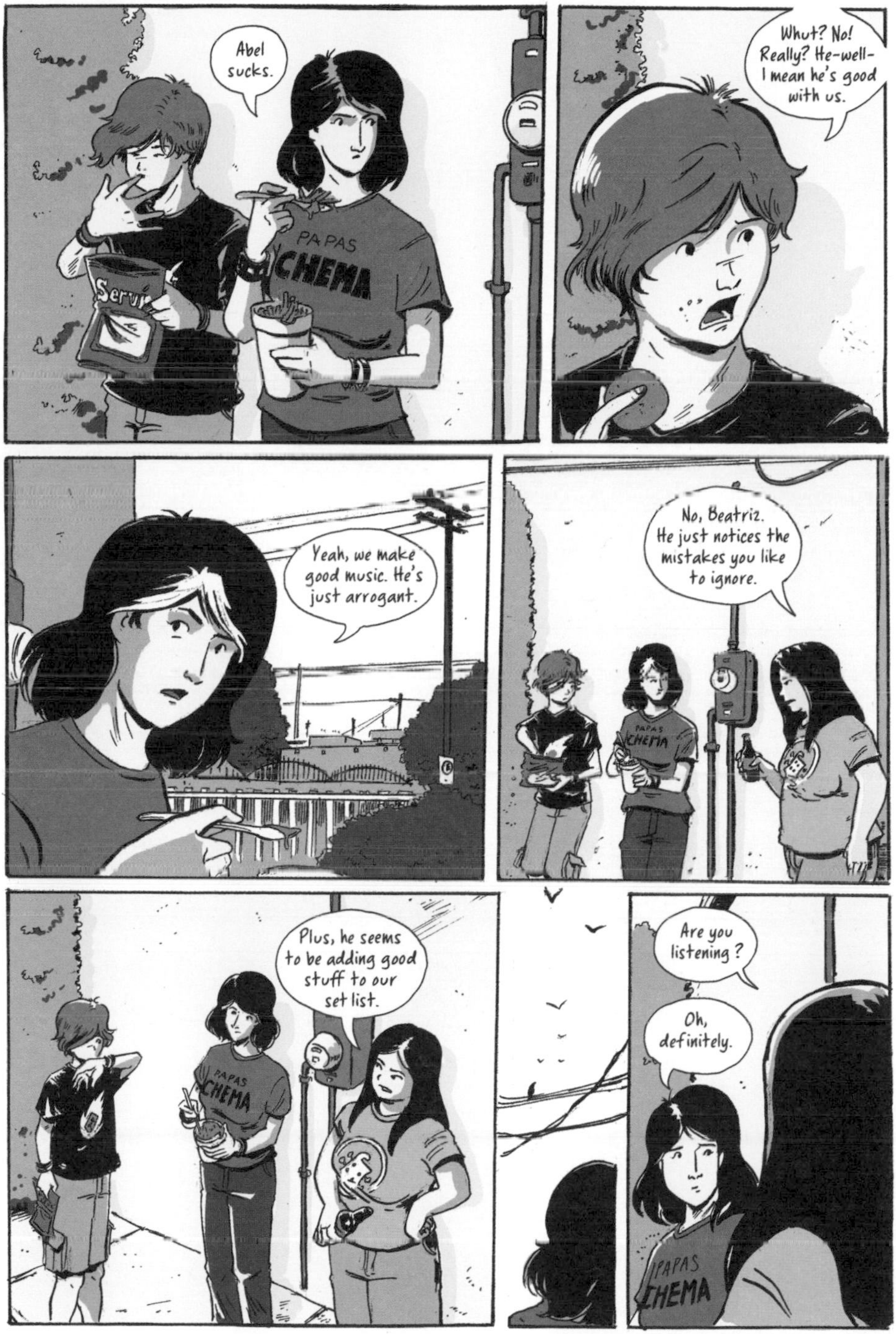
Abel sucks.
PAPAS CHEMA
Whut? No! Really? He-well- I mean he's good with us.
Yeah, we make good music. He's just arrogant.
No, Beatriz. He just notices the mistakes you like to ignore.
PAPAS CHEMA
Plus, he seems to be adding good stuff to our set list.
PAPAS CHEMA
Are you listening?
Oh, definitely.
PAPAS CHEMA

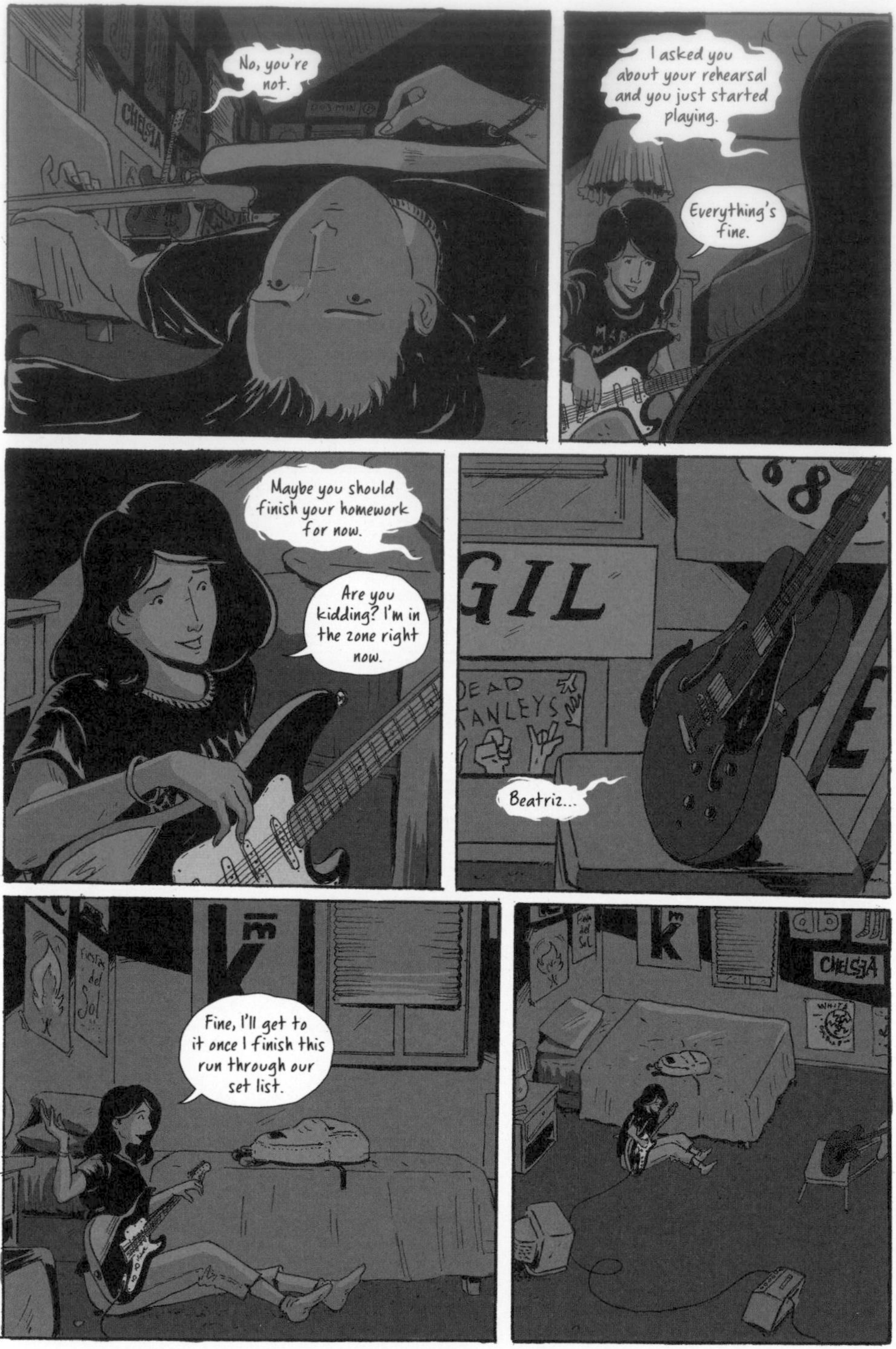
No, you're not.
I asked you about your rehearsal and you just started playing.
Everything's fine.
Maybe you should finish your homework for now.
Are you kidding? I'm in the zone right now.
Beatriz...
Fine, I'll get to it once I finish this run through our set list.

Gibson

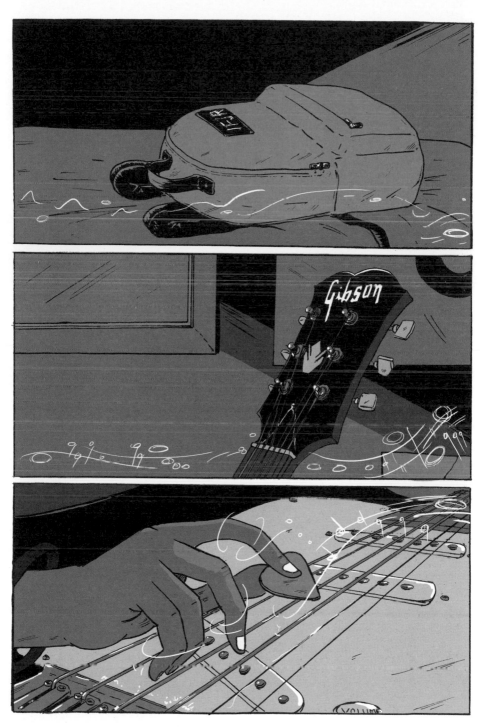

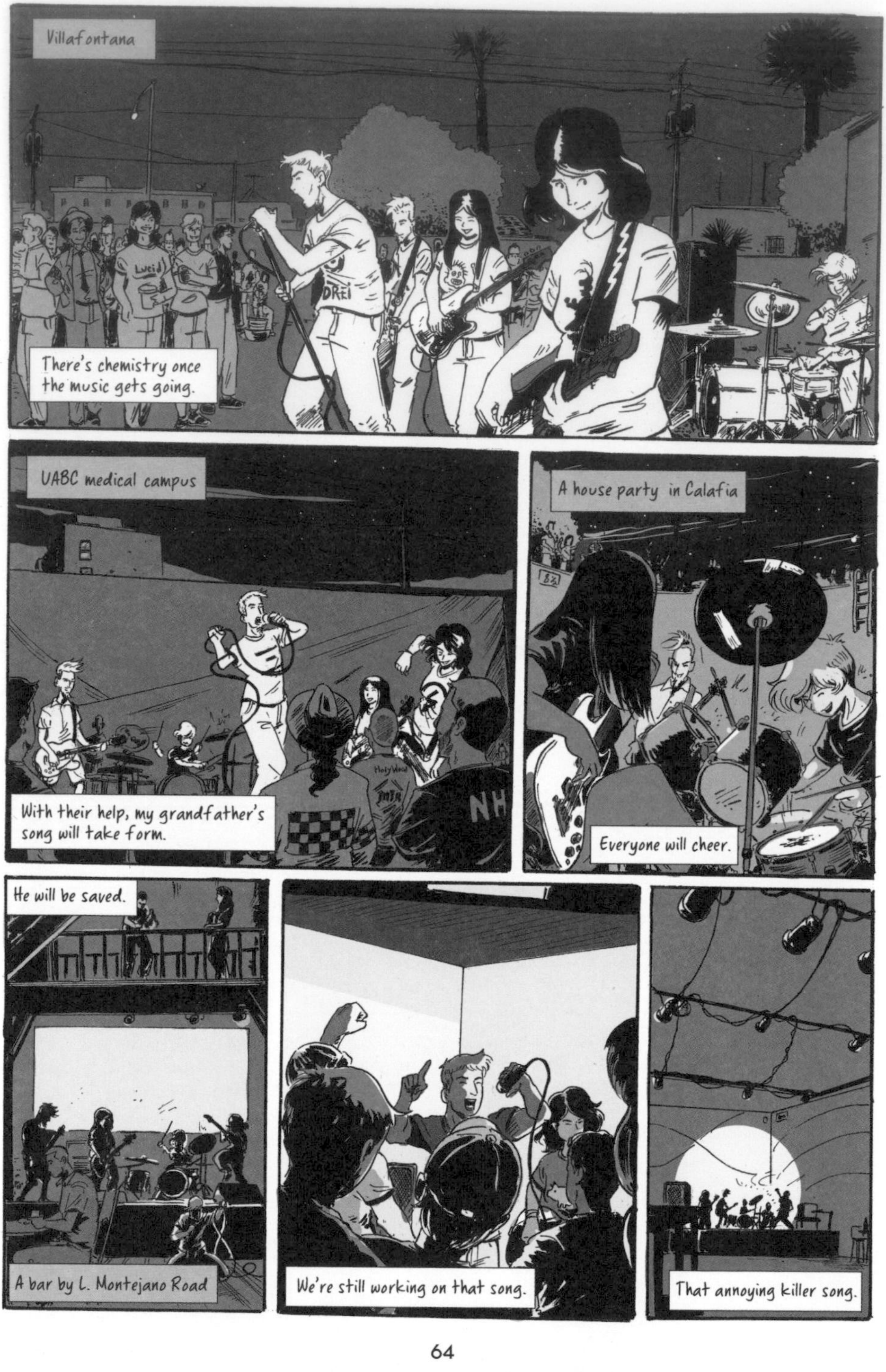
Villafontana
Lucid
DREI
There's chemistry once the music gets going.
UABC medical campus
NH
With their help, my grandfather's song will take form.
A house party in Calafia
Everyone will cheer.
He will be saved.
A bar by L. Montejano Road
We're still working on that song.
That annoying killer song.

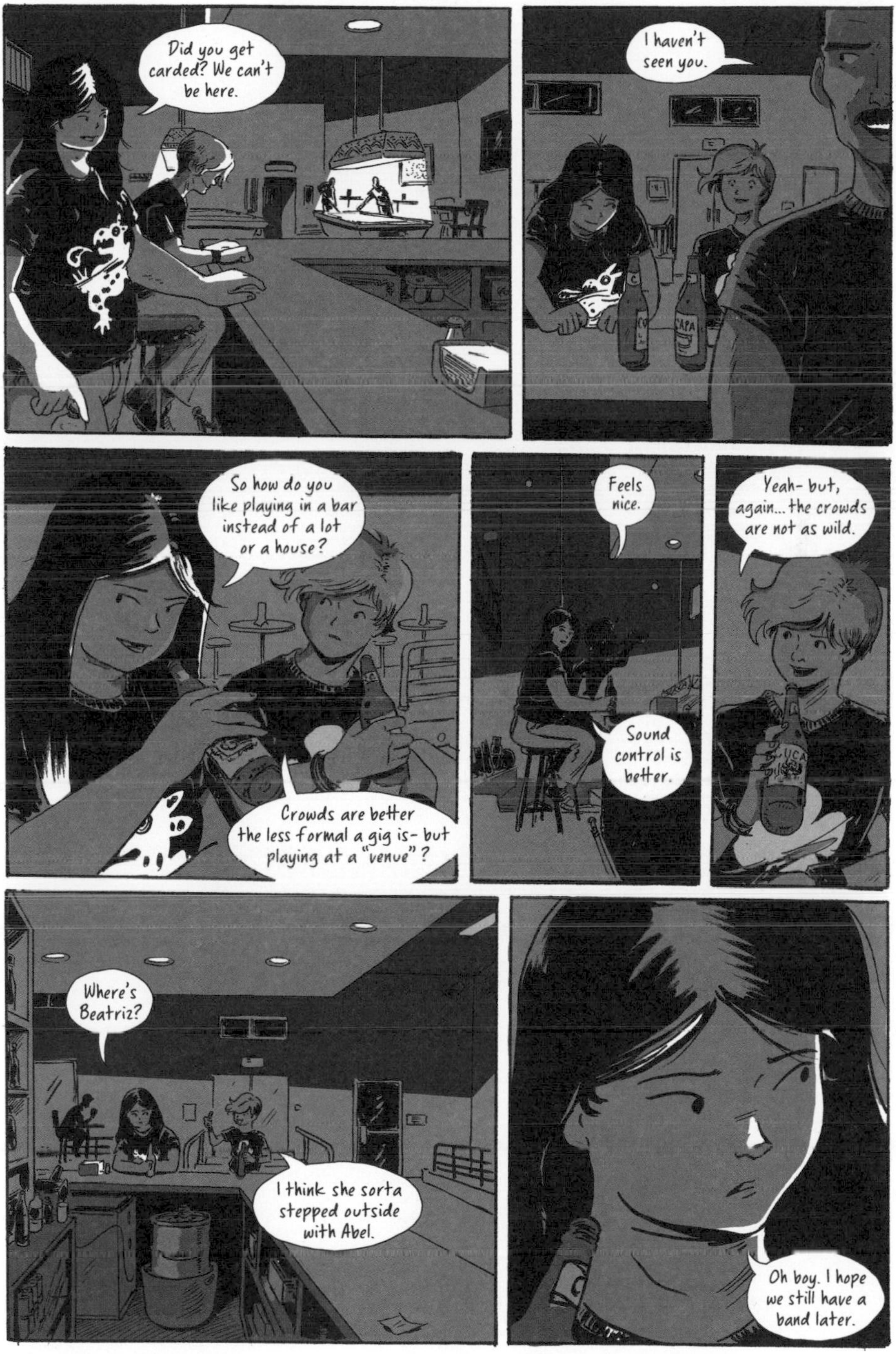
Did you get carded? We can't be here.
I haven't seen you.
So how do you like playing in a bar instead of a lot or a house?
Crowds are better the less formal a gig is- but playing at a "venue"?
Feels nice.
Sound control is better.
Yeah- but, again... the crowds are not as wild.
Where's Beatriz?
I think she sorta stepped outside with Abel.
Oh boy. I hope we still have a band later.

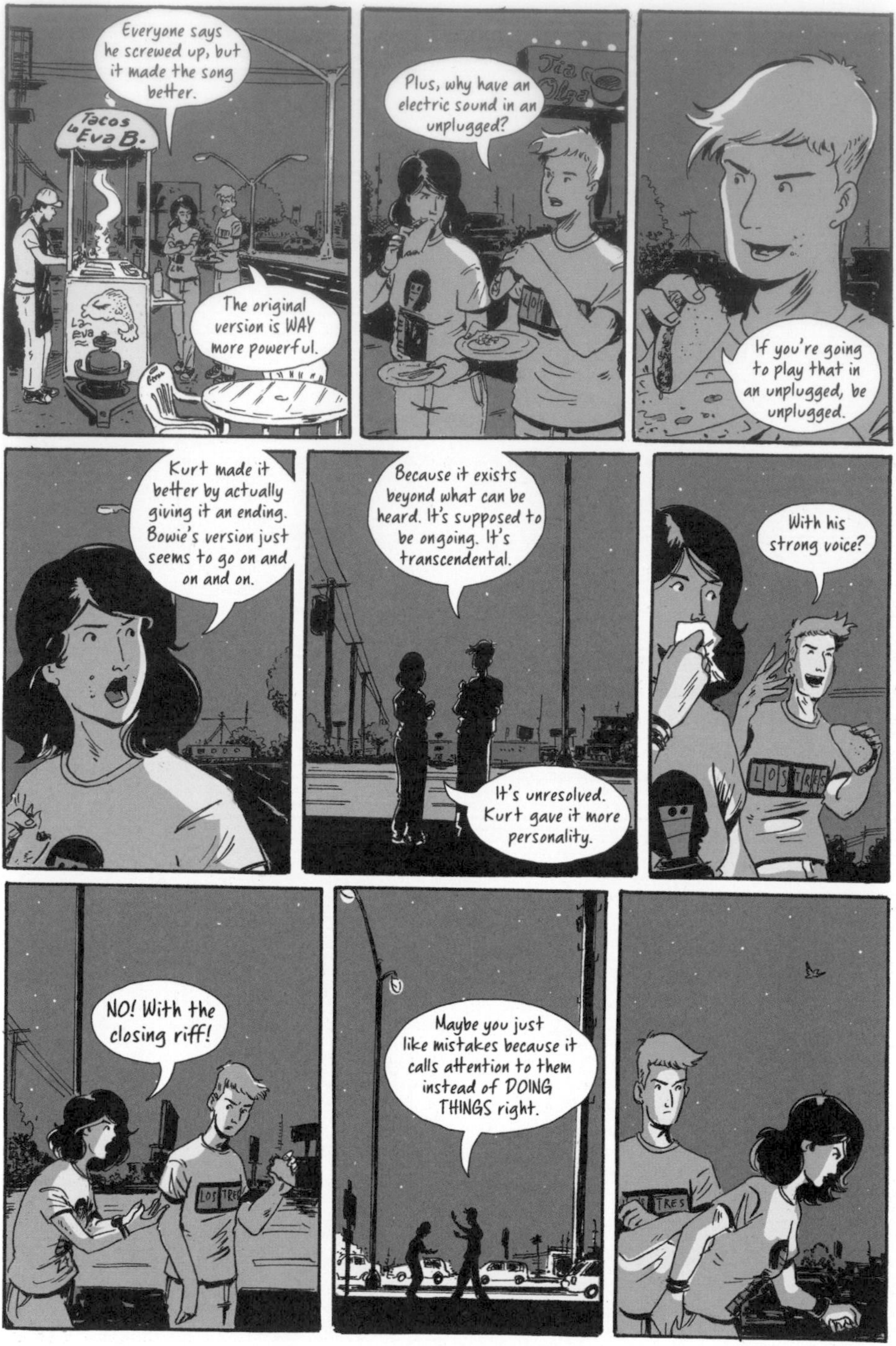
Everyone says he screwed up, but it made the song better.
Tacos La Eva B.
Tia Olga
Plus, why have an electric sound in an unplugged?
The original version is WAY more powerful.
If you're going to play that in an unplugged, be unplugged.
Kurt made it better by actually giving it an ending. Bowie's version just seems to go on and on and on.
Because it exists beyond what can be heard. It's supposed to be ongoing. It's transcendental.
It's unresolved. Kurt gave it more personality.
With his strong voice?
LOS TRES
NO! With the closing riff!
Maybe you just like mistakes because it calls attention to them instead of DOING THINGS right.

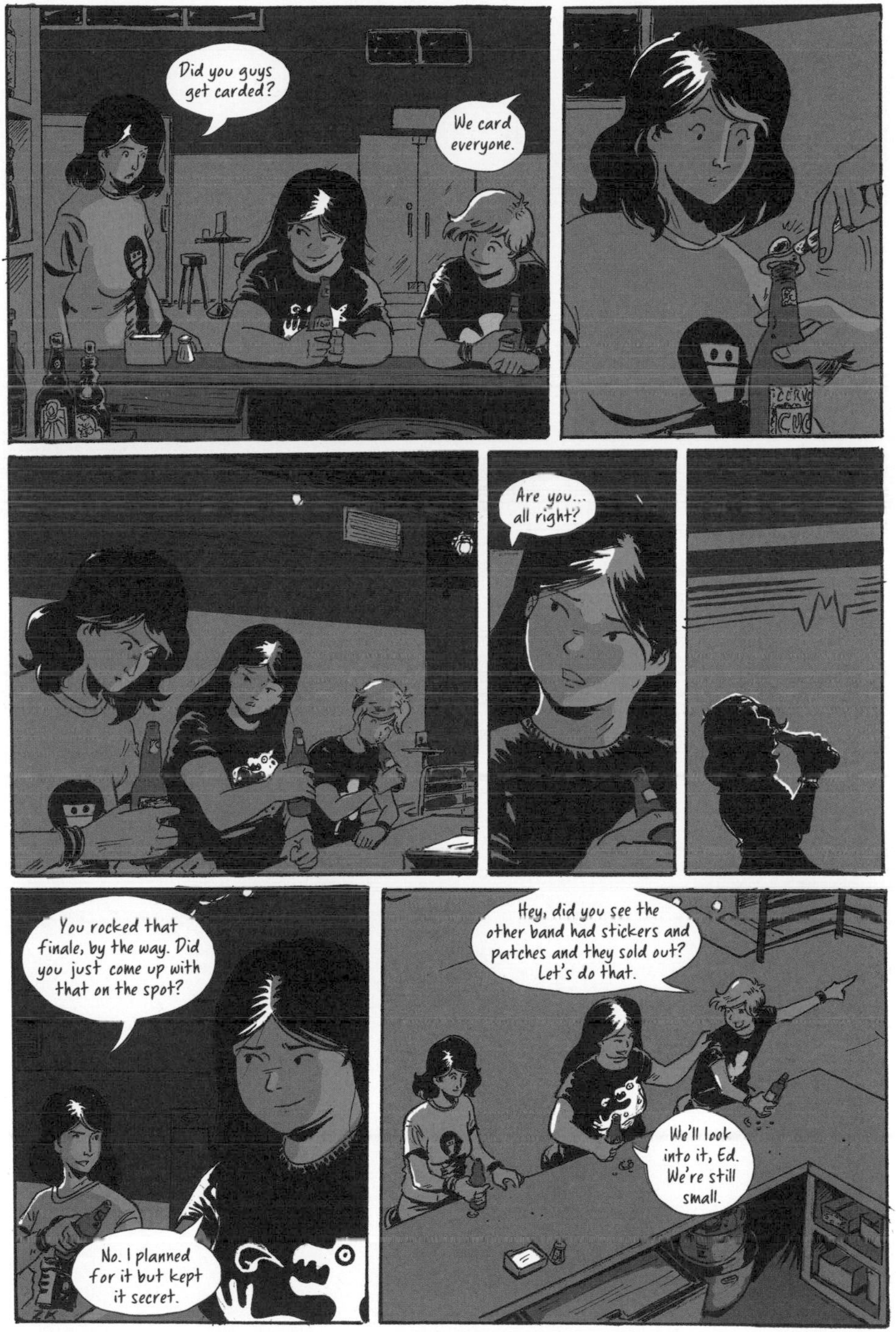

Did you guys get carded?
We card everyone.
Are you... all right?
You rocked that finale, by the way. Did you just come up with that on the spot?
No. I planned for it but kept it secret.
Hey, did you see the other band had stickers and patches and they sold out? Let's do that.
We'll look into it, Ed. We're still small.

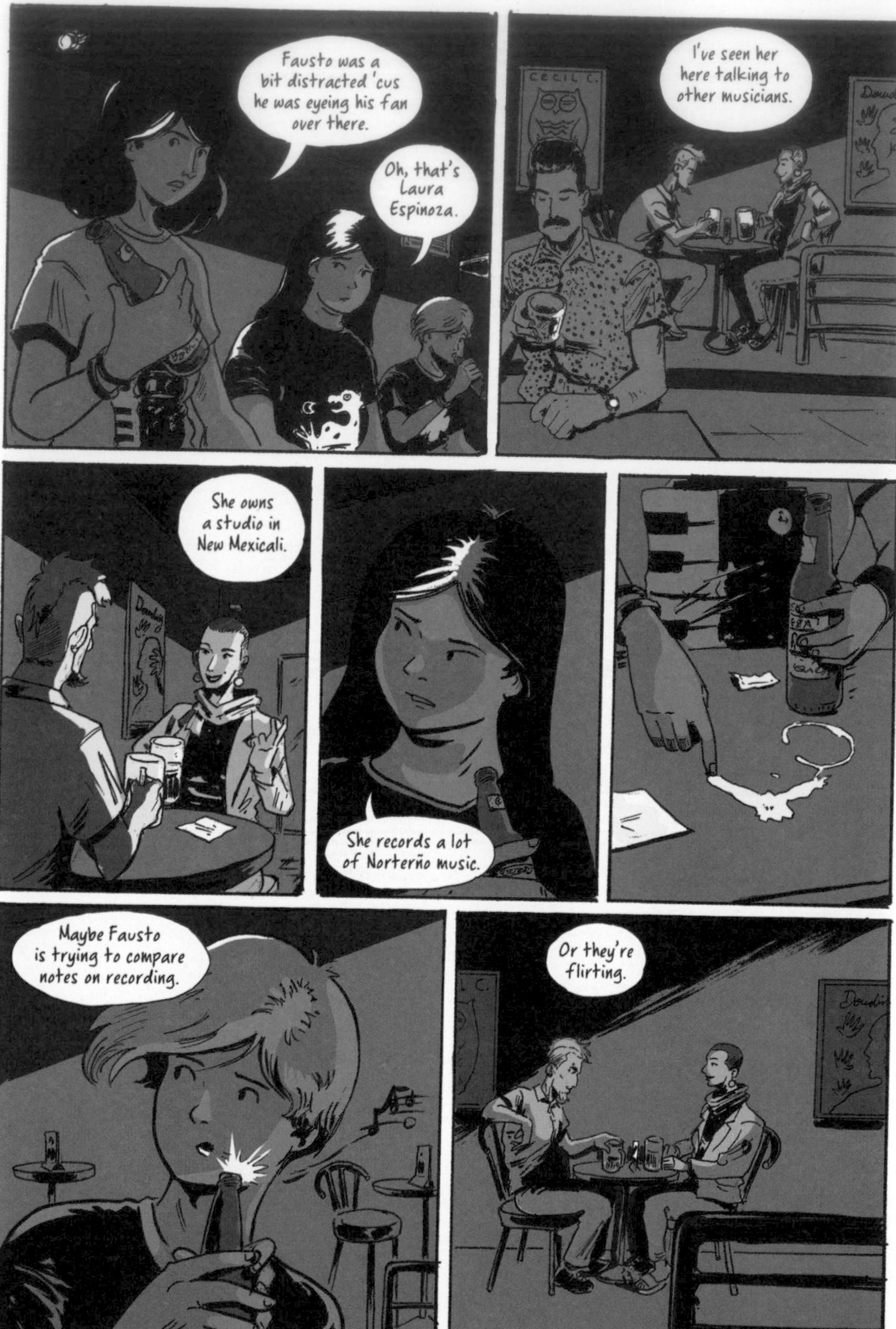

Fausto was a bit distracted 'cus he was eyeing his fan over there.
Oh, that's Laura Espinoza.
I've seen her here talking to other musicians.
She owns a studio in New Mexicali.
She records a lot of Norteño music.
Maybe Fausto is trying to compare notes on recording.
Or they're flirting.

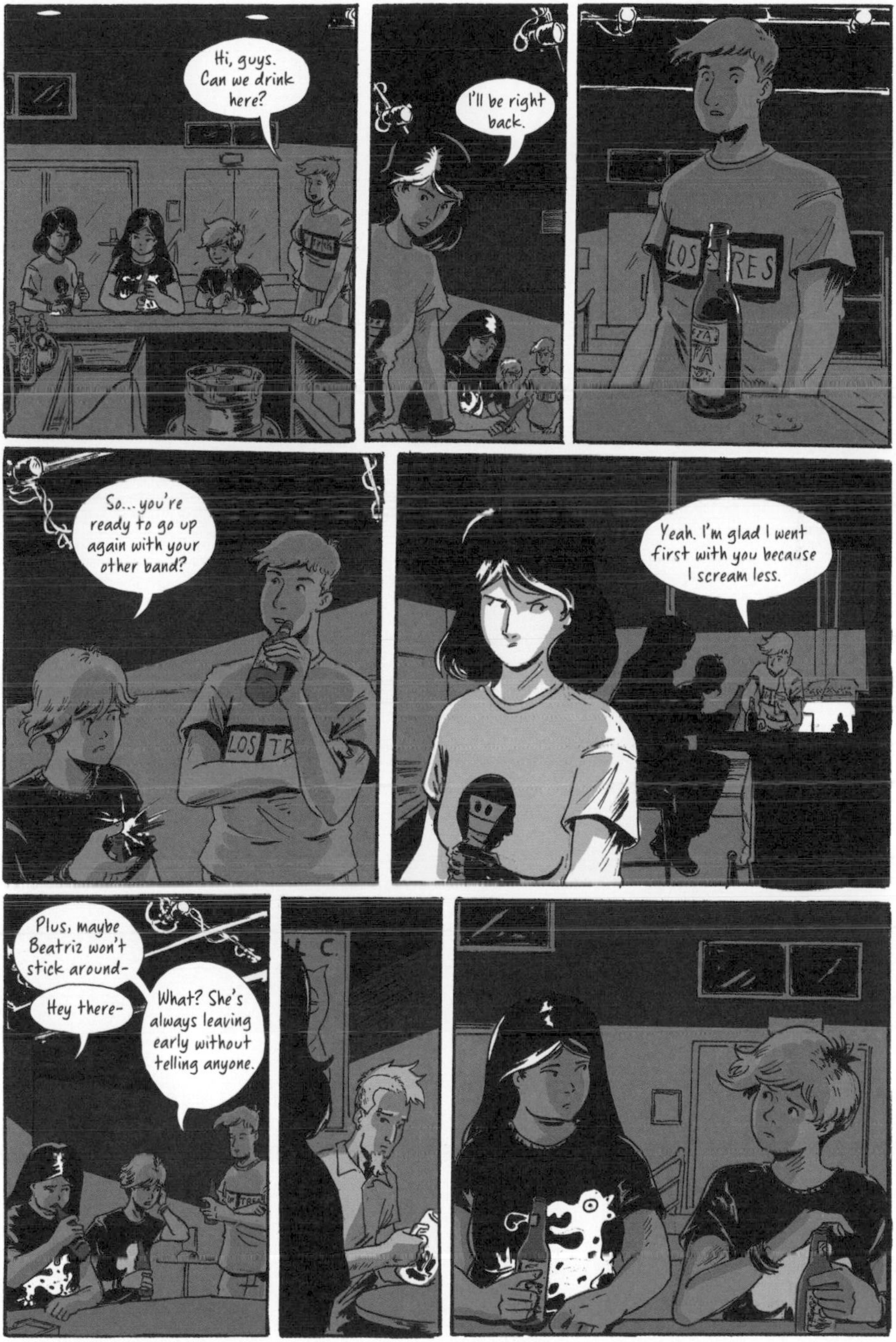
Hi, guys. Can we drink here?
I'll be right back.
LOS TRES
So... you're ready to go up again with your other band?
Yeah. I'm glad I went first with you because I scream less.
Plus, maybe Beatriz won't stick around-
What? She's always leaving early without telling anyone.
Hey there-

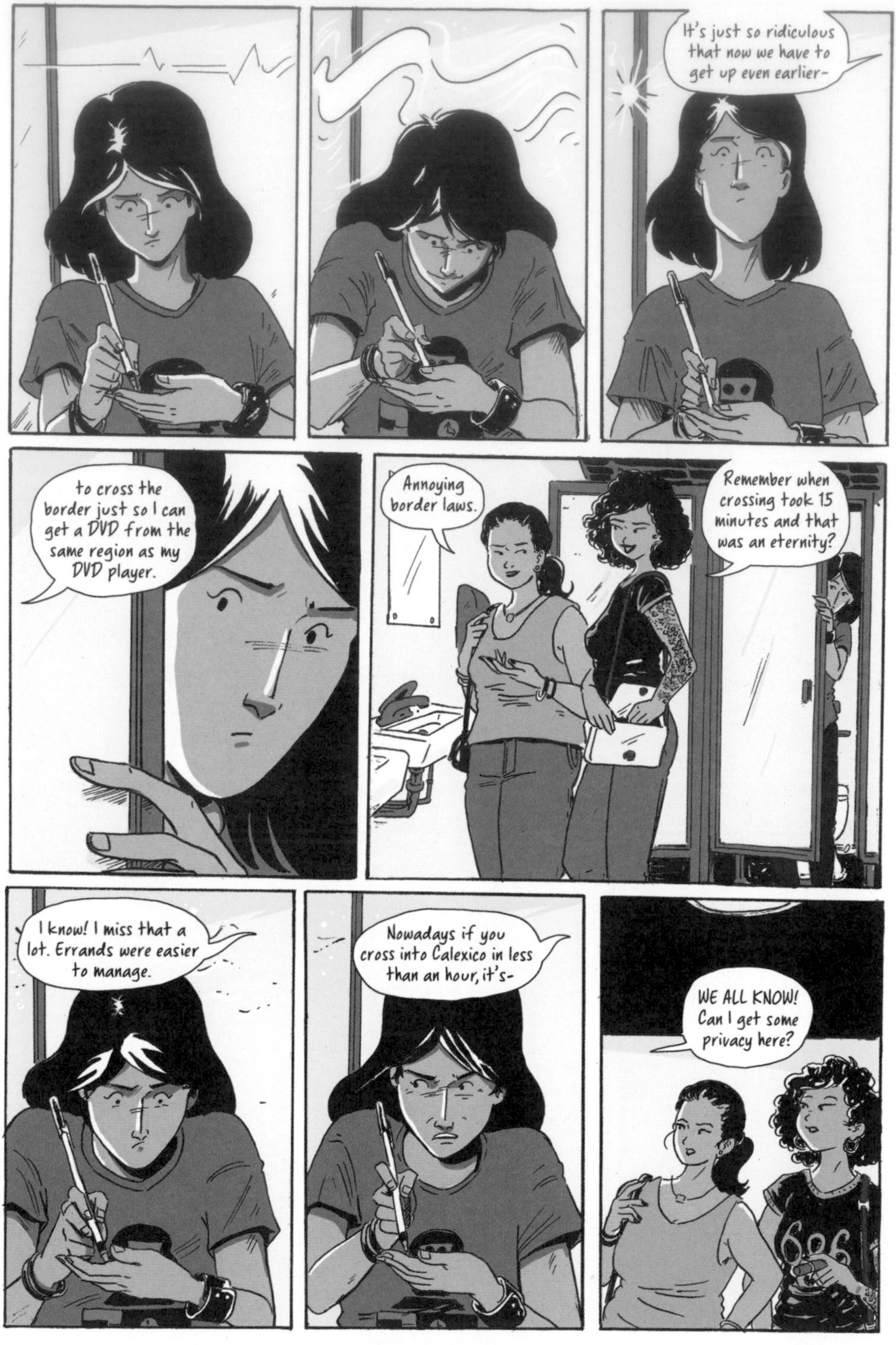
It's just so ridiculous that now we have to get up even earlier-
to cross the border just so I can get a DVD from the same region as my DVD player.
Annoying border laws.
Remember when crossing took 15 minutes and that was an eternity?
I know! I miss that a lot. Errands were easier to manage.
Nowadays if you cross into Calexico in less than an hour, it's-
WE ALL KNOW! Can I get some privacy here?
606

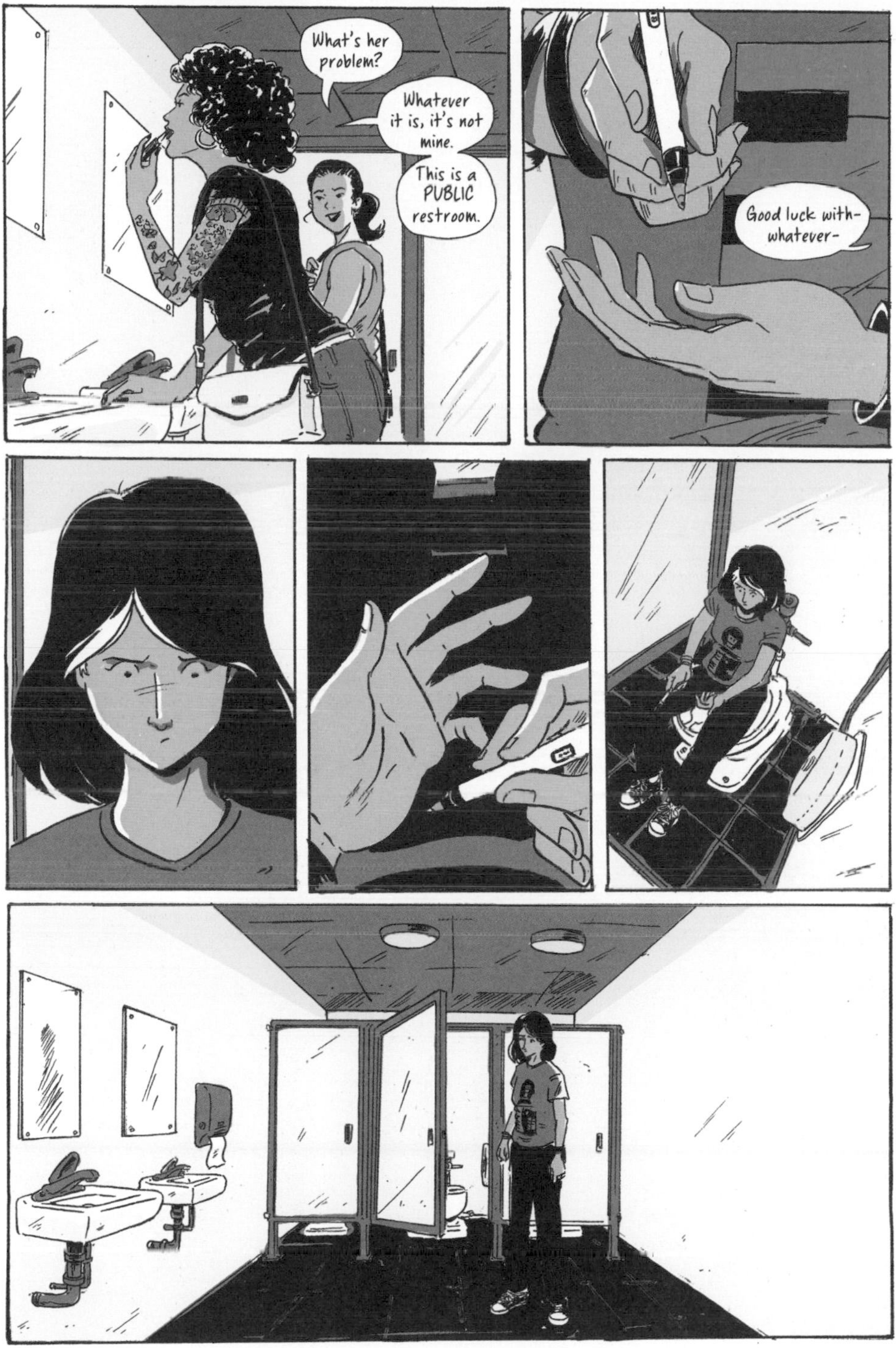
What's her problem?
Whatever it is, it's not mine.
This is a PUBLIC restroom.
Good luck with-whatever-

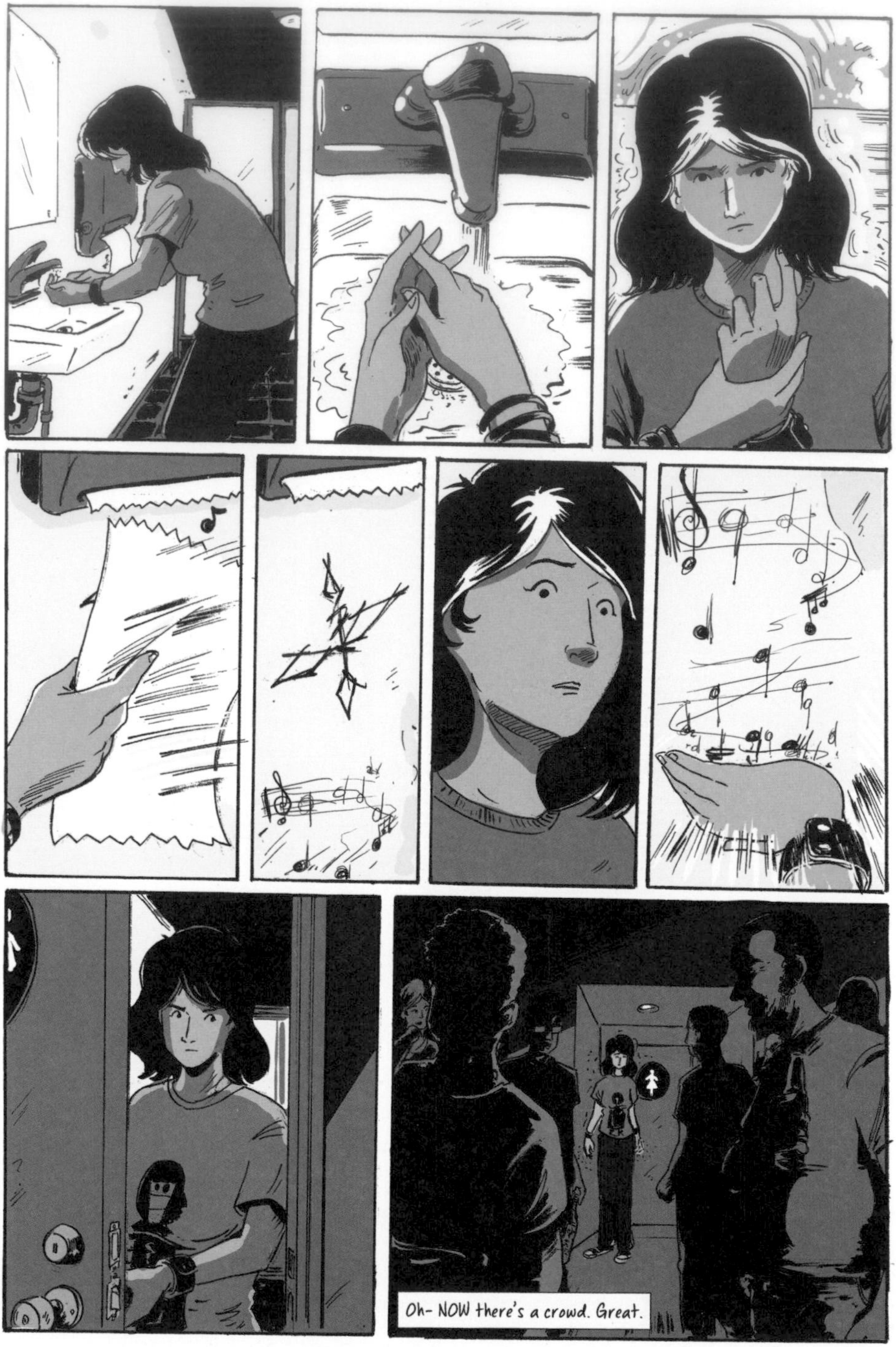
Oh- NOW there's a crowd. Great.

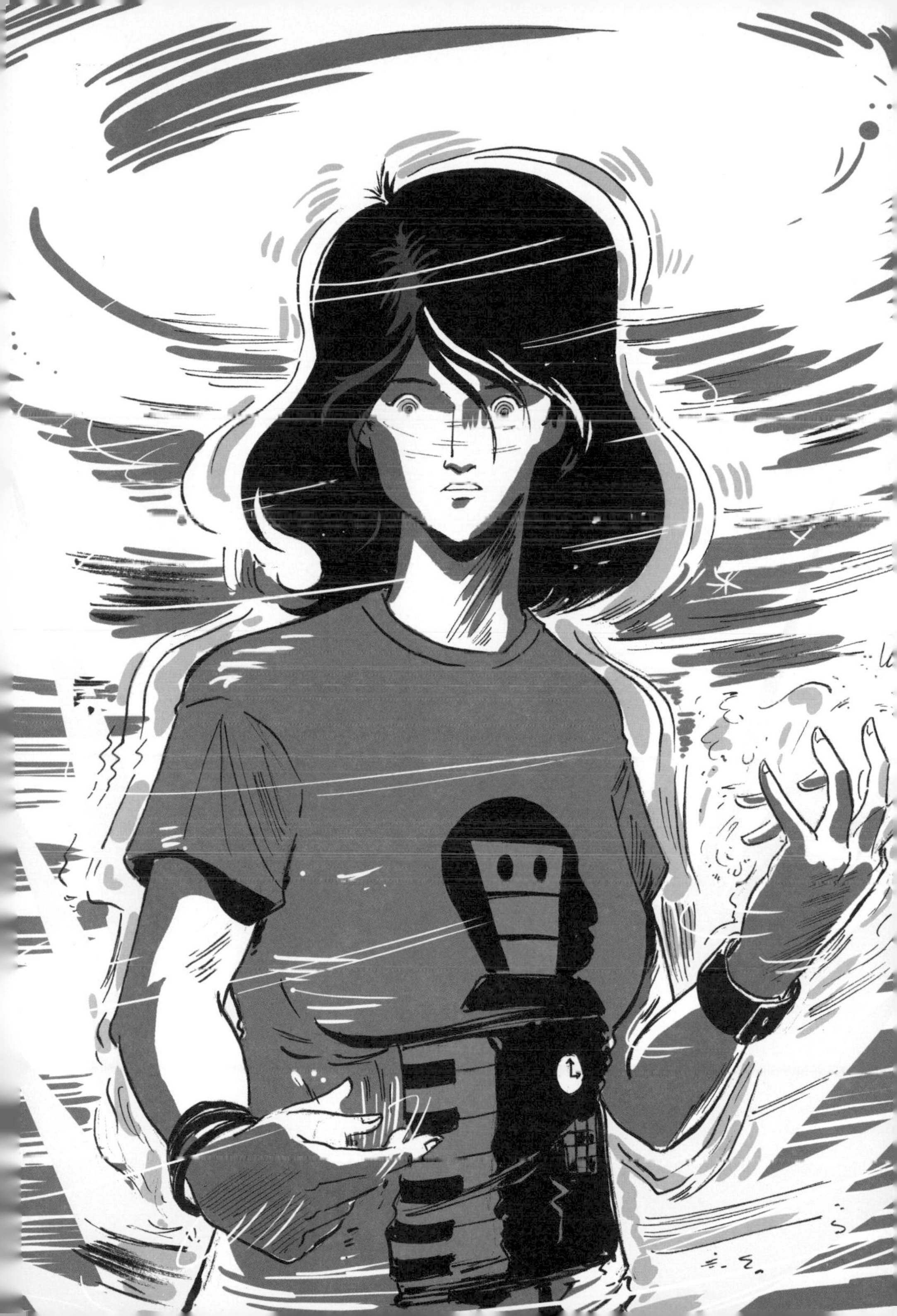

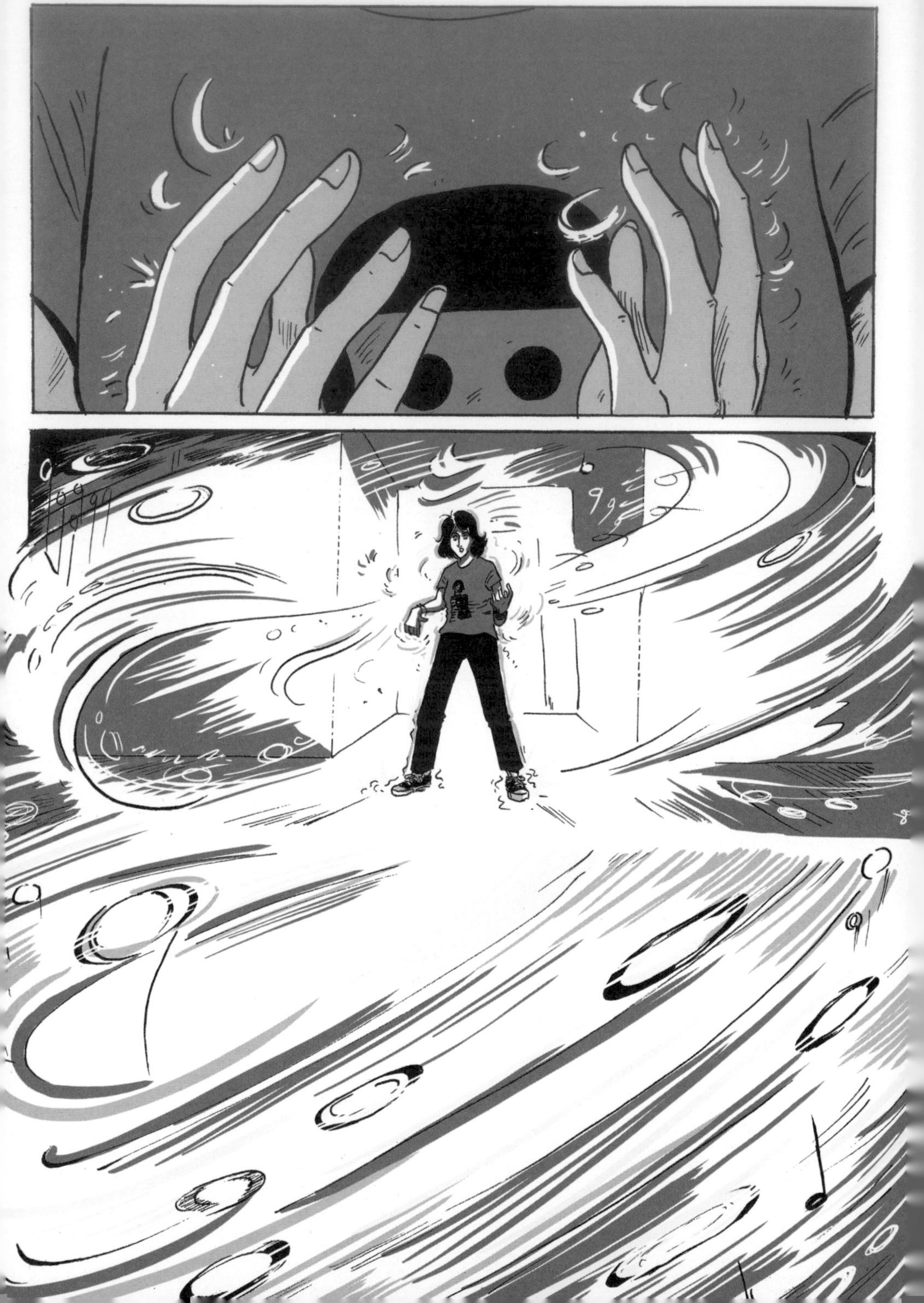

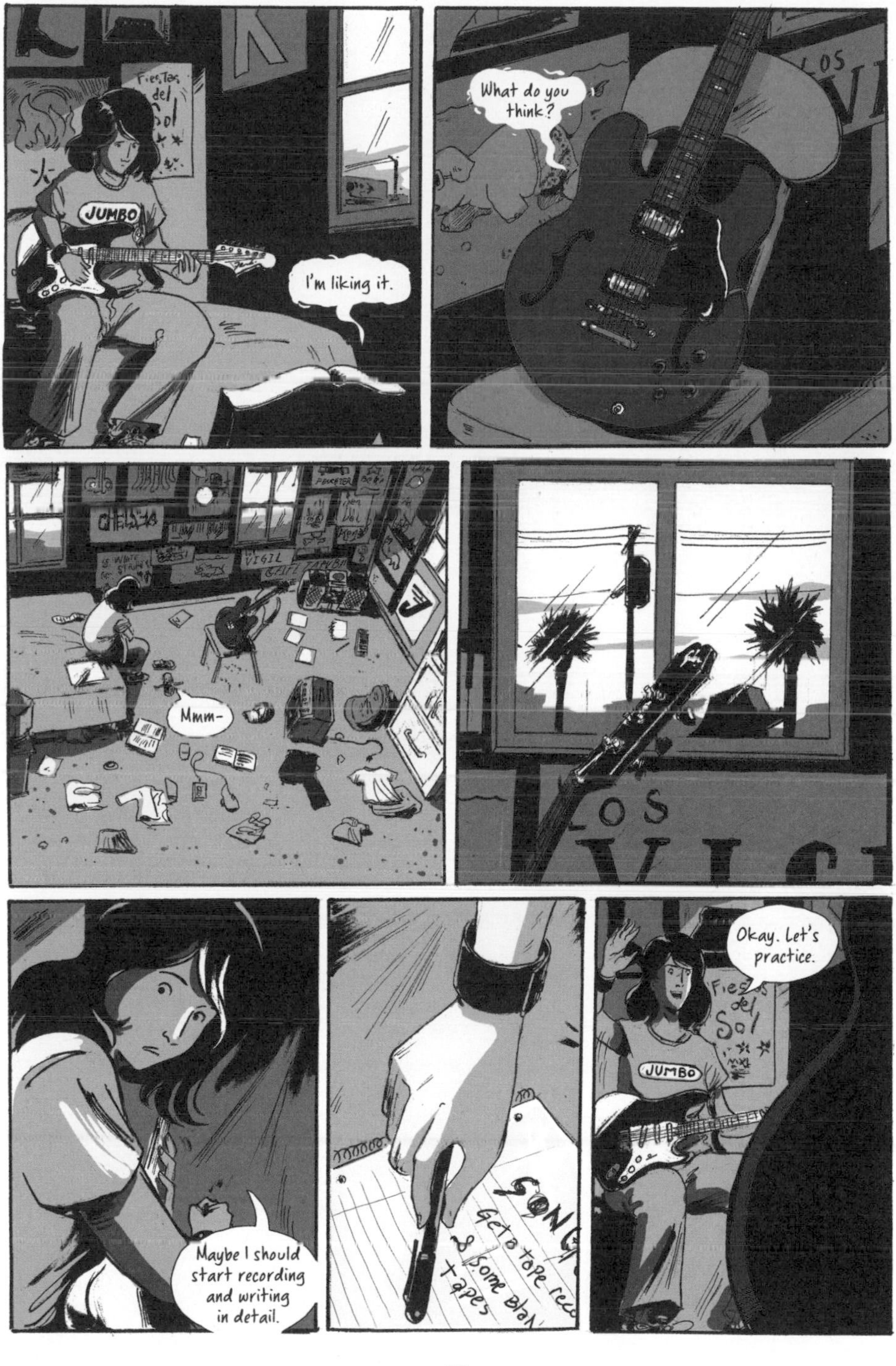

Fiestas del Sol
JUMBO
I'm liking it.
LOS
What do you think?
CHELSEA
VIGIL
Mmm-
LOS
Maybe I should start recording and writing in detail.
SONG
Get a tape reco
& some blan
tapes
Okay. Let's practice.
Fiestas del Sol
JUMBO

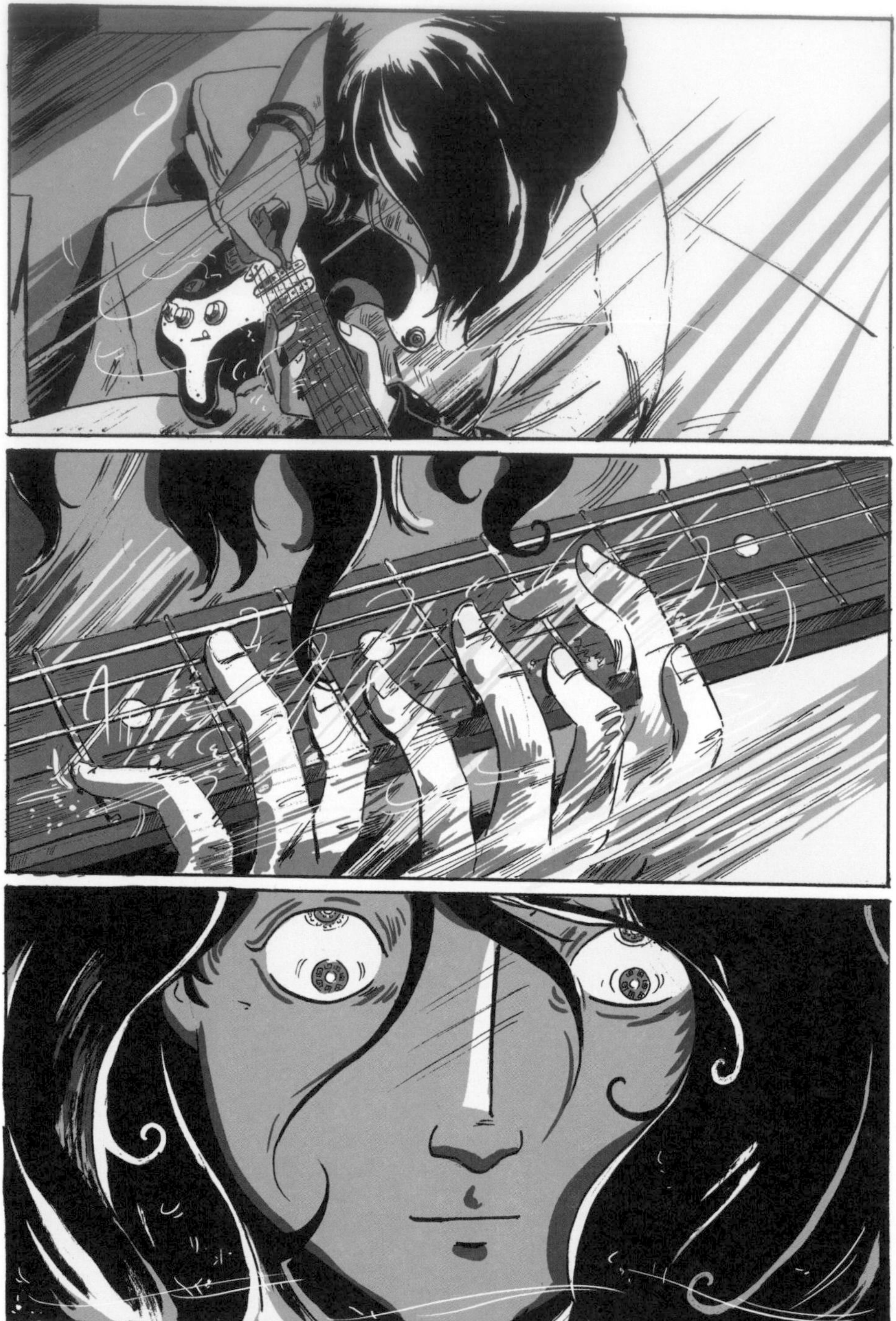

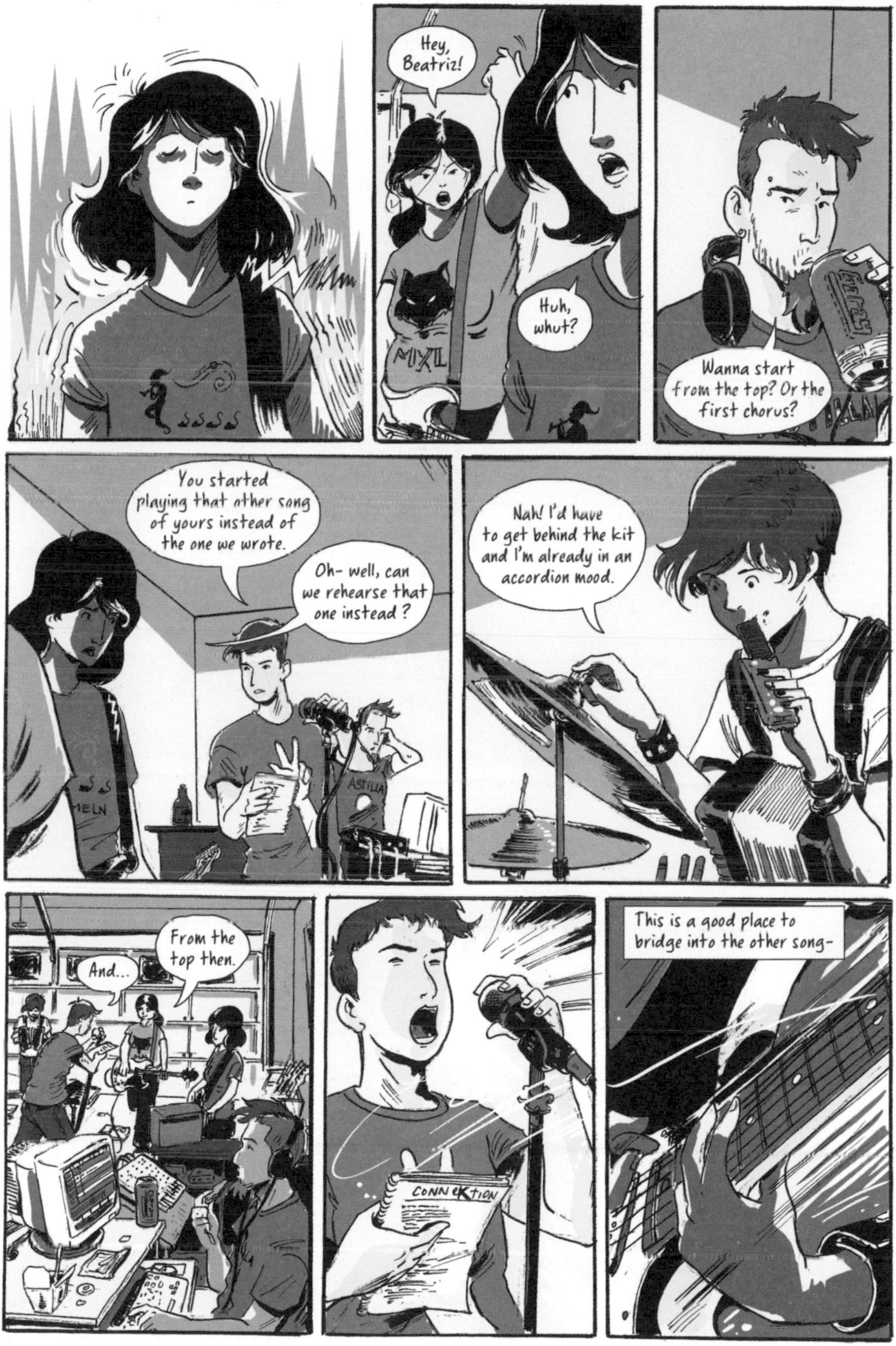
Hey, Beatriz!
Huh, whut?
Wanna start from the top? Or the first chorus?
You started playing that other song of yours instead of the one we wrote.
Oh- well, can we rehearse that one instead ?
Nah! I'd have to get behind the kit and I'm already in an accordion mood.
From the top then.
And...
CONNEKTION
This is a good place to bridge into the other song-

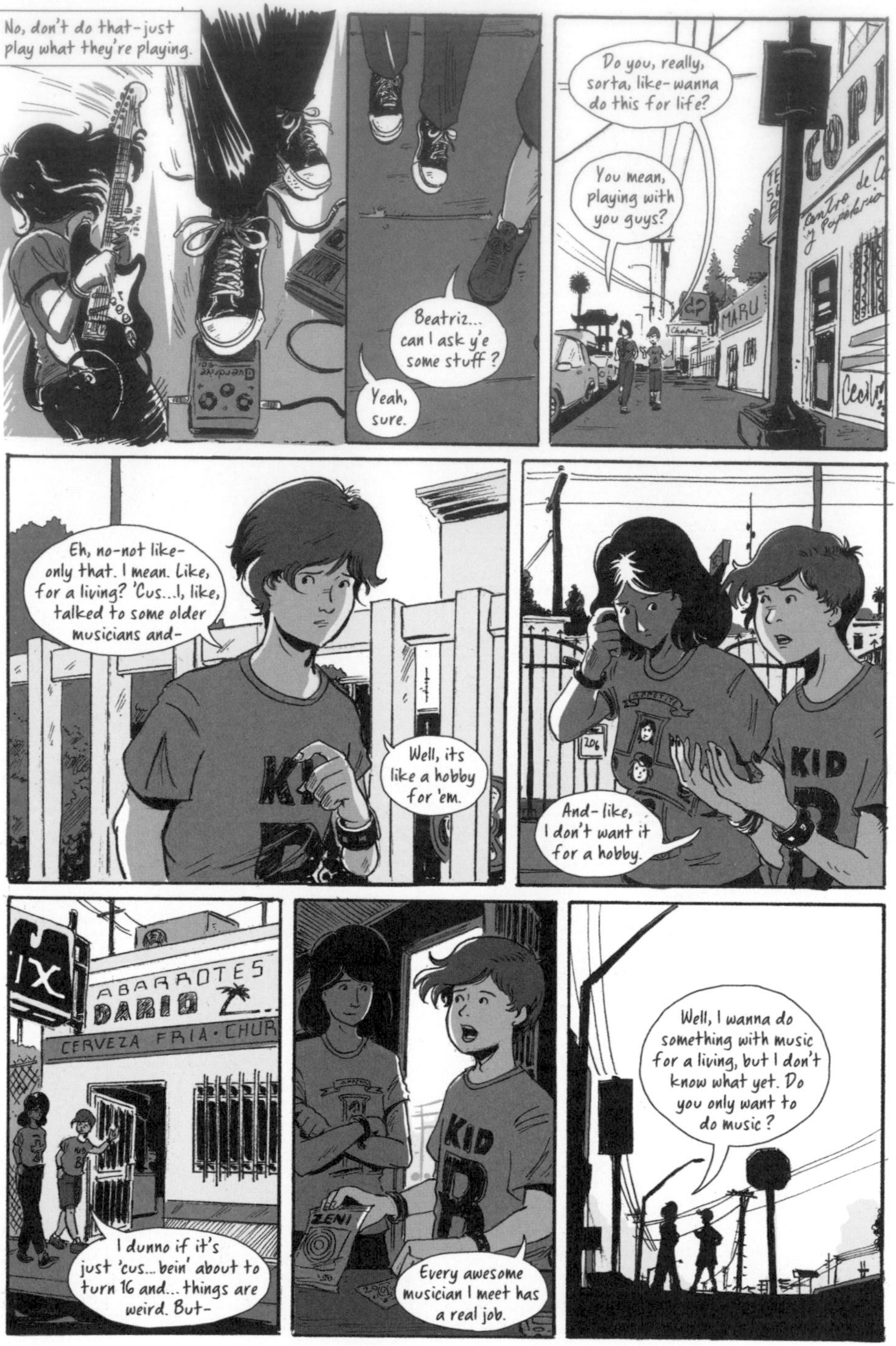
No, don't do that-just play what they're playing.
Overdrive 501
Beatriz... can I ask y'e some stuff?
Yeah, sure.
Do you, really, sorta, like-wanna do this for life?
You mean, playing with you guys?
COPI
Centro de Co
y Papeleria
MARU
Cecil
Eh, no-not like-only that. I mean. Like, for a living? 'Cus...I, like, talked to some older musicians and-
Well, its like a hobby for 'em.
KID B
And-like, I don't want it for a hobby.
ABARROTES DARIO
CERVEZA FRIA · CHUR
I dunno if it's just 'cus... bein' about to turn 16 and... things are weird. But-
ZENI
Every awesome musician I meet has a real job.
Well, I wanna do something with music for a living, but I don't know what yet. Do you only want to do music?

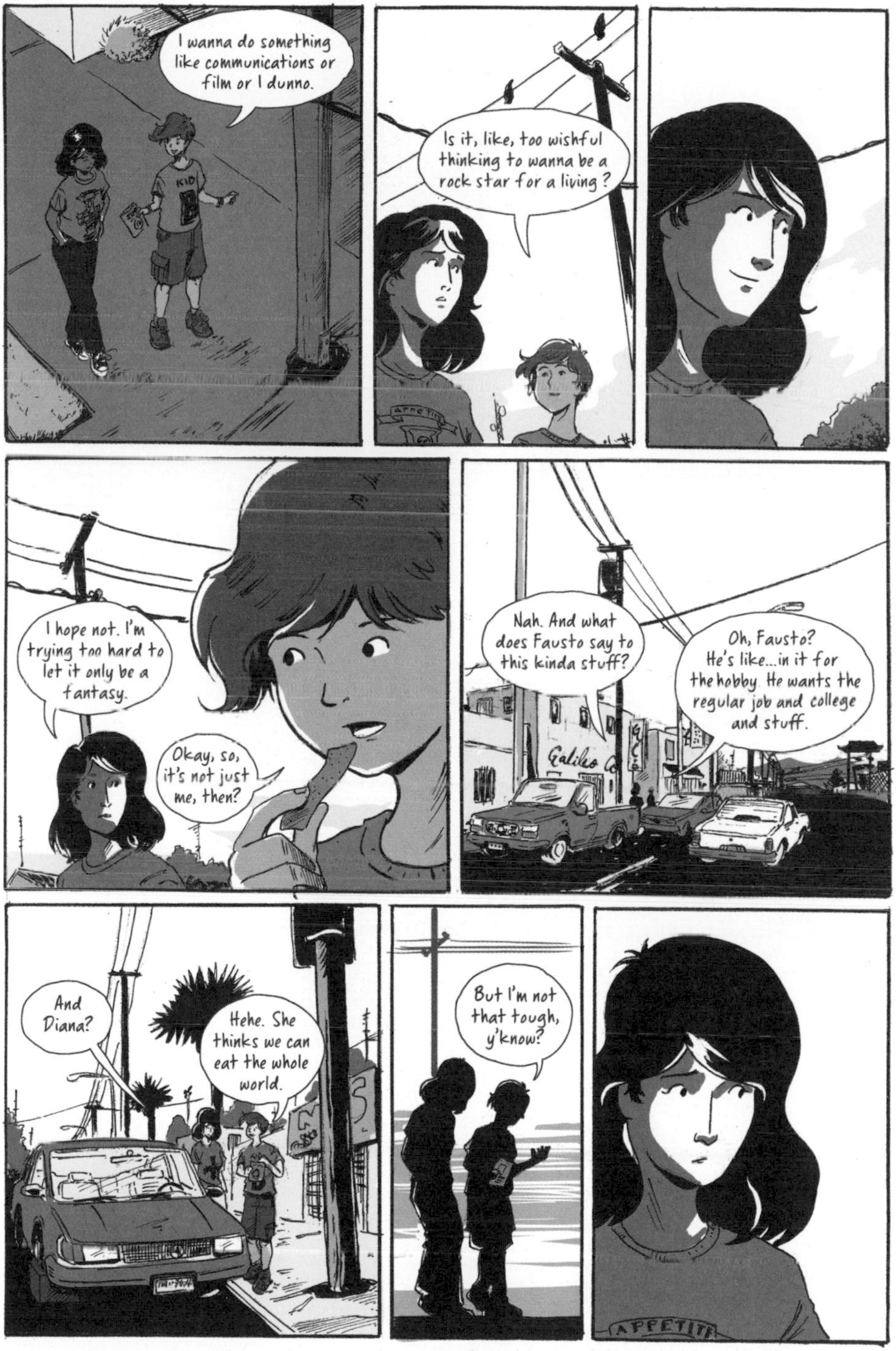

I wanna do something like communications or film or I dunno.
Is it, like, too wishful thinking to wanna be a rock star for a living?
I hope not. I'm trying too hard to let it only be a fantasy.
Okay, so, it's not just me, then?
Nah. And what does Fausto say to this kinda stuff?
Oh, Fausto? He's like...in it for the hobby. He wants the regular job and college and stuff.
And Diana?
Hehe. She thinks we can eat the whole world.
But I'm not that tough, y'know?

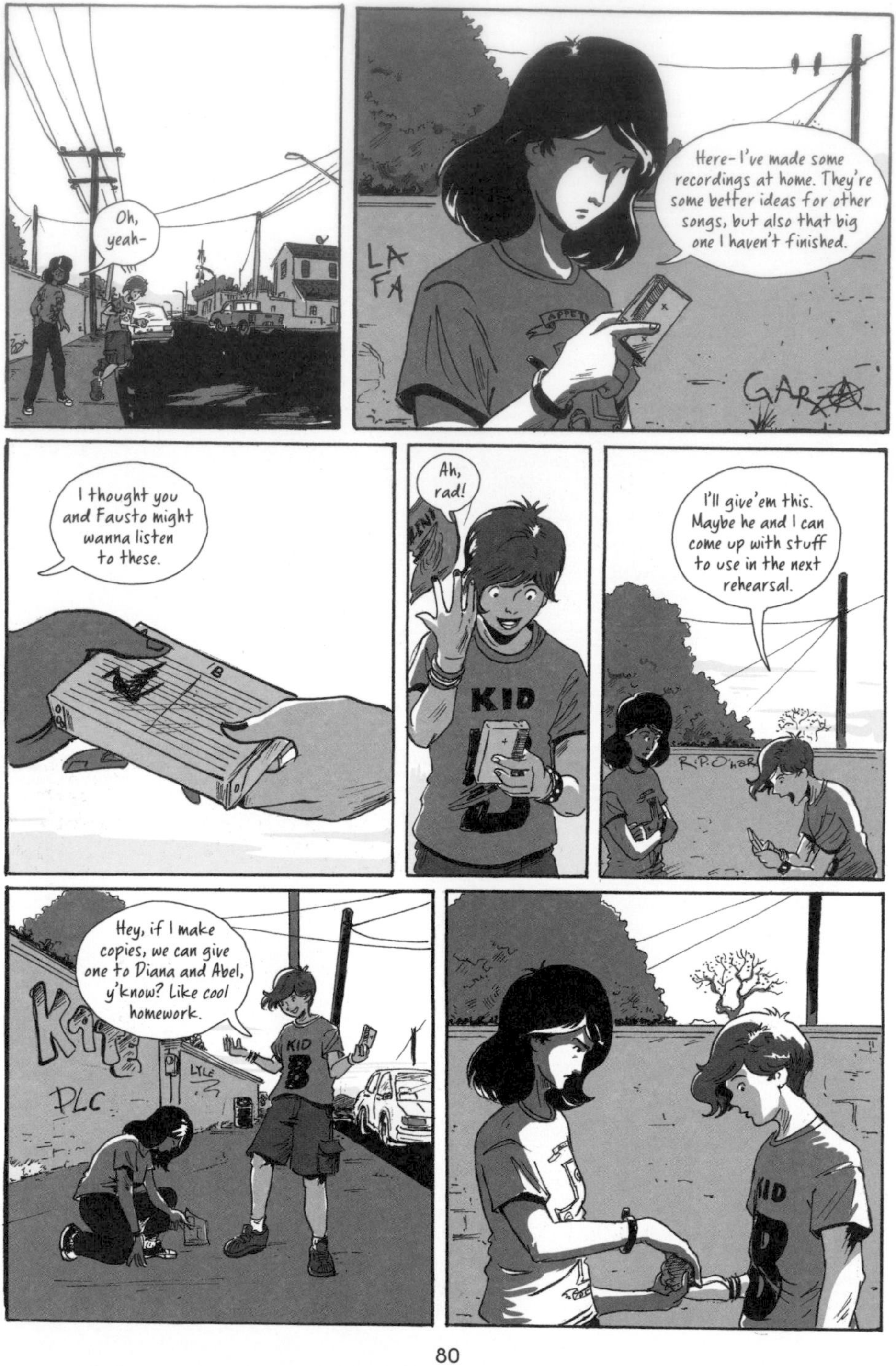
Oh, yeah-
Here- I've made some recordings at home. They're some better ideas for other songs, but also that big one I haven't finished.
LA FA
GARZA
I thought you and Fausto might wanna listen to these.
Ah, rad!
KID B
I'll give'em this. Maybe he and I can come up with stuff to use in the next rehearsal.
R.I.P. O'hara
Hey, if I make copies, we can give one to Diana and Abel, y'know? Like cool homework.
PLC
LYLE
KID B
KID

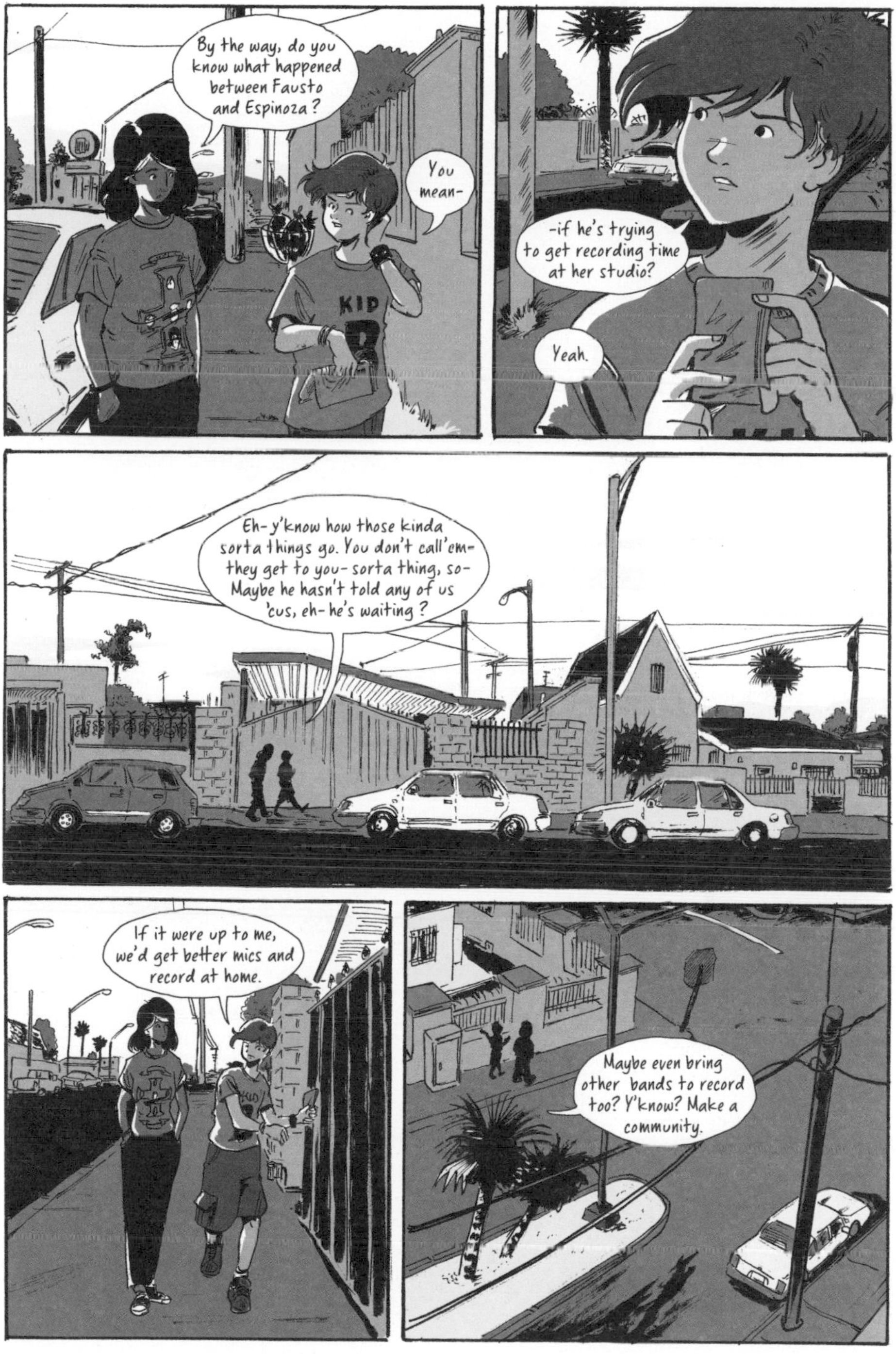
By the way, do you know what happened between Fausto and Espinoza?
You mean-
-if he's trying to get recording time at her studio?
Yeah.
Eh- y'know how those kinda sorta things go. You don't call'em- they get to you- sorta thing, so- Maybe he hasn't told any of us 'cus, eh- he's waiting?
If it were up to me, we'd get better mics and record at home.
Maybe even bring other bands to record too? Y'know? Make a community.

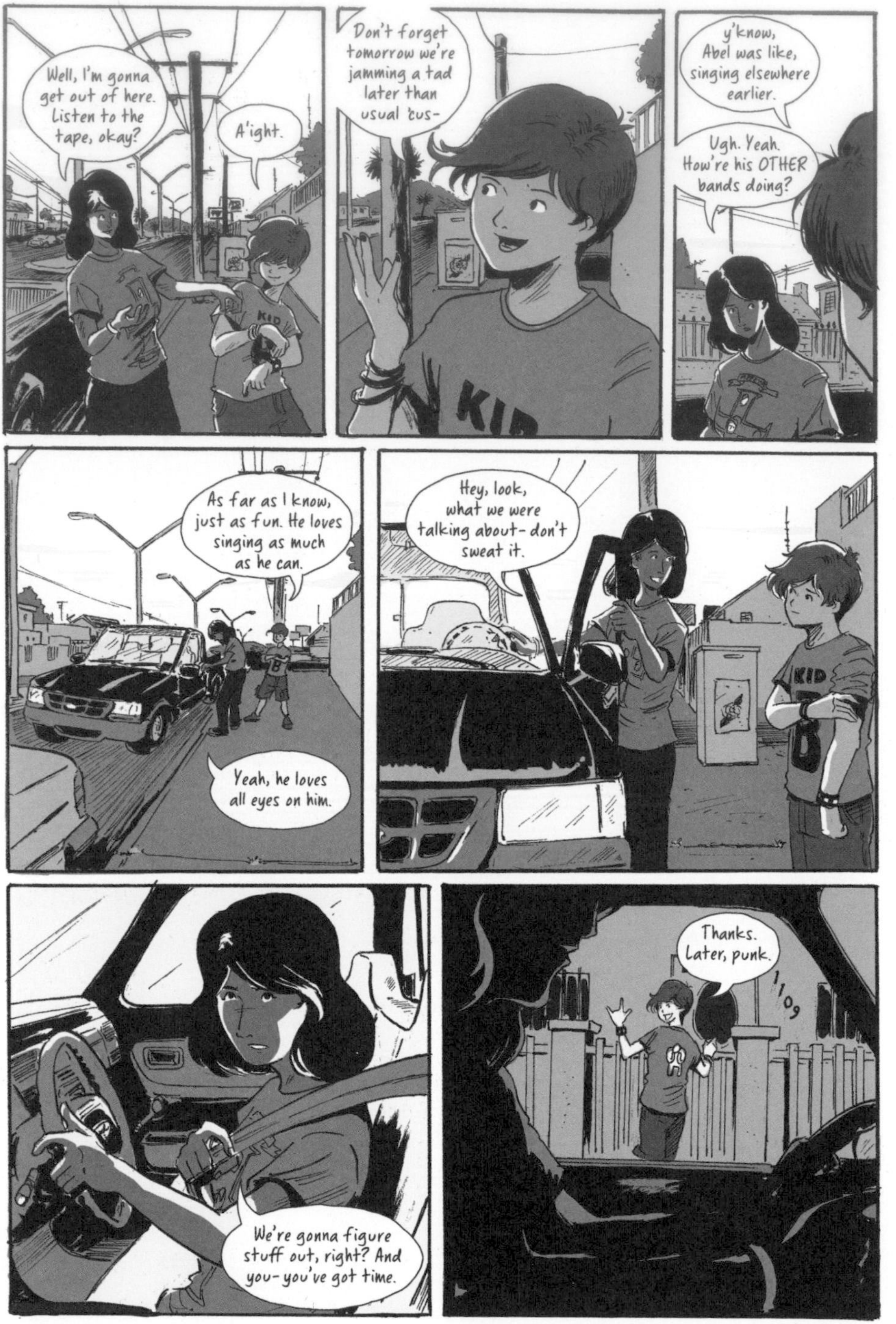
Well, I'm gonna get out of here. Listen to the tape, okay?
A'ight.
Don't forget tomorrow we're jamming a tad later than usual 'cus-
y'know, Abel was like, singing elsewhere earlier.
Ugh. Yeah. How're his OTHER bands doing?
As far as I know, just as fun. He loves singing as much as he can.
Yeah, he loves all eyes on him.
Hey, look, what we were talking about- don't sweat it.
We're gonna figure stuff out, right? And you- you've got time.
Thanks. Later, punk.
1109

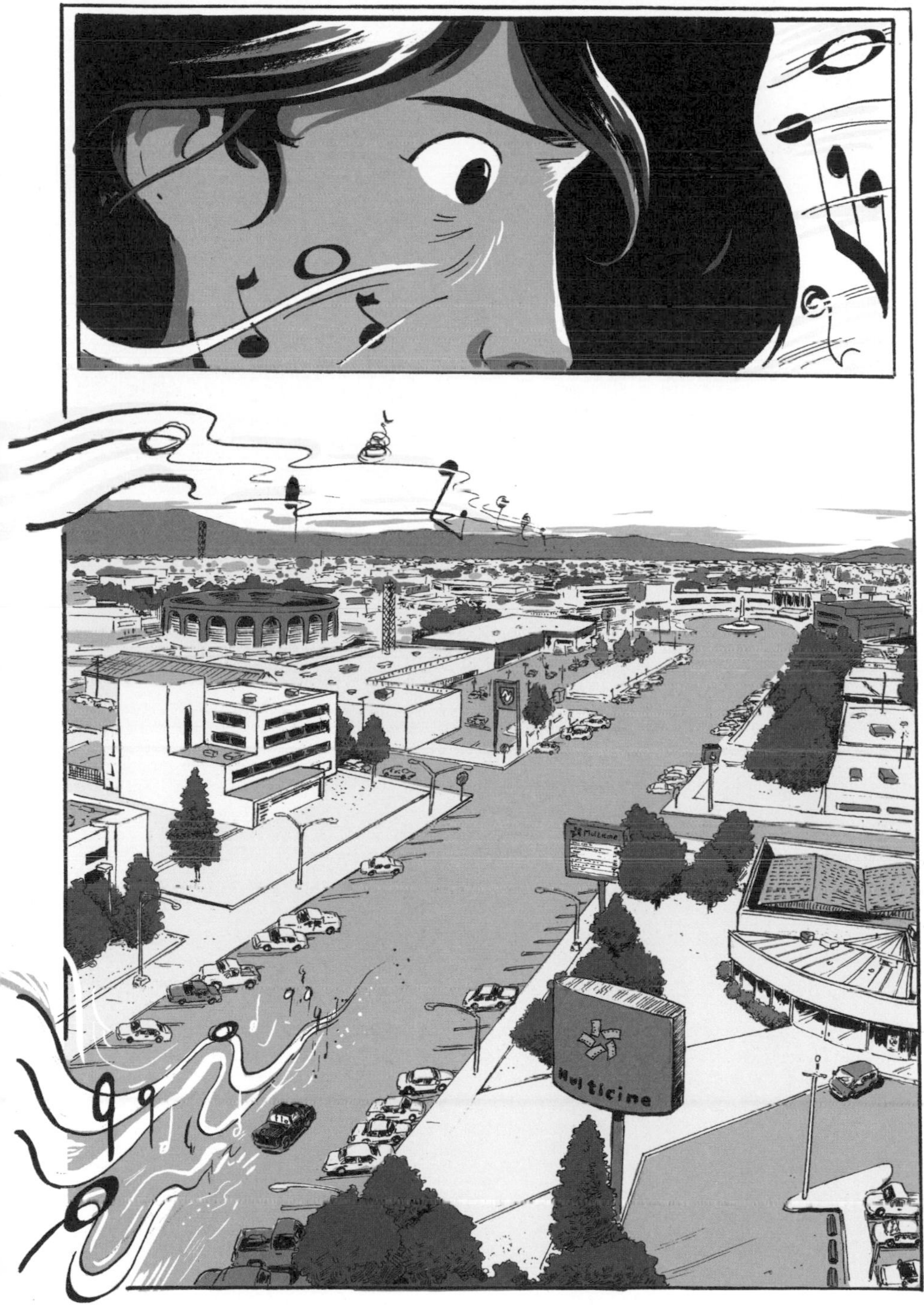
Multicine

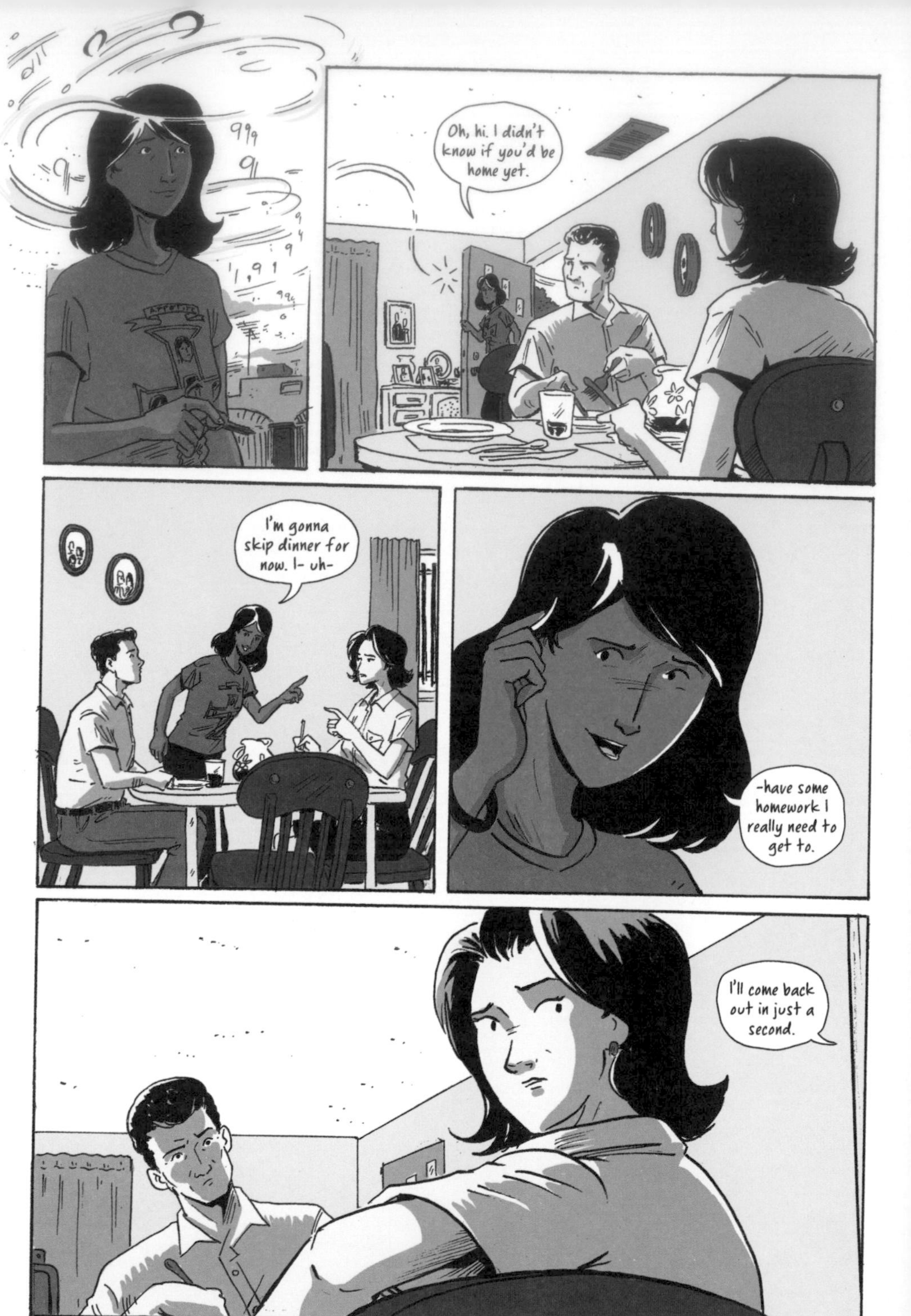
Oh, hi. I didn't know if you'd be home yet.
I'm gonna skip dinner for now. I- uh-
-have some homework I really need to get to.
I'll come back out in just a second.

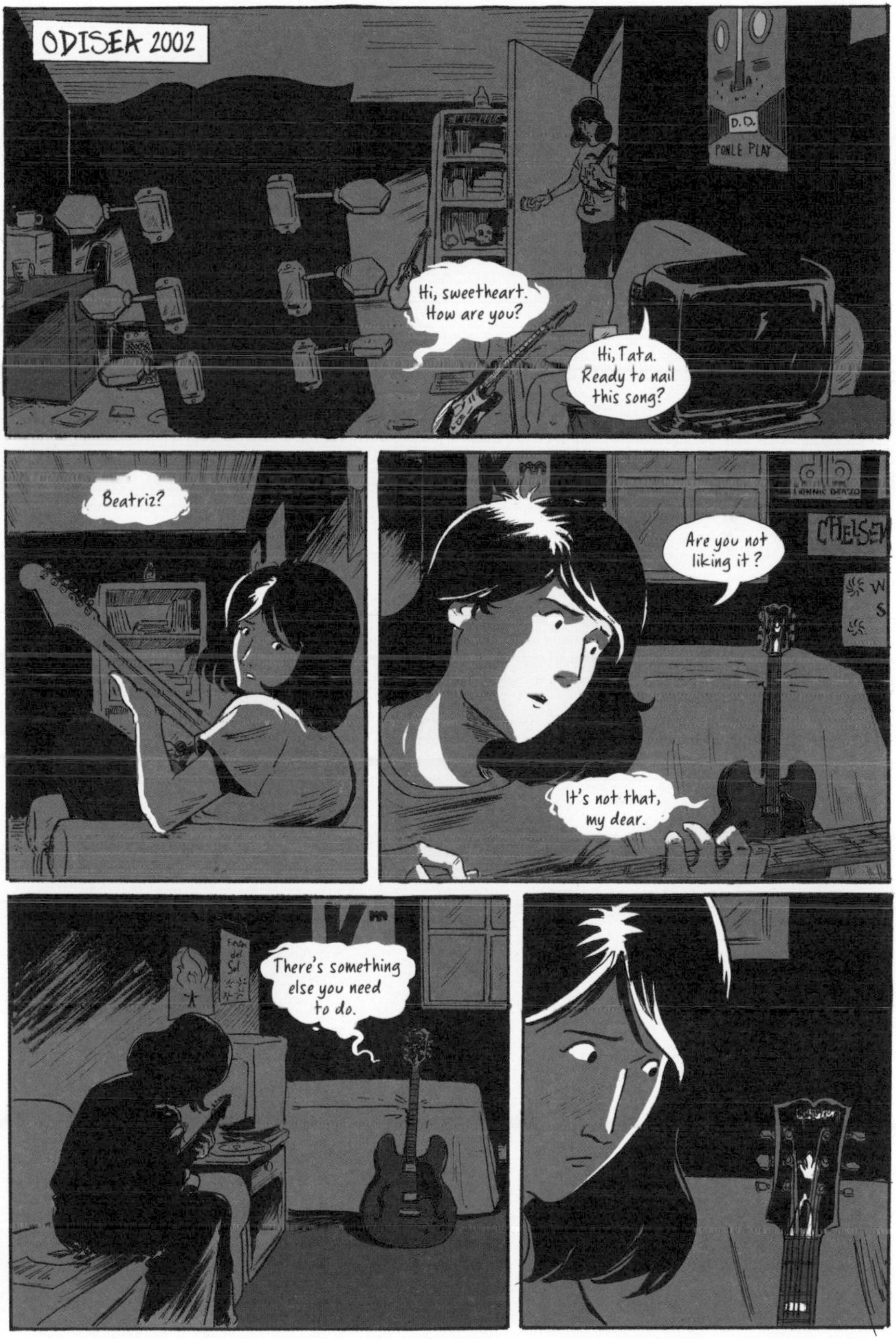

ODISEA 2002
D. D.
PONLE PLAY
Hi, sweetheart. How are you?
Hi, Tata. Ready to nail this song?
Beatriz?
CHELSEA
Are you not liking it?
It's not that, my dear.
There's something else you need to do.

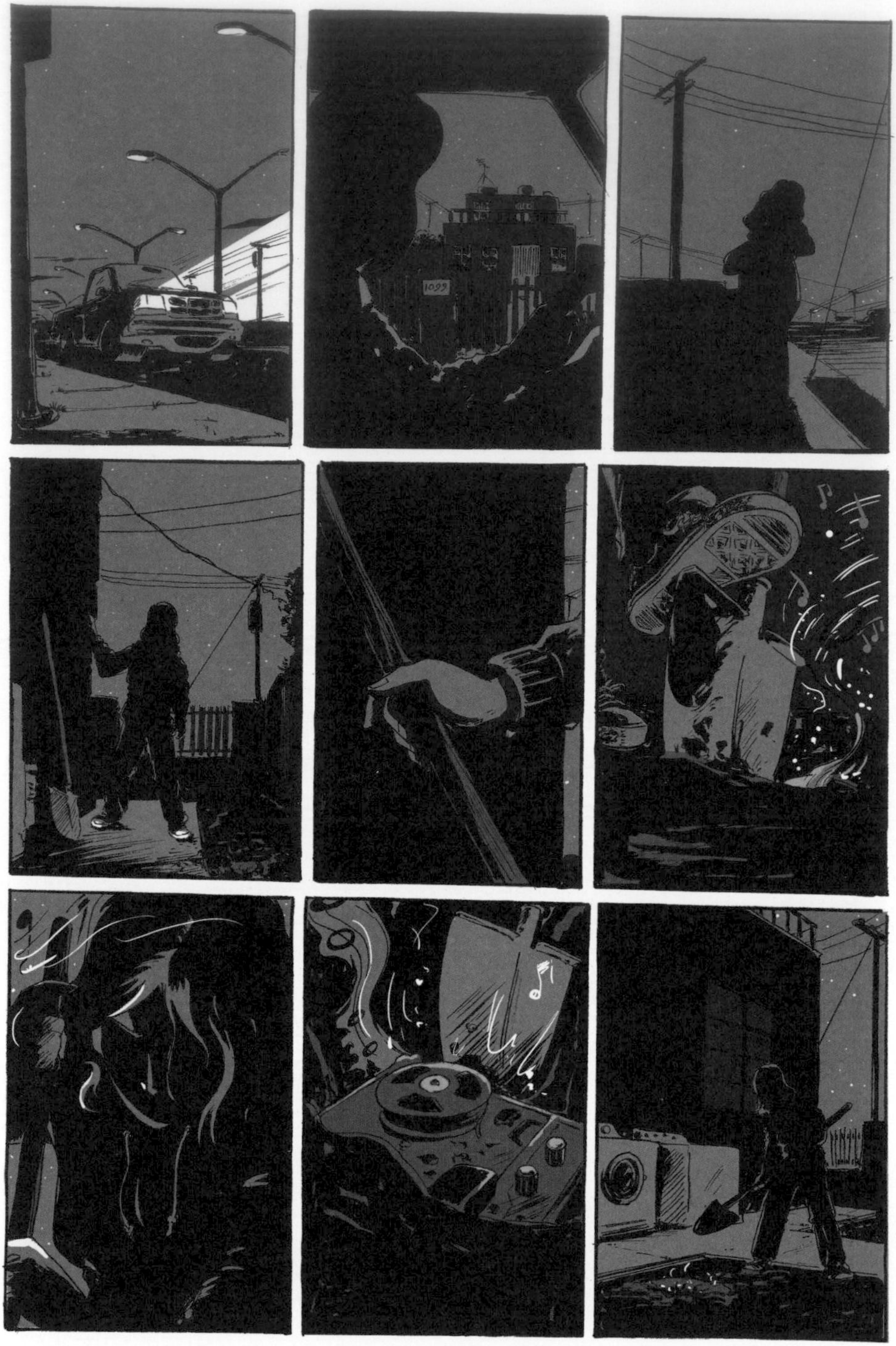

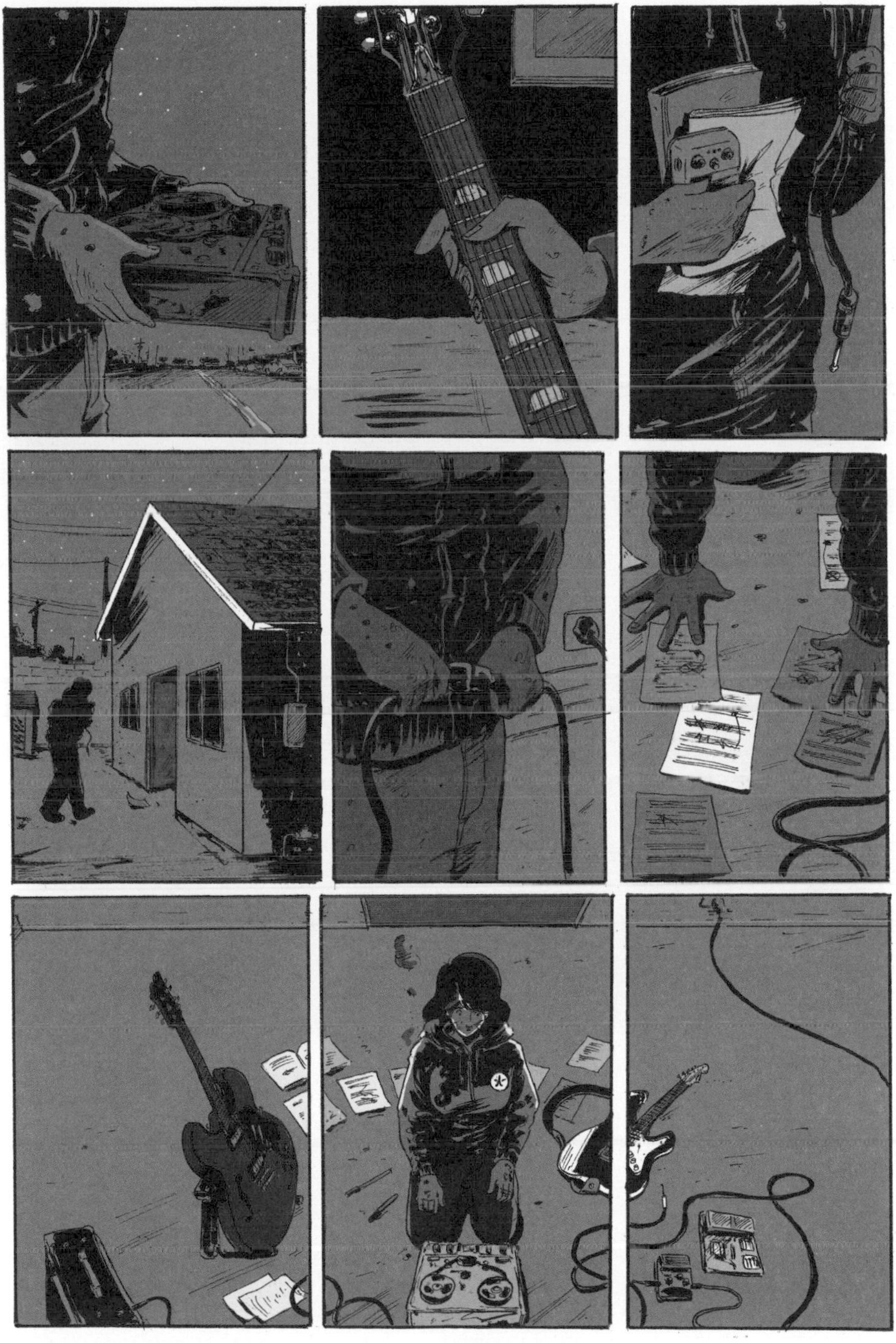

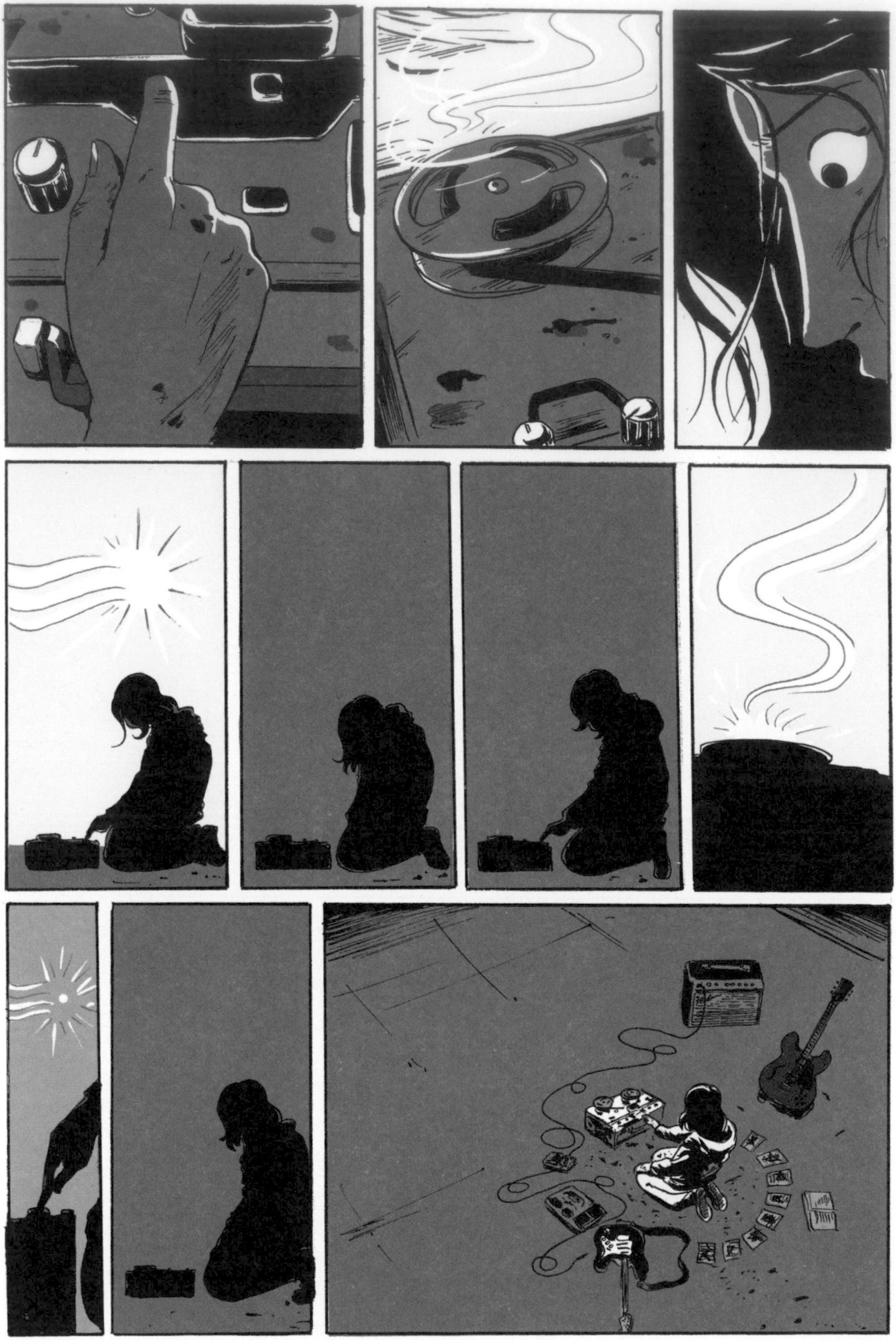

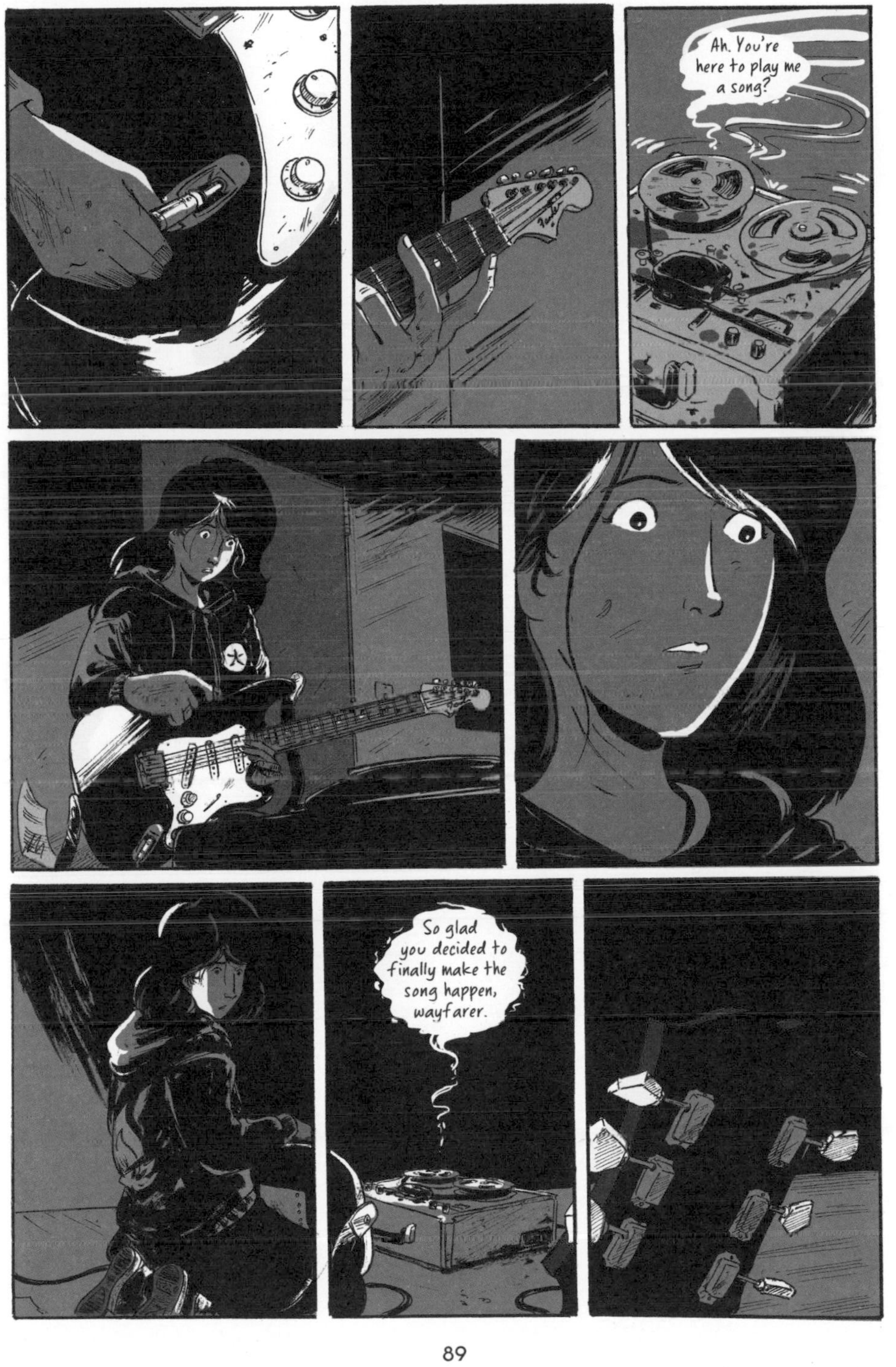
Ah. You're here to play me a song?
So glad you decided to finally make the song happen, wayfarer.

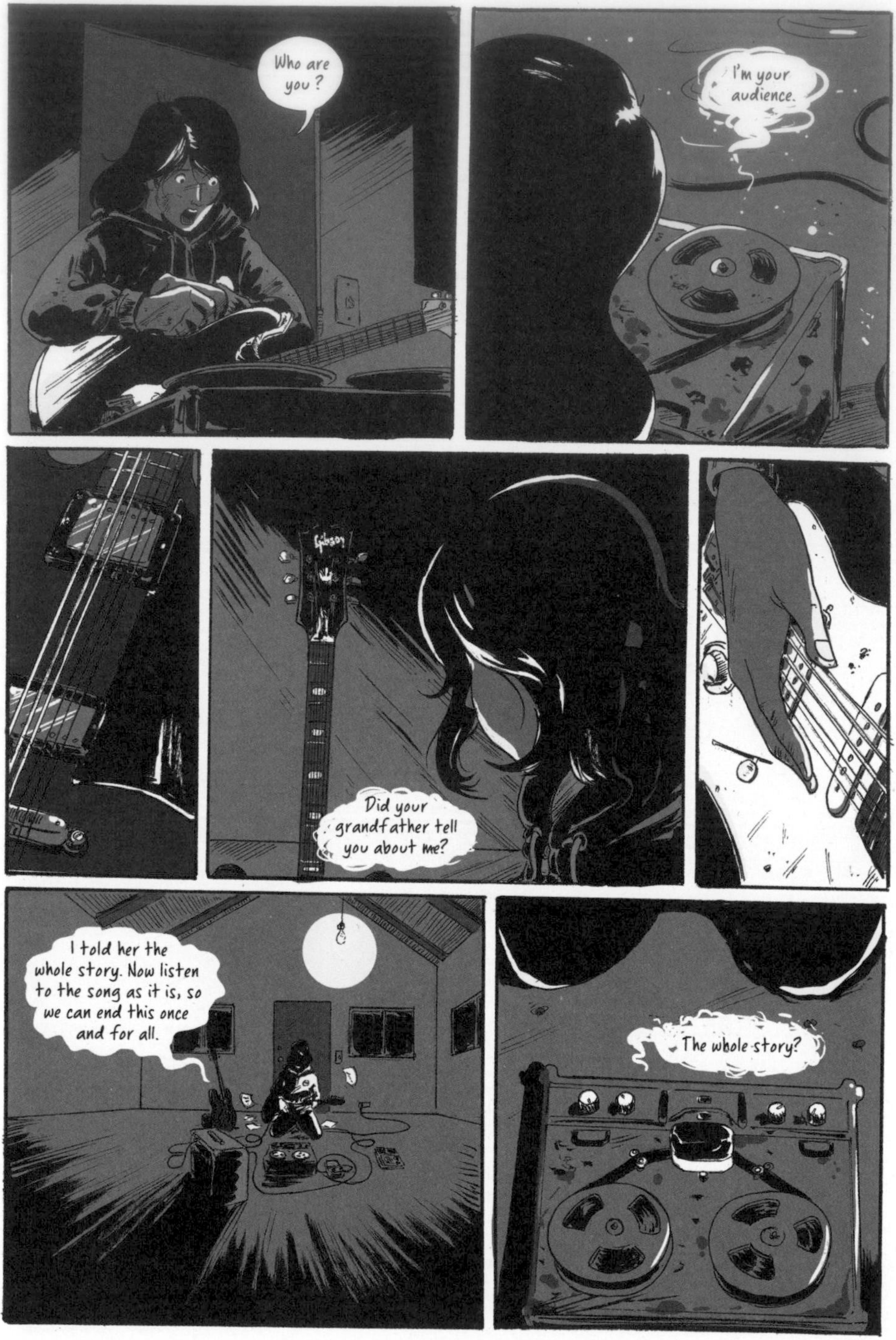
Who are you ?
I'm your audience.
Did your grandfather tell you about me?
I told her the whole story. Now listen to the song as it is, so we can end this once and for all.
The whole story?

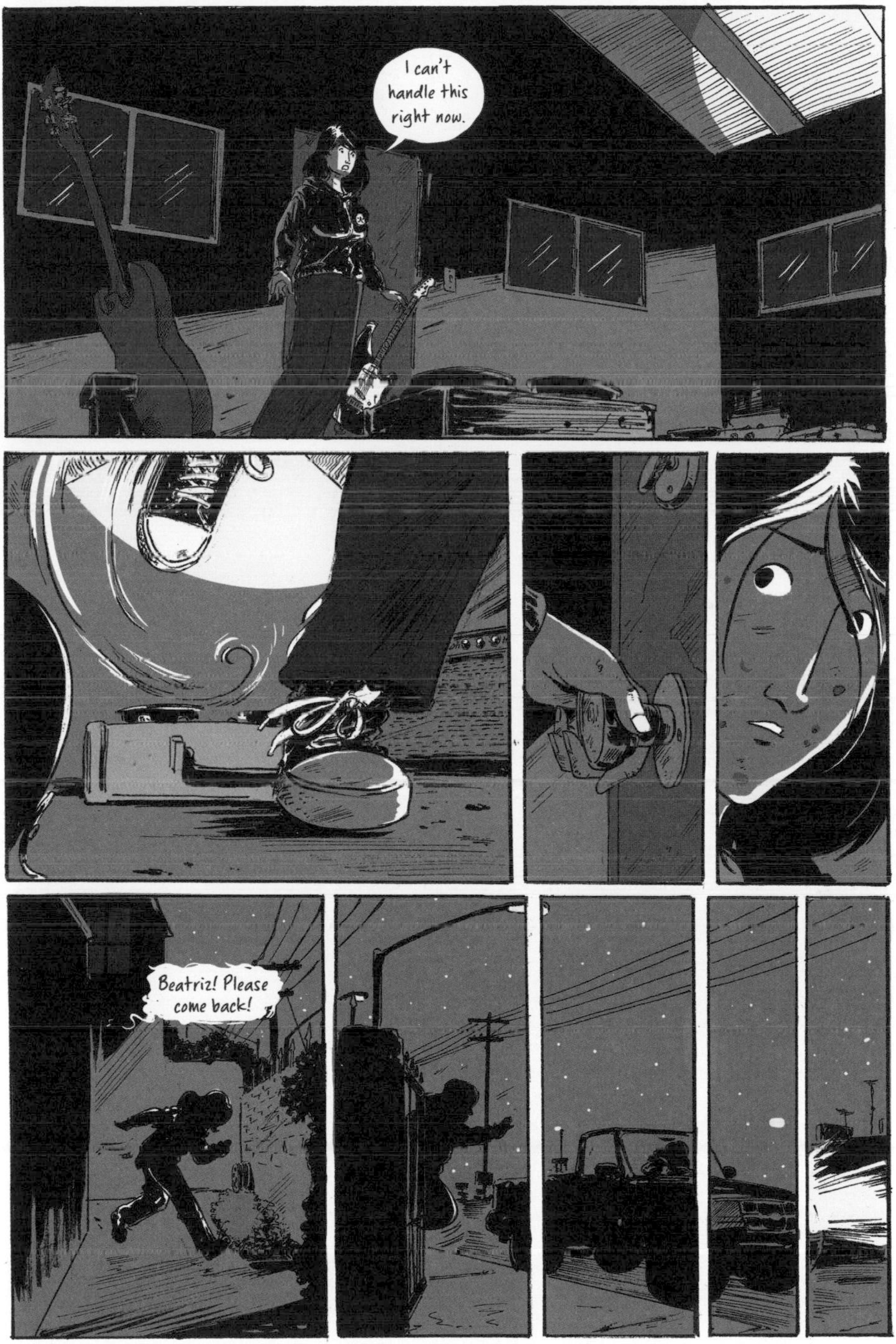
I can't handle this right now.
Beatriz! Please come back!

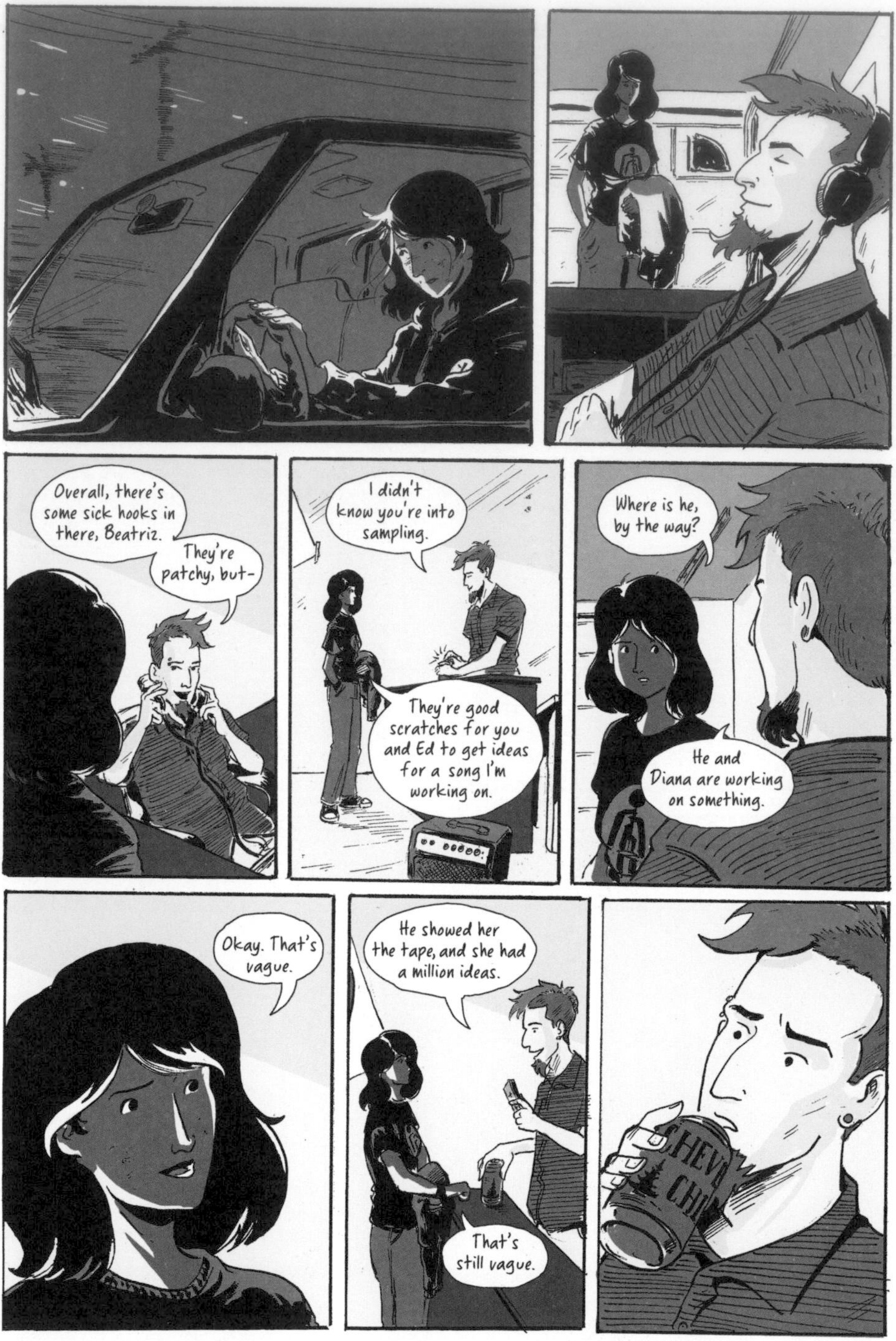
Overall, there's some sick hooks in there, Beatriz.
They're patchy, but-
I didn't know you're into sampling.
They're good scratches for you and Ed to get ideas for a song I'm working on.
Where is he, by the way?
He and Diana are working on something.
Okay. That's vague.
He showed her the tape, and she had a million ideas.
That's still vague.

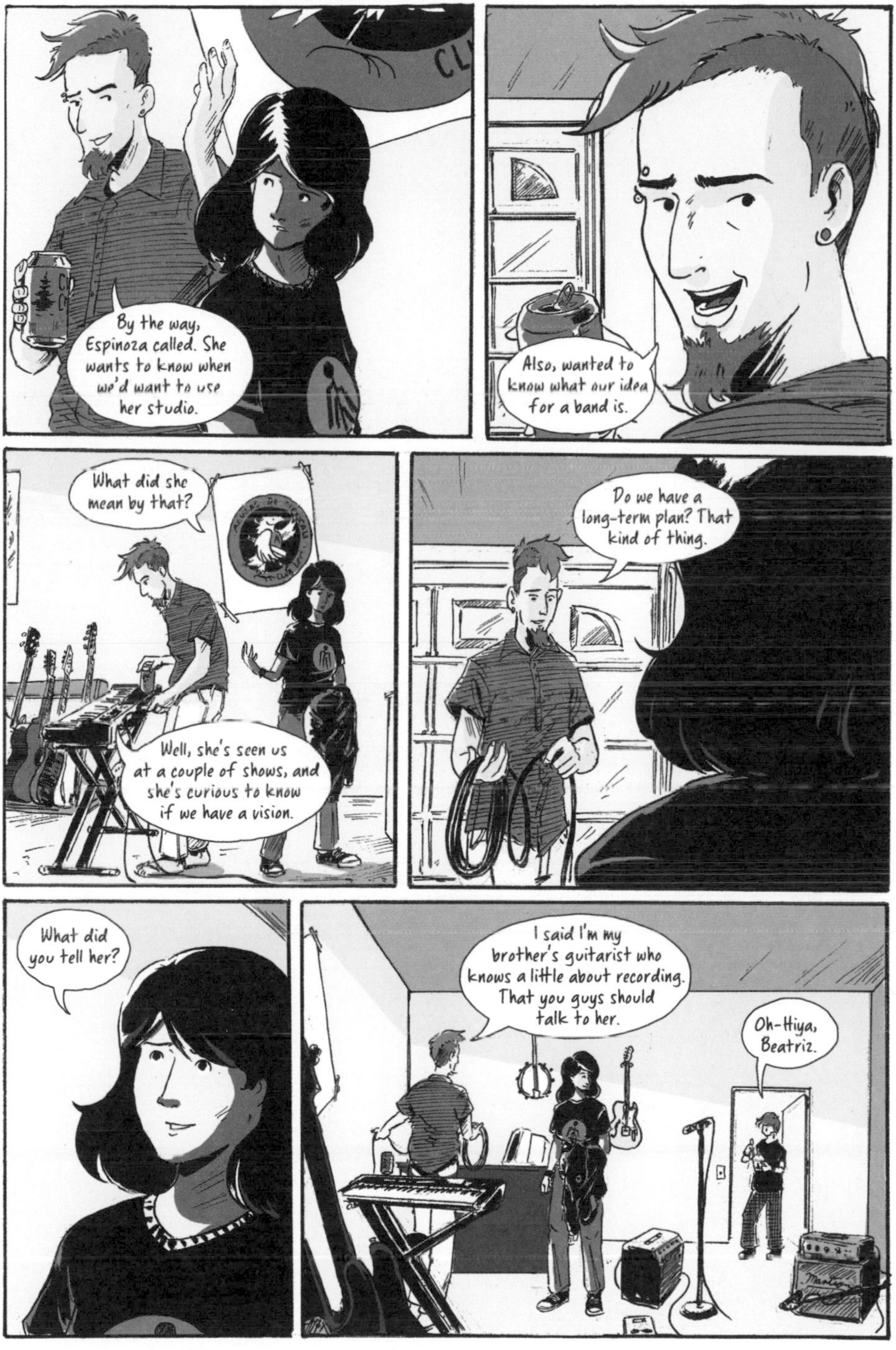
By the way, Espinoza called. She wants to know when we'd want to use her studio.
Also, wanted to know what our idea for a band is.
What did she mean by that?
Well, she's seen us at a couple of shows, and she's curious to know if we have a vision.
Do we have a long-term plan? That kind of thing.
What did you tell her?
I said I'm my brother's guitarist who knows a little about recording. That you guys should talk to her.
Oh-Hiya, Beatriz.

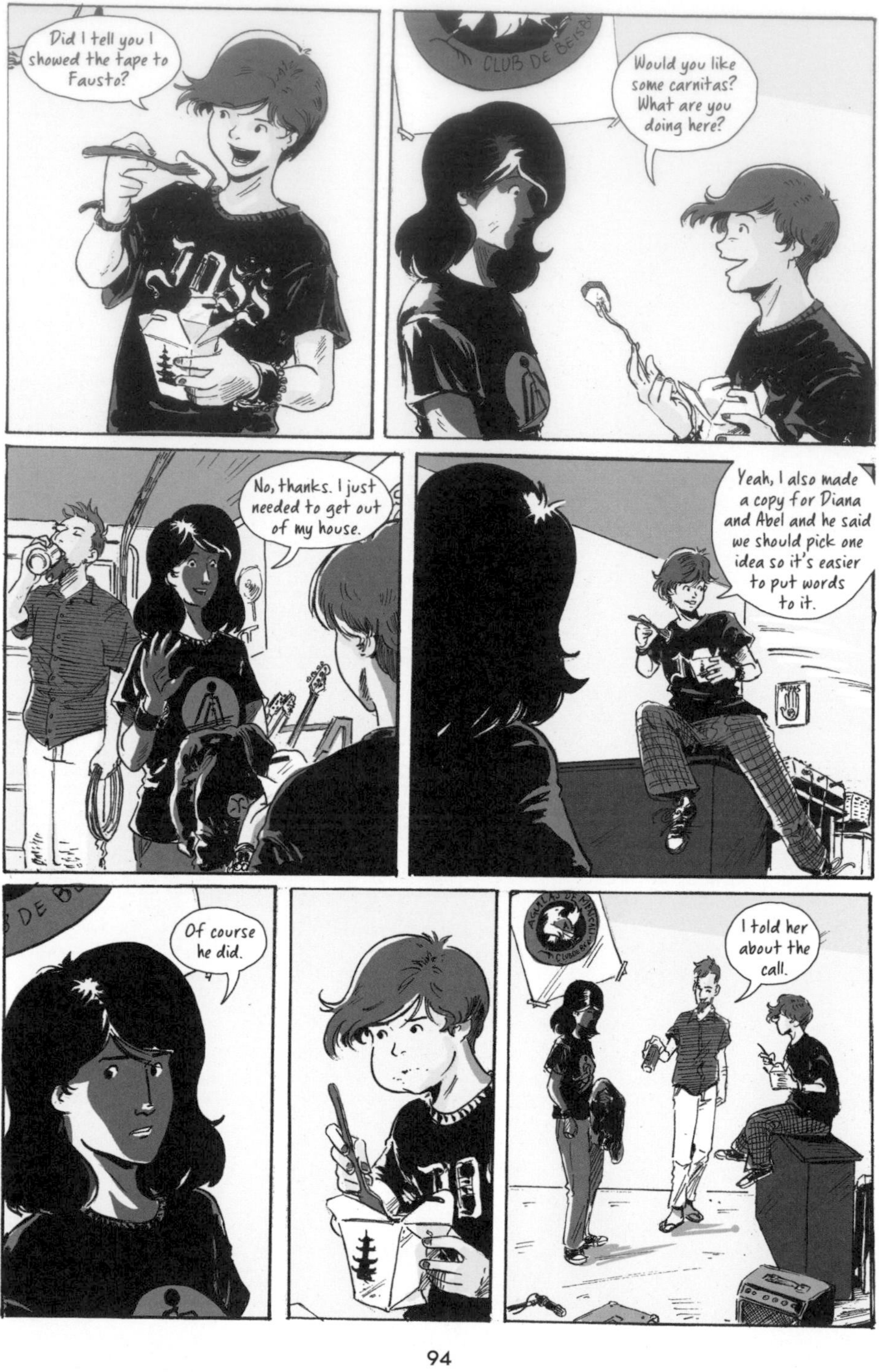
Did I tell you I showed the tape to Fausto?
CLUB DE BEISB
Would you like some carnitas? What are you doing here?
No, thanks. I just needed to get out of my house.
Yeah, I also made a copy for Diana and Abel and he said we should pick one idea so it's easier to put words to it.
DE B
Of course he did.
I told her about the call.

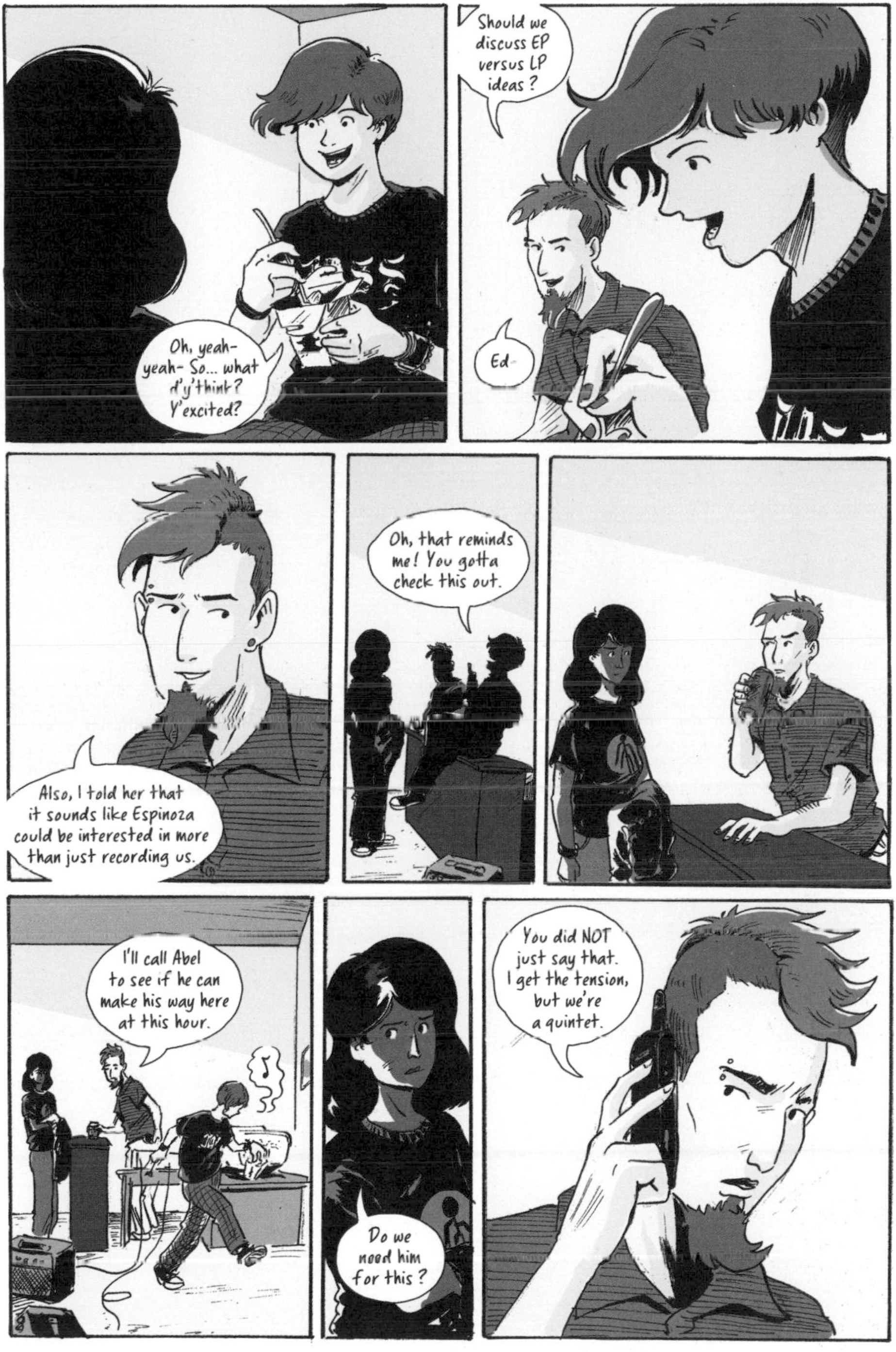
Oh, yeah- yeah- So... what d'y'think? Y'excited?
Should we discuss EP versus LP ideas?
Ed-
Also, I told her that it sounds like Espinoza could be interested in more than just recording us.
Oh, that reminds me! You gotta check this out.
I'll call Abel to see if he can make his way here at this hour.
Do we need him for this?
You did NOT just say that. I get the tension, but we're a quintet.

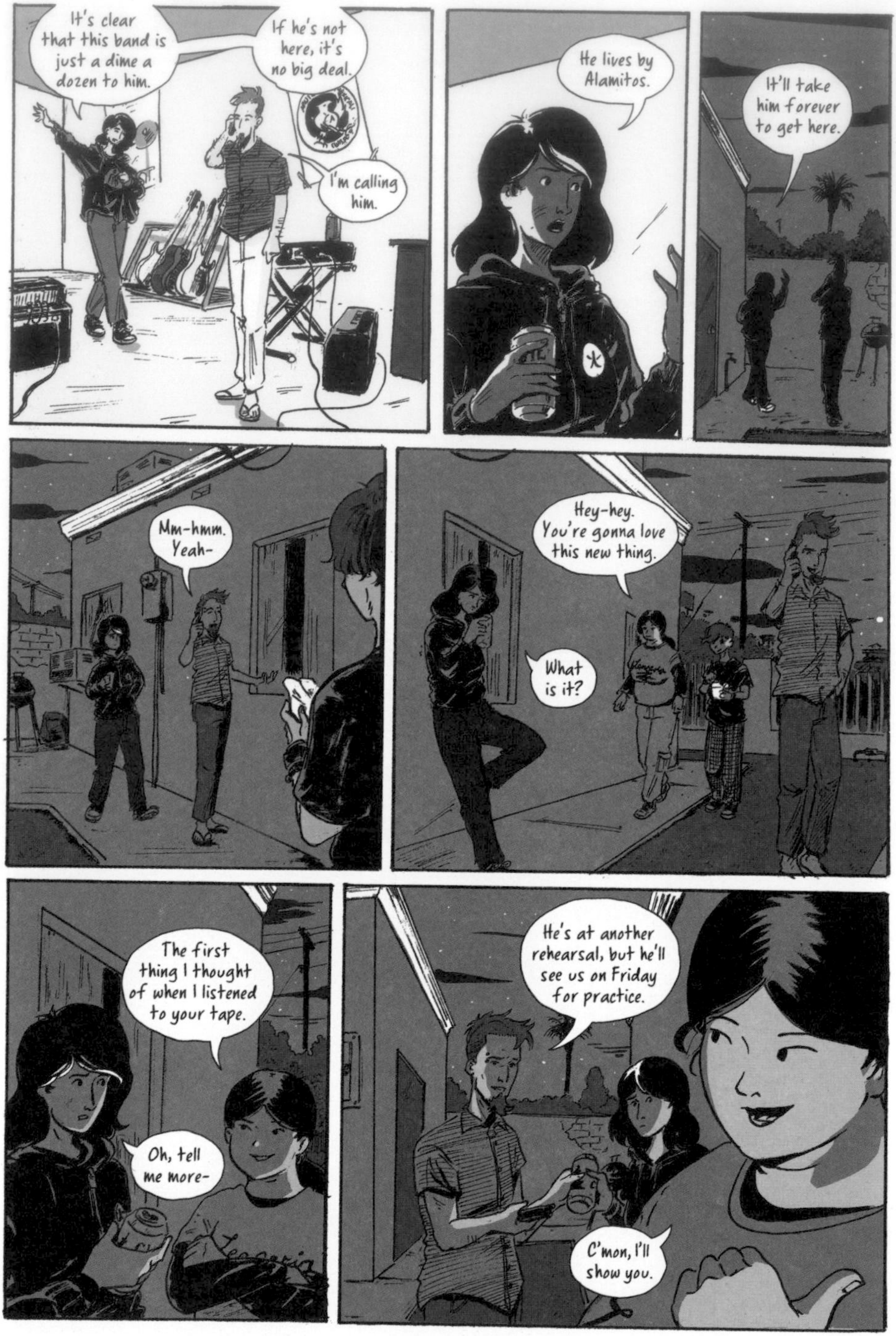
It's clear that this band is just a dime a dozen to him.
If he's not here, it's no big deal.
I'm calling him.
He lives by Alamitos.
It'll take him forever to get here.
Mm-hmm. Yeah-
Hey-hey. You're gonna love this new thing.
What is it?
The first thing I thought of when I listened to your tape.
Oh, tell me more-
He's at another rehearsal, but he'll see us on Friday for practice.
C'mon, I'll show you.

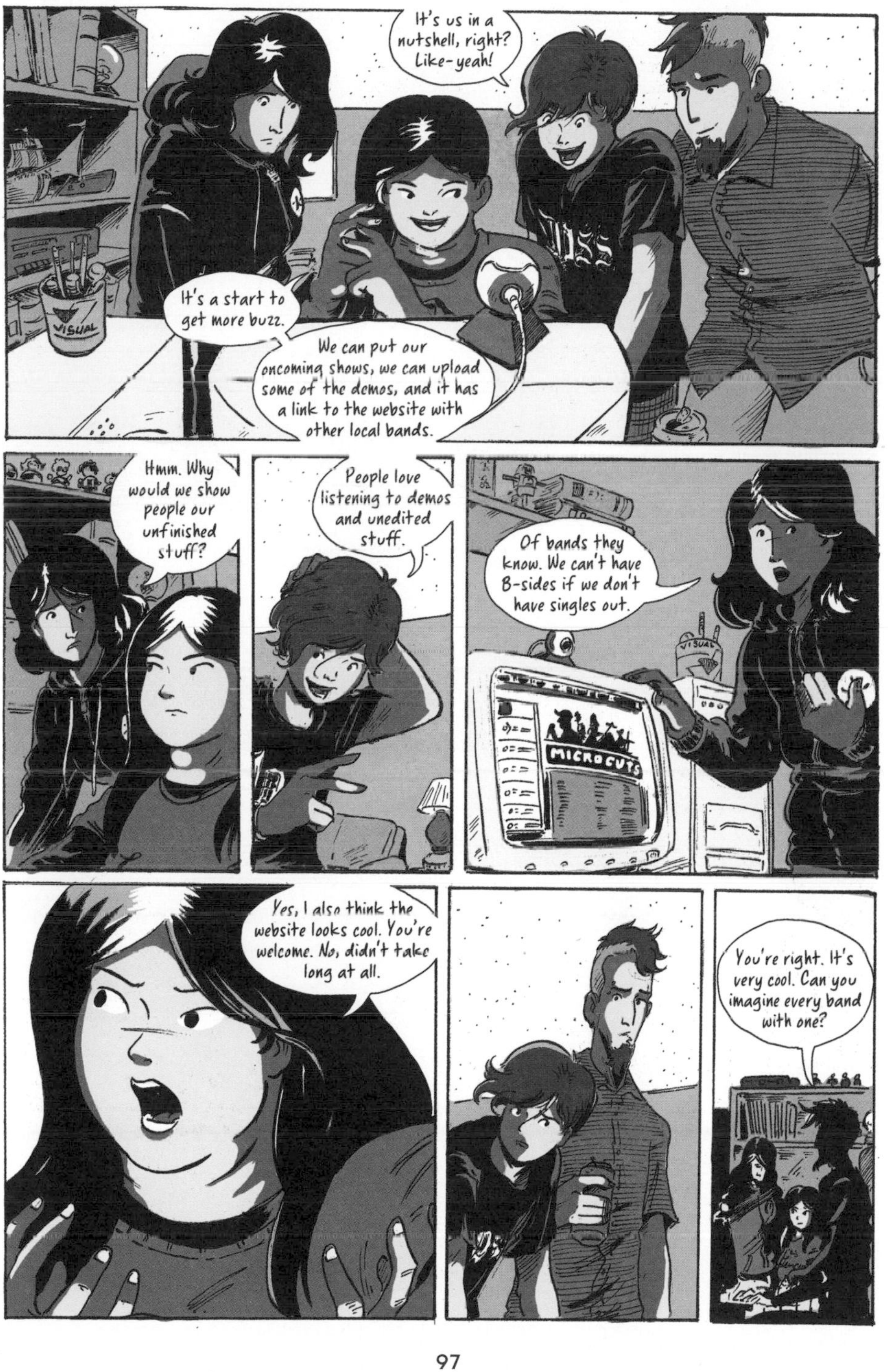
It's us in a nutshell, right? Like-yeah!
It's a start to get more buzz.
We can put our oncoming shows, we can upload some of the demos, and it has a link to the website with other local bands.
Hmm. Why would we show people our unfinished stuff?
People love listening to demos and unedited stuff.
Of bands they know. We can't have B-sides if we don't have singles out.
MICROCUTS
Yes, I also think the website looks cool. You're welcome. No, didn't take long at all.
You're right. It's very cool. Can you imagine every band with one?

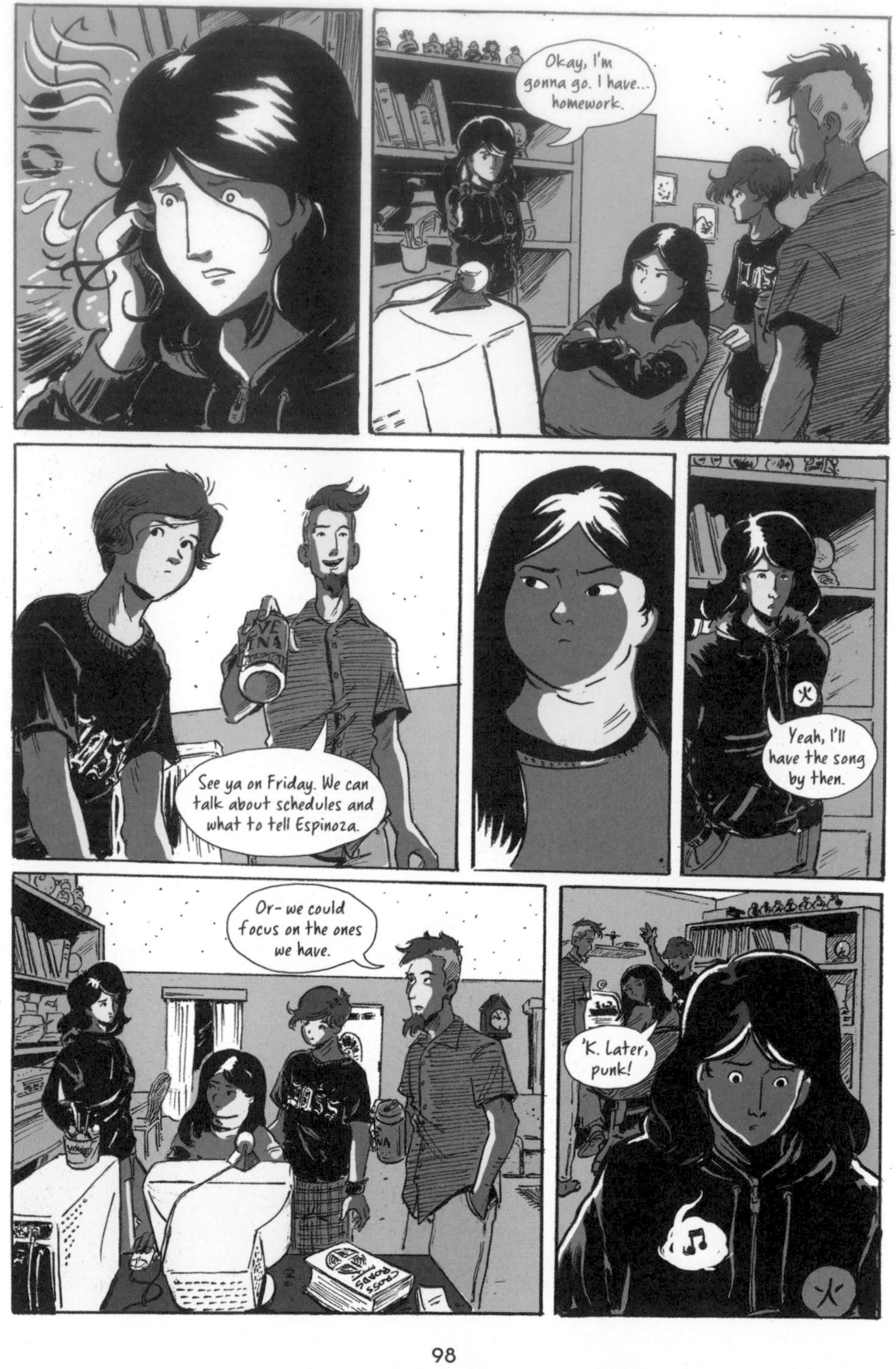
Okay, I'm gonna go. I have... homework.
See ya on Friday. We can talk about schedules and what to tell Espinoza.
Yeah, I'll have the song by then.
Or- we could focus on the ones we have.
'K. Later, punk!

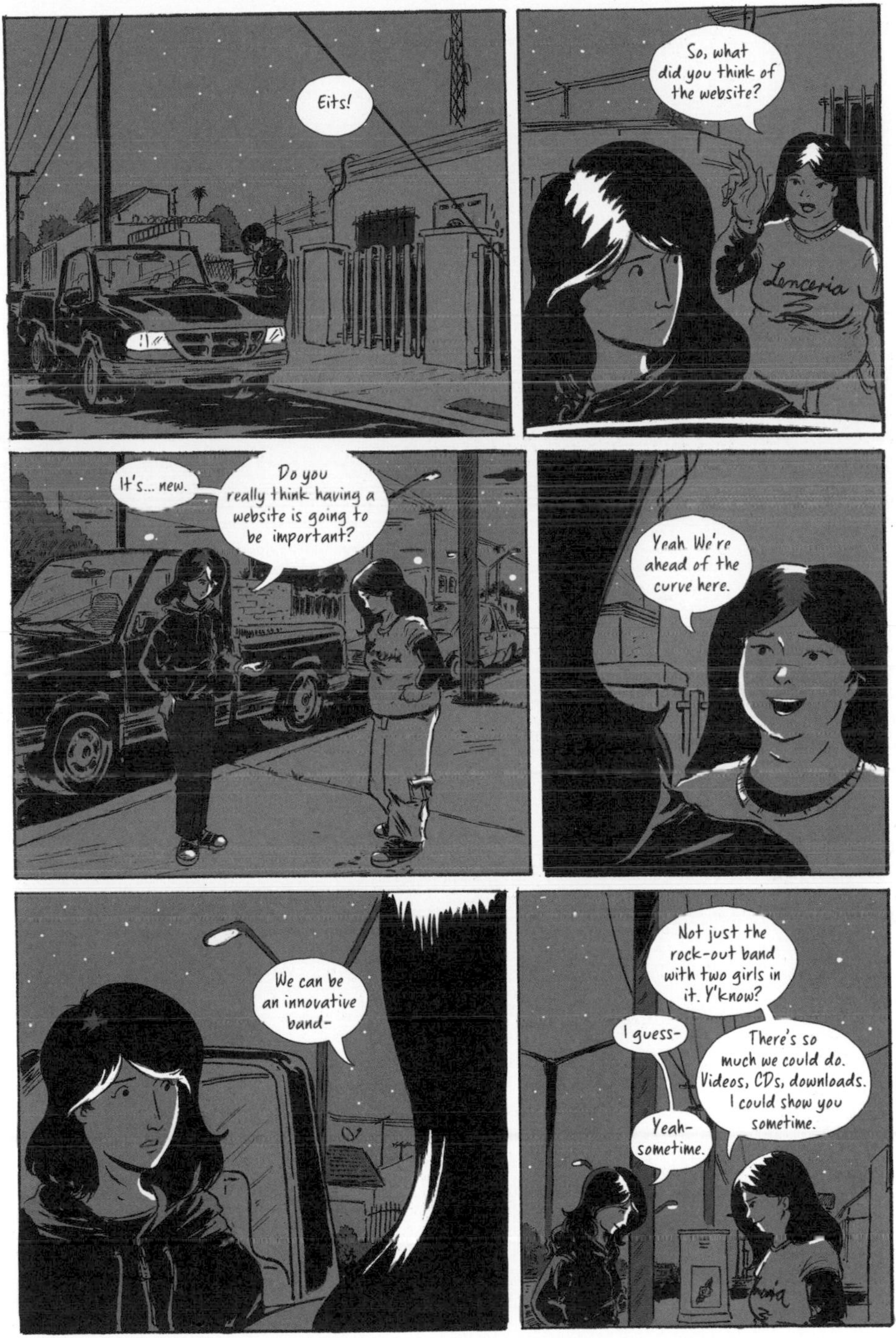
Eits!
So, what did you think of the website?
Lenceria
It's... new.
Do you really think having a website is going to be important?
Yeah. We're ahead of the curve here.
We can be an innovative band-
Not just the rock-out band with two girls in it. Y'know?
I guess-
There's so much we could do. Videos, CDs, downloads. I could show you sometime.
Yeah- sometime.

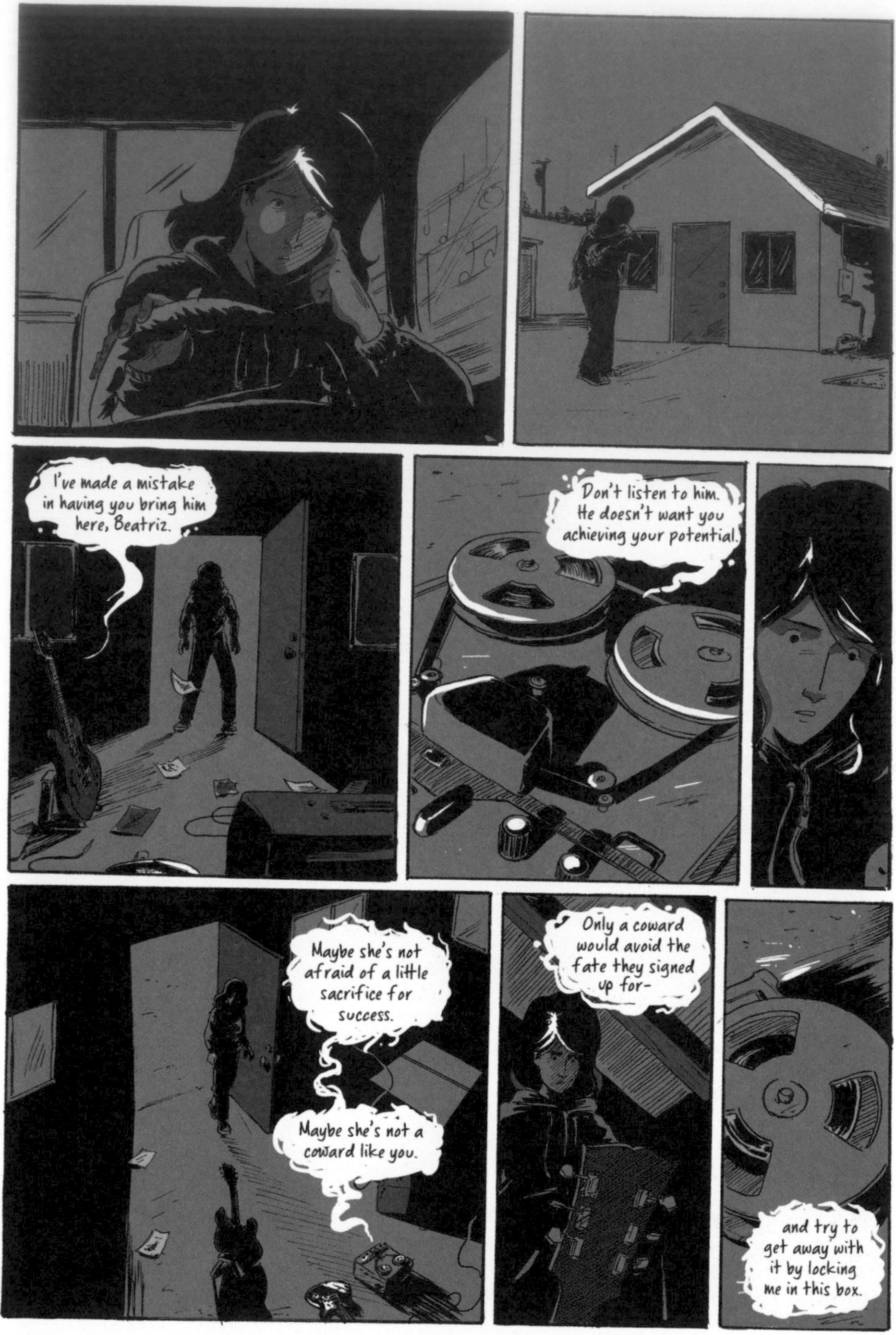
I've made a mistake in having you bring him here, Beatriz.
Don't listen to him. He doesn't want you achieving your potential.
Maybe she's not afraid of a little sacrifice for success.
Maybe she's not a coward like you.
Only a coward would avoid the fate they signed up for-
and try to get away with it by locking me in this box.

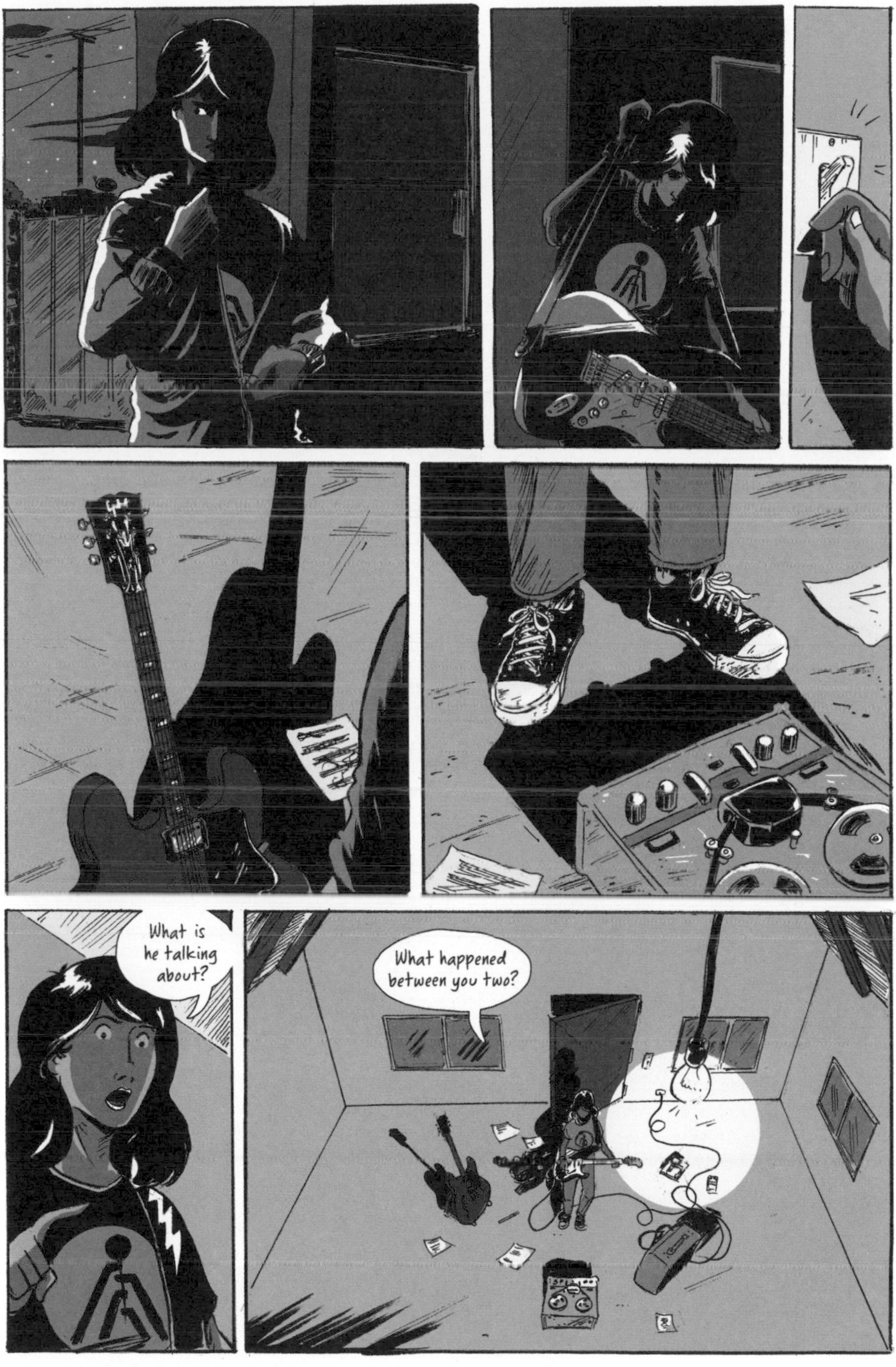
What is he talking about?
What happened between you two?

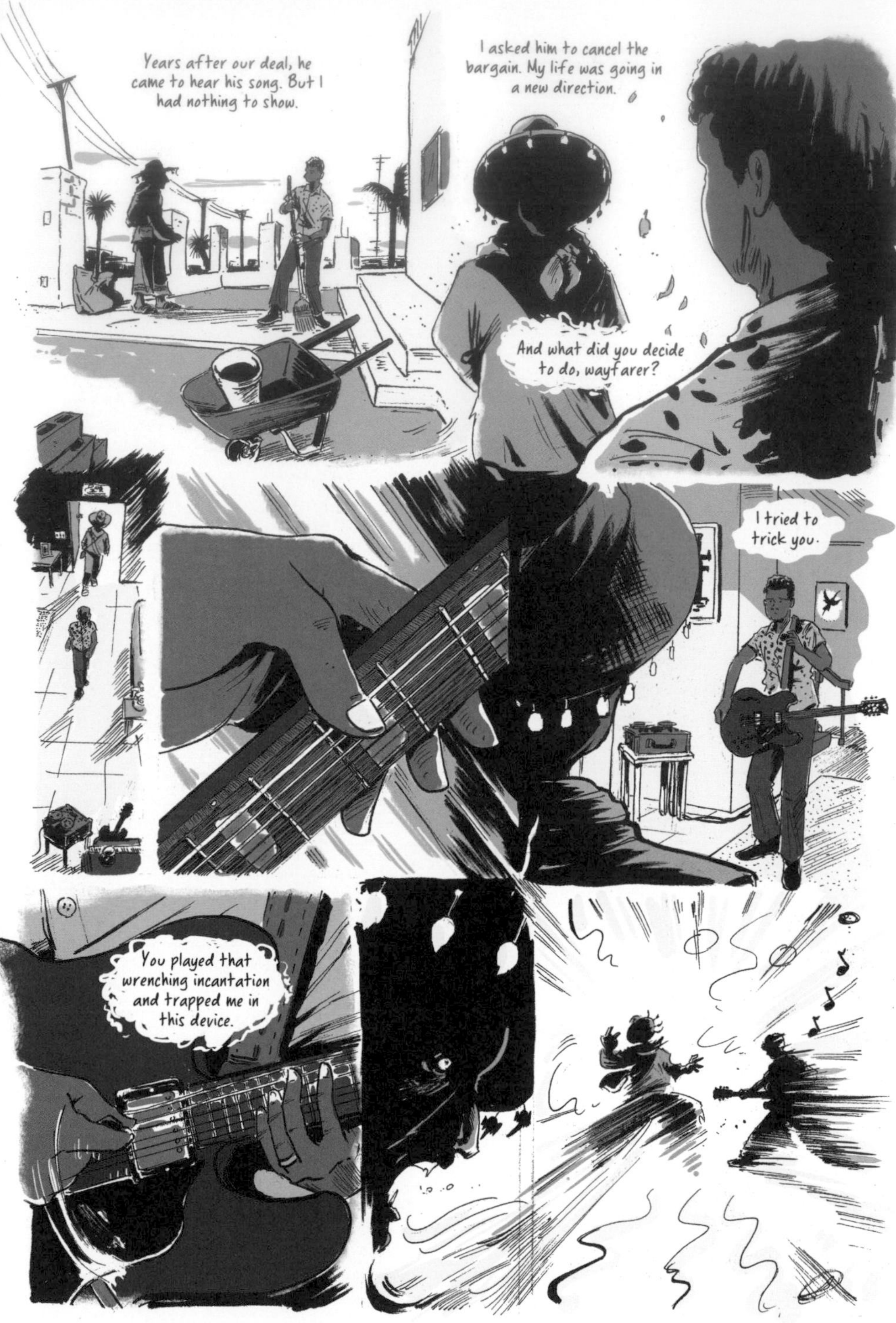
Years after our deal, he came to hear his song. But I had nothing to show.
I asked him to cancel the bargain. My life was going in a new direction.
And what did you decide to do, wayfarer?
I tried to trick you.
You played that wrenching incantation and trapped me in this device.

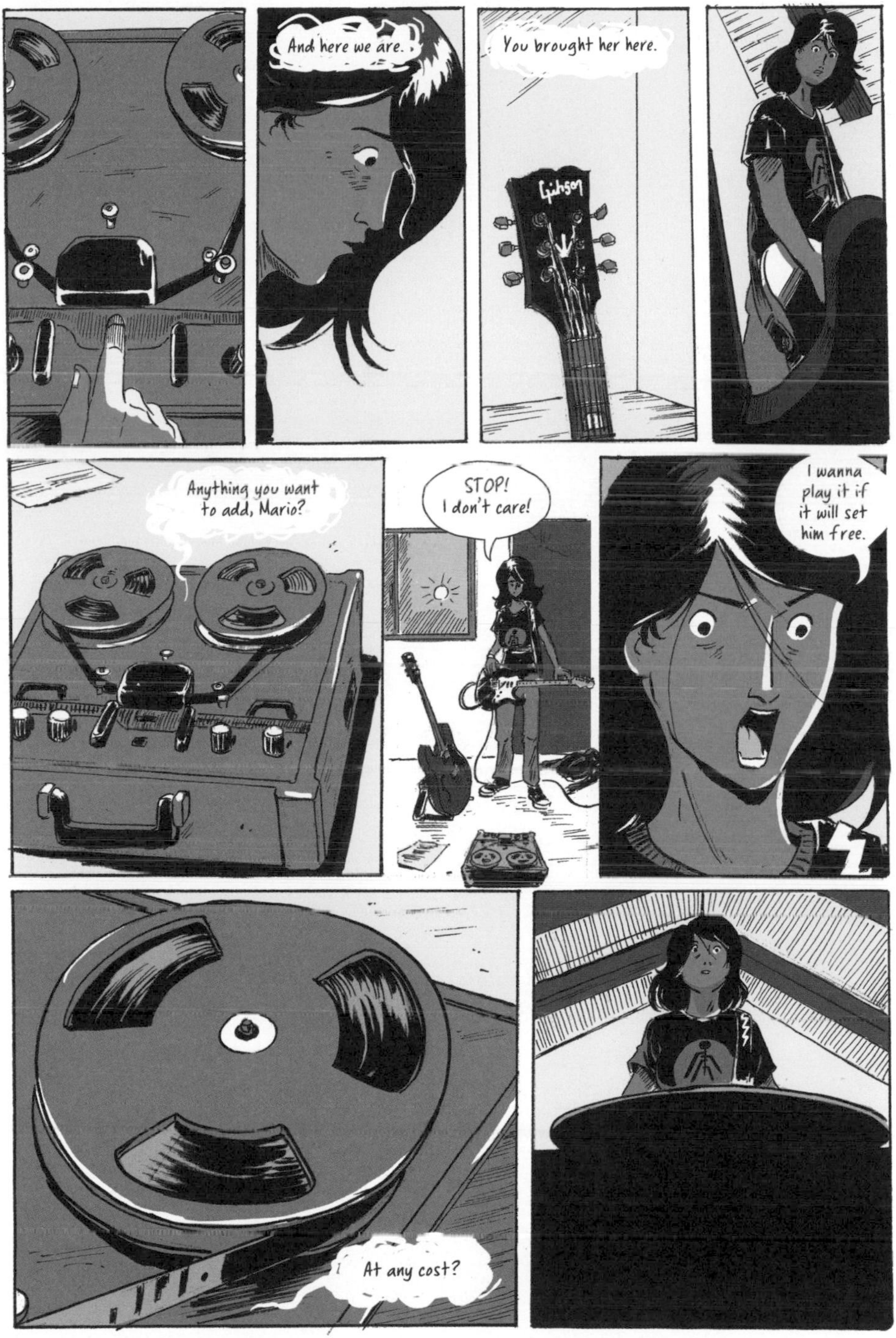
And here we are.
You brought her here.
Gibson
Anything you want to add, Mario?
STOP! I don't care!
I wanna play it if it will set him free.
At any cost?

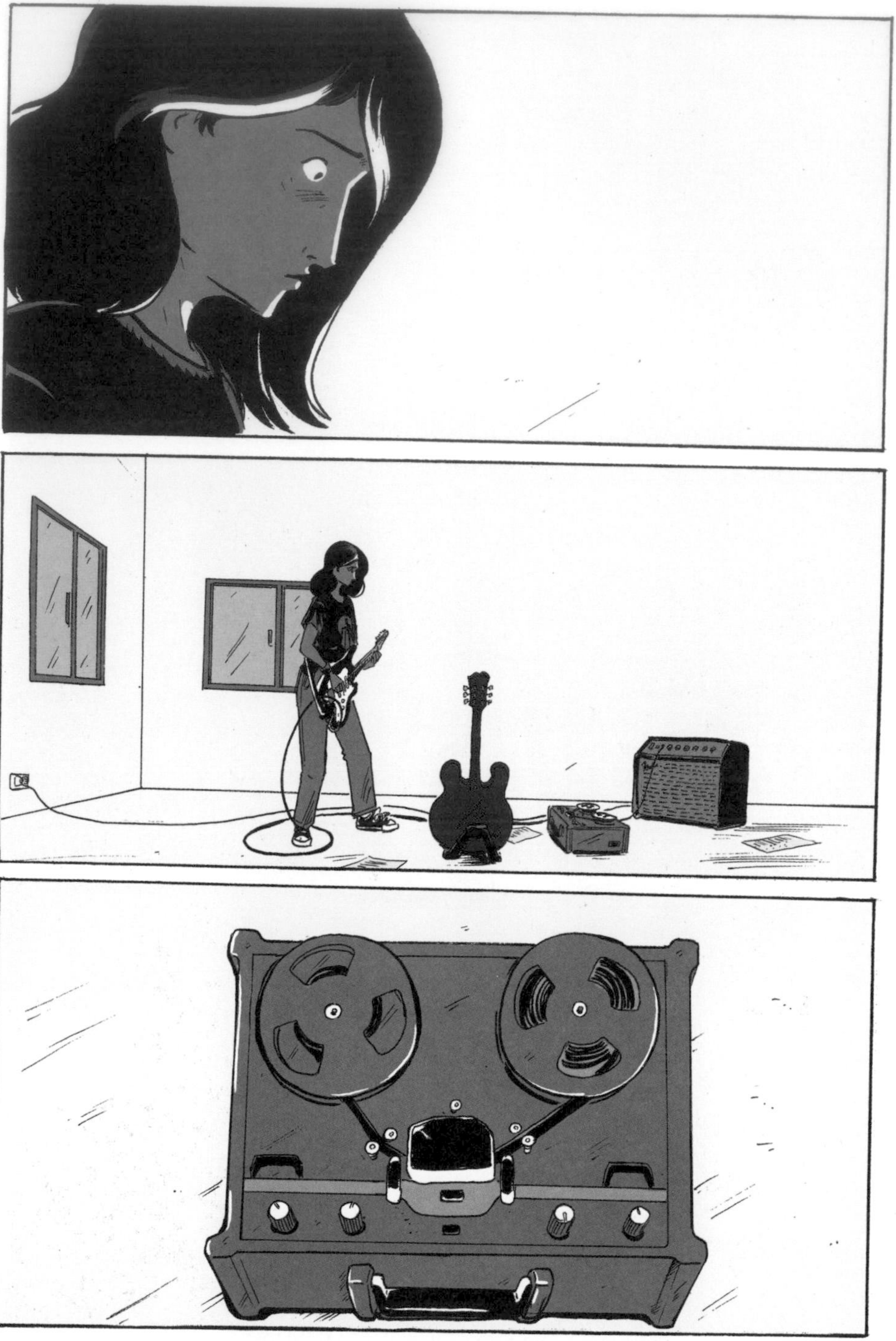

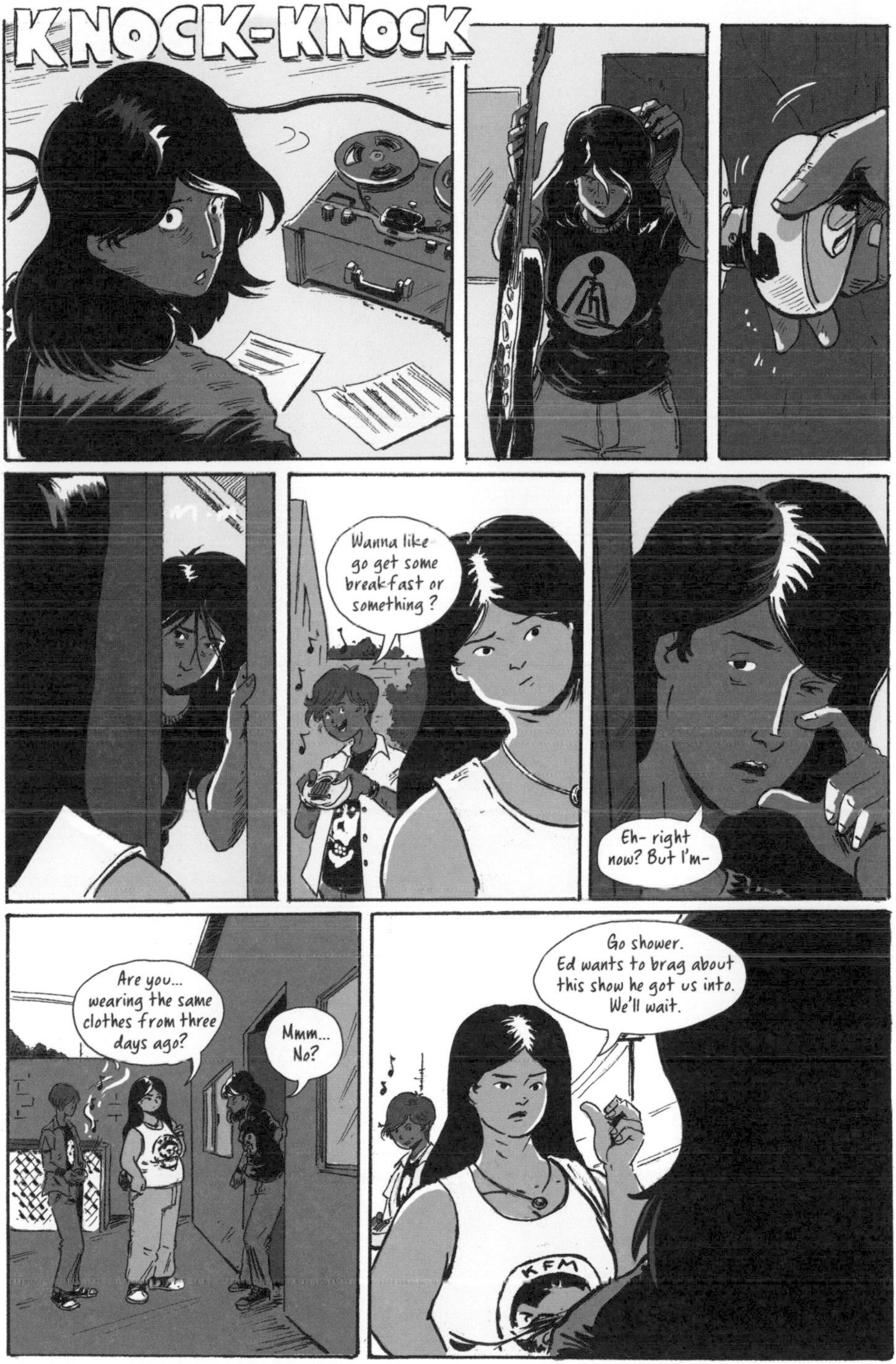
KNOCK-KNOCK
Wanna like go get some breakfast or something?
Eh- right now? But I'm-
Are you... wearing the same clothes from three days ago?
Mmm... No?
Go shower. Ed wants to brag about this show he got us into. We'll wait.
KFM

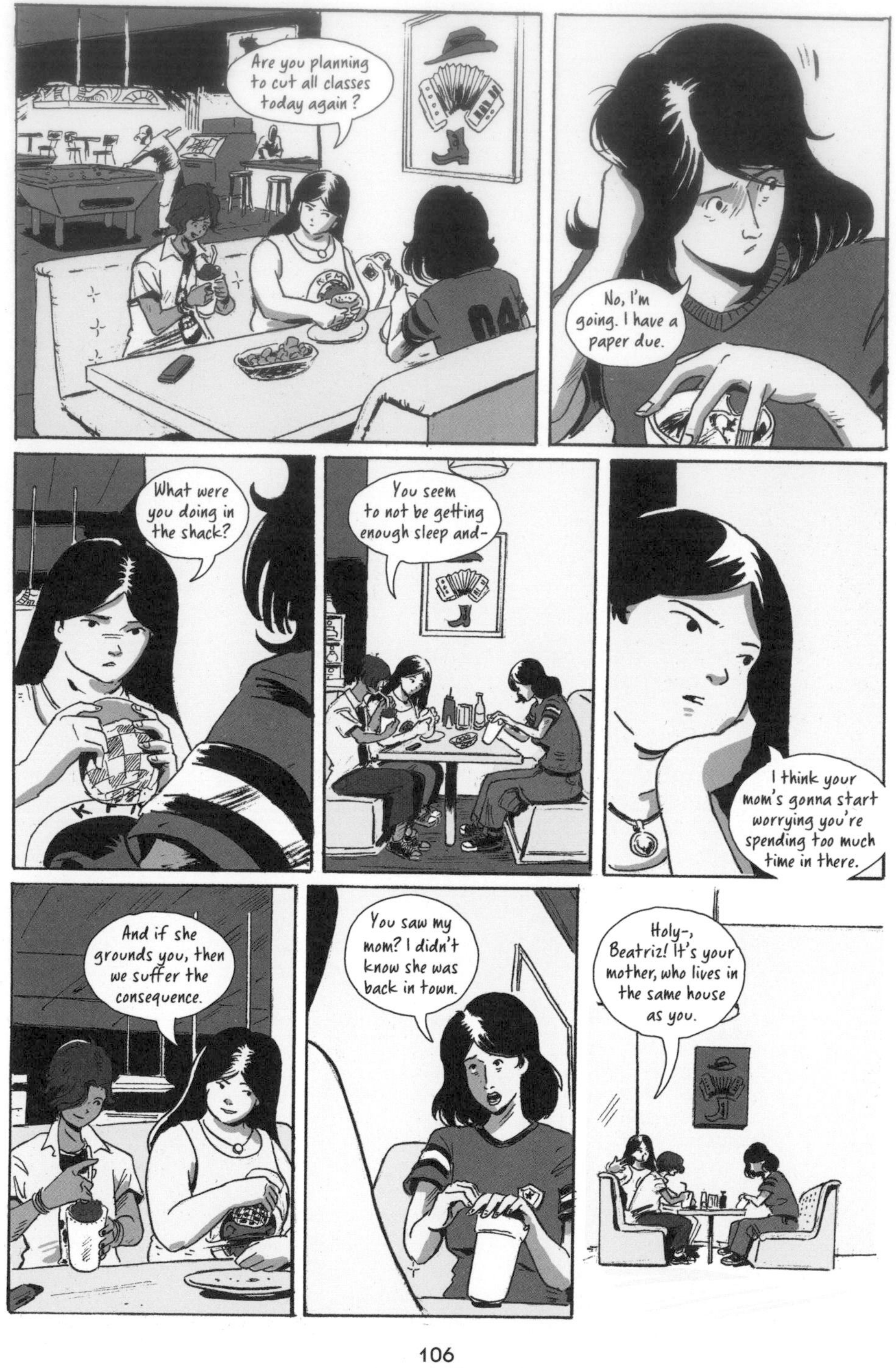
Are you planning to cut all classes today again?
No, I'm going. I have a paper due.
What were you doing in the shack?
You seem to not be getting enough sleep and-
I think your mom's gonna start worrying you're spending too much time in there.
And if she grounds you, then we suffer the consequence.
You saw my mom? I didn't know she was back in town.
Holy-, Beatriz! It's your mother, who lives in the same house as you.

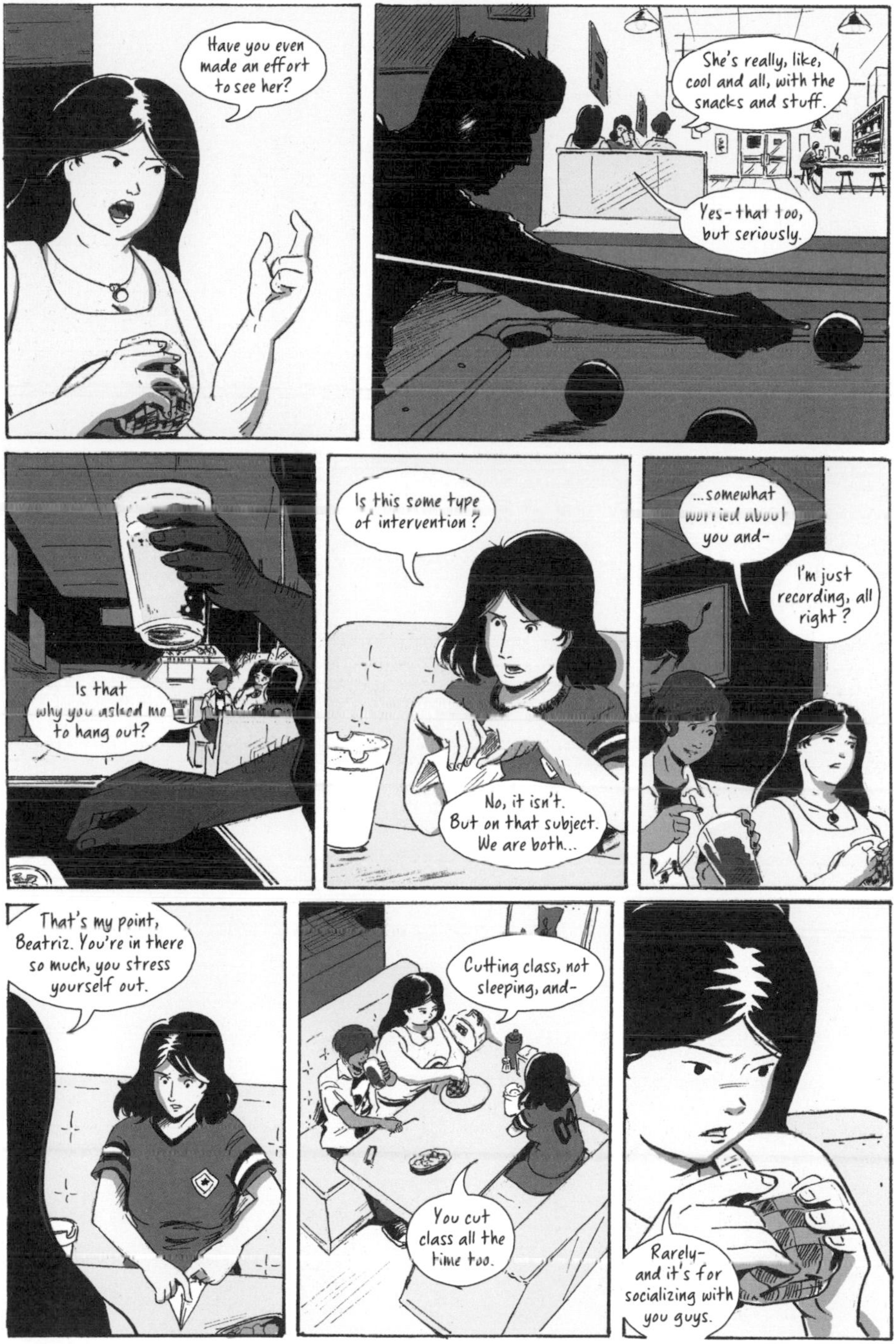
Have you even made an effort to see her?
She's really, like, cool and all, with the snacks and stuff.
Yes-that too, but seriously.
Is that why you asked me to hang out?
Is this some type of intervention?
No, it isn't. But on that subject. We are both...
...somewhat worried about you and-
I'm just recording, all right?
That's my point, Beatriz. You're in there so much, you stress yourself out.
Cutting class, not sleeping, and-
You cut class all the time too.
Rarely- and it's for socializing with you guys.

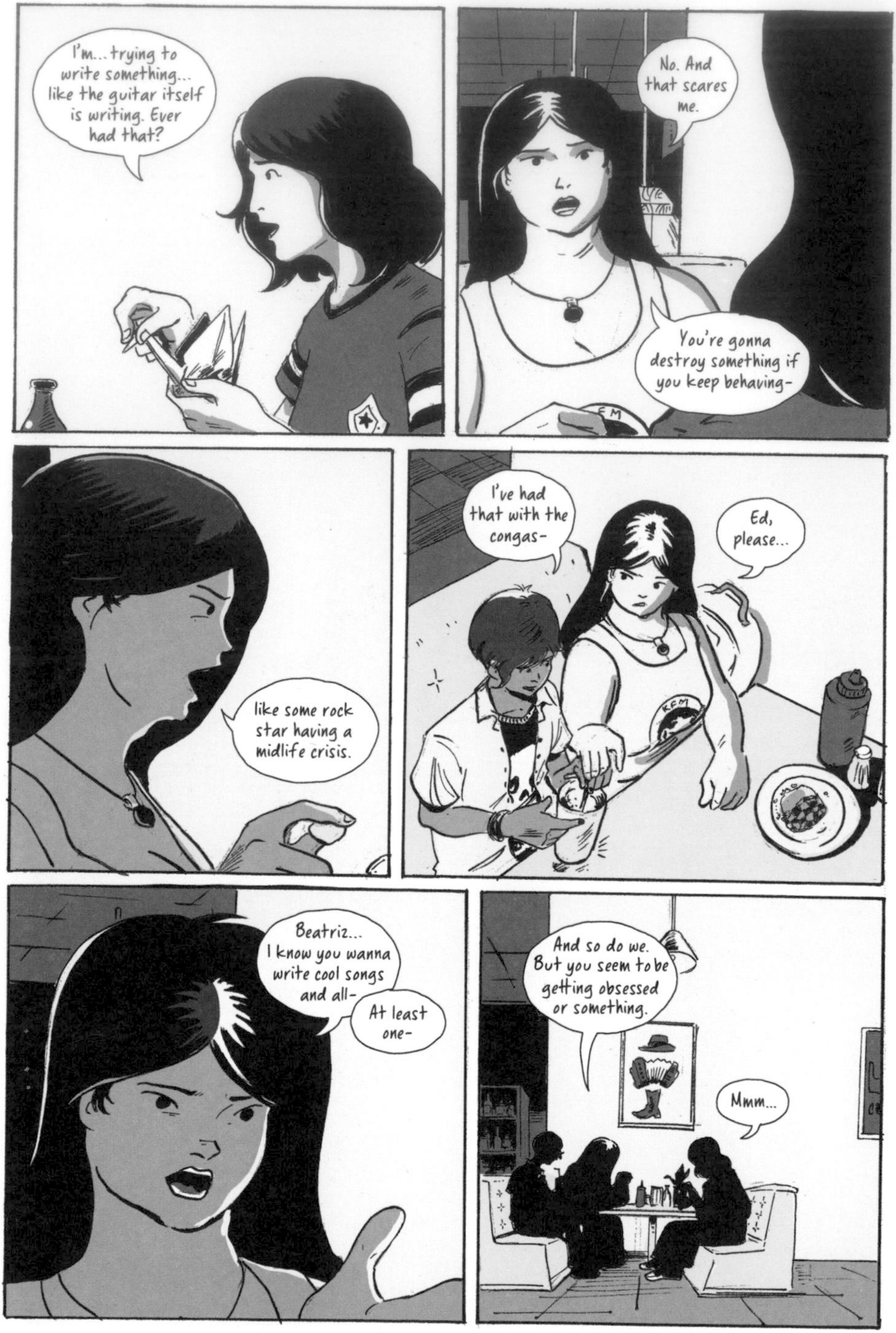

I'm... trying to write something... like the guitar itself is writing. Ever had that?
No. And that scares me.
You're gonna destroy something if you keep behaving-
like some rock star having a midlife crisis.
I've had that with the congas-
Ed, please...
Beatriz... I know you wanna write cool songs and all-
At least one-
And so do we. But you seem to be getting obsessed or something.
Mmm...

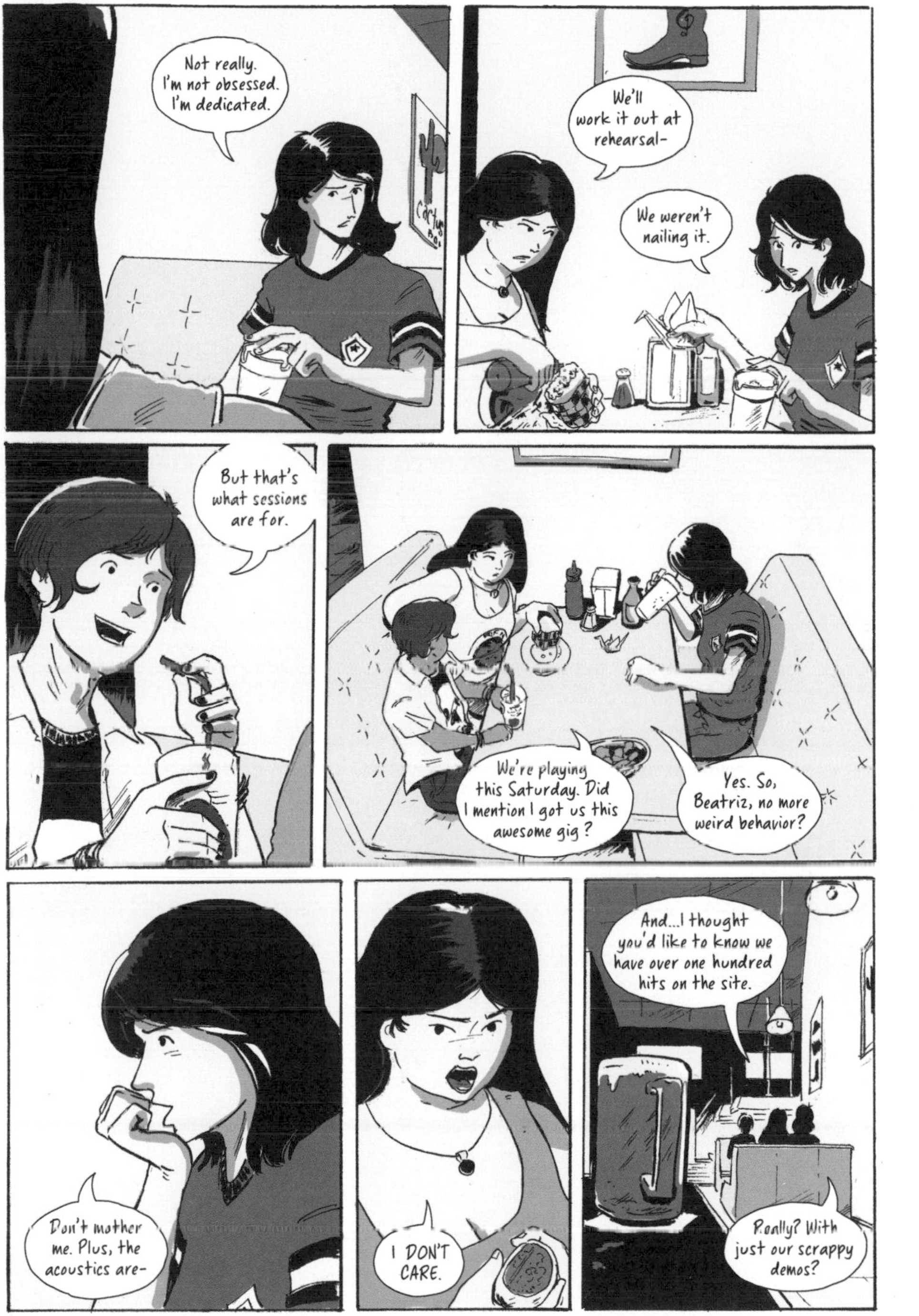

Not really. I'm not obsessed. I'm dedicated.
We'll work it out at rehearsal-
We weren't nailing it.
But that's what sessions are for.
We're playing this Saturday. Did I mention I got us this awesome gig?
Yes. So, Beatriz, no more weird behavior?
Don't mother me. Plus, the acoustics are-
I DON'T CARE.
And...I thought you'd like to know we have over one hundred hits on the site.
Really? With just our scrappy demos?

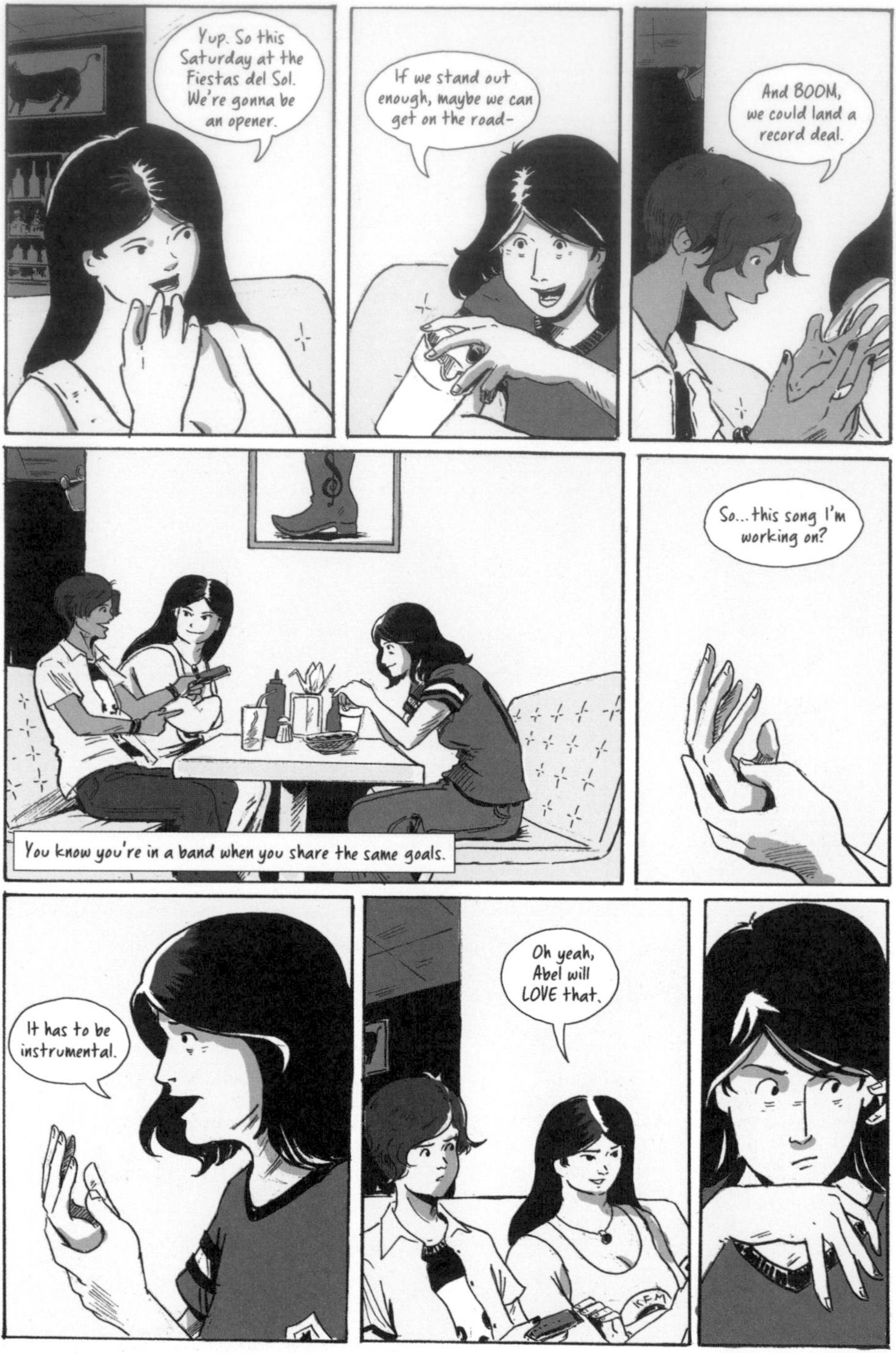
Yup. So this Saturday at the Fiestas del Sol. We're gonna be an opener.
If we stand out enough, maybe we can get on the road-
And BOOM, we could land a record deal.
You know you're in a band when you share the same goals.
So... this song I'm working on?
It has to be instrumental.
Oh yeah, Abel will LOVE that.

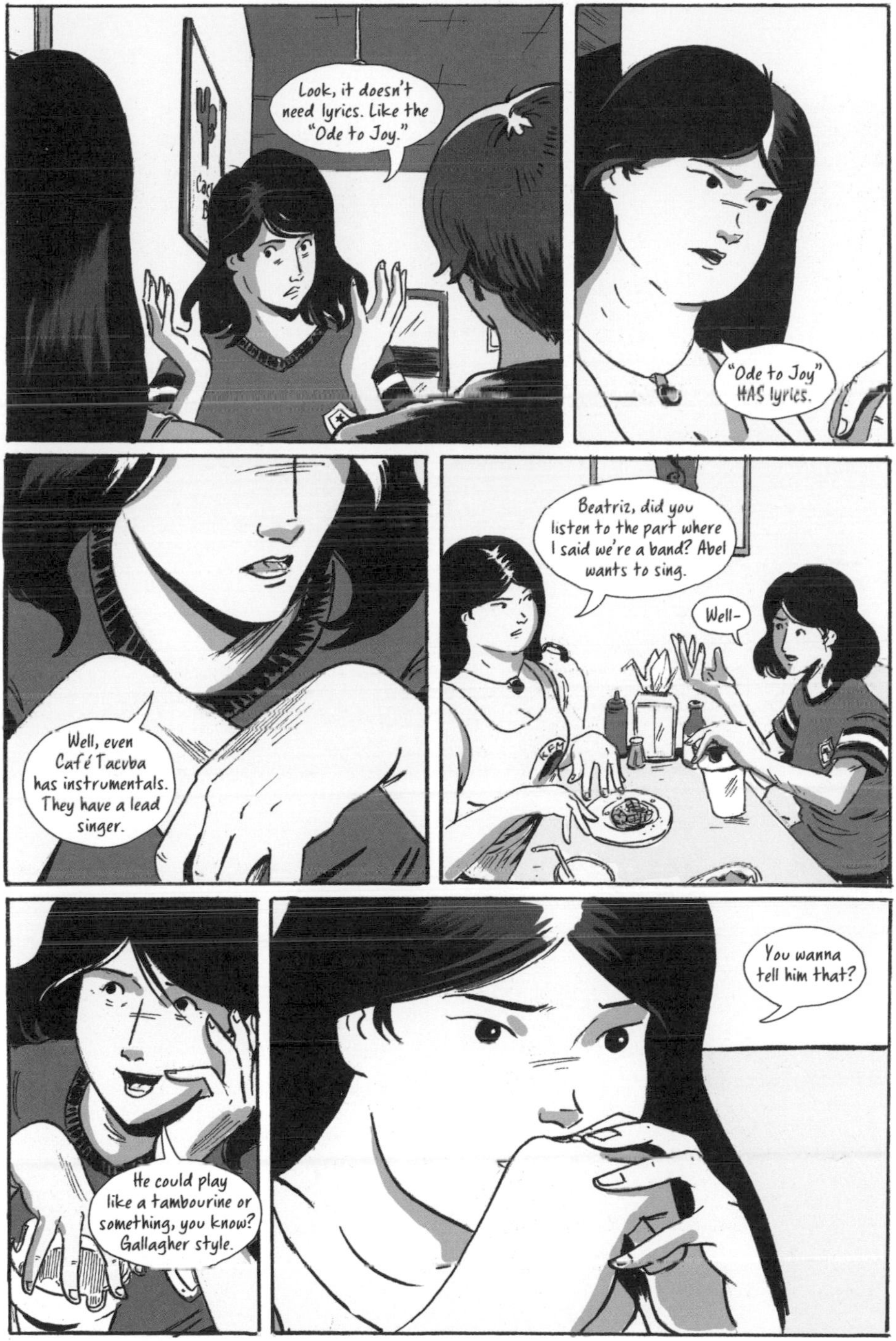
Look, it doesn't need lyrics. Like the "Ode to Joy."
"Ode to Joy" HAS lyrics.
Well, even Café Tacuba has instrumentals. They have a lead singer.
Beatriz, did you listen to the part where I said we're a band? Abel wants to sing.
Well-
He could play like a tambourine or something, you know? Gallagher style.
You wanna tell him that?

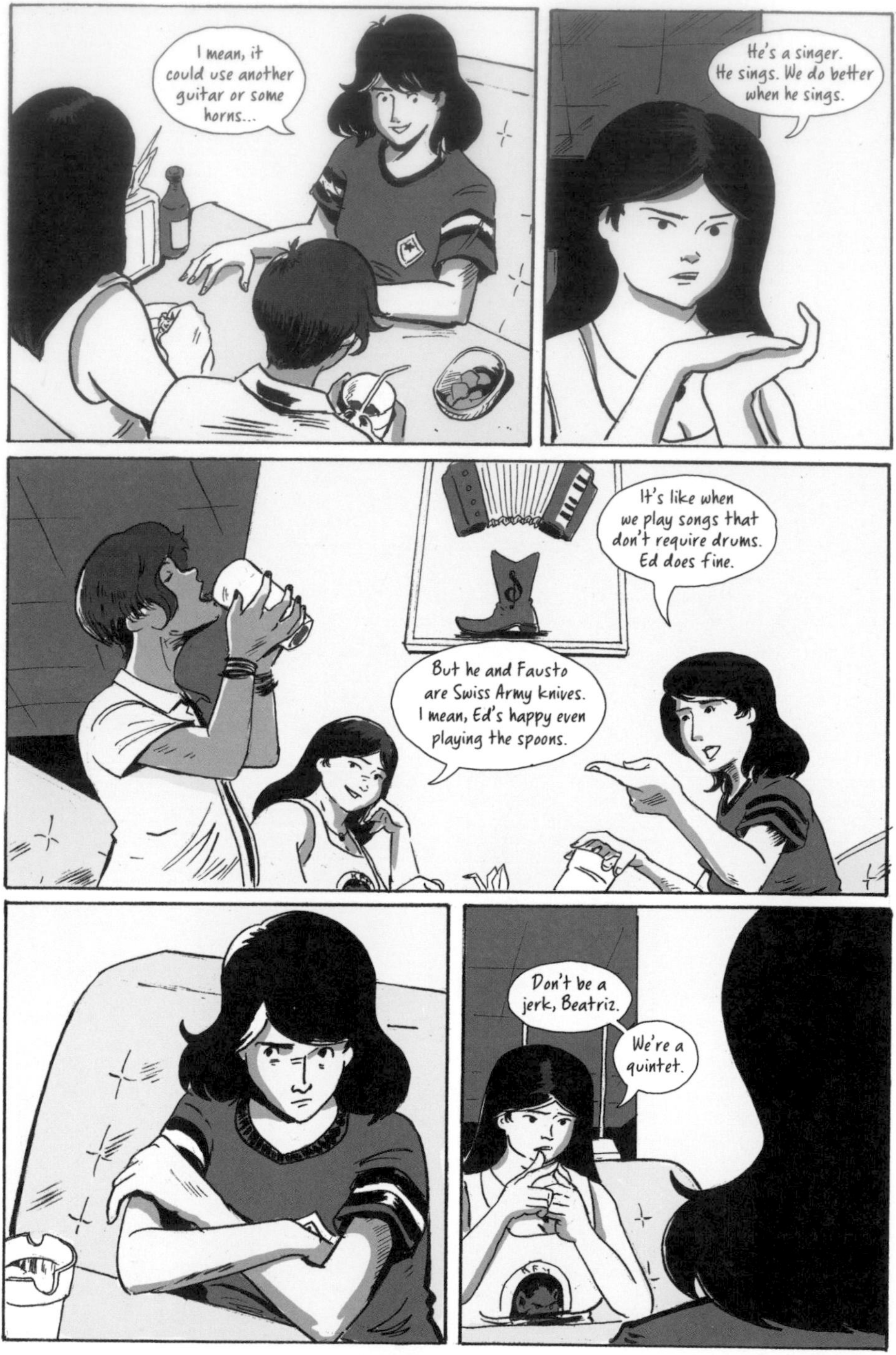
I mean, it could use another guitar or some horns...
He's a singer. He sings. We do better when he sings.
It's like when we play songs that don't require drums. Ed does fine.
But he and Fausto are Swiss Army knives. I mean, Ed's happy even playing the spoons.
Don't be a jerk, Beatriz.
We're a quintet.

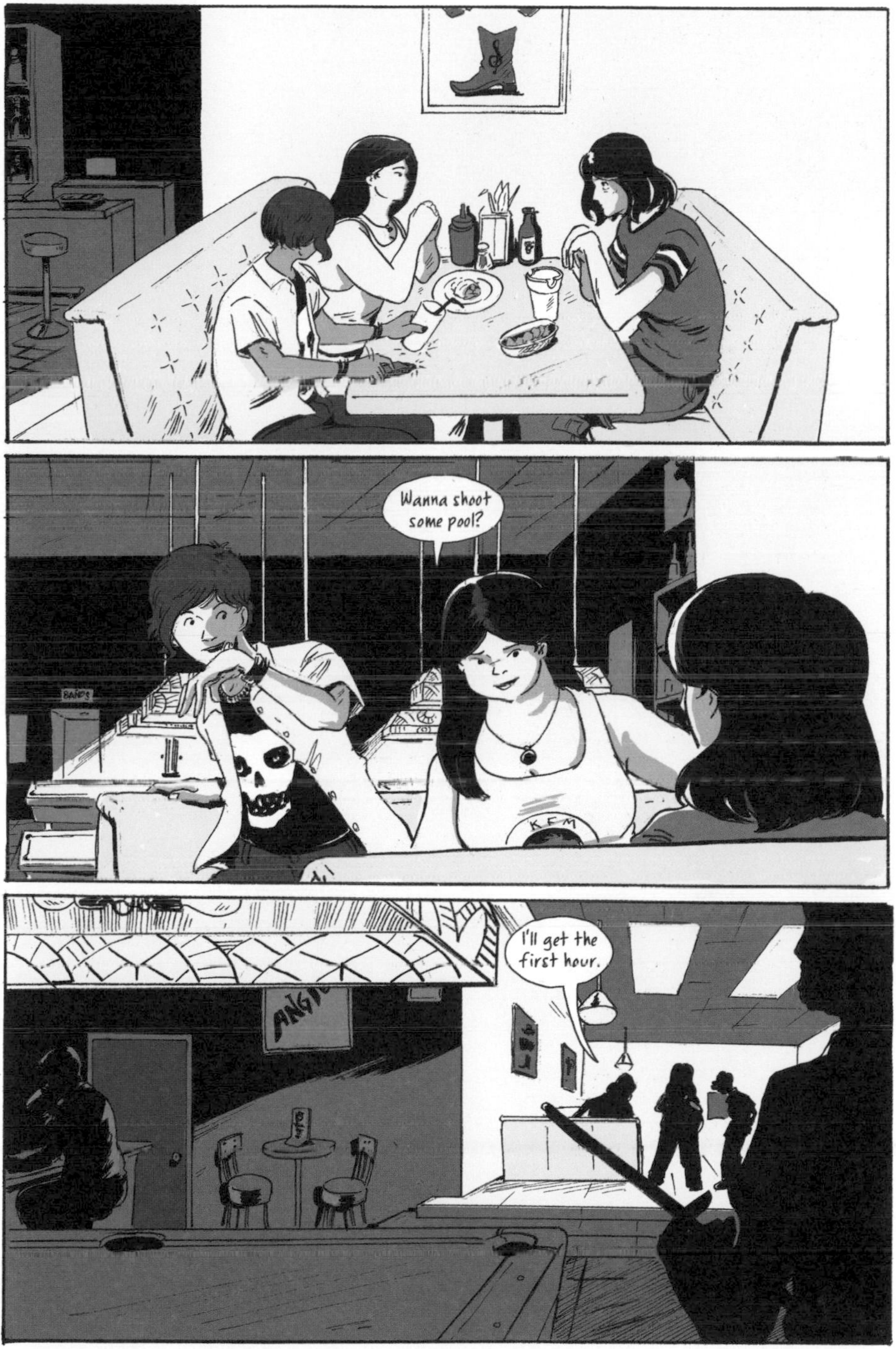
Wanna shoot some pool?
I'll get the first hour.

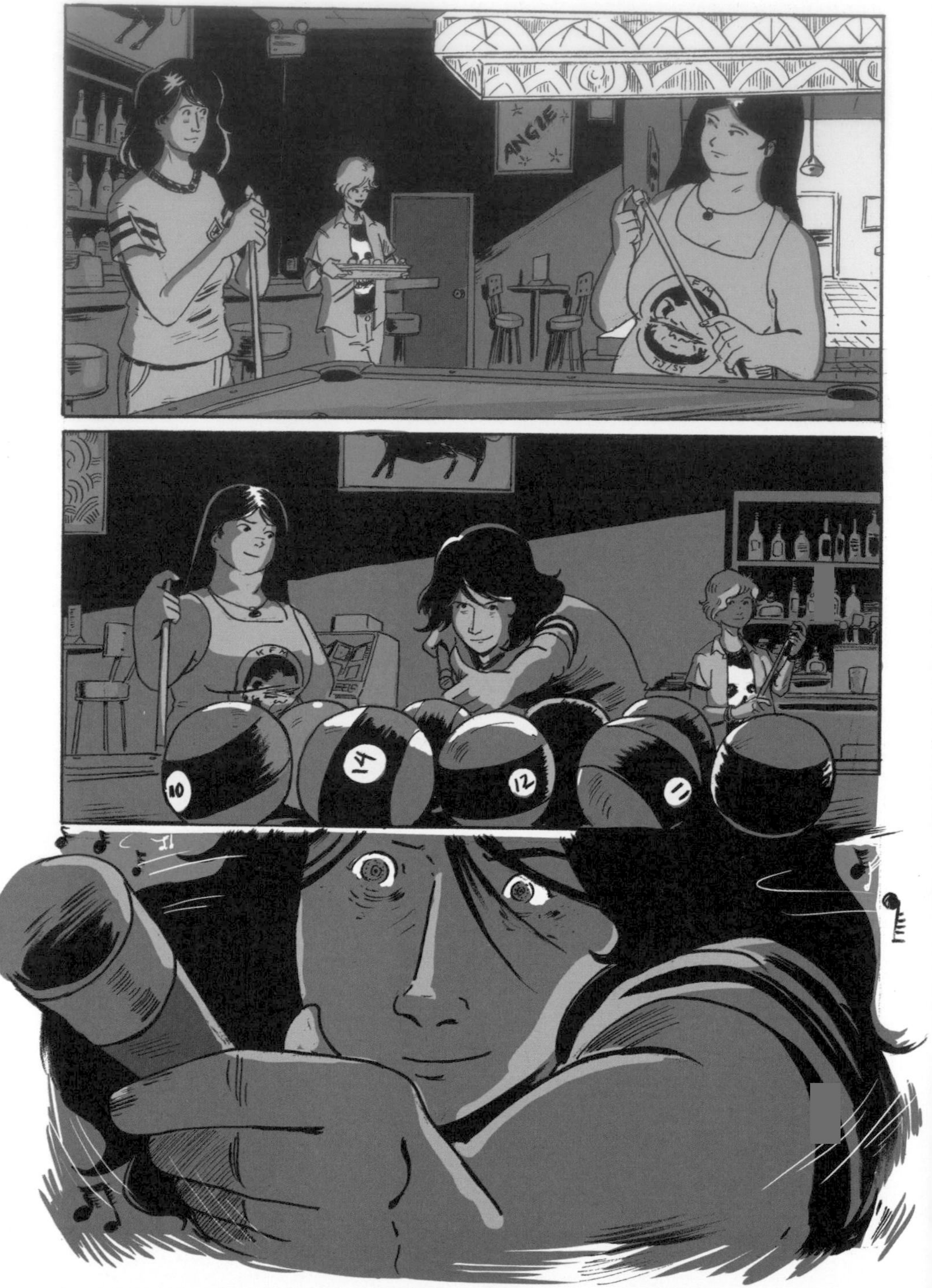
ANGIE
KFM
10
14
12
11

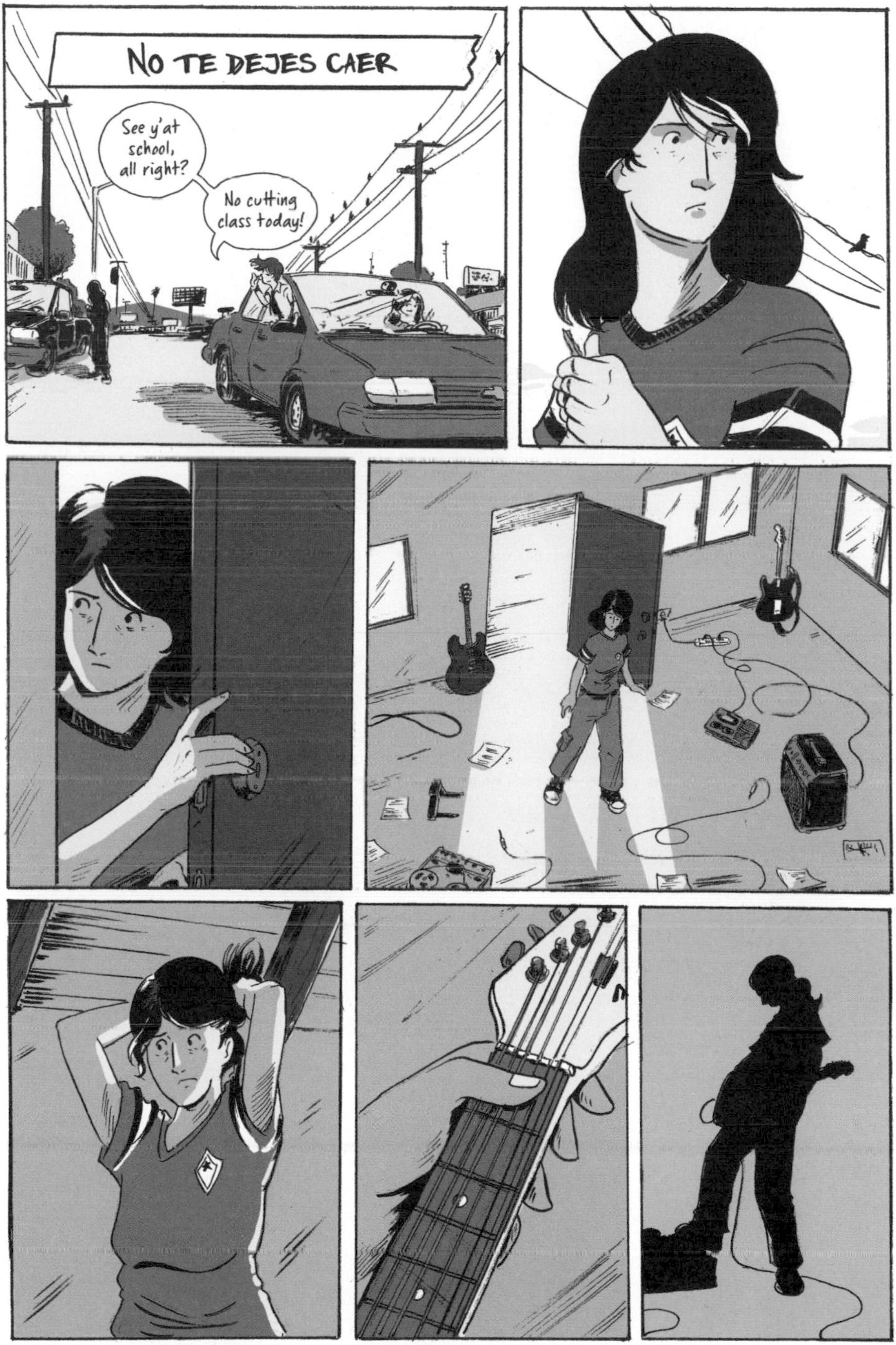
NO TE DEJES CAER
See y'at school, all right?
No cutting class today!

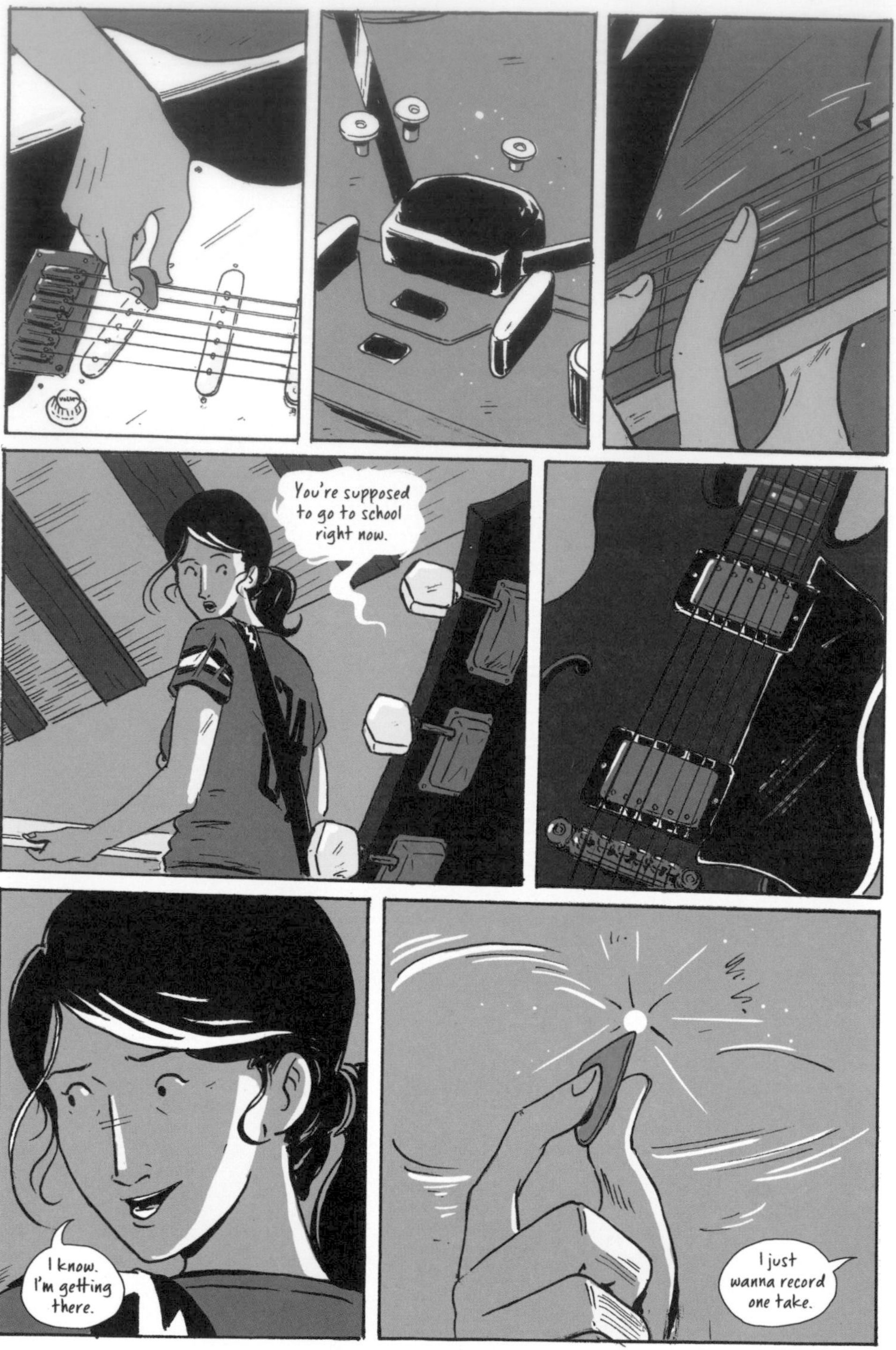
You're supposed to go to school right now.
I know. I'm getting there.
I just wanna record one take.

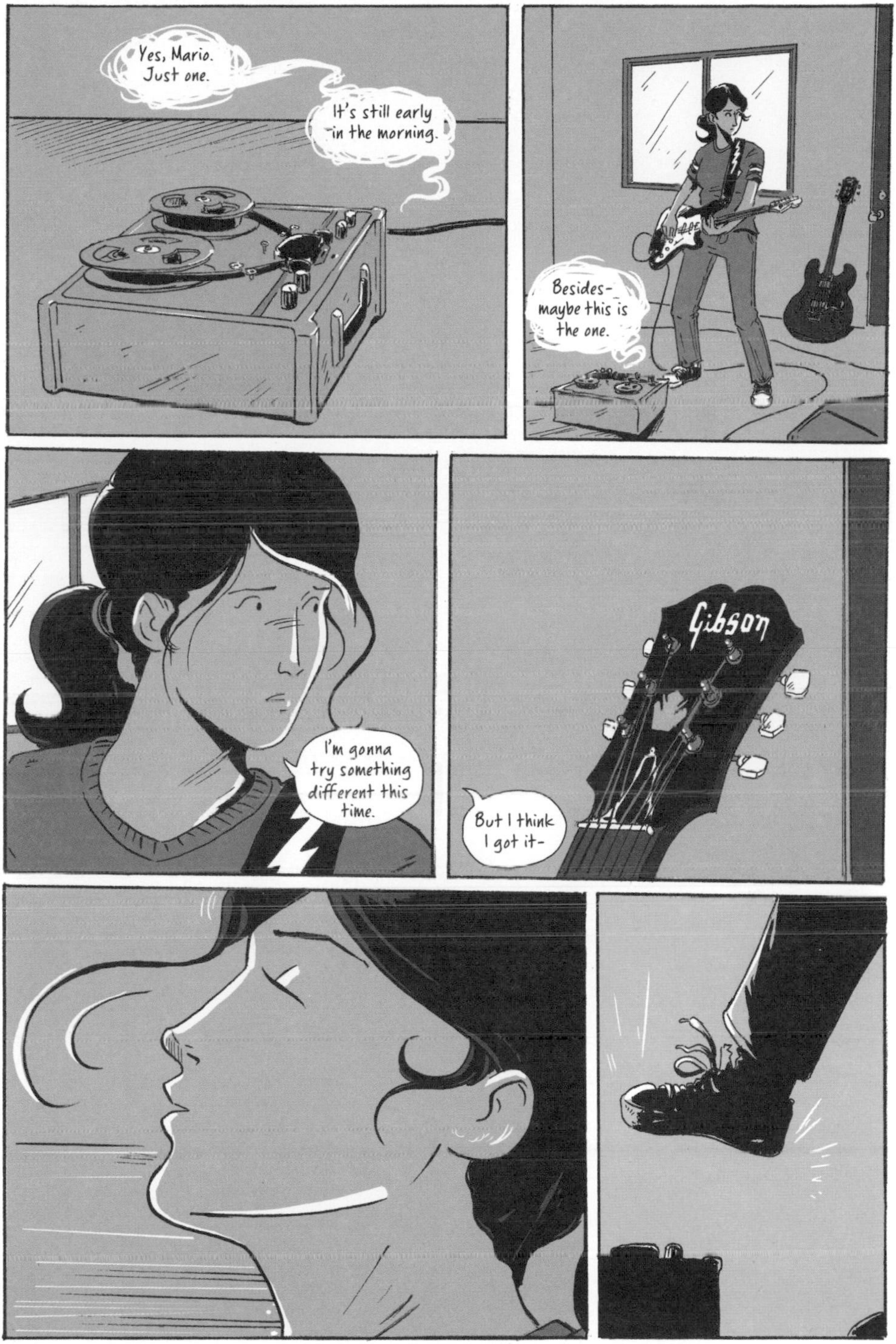
Yes, Mario. Just one.
It's still early in the morning.
Besides- maybe this is the one.
I'm gonna try something different this time.
Gibson
But I think I got it-

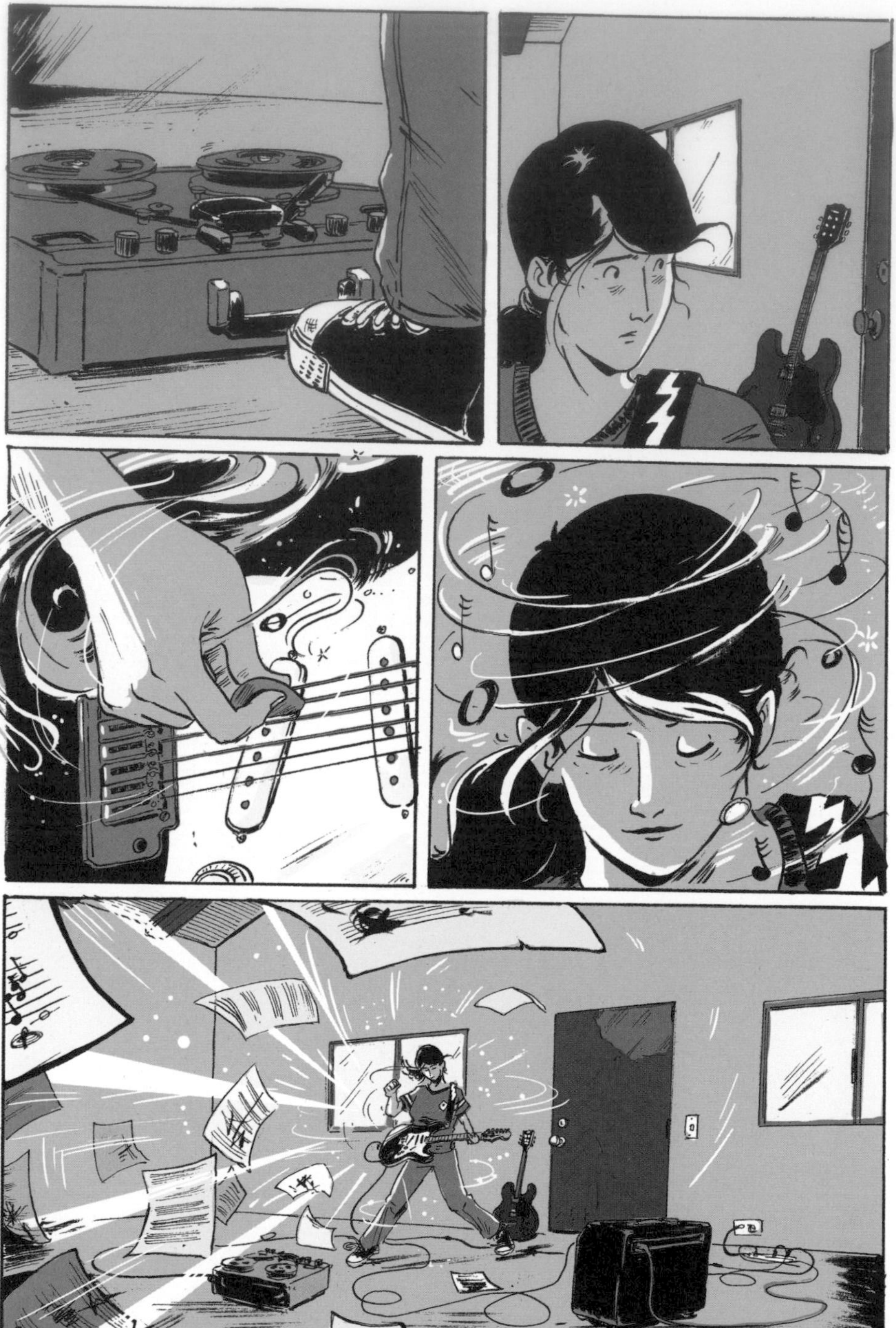

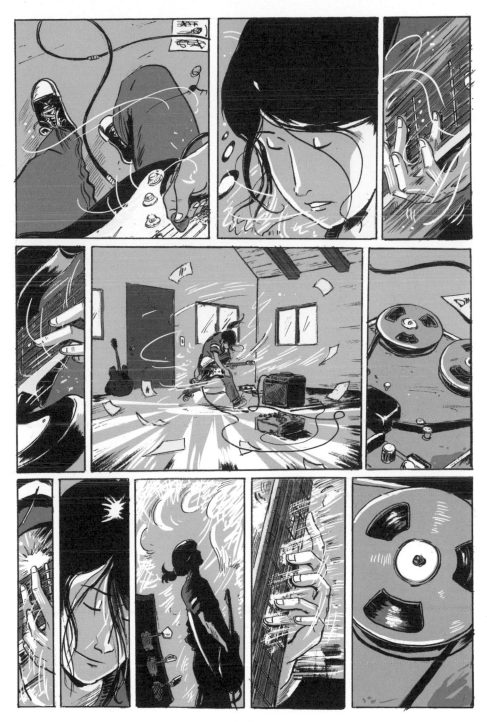

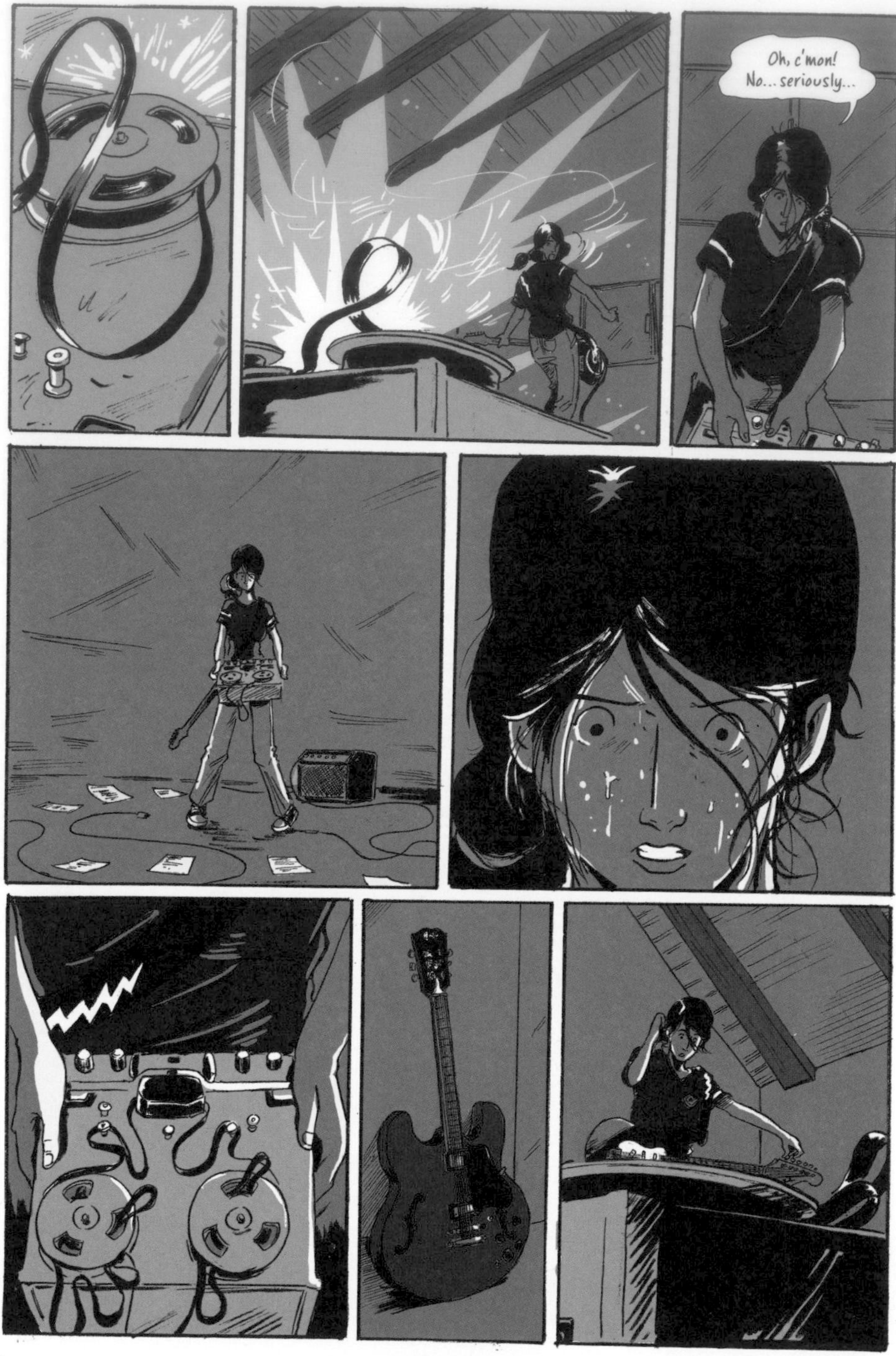
Oh, c'mon!
No... seriously...

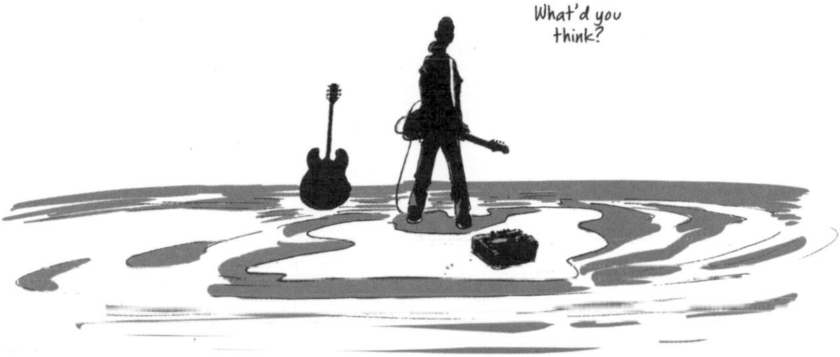
What'd you think?

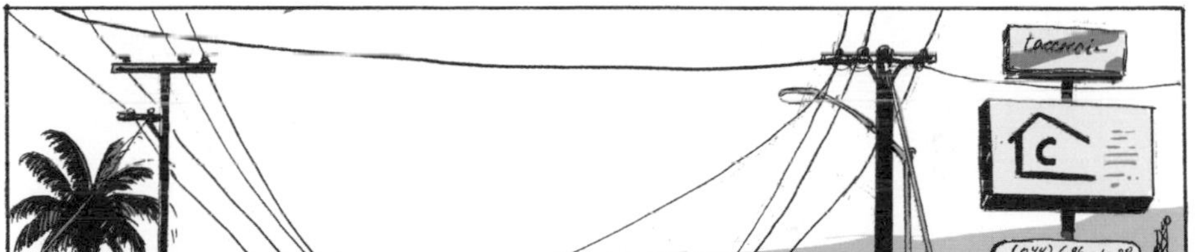
DR. Torres
RESOLANA
(044) 686-1-98

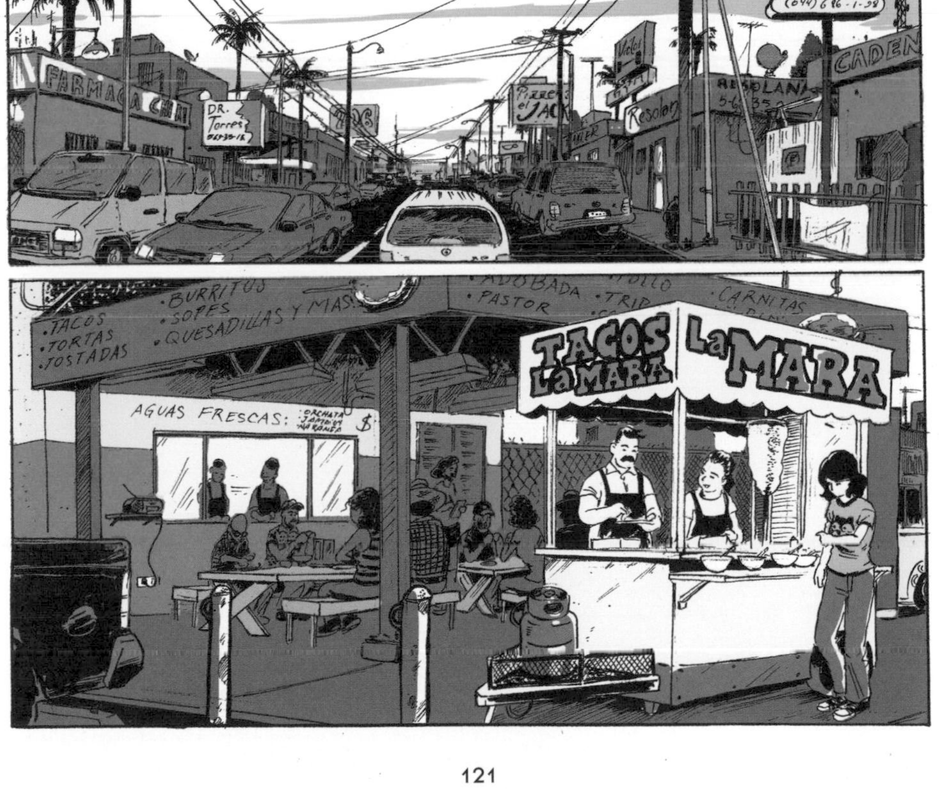
•TACOS
•TORTAS
•TOSTADAS
•BURRITOS
•SOPES
•QUESADILLAS Y MAS
•ADOBADA
•PASTOR
CARNITAS
TACOS La MARA
La MARA
AGUAS FRESCAS:

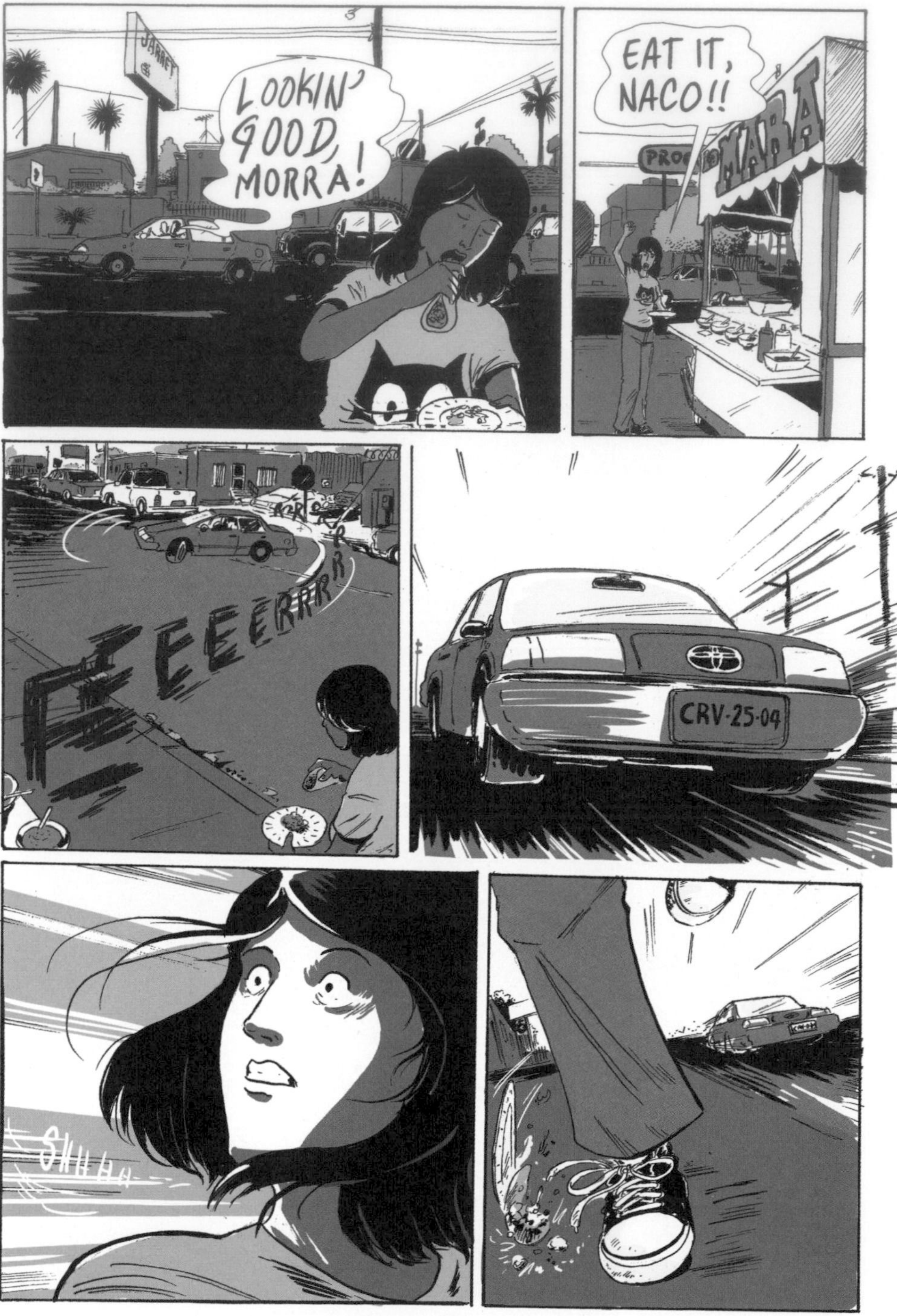
LOOKIN' GOOD, MORRA!
EAT IT, NACO!!
EEEERRRR
CRV-25-04
SHHHH

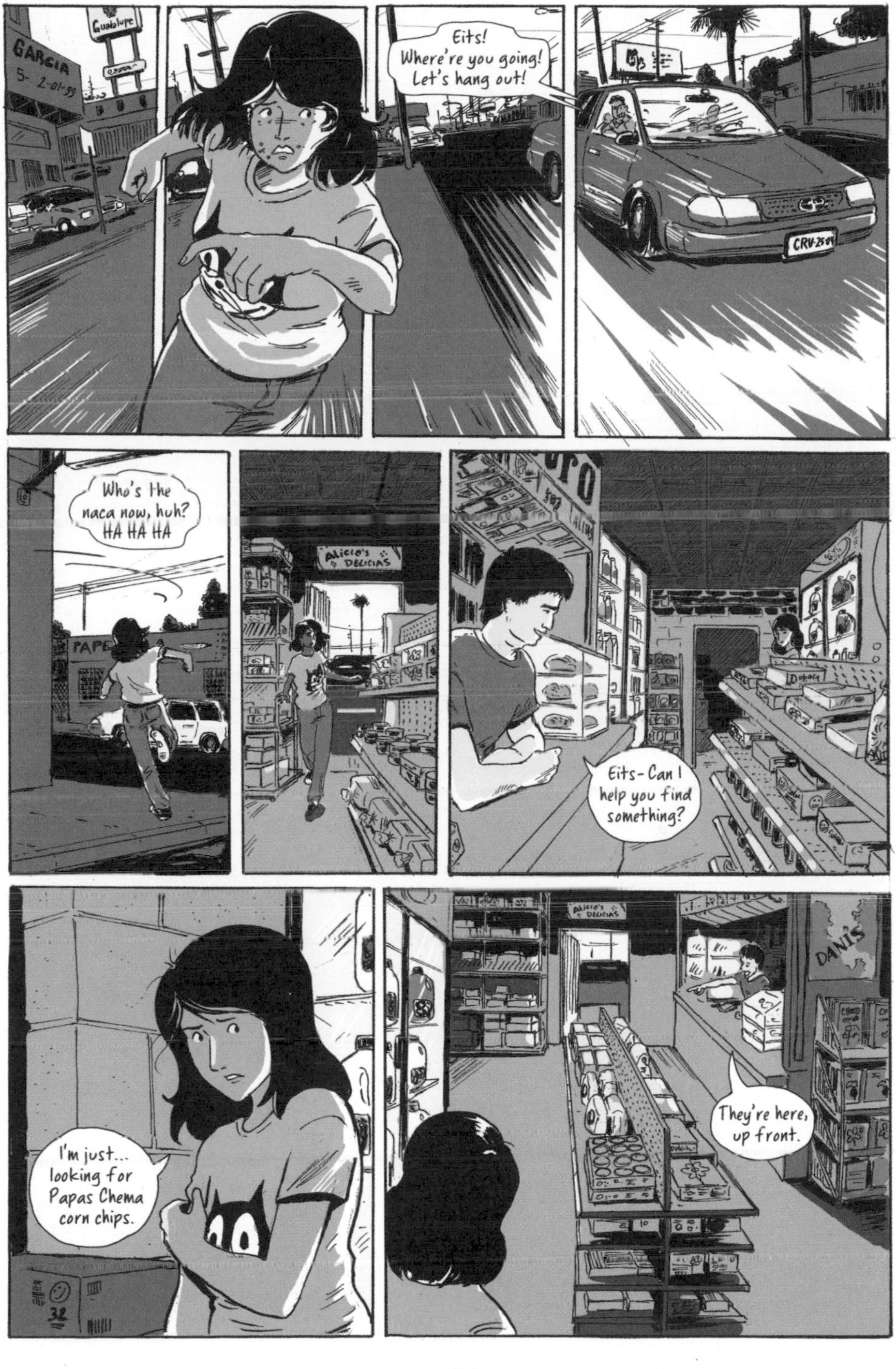
Eits! Where're you going! Let's hang out!
Who's the naca now, huh? HA HA HA
Eits- Can I help you find something?
I'm just... looking for Papas Chema corn chips.
They're here, up front.

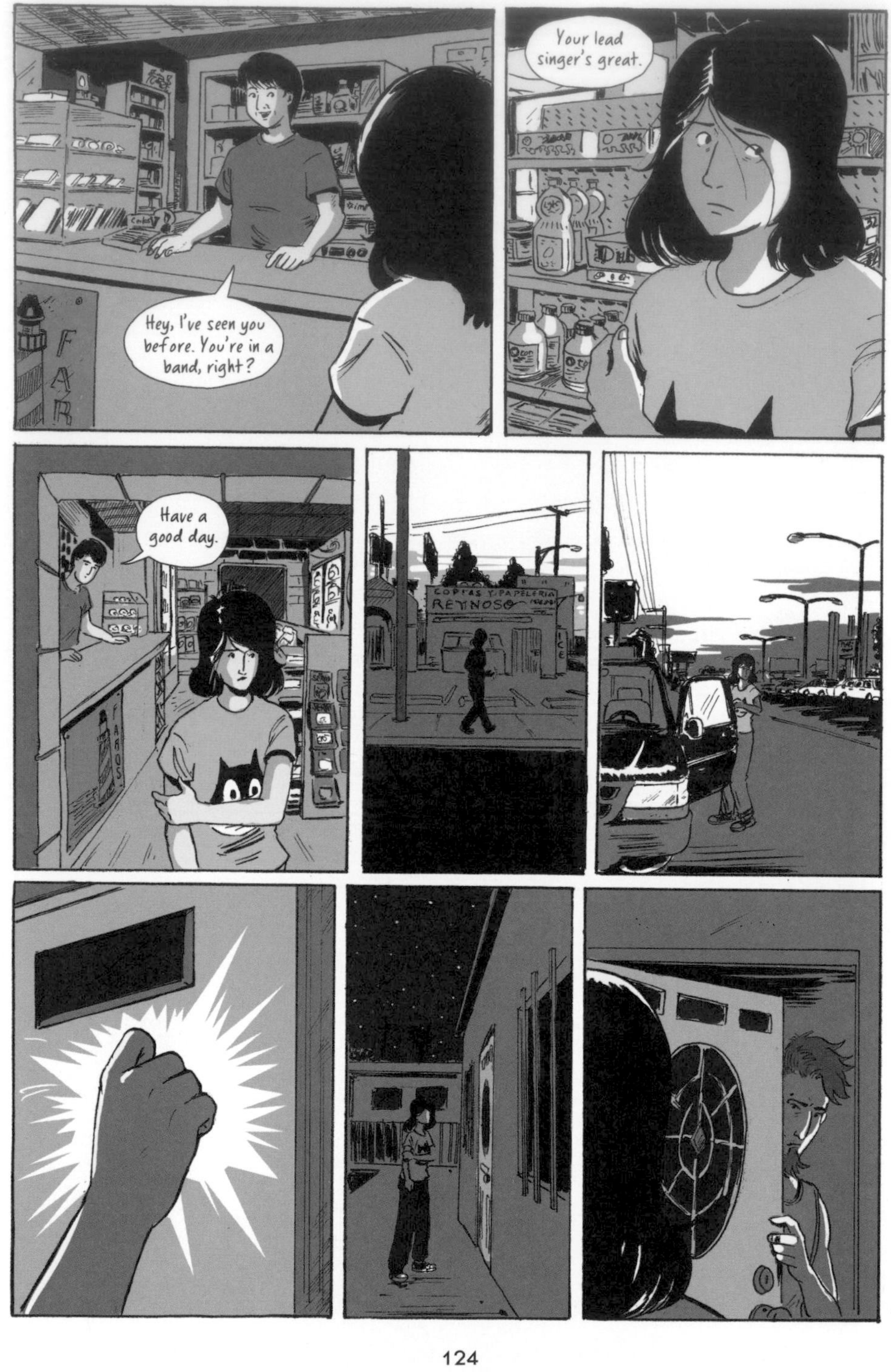
Hey, I've seen you before. You're in a band, right?
Your lead singer's great.
Have a good day.
COPIAS Y PAPELERIA
REYNOSO

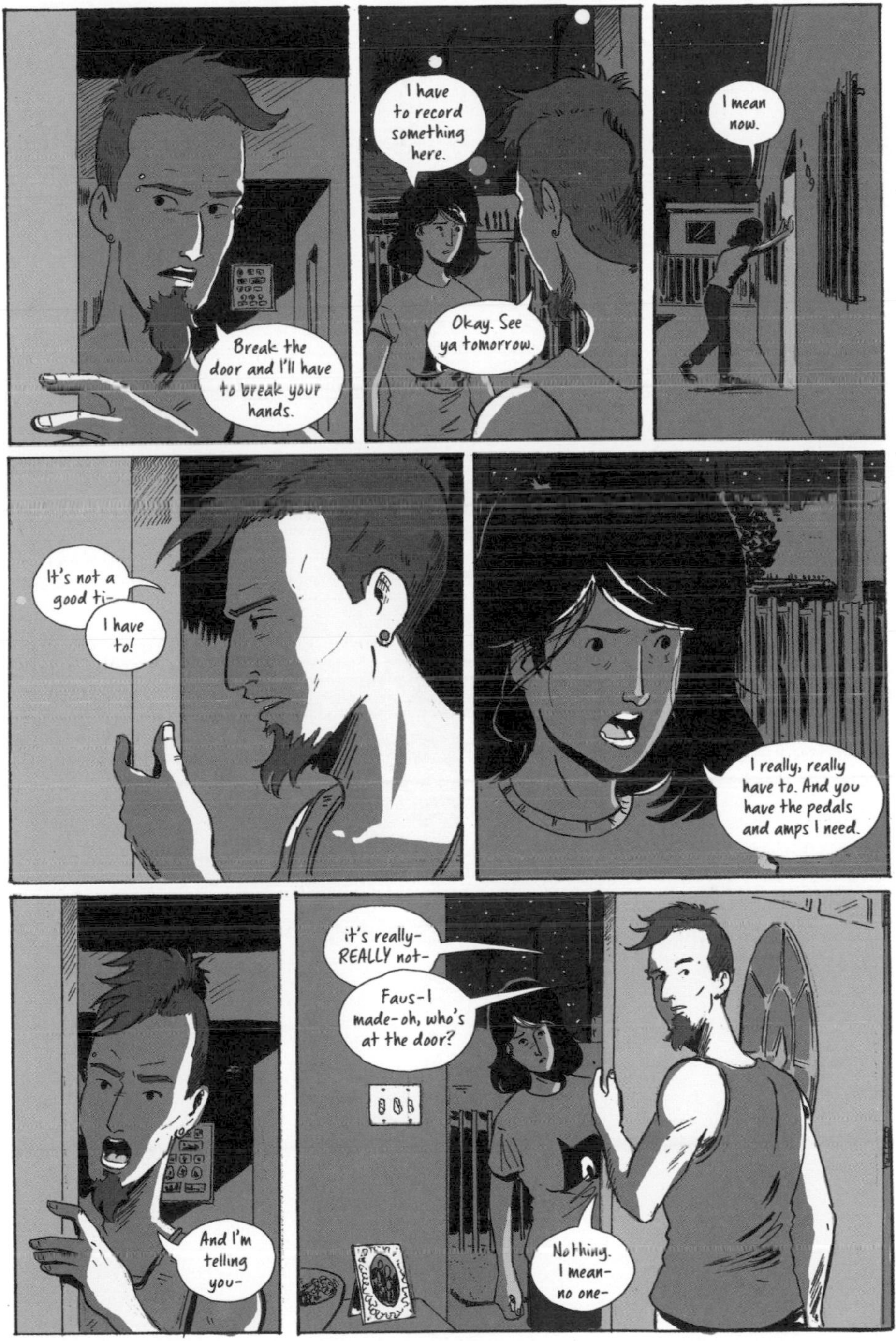
Break the door and I'll have to break your hands.
I have to record something here.
Okay. See ya tomorrow.
I mean now.
It's not a good ti-
I have to!
I really, really have to. And you have the pedals and amps I need.
And I'm telling you-
it's really- REALLY not-
Faus-I made-oh, who's at the door?
Nothing. I mean- no one-

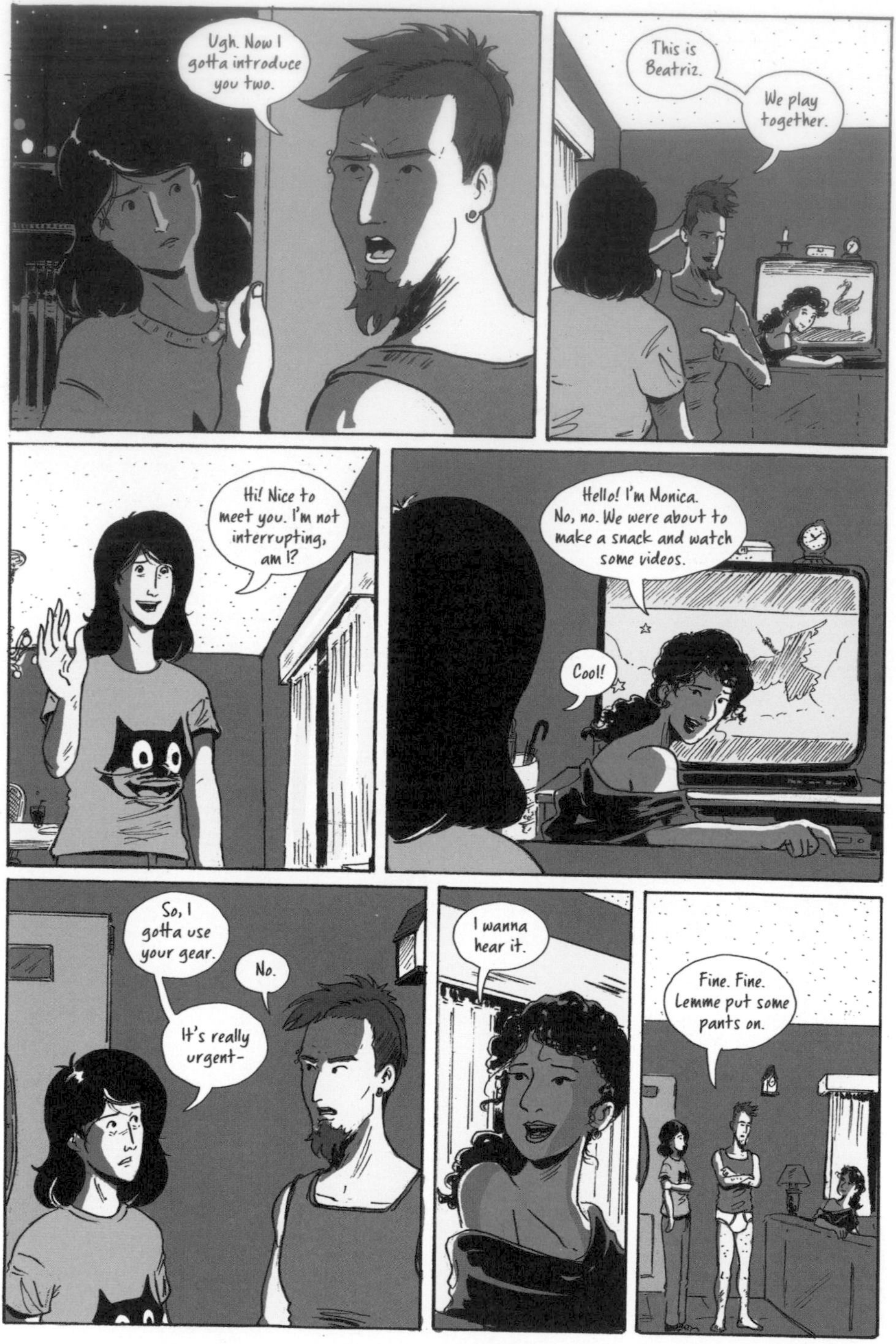
Ugh. Now I gotta introduce you two.
This is Beatriz.
We play together.
Hi! Nice to meet you. I'm not interrupting, am I?
Hello! I'm Monica. No, no. We were about to make a snack and watch some videos.
Cool!
So, I gotta use your gear.
No.
It's really urgent-
I wanna hear it.
Fine. Fine. Lemme put some pants on.

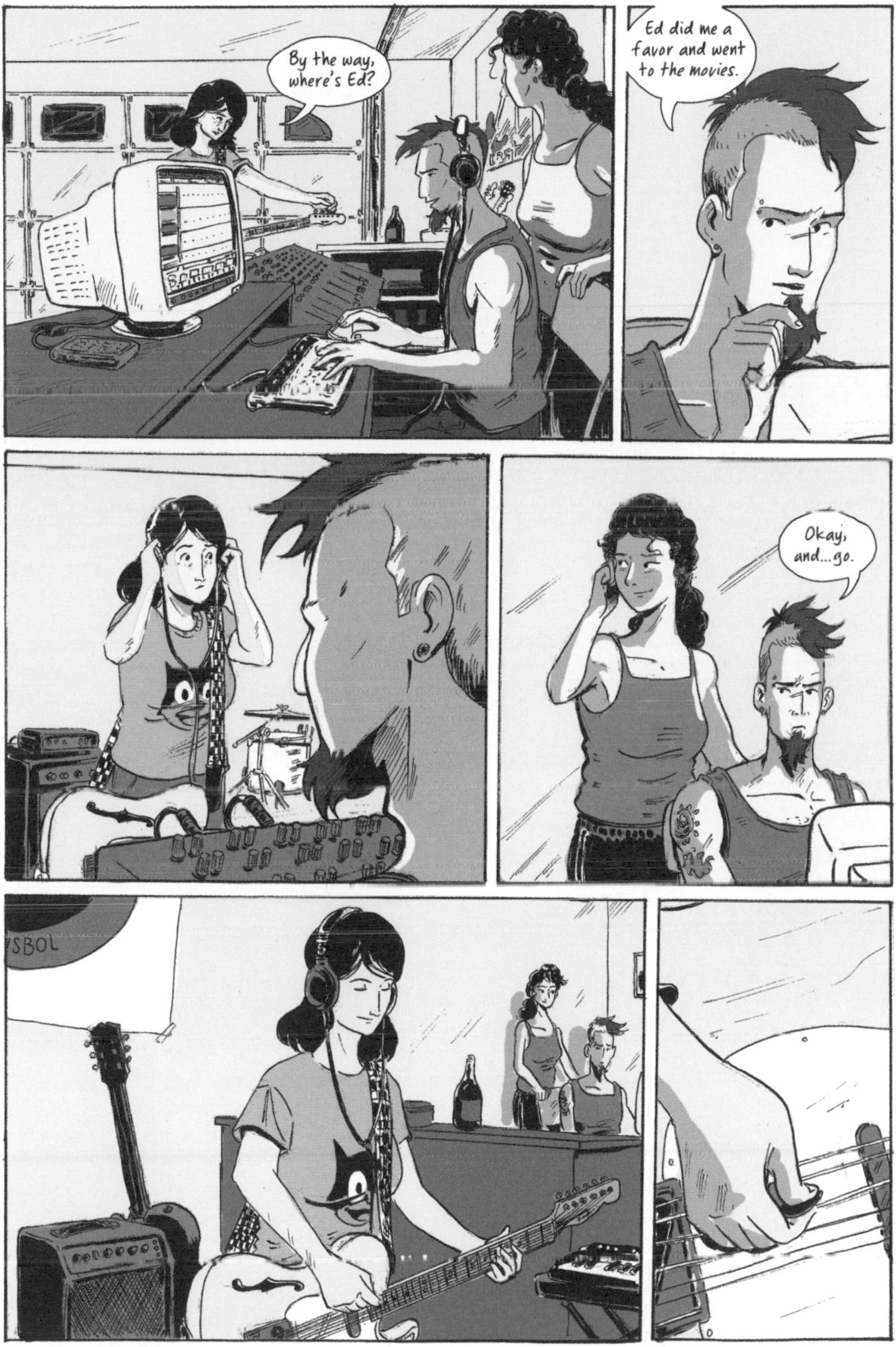
By the way, where's Ed?
Ed did me a favor and went to the movies.
Okay, and...go.
SBOL

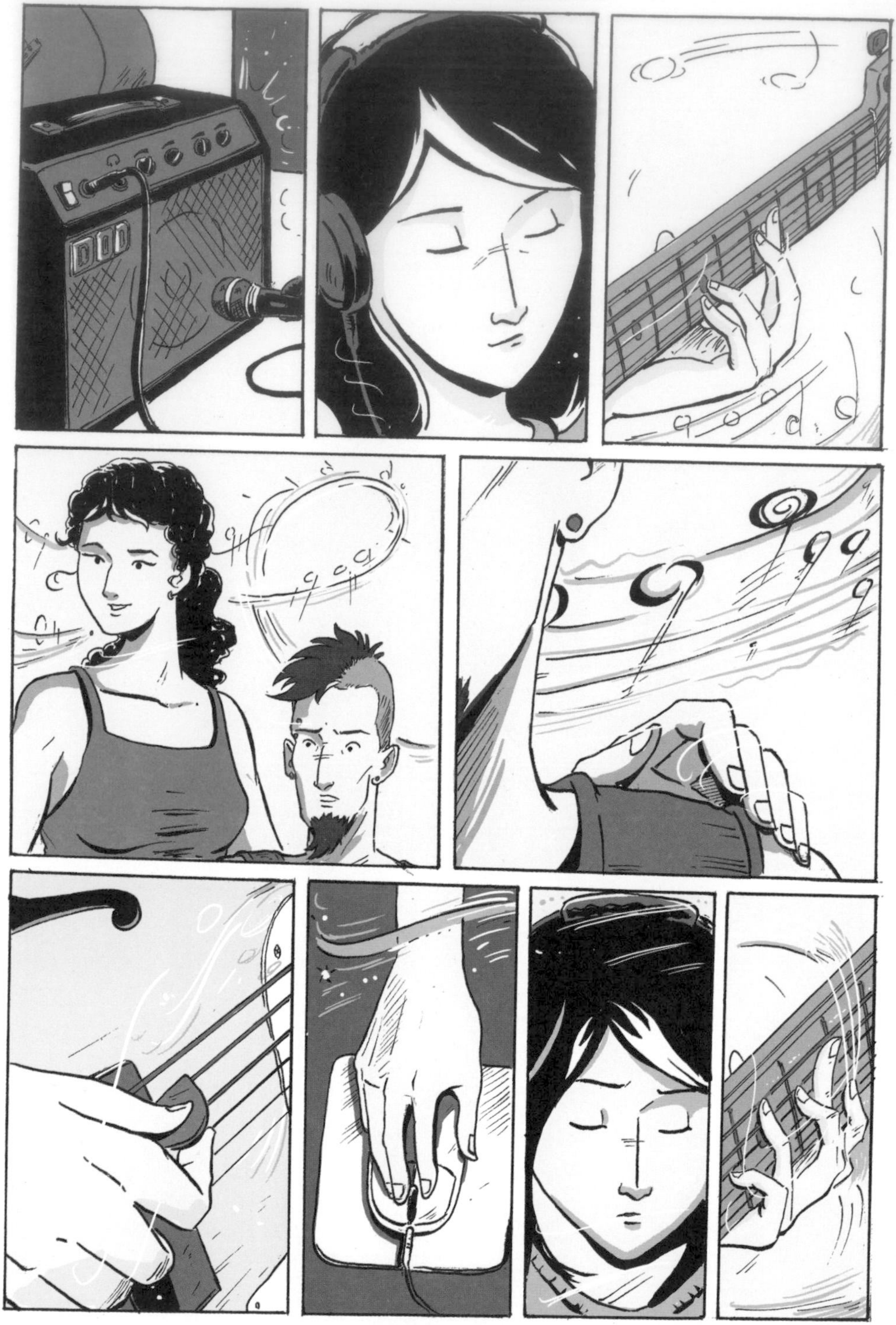

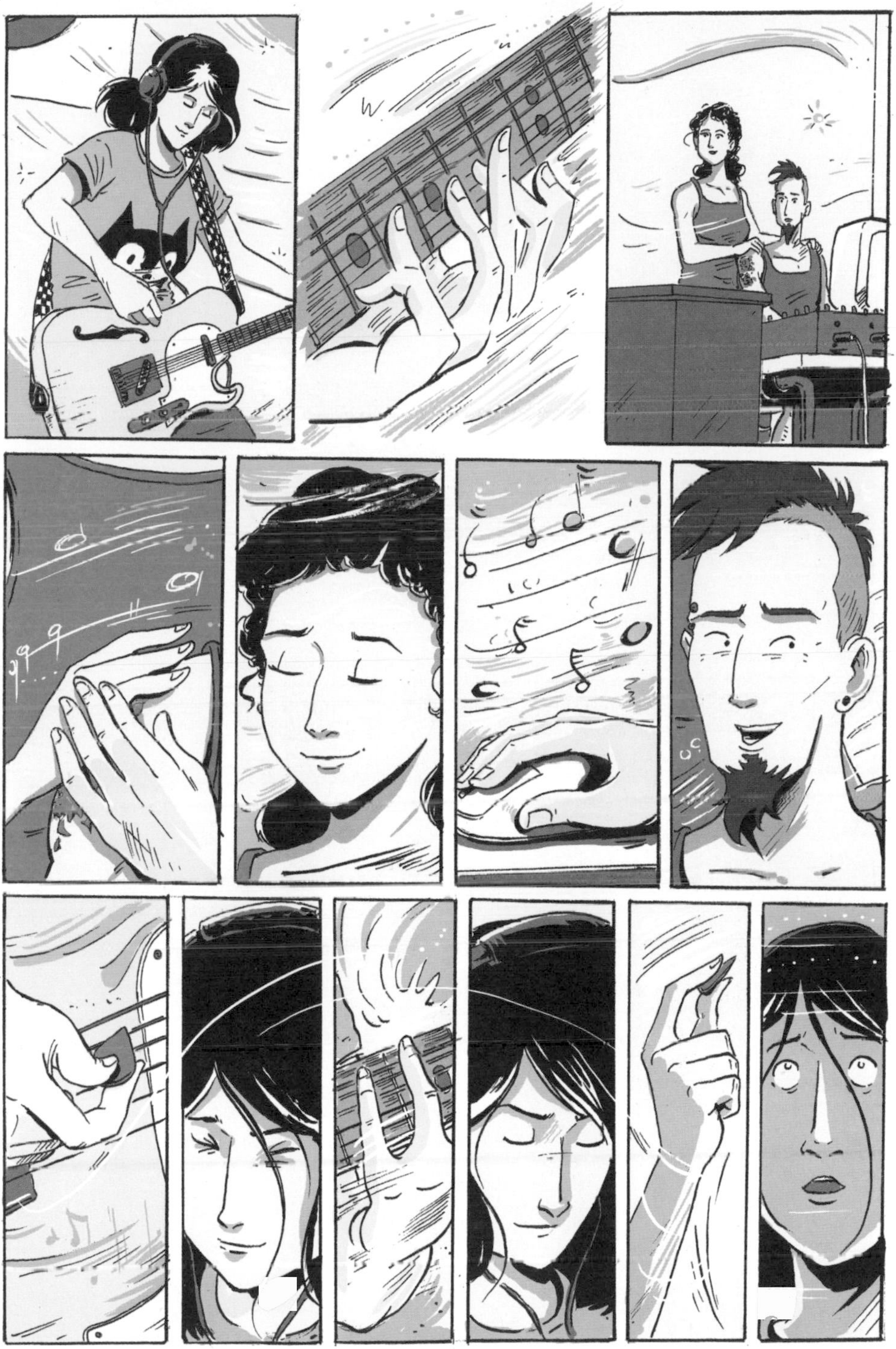

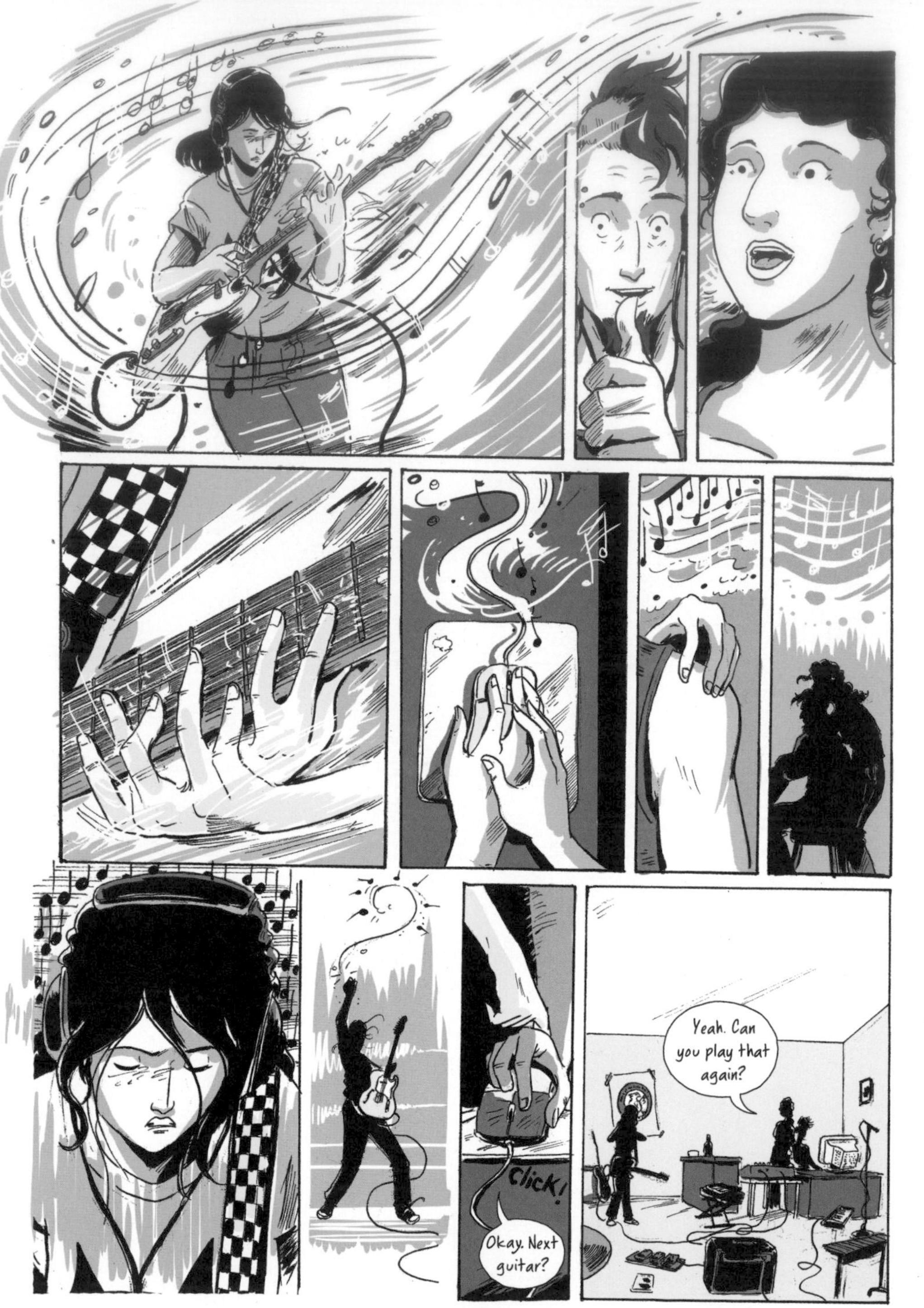
CLICK!
Okay. Next guitar?
Yeah. Can you play that again?

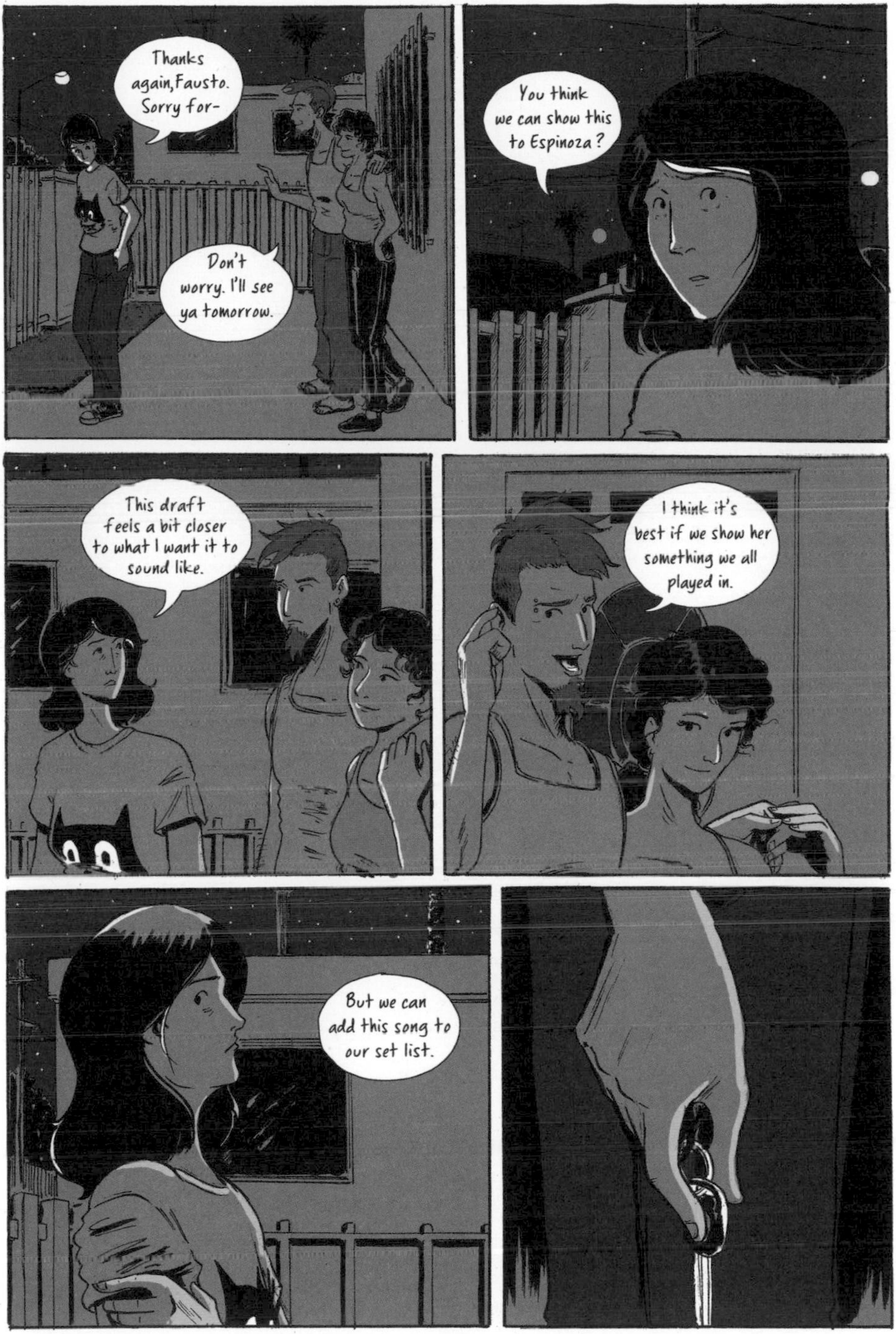
Thanks again, Fausto. Sorry for-
Don't worry. I'll see ya tomorrow.
You think we can show this to Espinoza?
This draft feels a bit closer to what I want it to sound like.
I think it's best if we show her something we all played in.
But we can add this song to our set list.

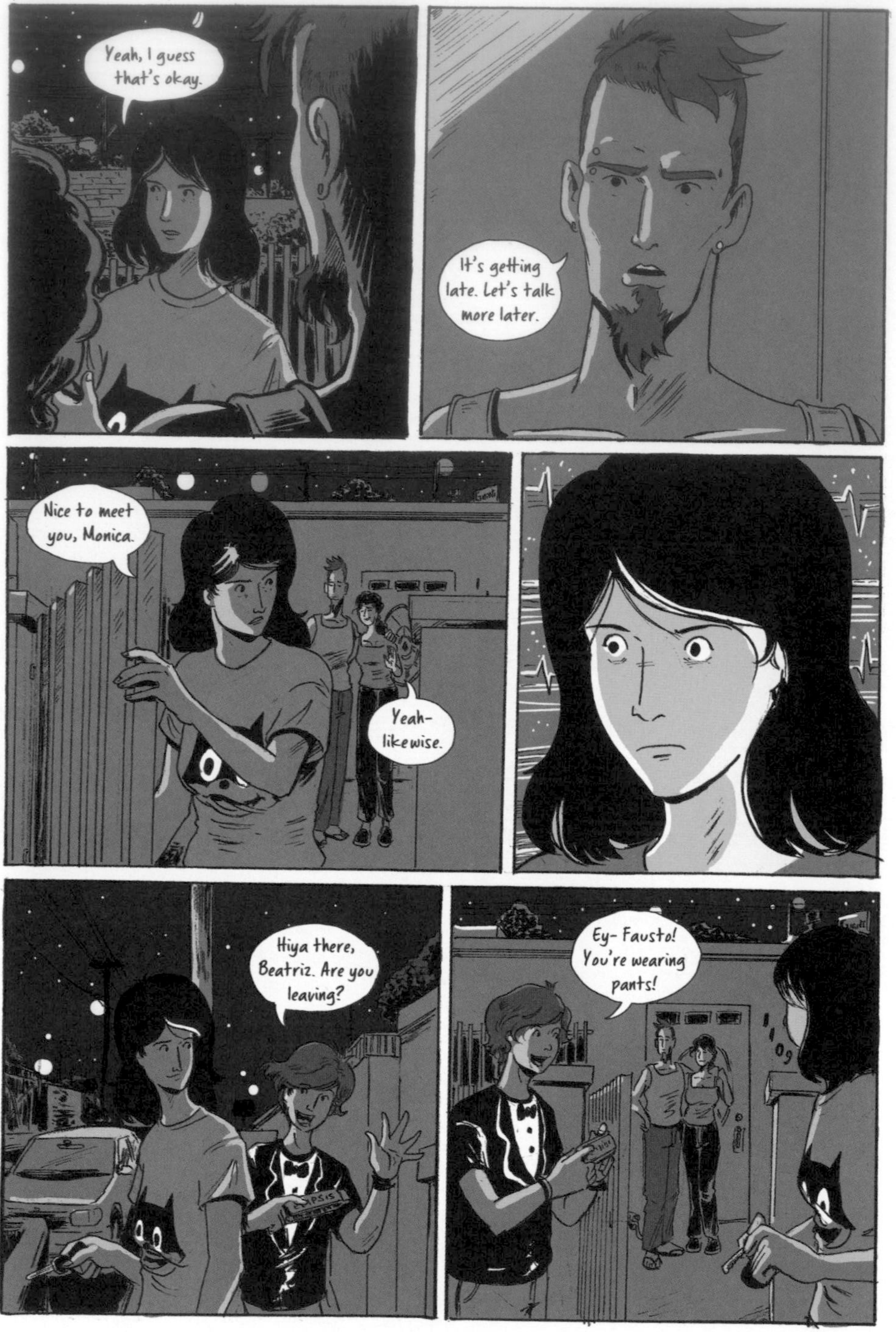
Yeah, I guess that's okay.
It's getting late. Let's talk more later.
Nice to meet you, Monica.
Yeah- likewise.
Hiya there, Beatriz. Are you leaving?
Ey- Fausto! You're wearing pants!

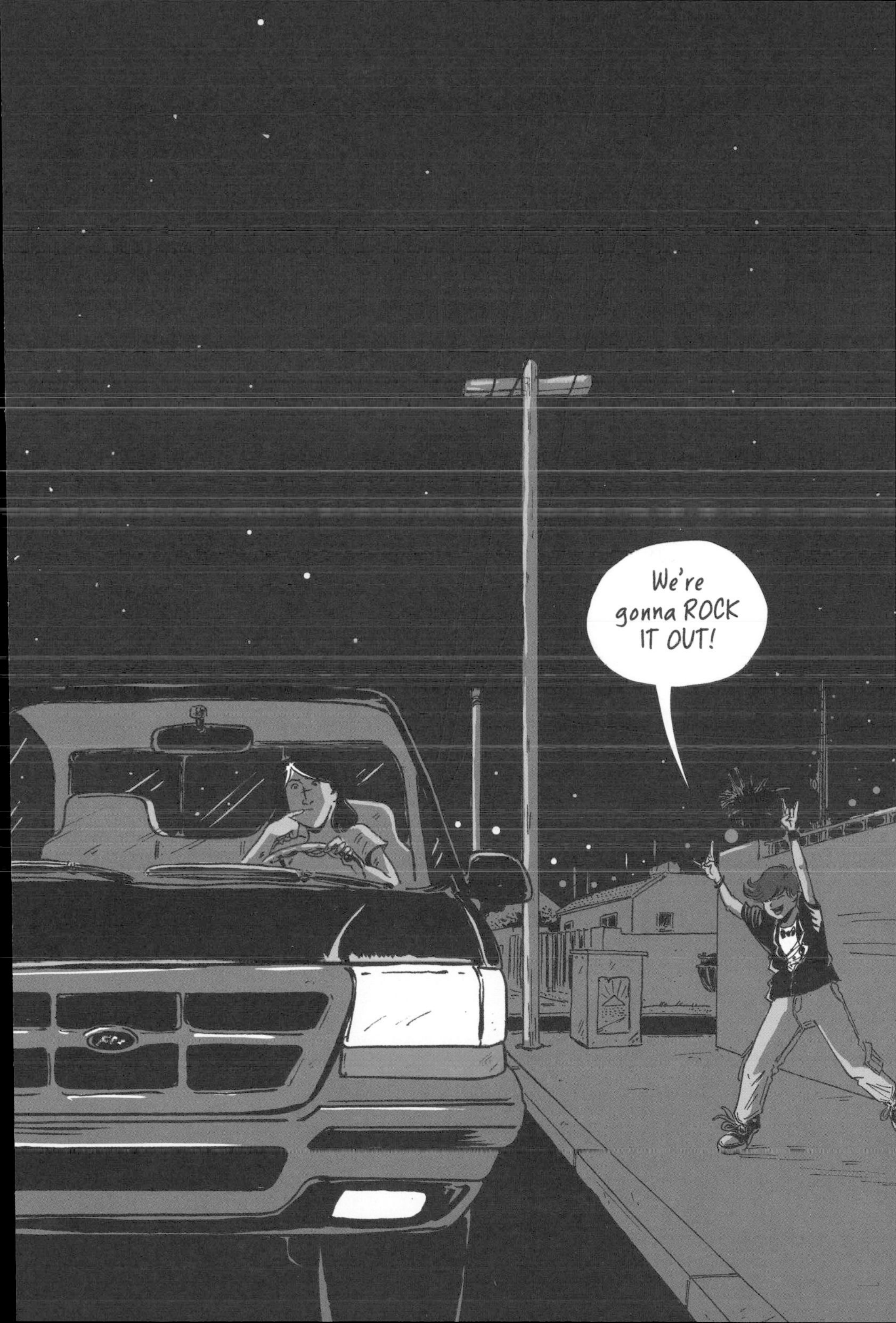
We're gonna ROCK IT OUT!

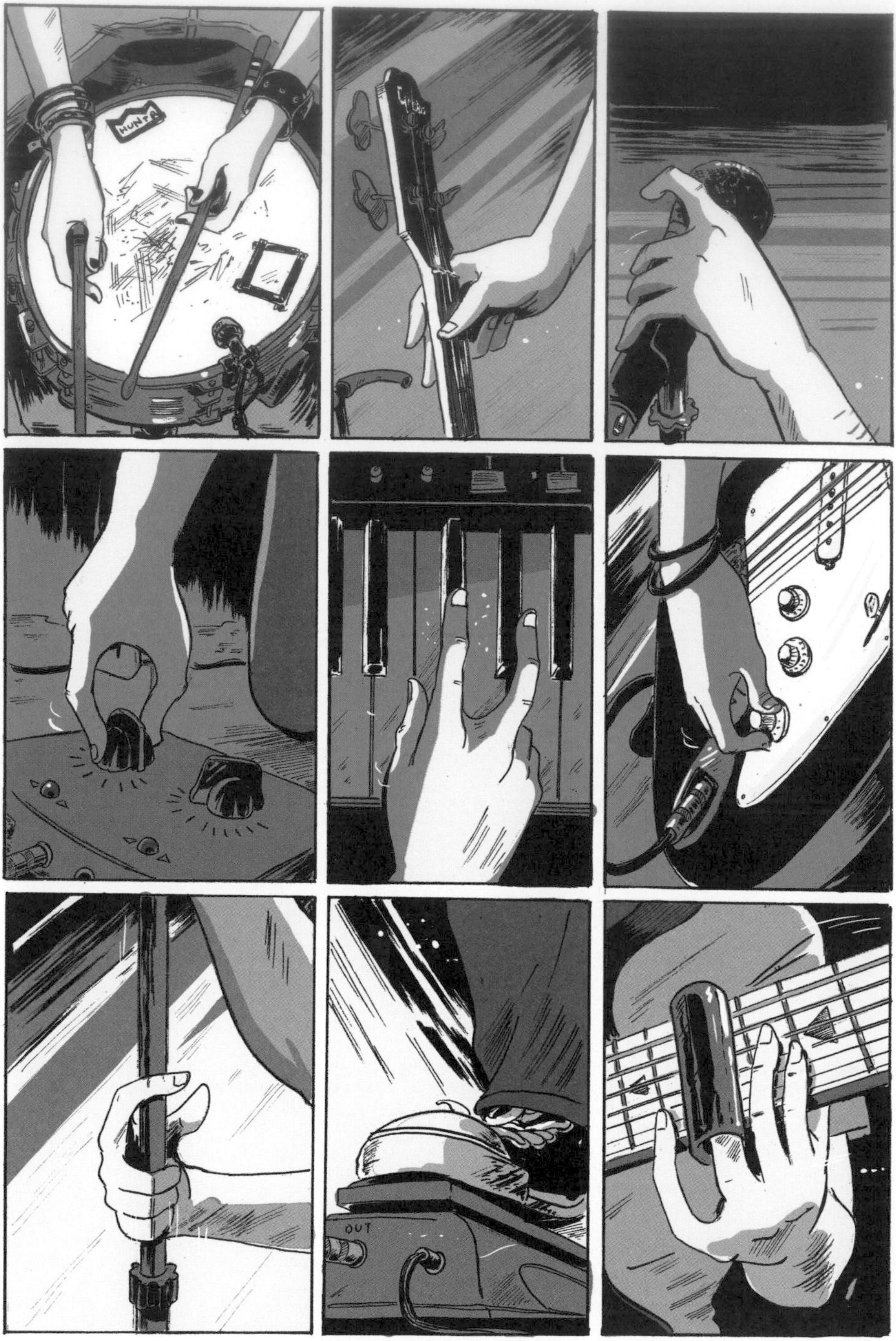
OUT

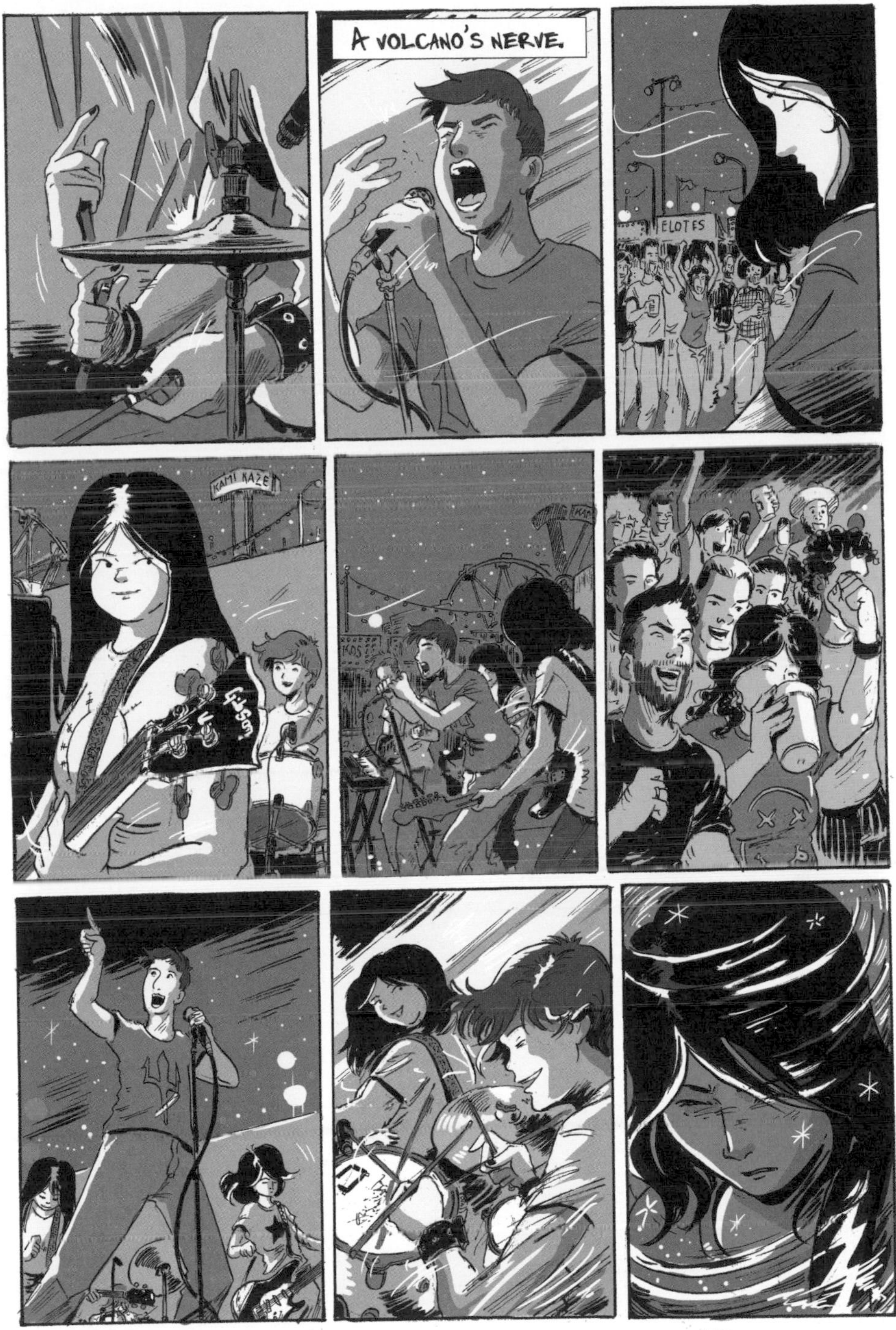
A VOLCANO'S NERVE.
ELOTES
KAMI KAZE

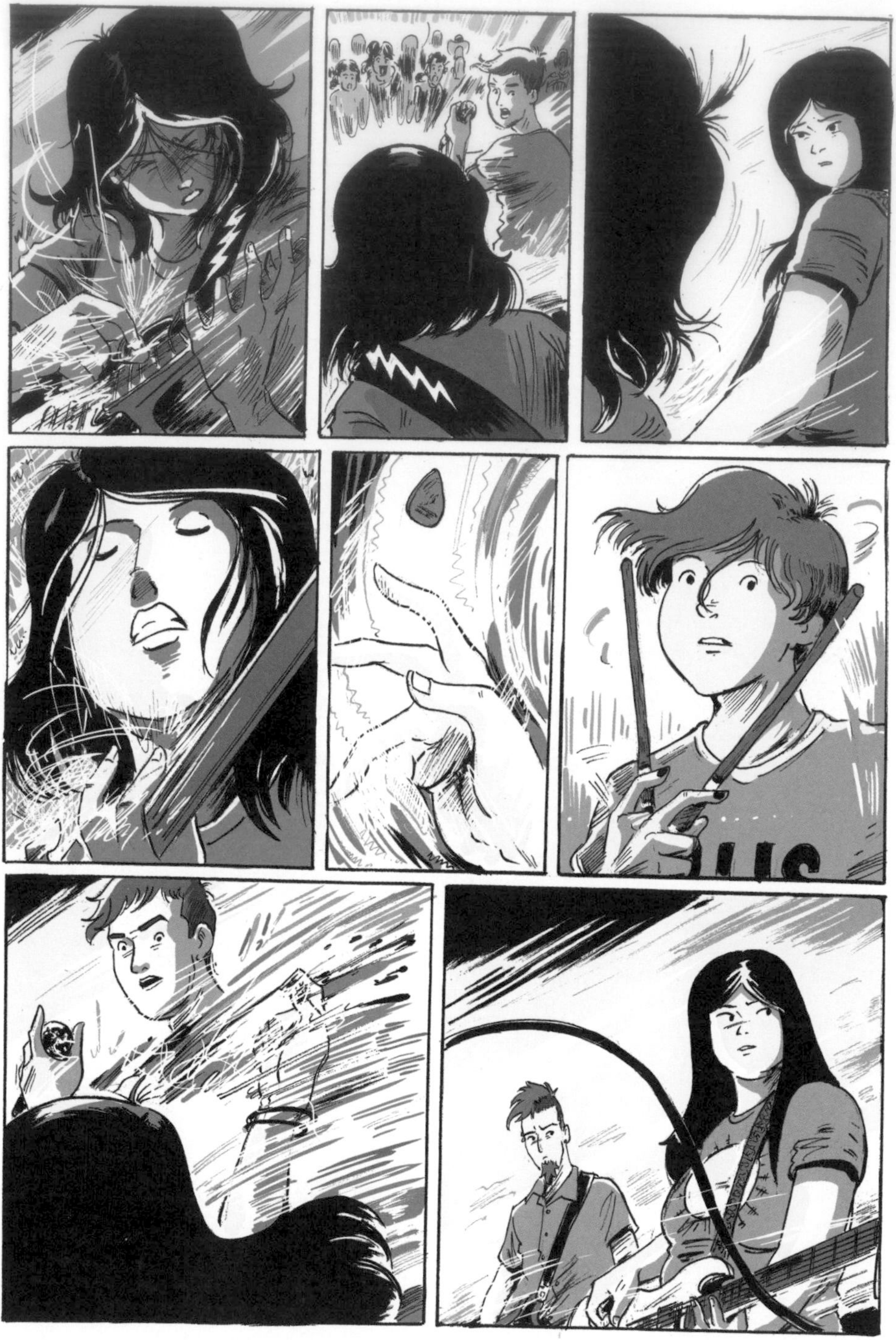

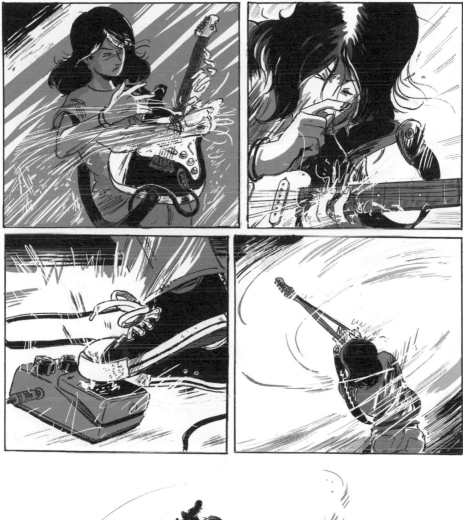

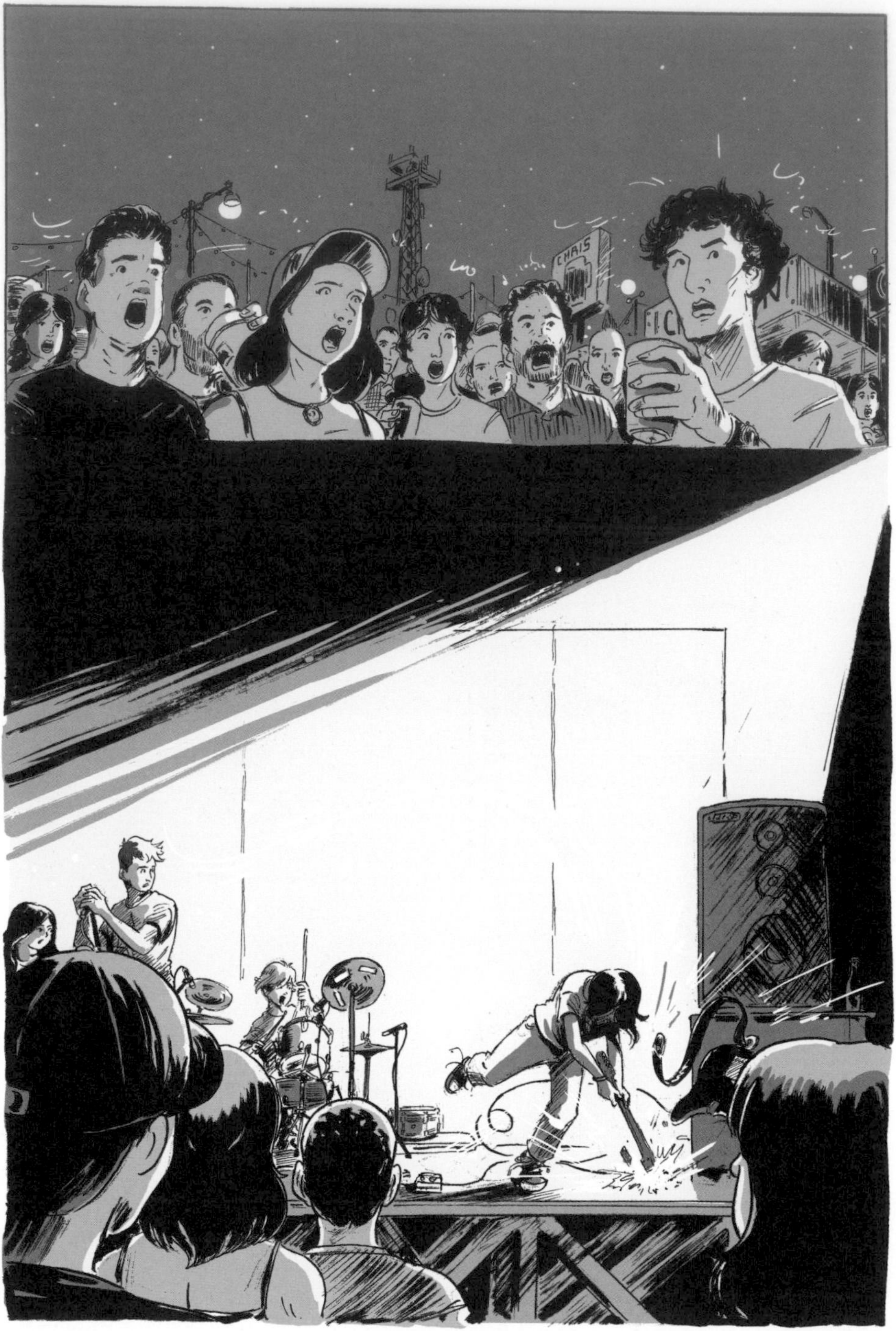
CHRIS

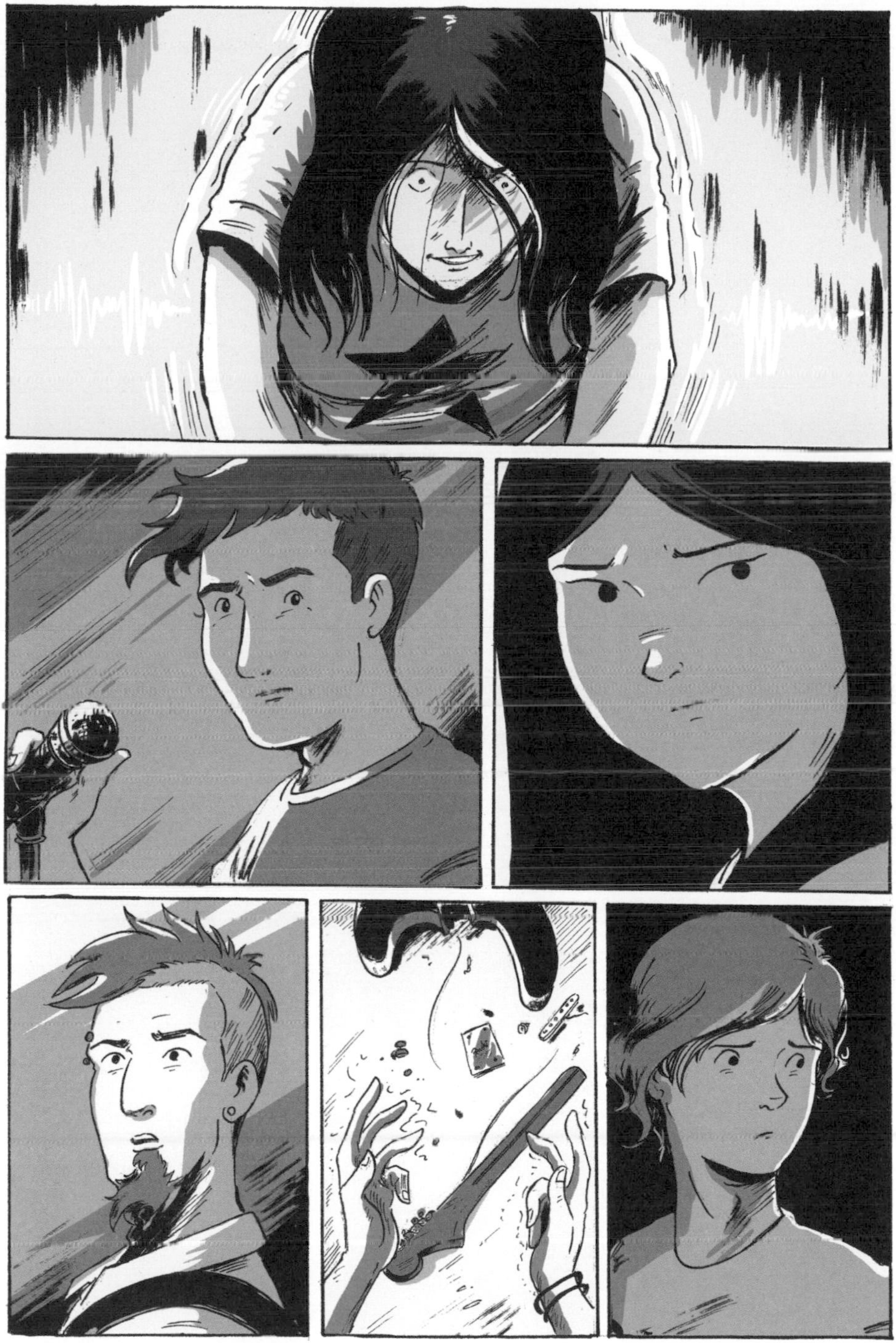

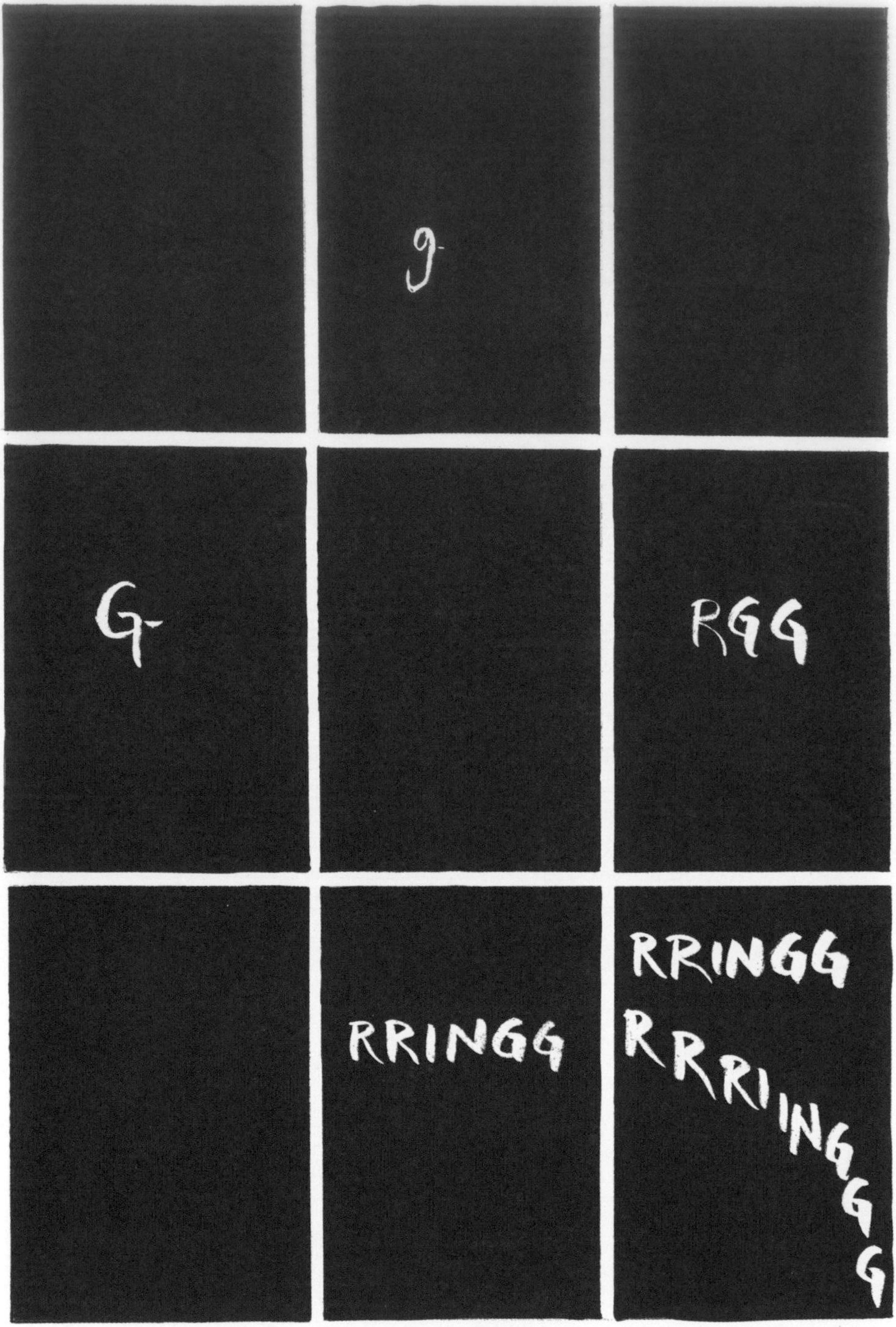
g
G
RGG
RRINGG
RRINGG
RRRIINGGG

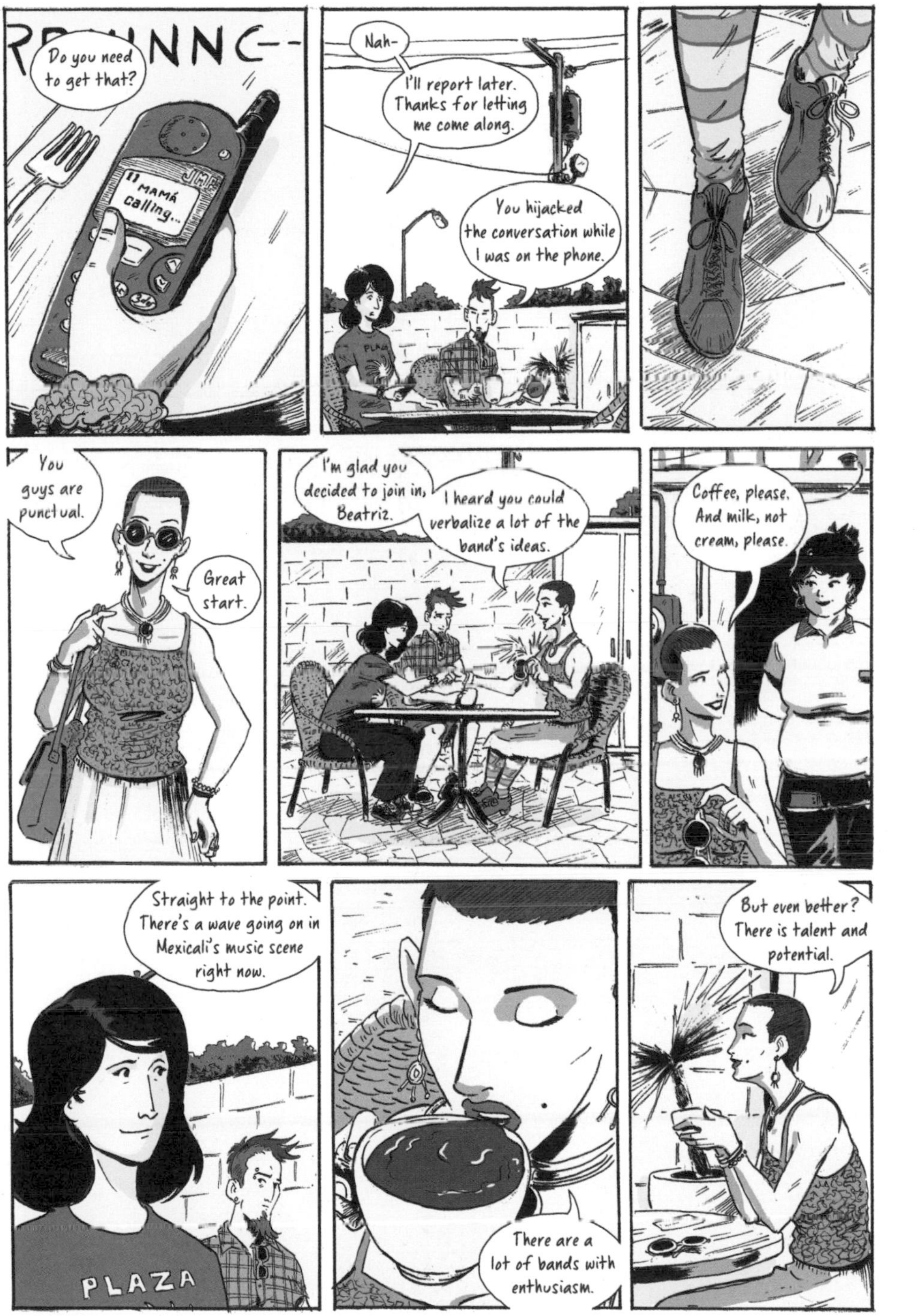
RRRINNG--
Do you need to get that?
MAMÁ calling...
Nah-
I'll report later. Thanks for letting me come along.
You hijacked the conversation while I was on the phone.
You guys are punctual.
Great start.
I'm glad you decided to join in, Beatriz.
I heard you could verbalize a lot of the band's ideas.
Coffee, please. And milk, not cream, please.
Straight to the point. There's a wave going on in Mexicali's music scene right now.
PLAZA
There are a lot of bands with enthusiasm.
But even better? There is talent and potential.

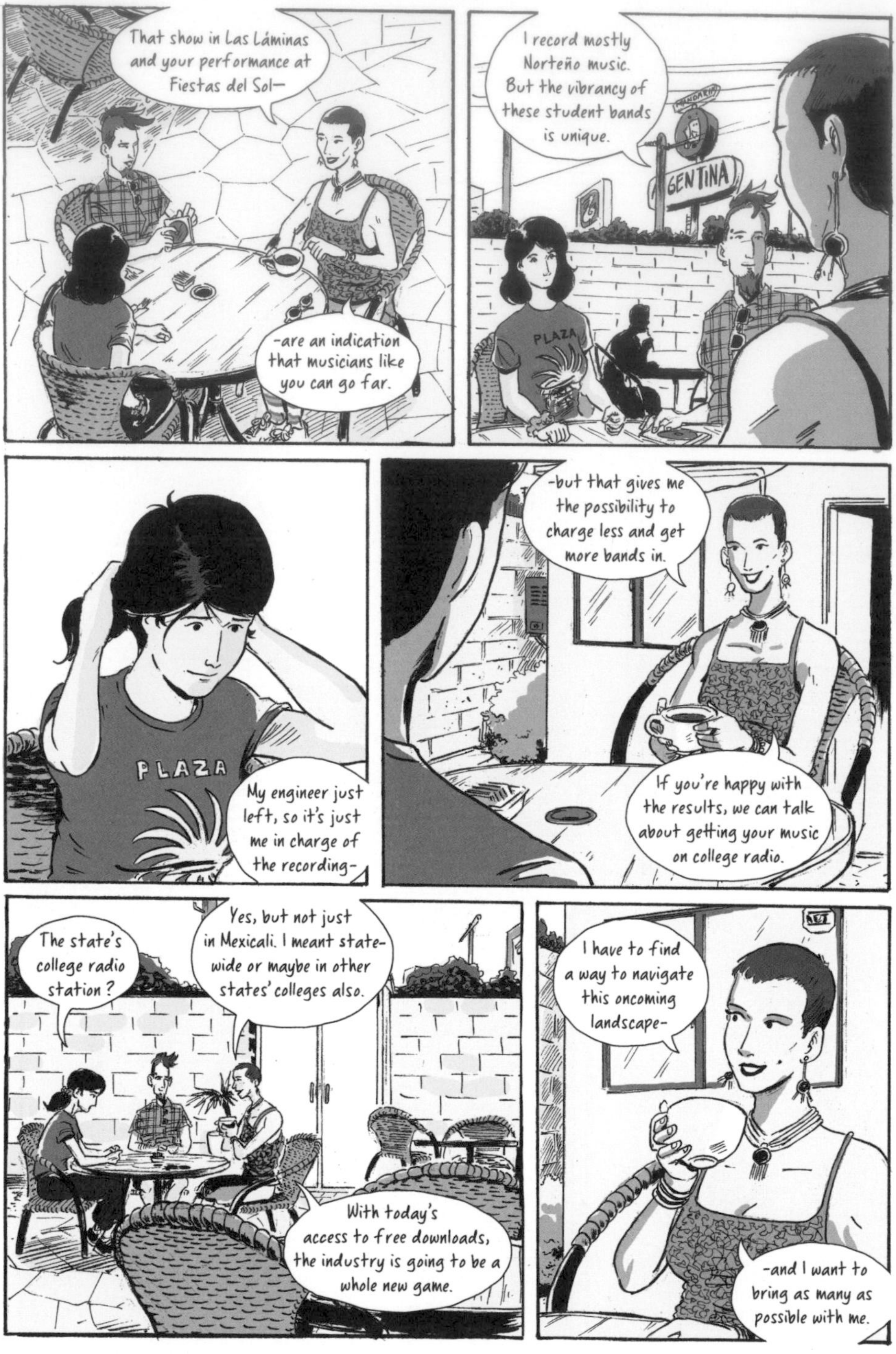
That show in Las Láminas and your performance at Fiestas del Sol—
-are an indication that musicians like you can go far.
I record mostly Norteño music. But the vibrancy of these student bands is unique.
GENTINA
PLAZA
PLAZA
My engineer just left, so it's just me in charge of the recording-
-but that gives me the possibility to charge less and get more bands in.
If you're happy with the results, we can talk about getting your music on college radio.
The state's college radio station?
Yes, but not just in Mexicali. I meant state-wide or maybe in other states' colleges also.
With today's access to free downloads, the industry is going to be a whole new game.
I have to find a way to navigate this oncoming landscape-
-and I want to bring as many as possible with me.

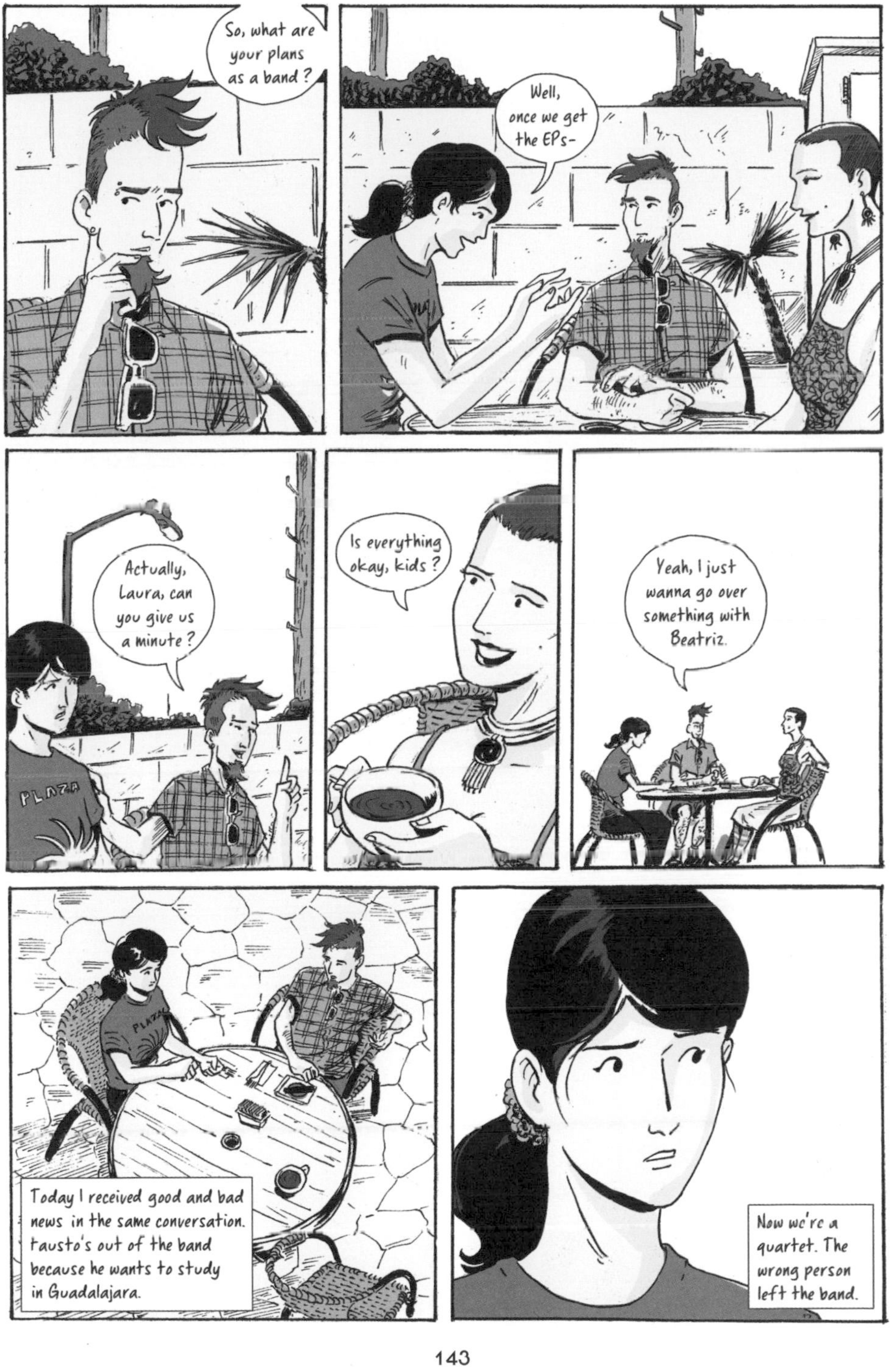

So, what are your plans as a band?
Well, once we get the EPs-
Actually, Laura, can you give us a minute?
Is everything okay, kids?
Yeah, I just wanna go over something with Beatriz.
Today I received good and bad news in the same conversation. Fausto's out of the band because he wants to study in Guadalajara.
Now we're a quartet. The wrong person left the band.

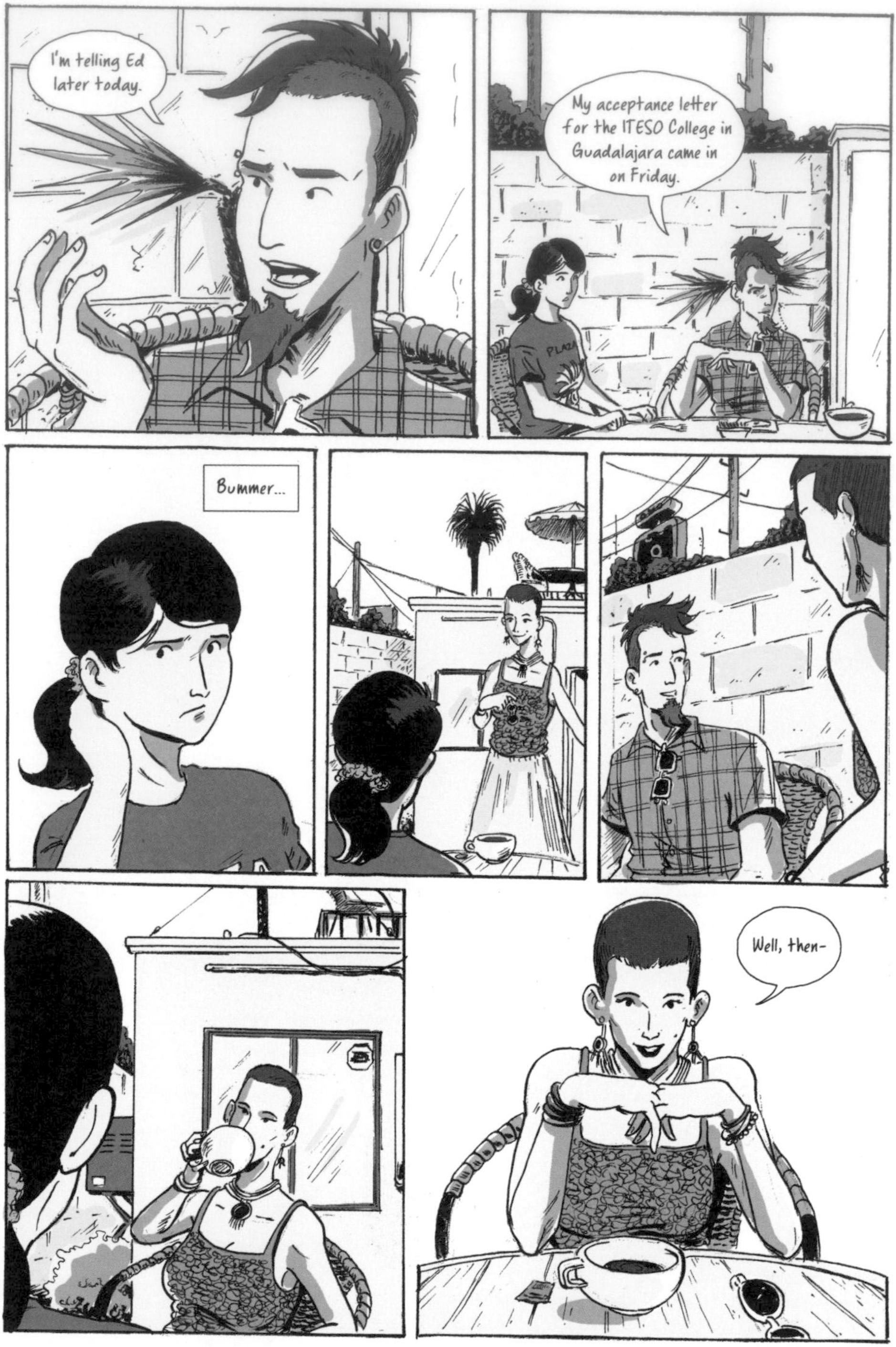
I'm telling Ed later today.
My acceptance letter for the ITESO College in Guadalajara came in on Friday.
PLAZA
Bummer...
Well, then-

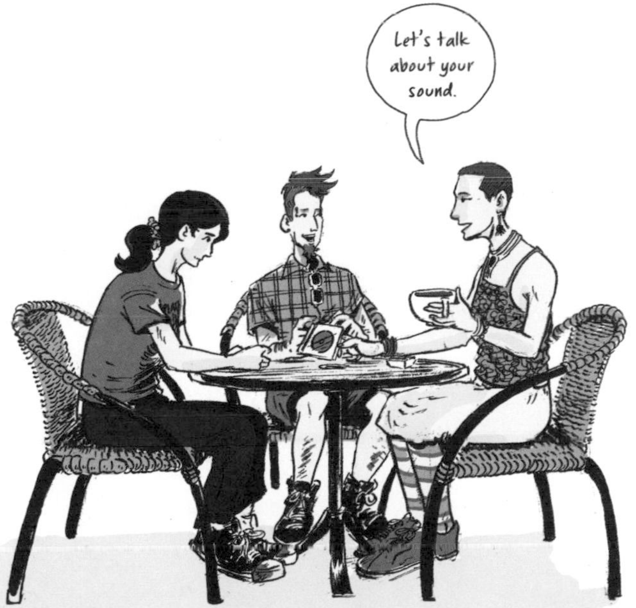
Let's talk about your sound.

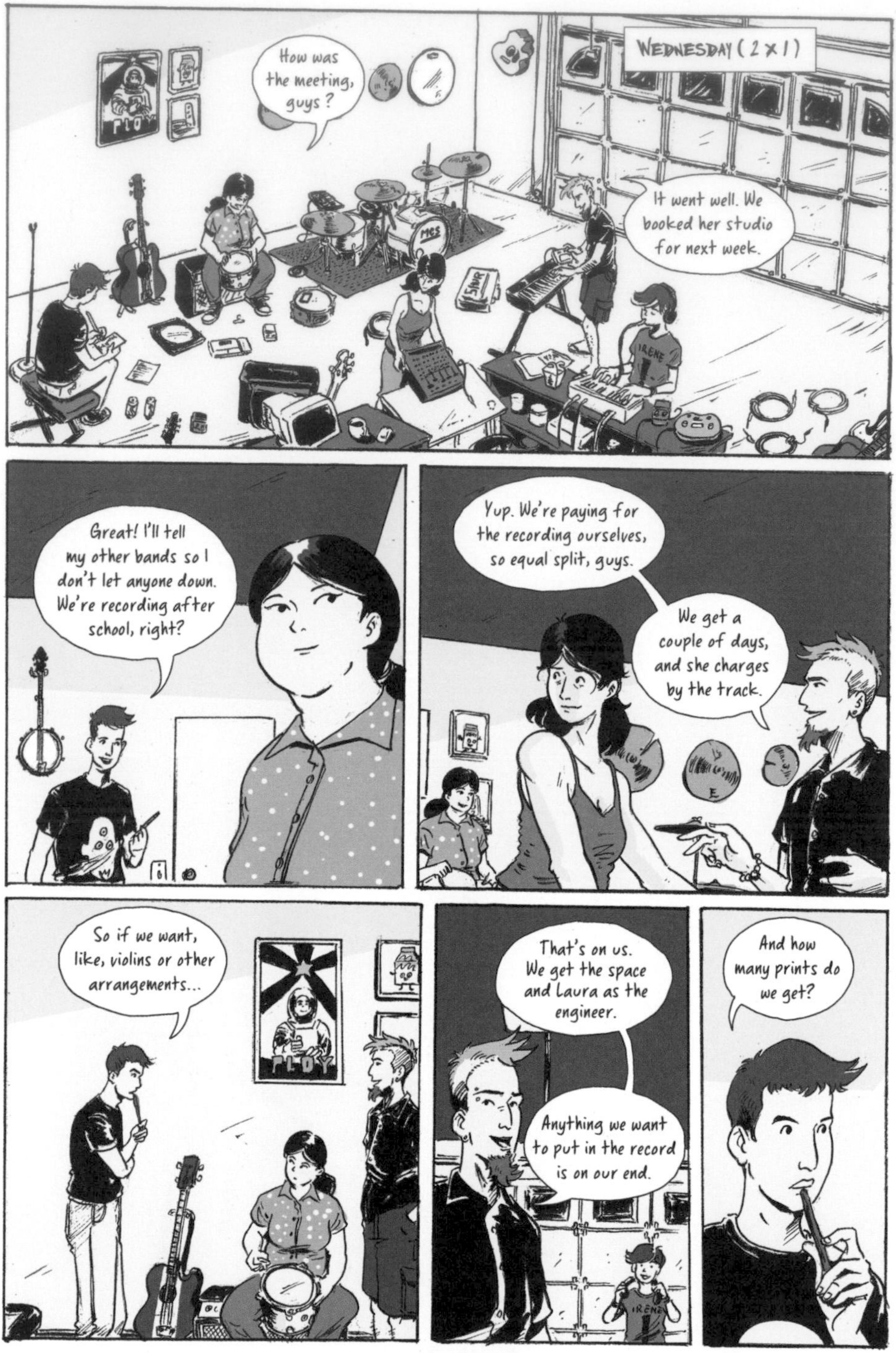
WEDNESDAY (2 x 1)
How was the meeting, guys?
It went well. We booked her studio for next week.
Great! I'll tell my other bands so I don't let anyone down. We're recording after school, right?
Yup. We're paying for the recording ourselves, so equal split, guys.
We get a couple of days, and she charges by the track.
So if we want, like, violins or other arrangements...
That's on us. We get the space and Laura as the engineer.
Anything we want to put in the record is on our end.
And how many prints do we get?

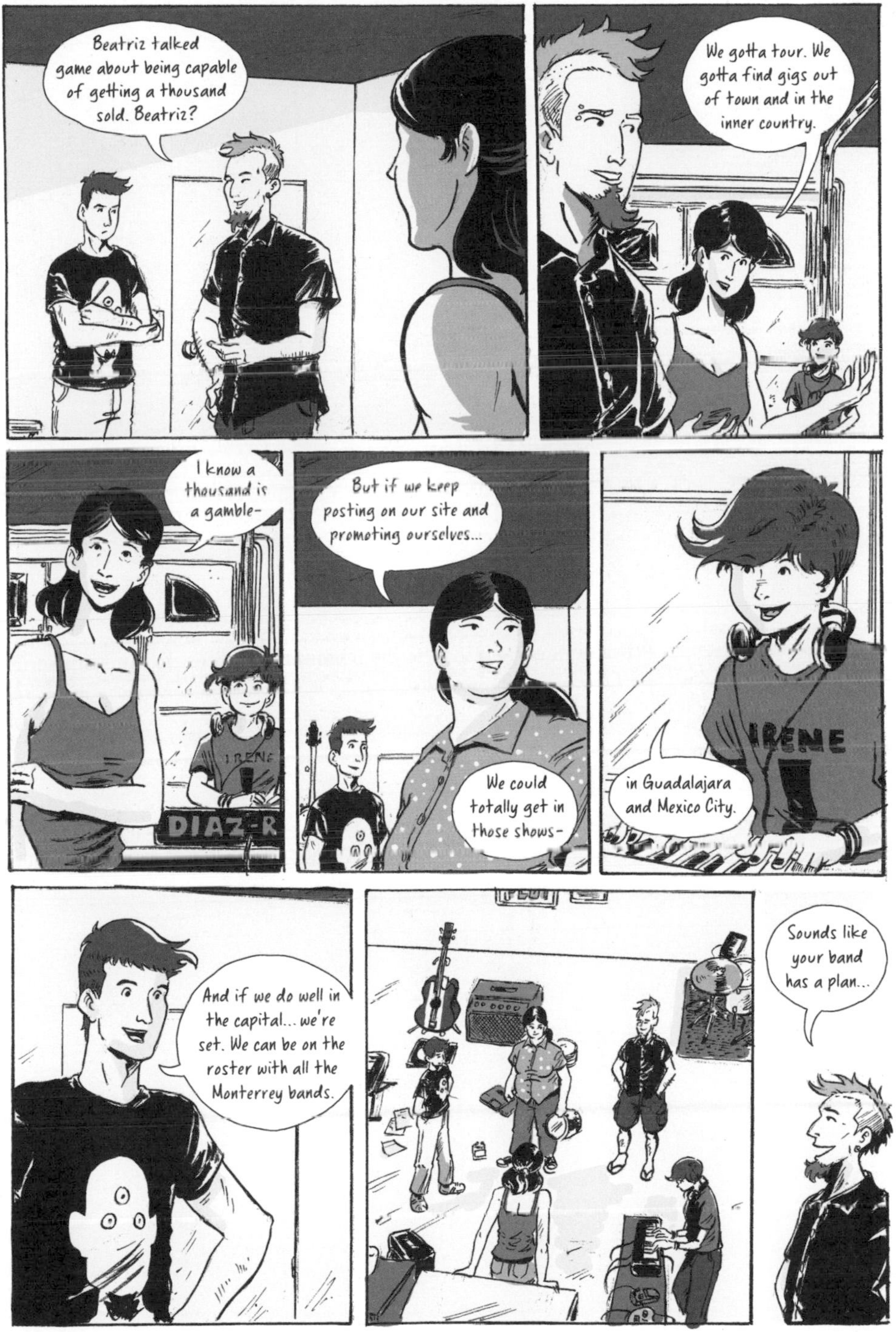
Beatriz talked game about being capable of getting a thousand sold. Beatriz?
We gotta tour. We gotta find gigs out of town and in the inner country.
I know a thousand is a gamble-
But if we keep posting on our site and promoting ourselves...
DIAZ-R
IRENE
We could totally get in those shows-
in Guadalajara and Mexico City.
IRENE
And if we do well in the capital... we're set. We can be on the roster with all the Monterrey bands.
Sounds like your band has a plan...

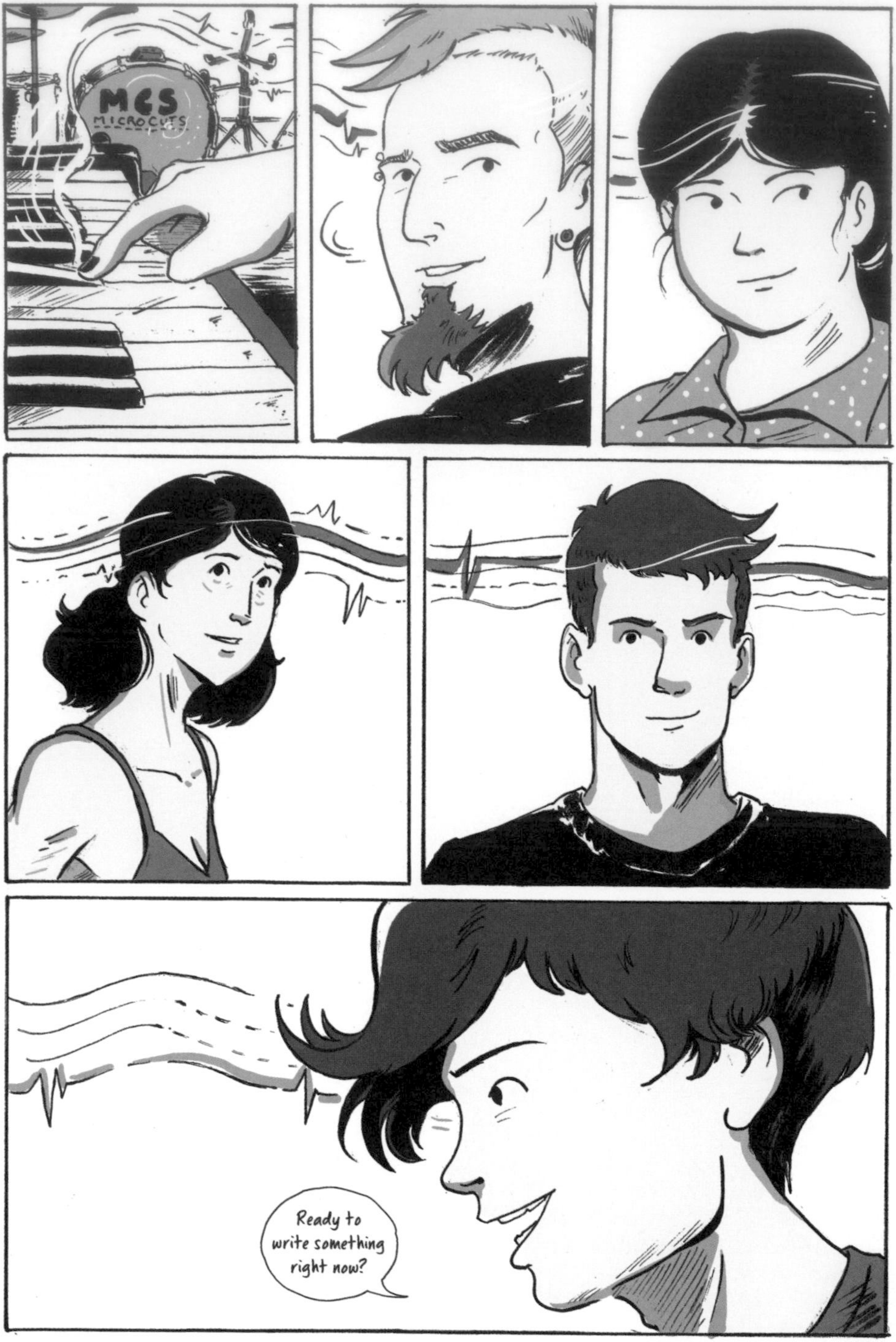
MCS
MICROCUTS
Ready to write something right now?

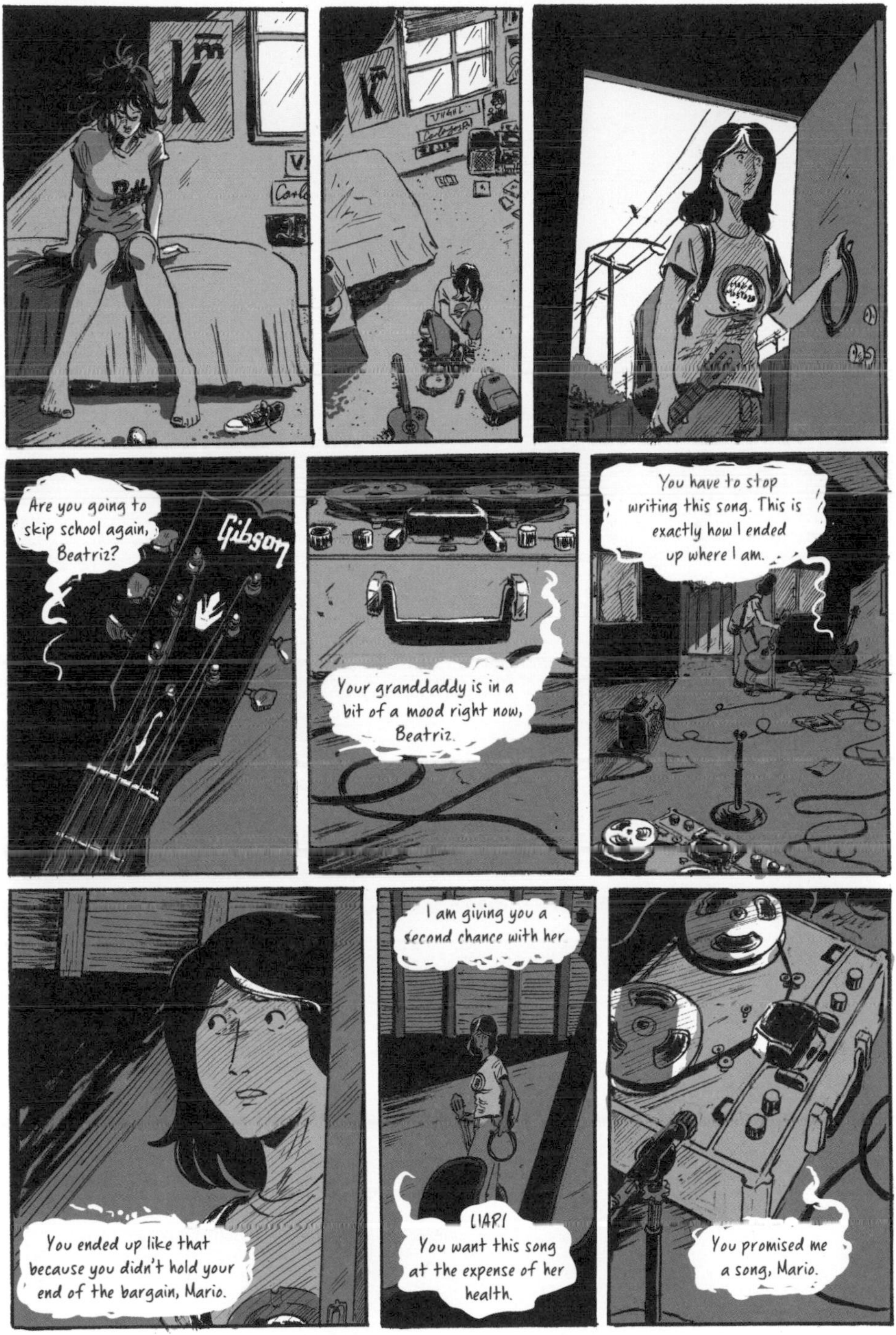
Are you going to skip school again, Beatriz?
Your granddaddy is in a bit of a mood right now, Beatriz.
You have to stop writing this song. This is exactly how I ended up where I am.
You ended up like that because you didn't hold your end of the bargain, Mario.
I am giving you a second chance with her
LIAR! You want this song at the expense of her health.
You promised me a song, Mario.

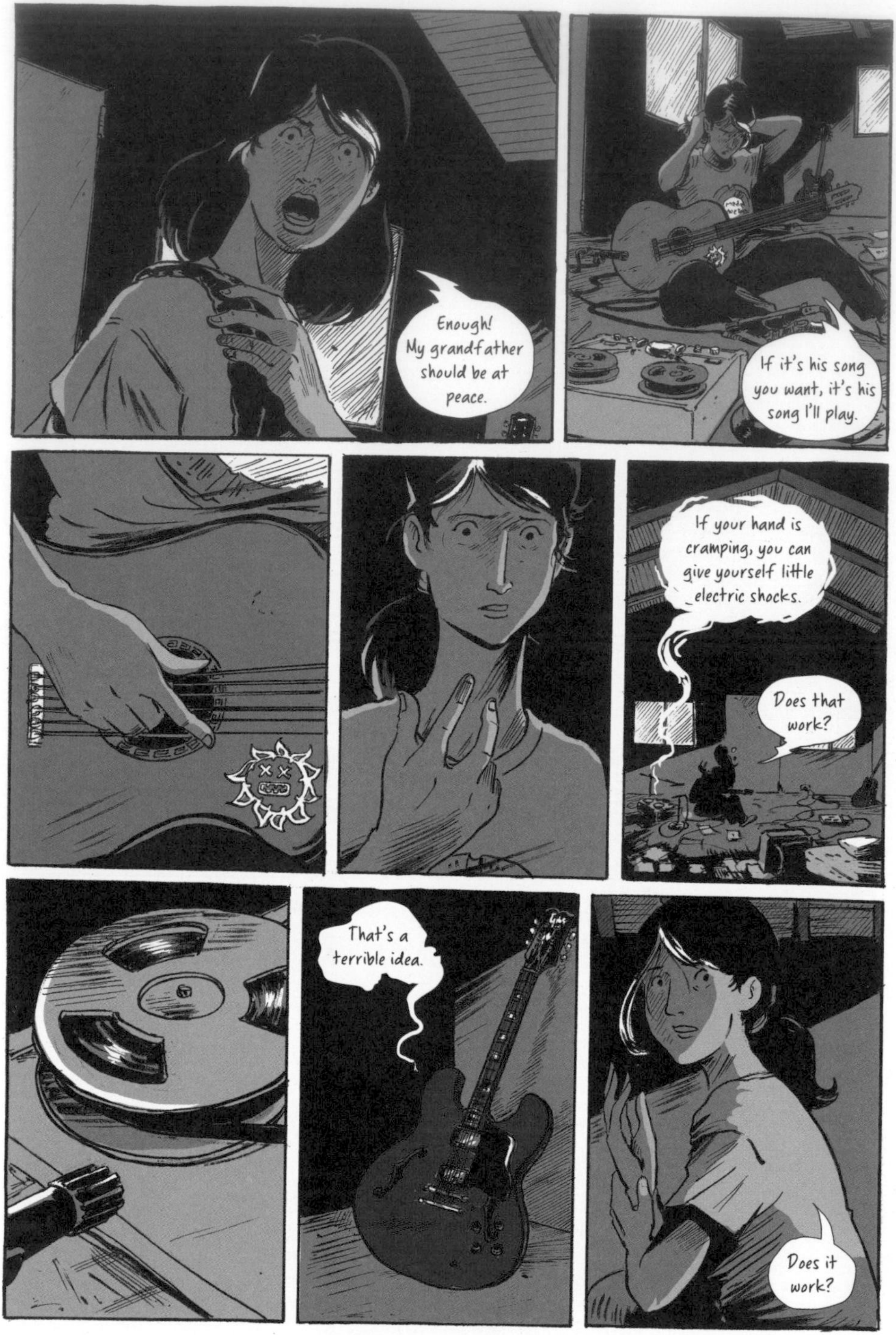

Enough! My grandfather should be at peace.
If it's his song you want, it's his song I'll play.
If your hand is cramping, you can give yourself little electric shocks.
Does that work?
That's a terrible idea.
Does it work?

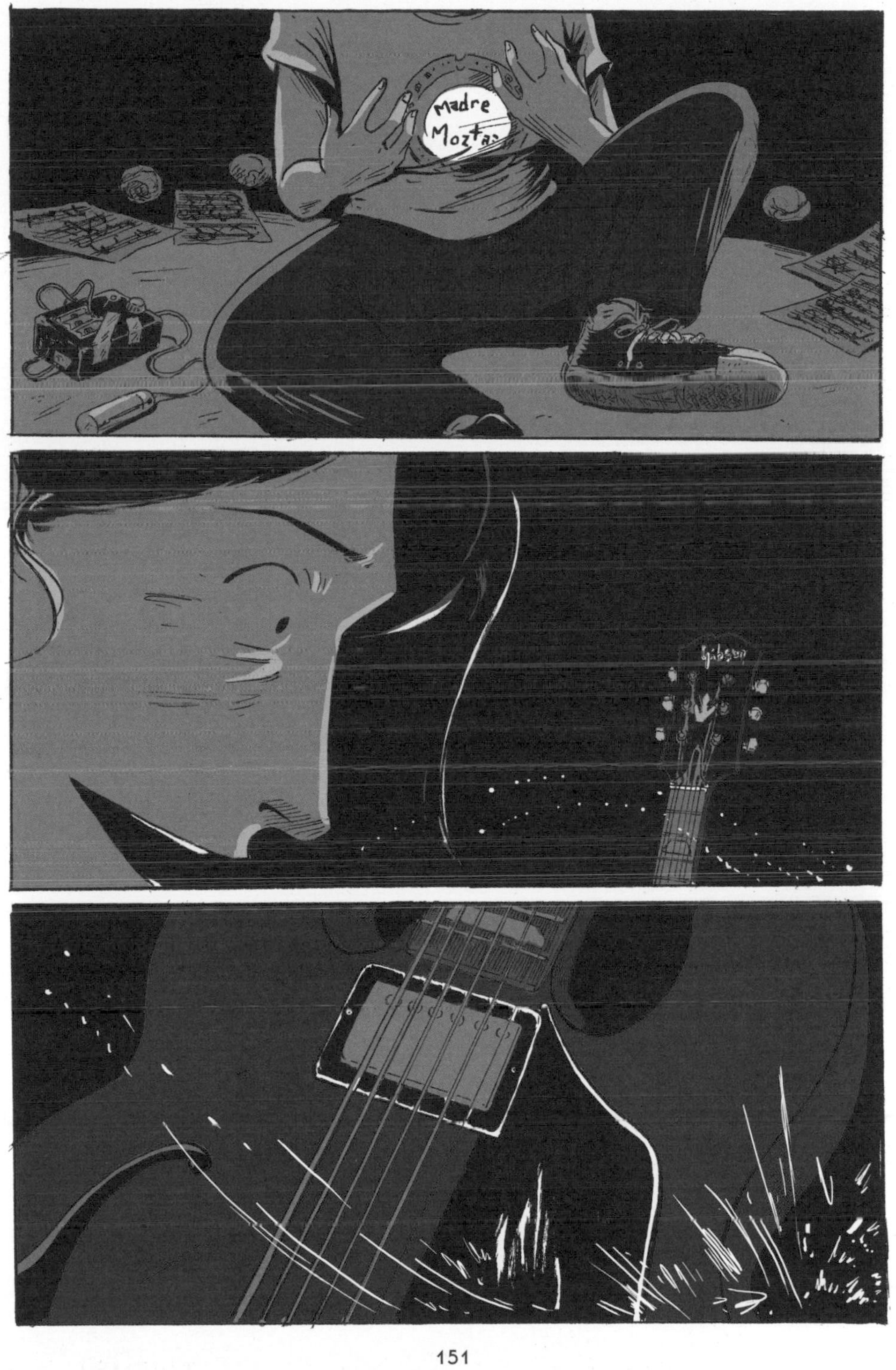
Madre

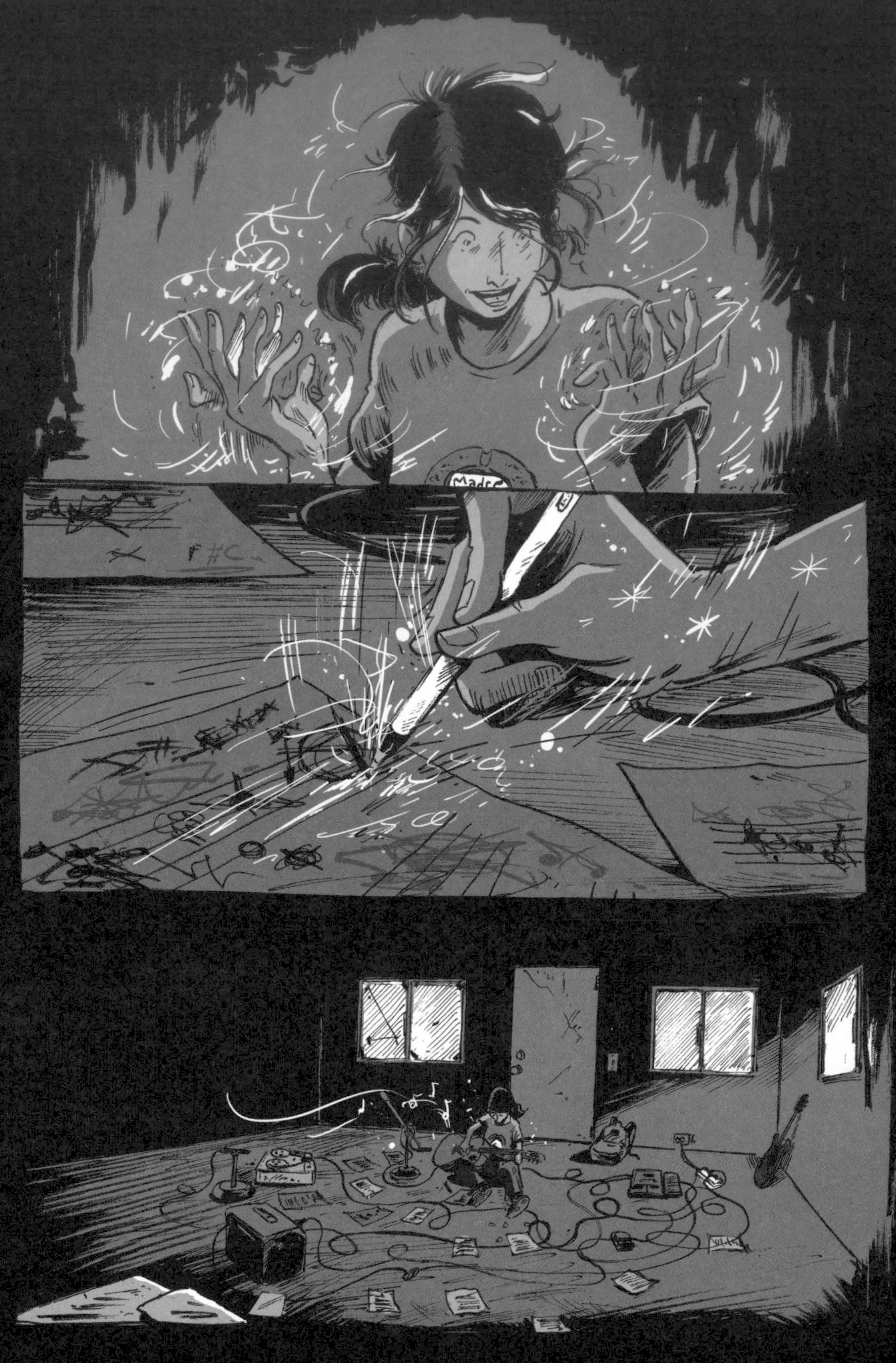

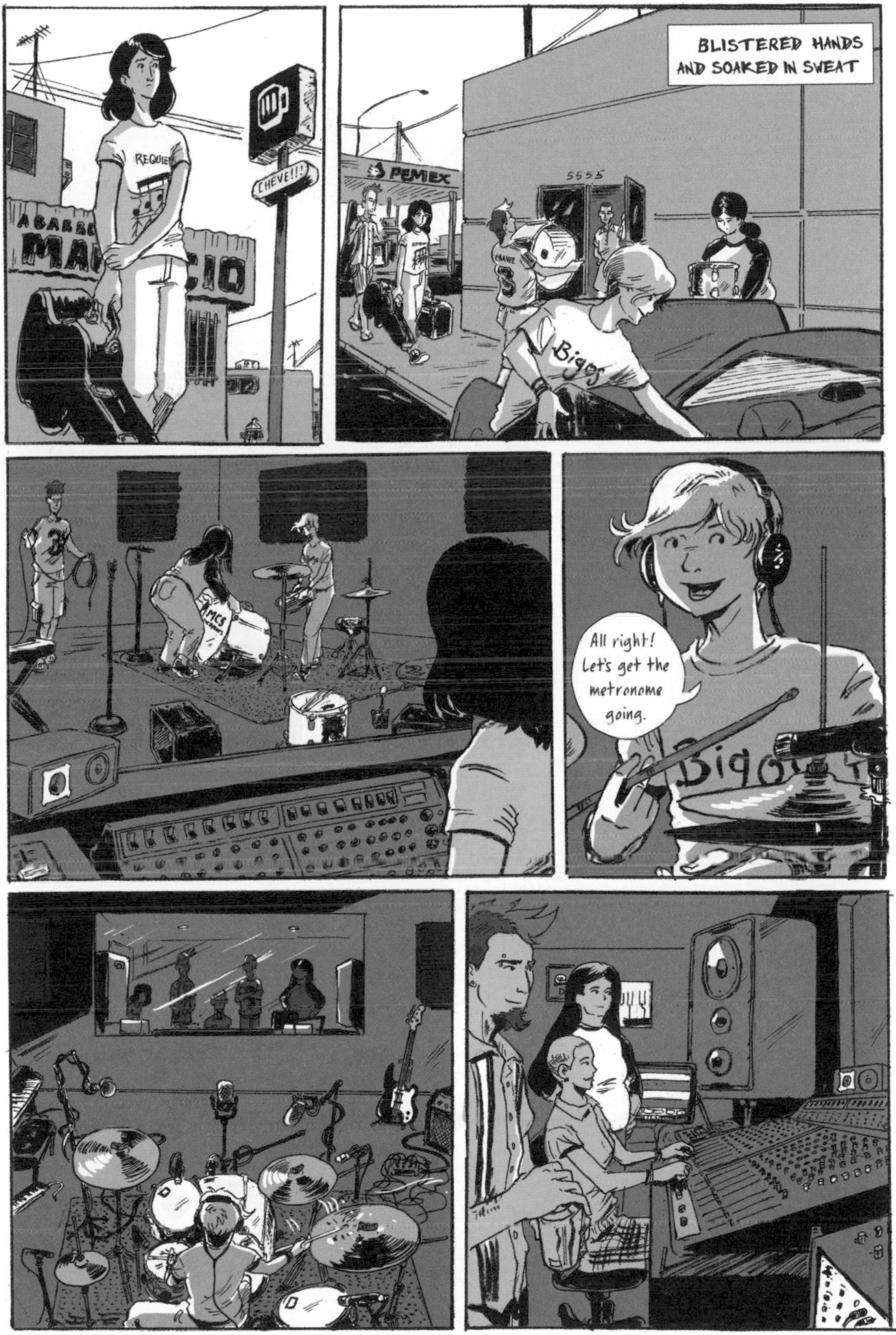
REQUIEM
CHEVE!!!
PEMEX
5555
BLISTERED HANDS AND SOAKED IN SWEAT
Biggs
All right! Let's get the metronome going.

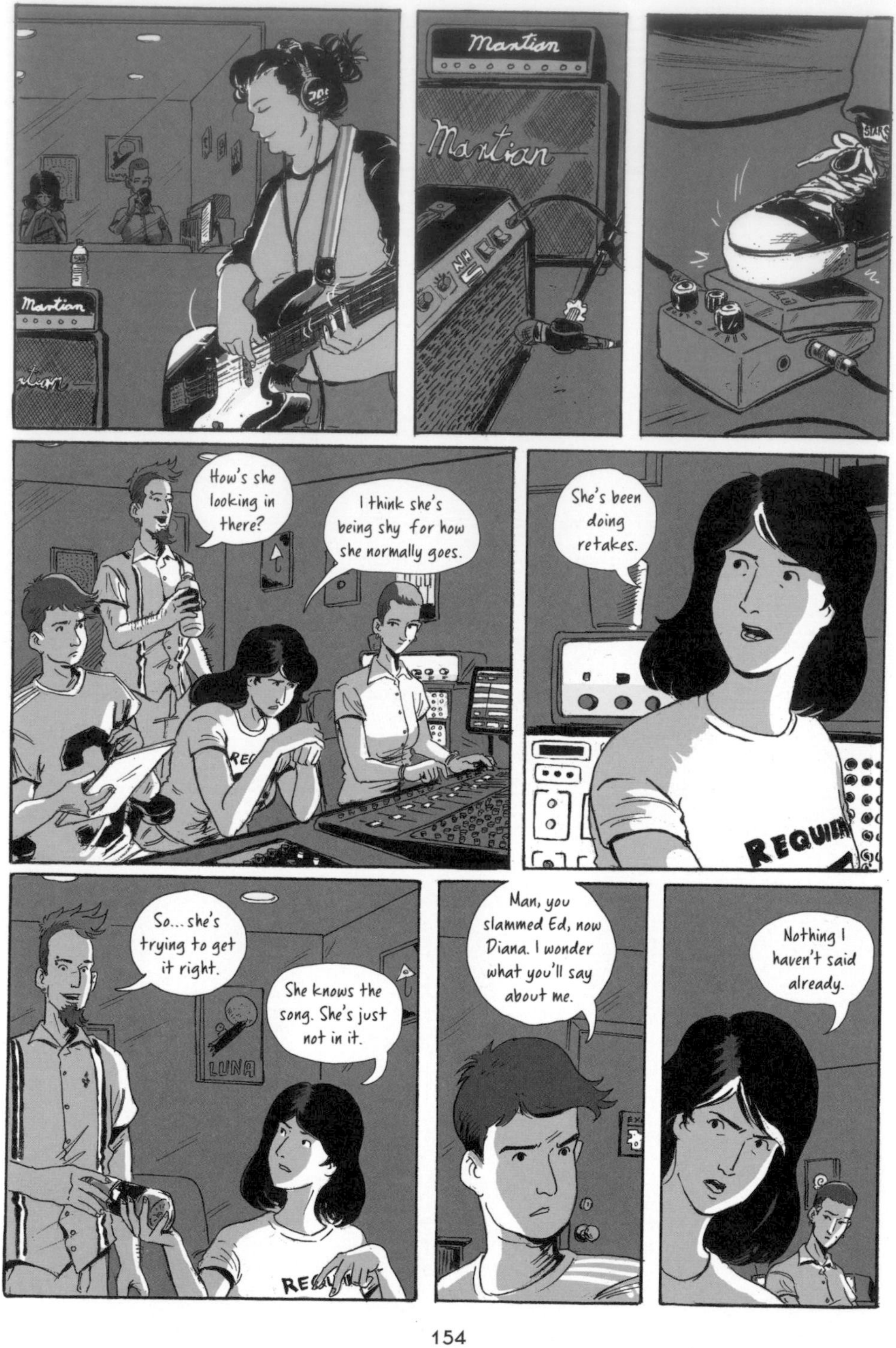
Mantian
Mantian
Mantian
How's she looking in there?
I think she's being shy for how she normally goes.
She's been doing retakes.
So... she's trying to get it right.
She knows the song. She's just not in it.
LUNA
Man, you slammed Ed, now Diana. I wonder what you'll say about me.
Nothing I haven't said already.

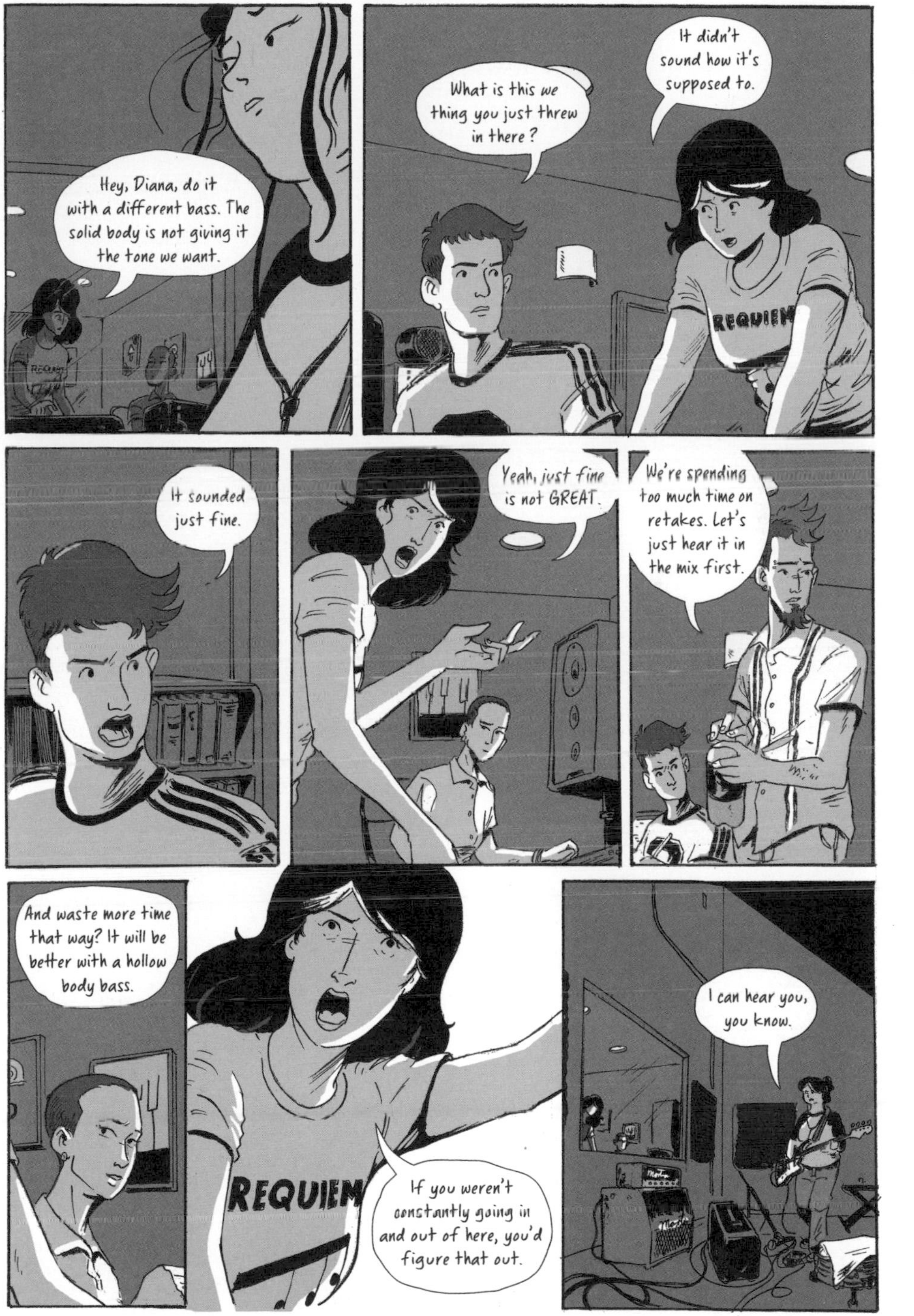
Hey, Diana, do it with a different bass. The solid body is not giving it the tone we want.
What is this we thing you just threw in there?
It didn't sound how it's supposed to.
It sounded just fine.
Yeah, just fine is not GREAT.
We're spending too much time on retakes. Let's just hear it in the mix first.
And waste more time that way? It will be better with a hollow body bass.
If you weren't constantly going in and out of here, you'd figure that out.
I can hear you, you know.

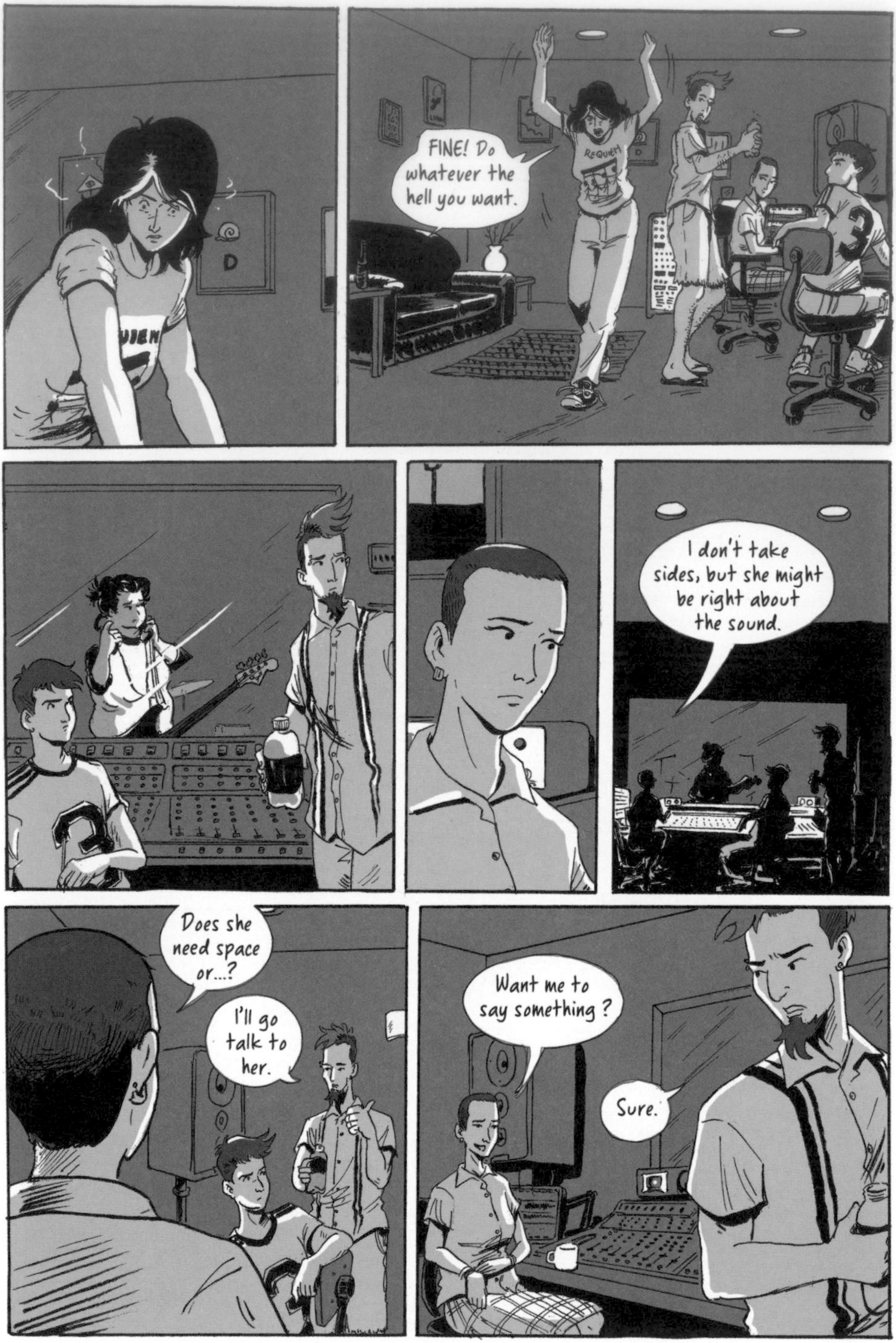

FINE! Do whatever the hell you want.
I don't take sides, but she might be right about the sound.
Does she need space or...?
I'll go talk to her.
Want me to say something ?
Sure.

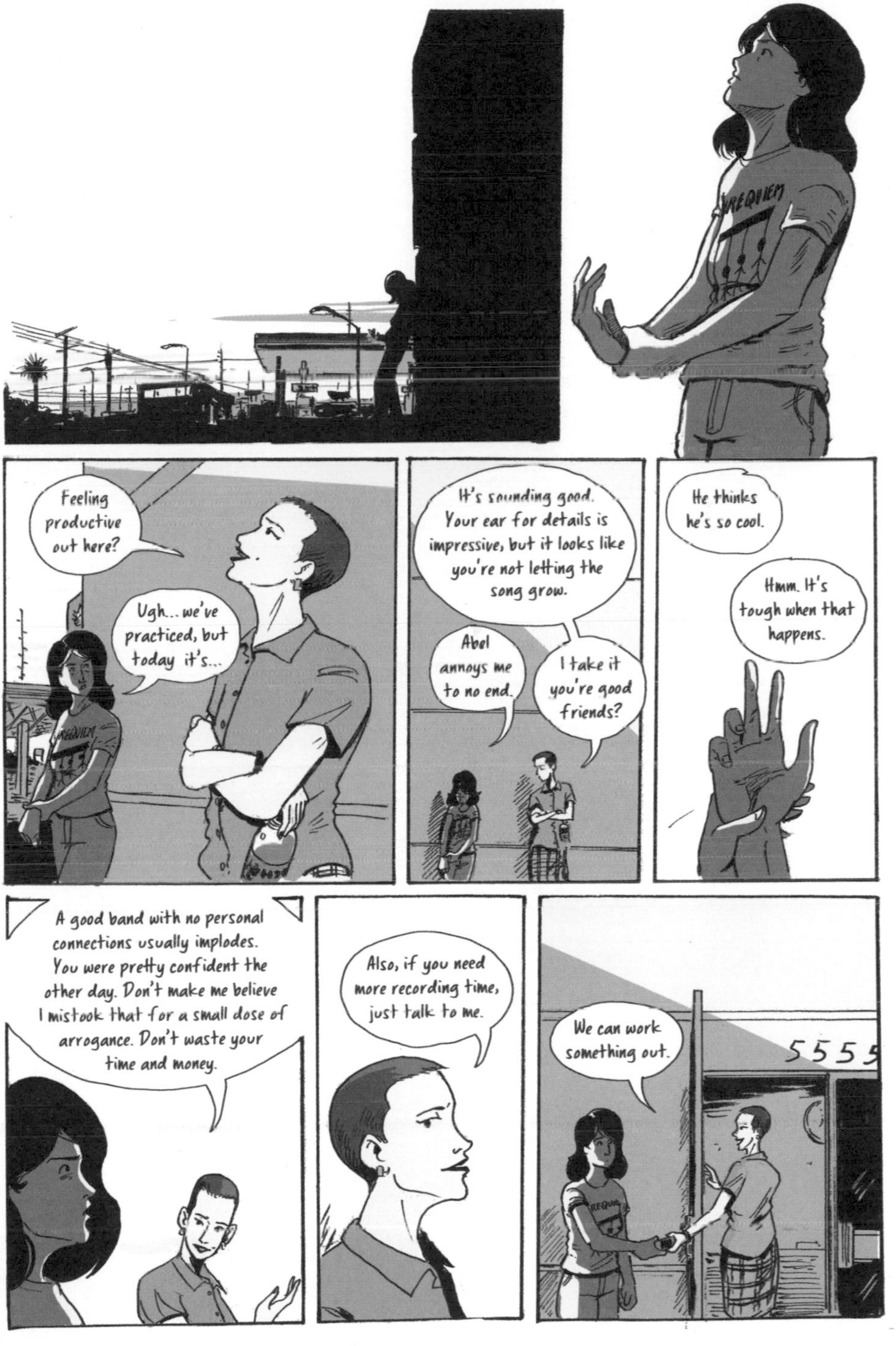

Feeling productive out here?
Ugh... we've practiced, but today it's...
It's sounding good. Your ear for details is impressive, but it looks like you're not letting the song grow.
Abel annoys me to no end.
I take it you're good friends?
He thinks he's so cool.
Hmm. It's tough when that happens.
A good band with no personal connections usually implodes. You were pretty confident the other day. Don't make me believe I mistook that for a small dose of arrogance. Don't waste your time and money.
Also, if you need more recording time, just talk to me.
We can work something out.
5555

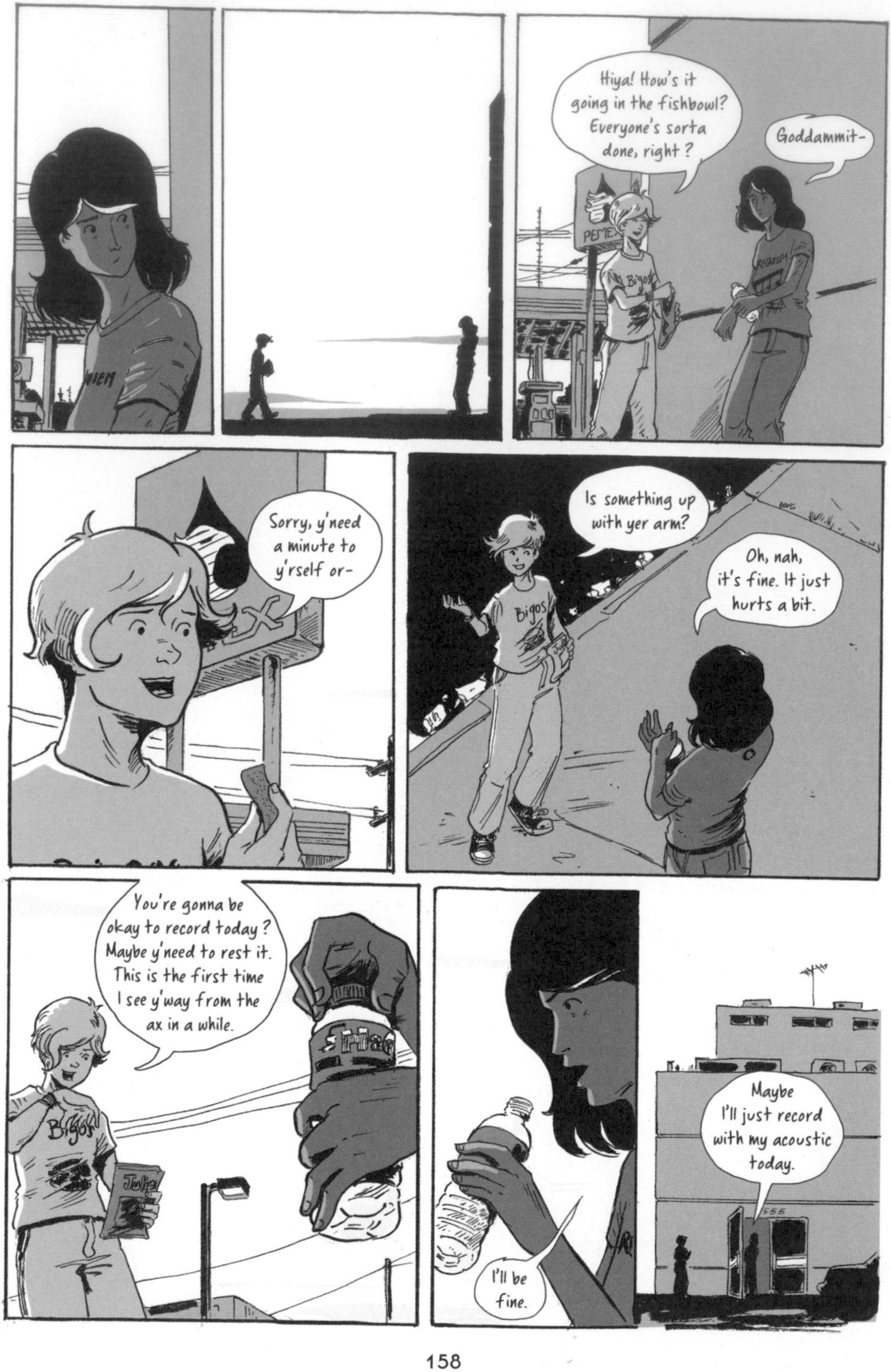

Hiya! How's it going in the fishbowl? Everyone's sorta done, right?
Goddammit-
Sorry, y'need a minute to y'rself or-
Is something up with yer arm?
Oh, nah, it's fine. It just hurts a bit.
You're gonna be okay to record today? Maybe y'need to rest it. This is the first time I see y'way from the ax in a while.
I'll be fine.
Maybe I'll just record with my acoustic today.

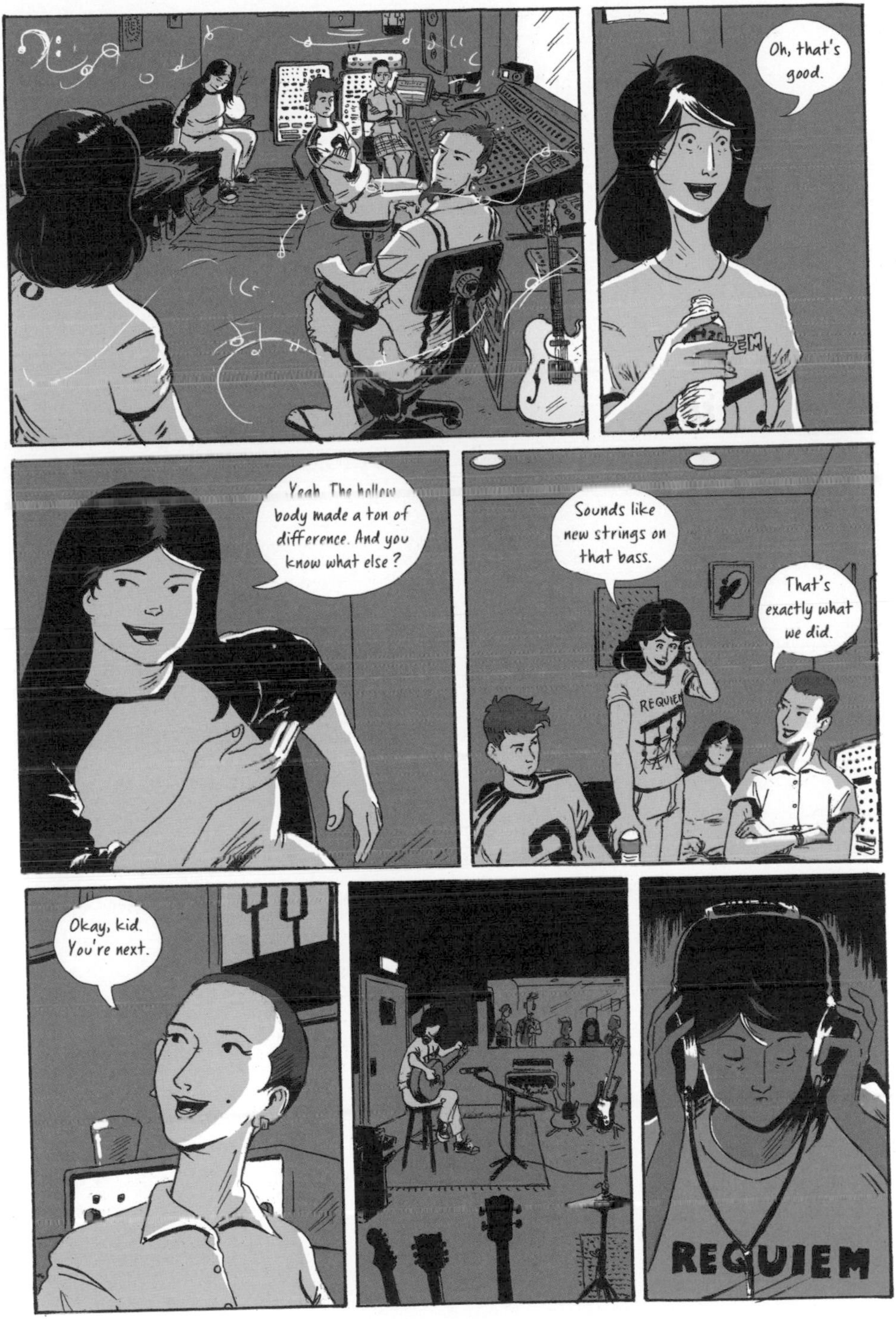
Oh, that's good.
Yeah. The hollow body made a ton of difference. And you know what else?
Sounds like new strings on that bass.
That's exactly what we did.
Okay, kid. You're next.
REQUIEM

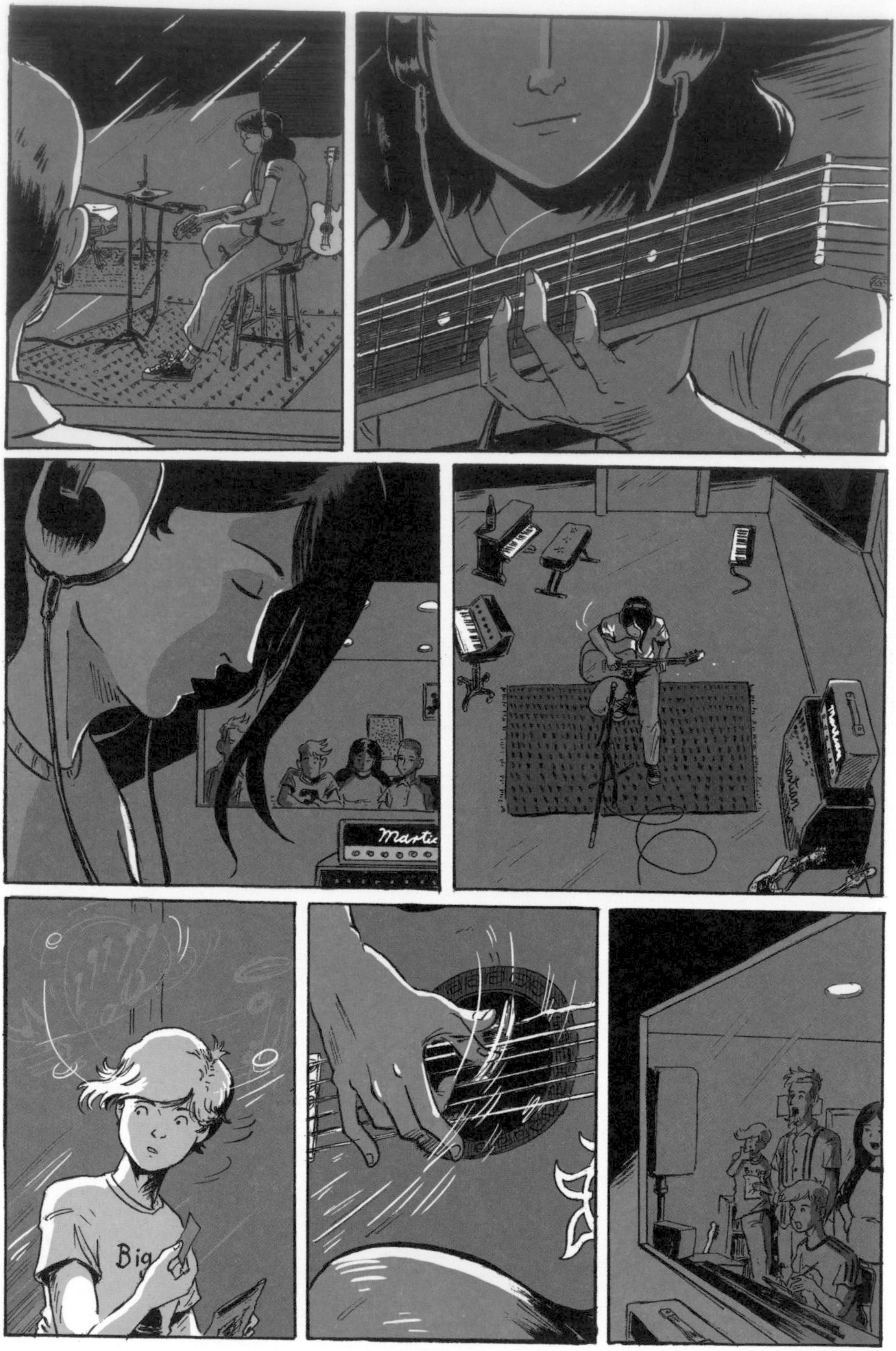
Big

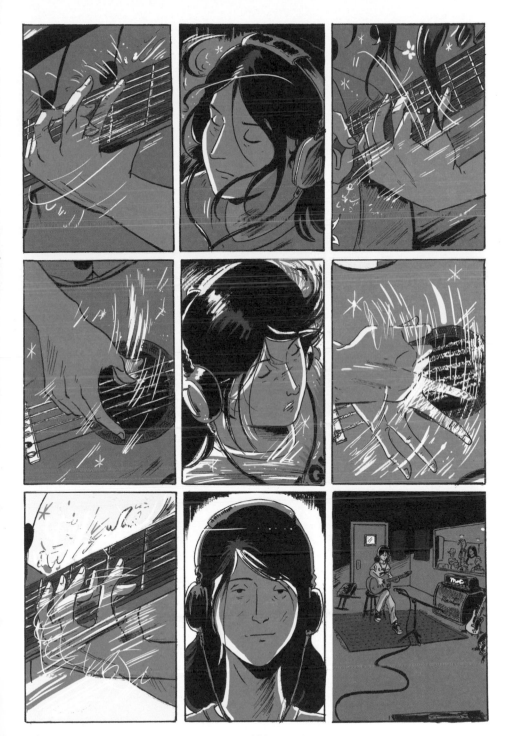

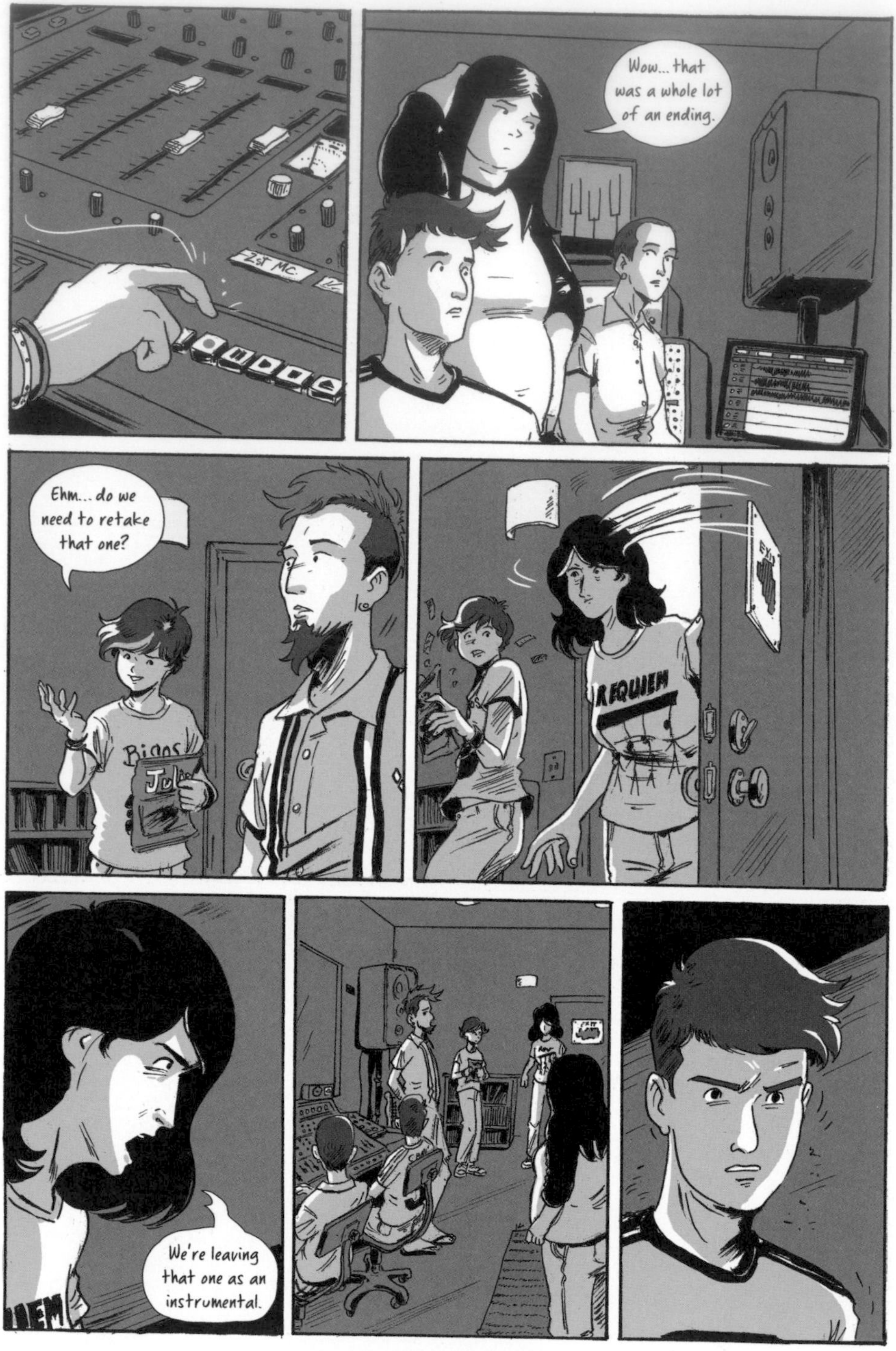

2ST MC.
Wow... that was a whole lot of an ending.
Ehm... do we need to retake that one?
REQUIEM
We're leaving that one as an instrumental.

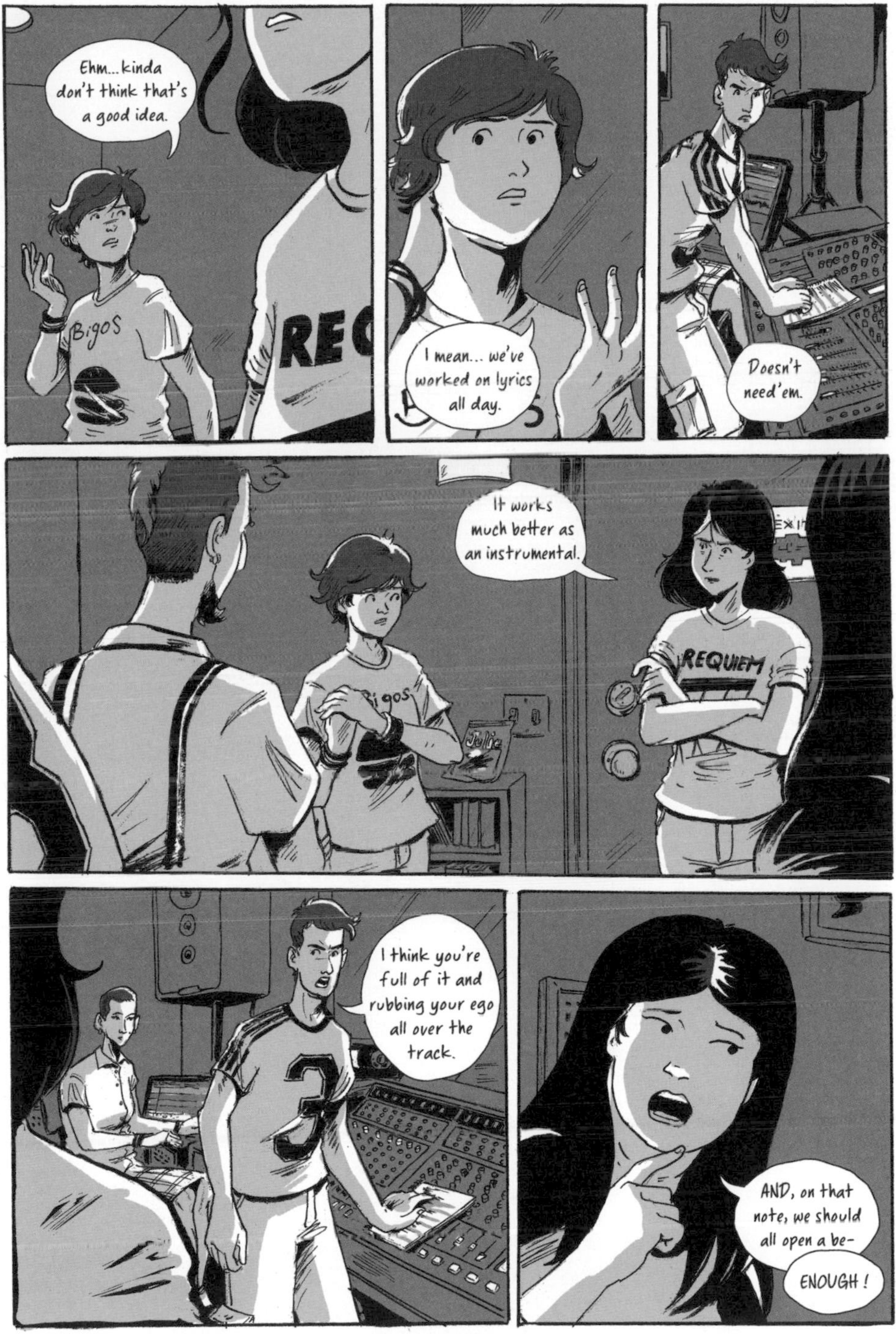
Ehm...kinda don't think that's a good idea.
REQ
Bigos
I mean... we've worked on lyrics all day.
Doesn't need'em.
It works much better as an instrumental.
REQUIEM
Bigos
I think you're full of it and rubbing your ego all over the track.
AND, on that note, we should all open a be-
ENOUGH!

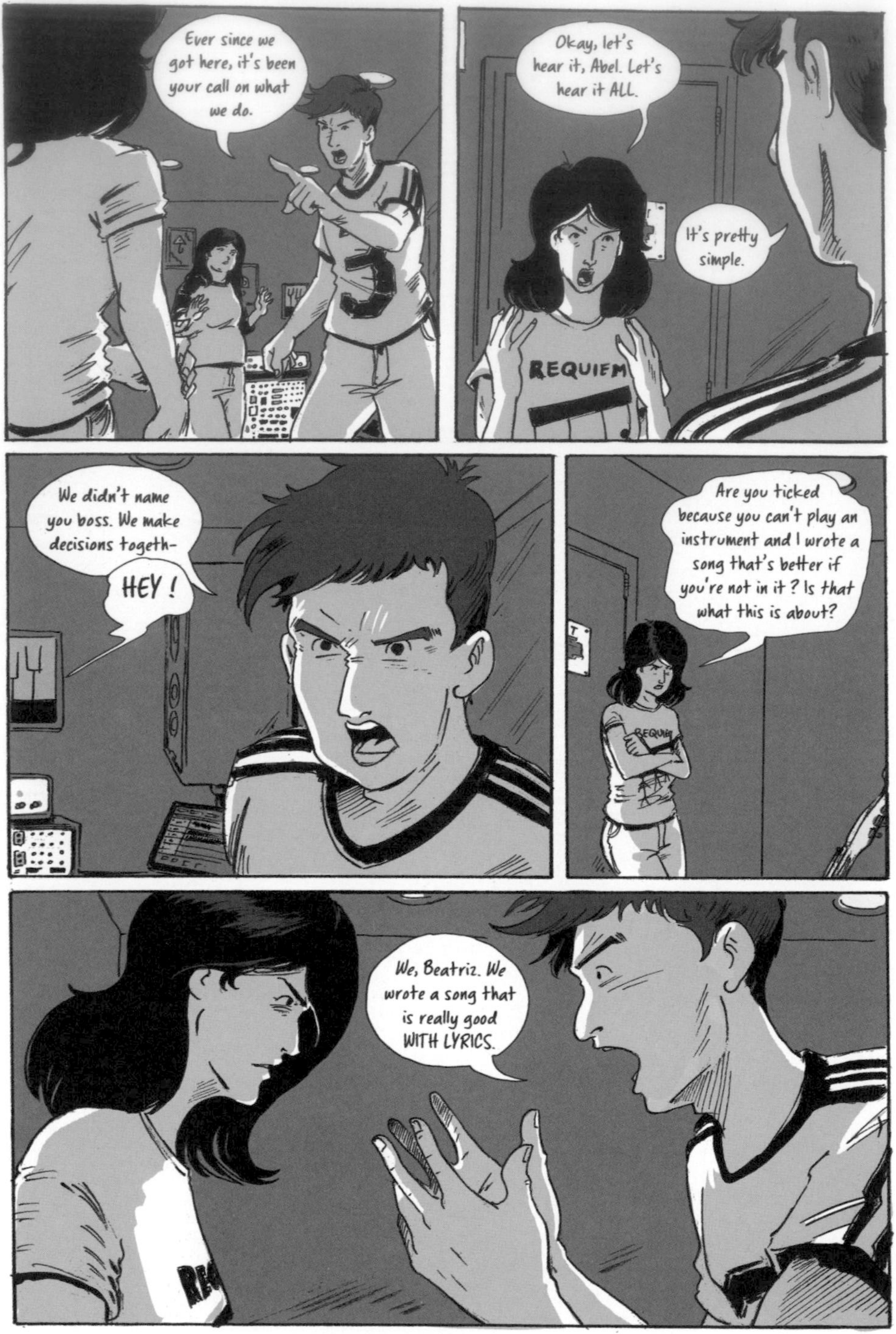
Ever since we got here, it's been your call on what we do.
Okay, let's hear it, Abel. Let's hear it ALL.
It's pretty simple.
REQUIEM
We didn't name you boss. We make decisions togeth-
HEY!
Are you ticked because you can't play an instrument and I wrote a song that's better if you're not in it? Is that what this is about?
We, Beatriz. We wrote a song that is really good WITH LYRICS.

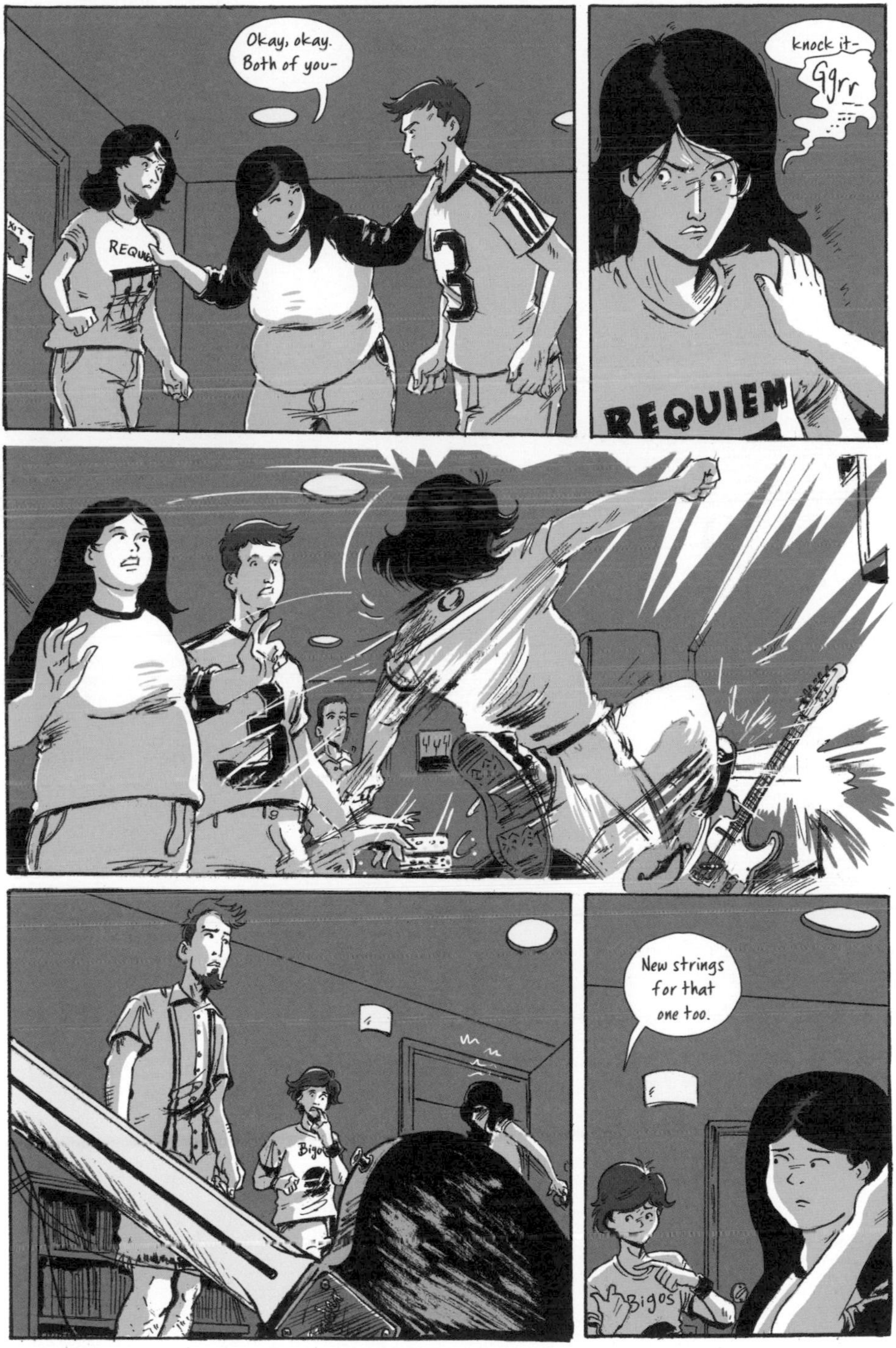
Okay, okay. Both of you-
knock it-
Ggrr
REQUIEM
New strings for that one too.
Bigos

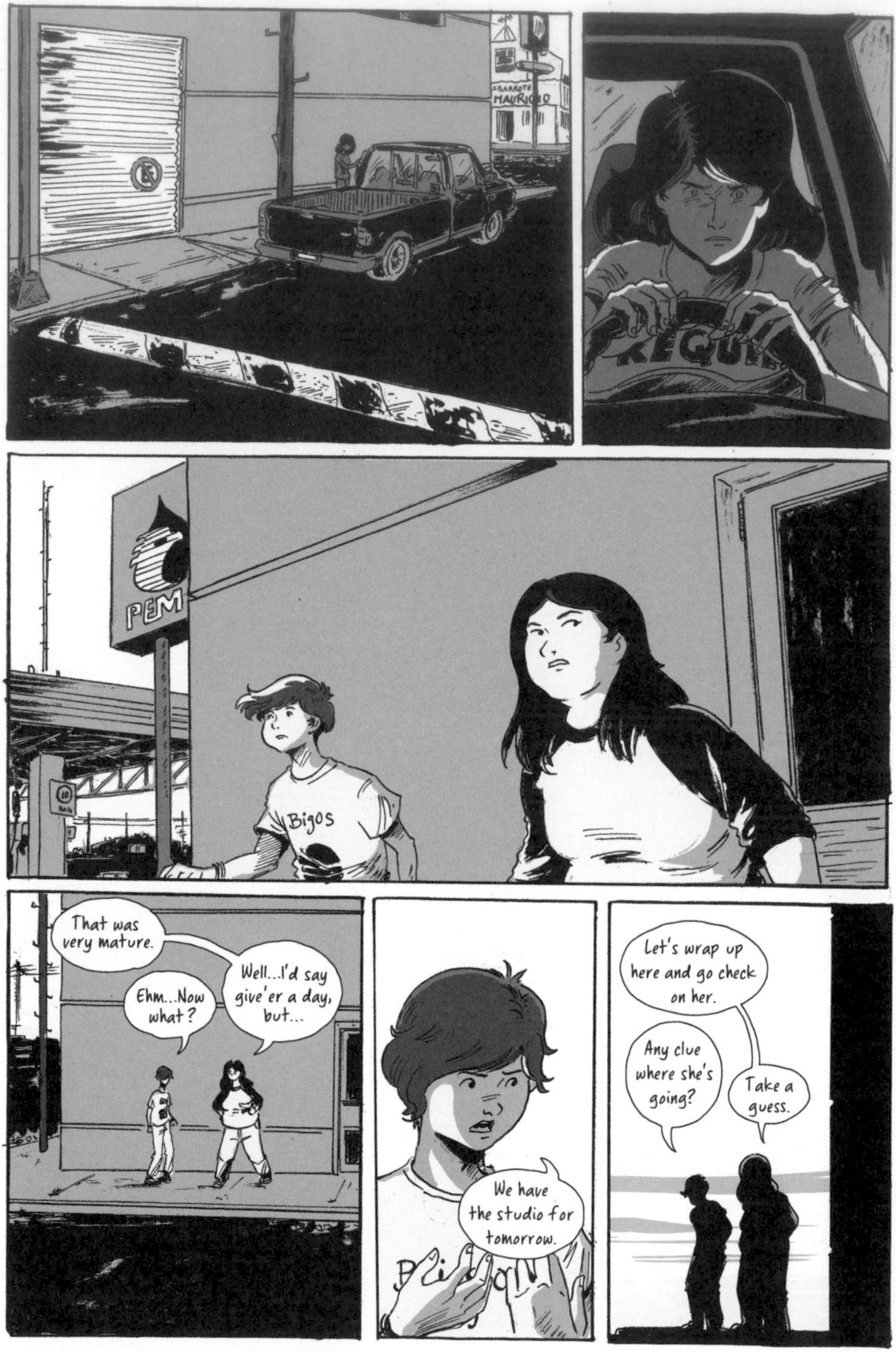
ABARROTES
MAURICIO
PREQUE
PEM
Bigos
That was very mature.
Ehm...Now what?
Well...I'd say give'er a day, but...
We have the studio for tomorrow.
Let's wrap up here and go check on her.
Any clue where she's going?
Take a guess.

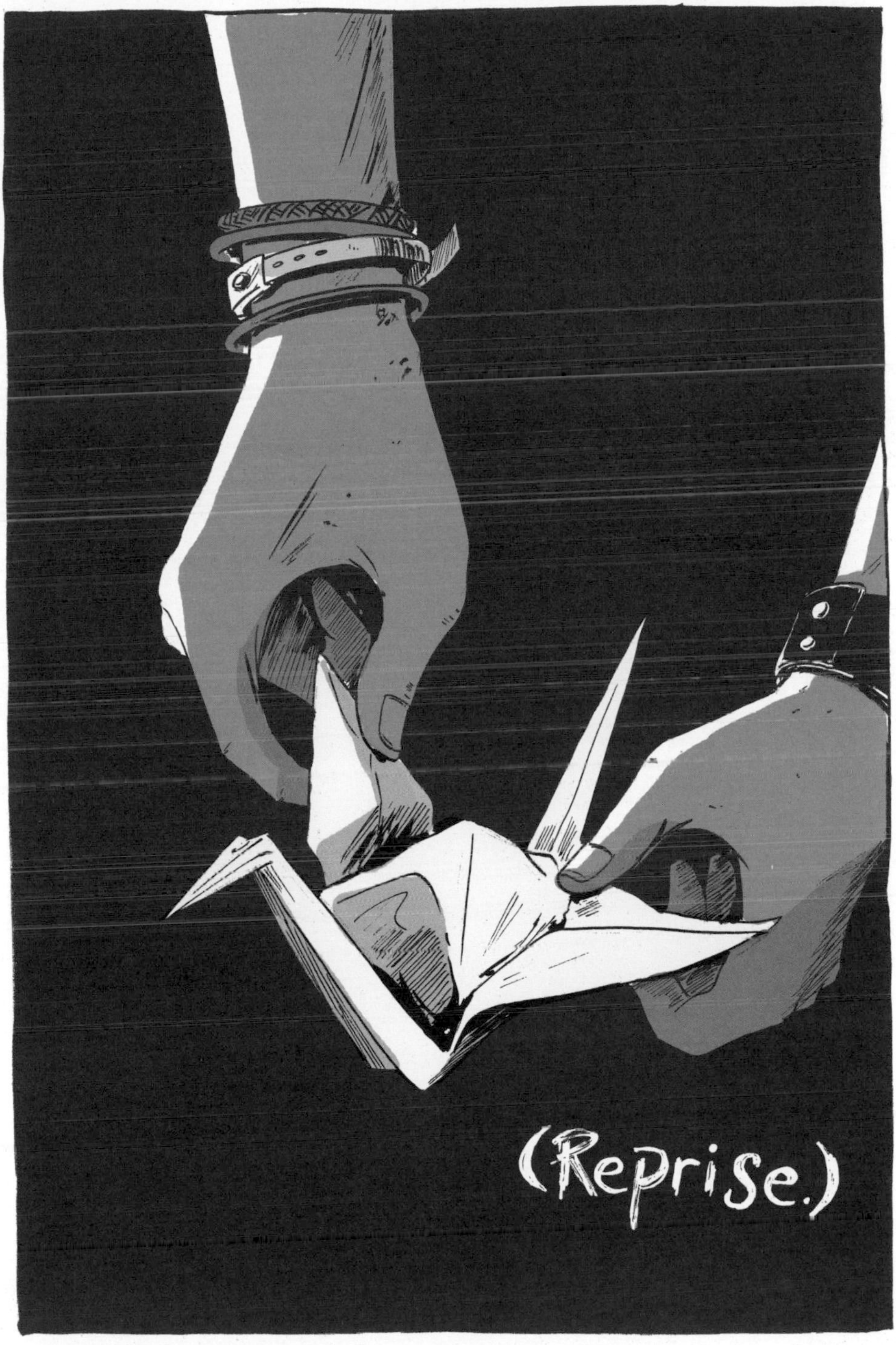
(Reprise.)

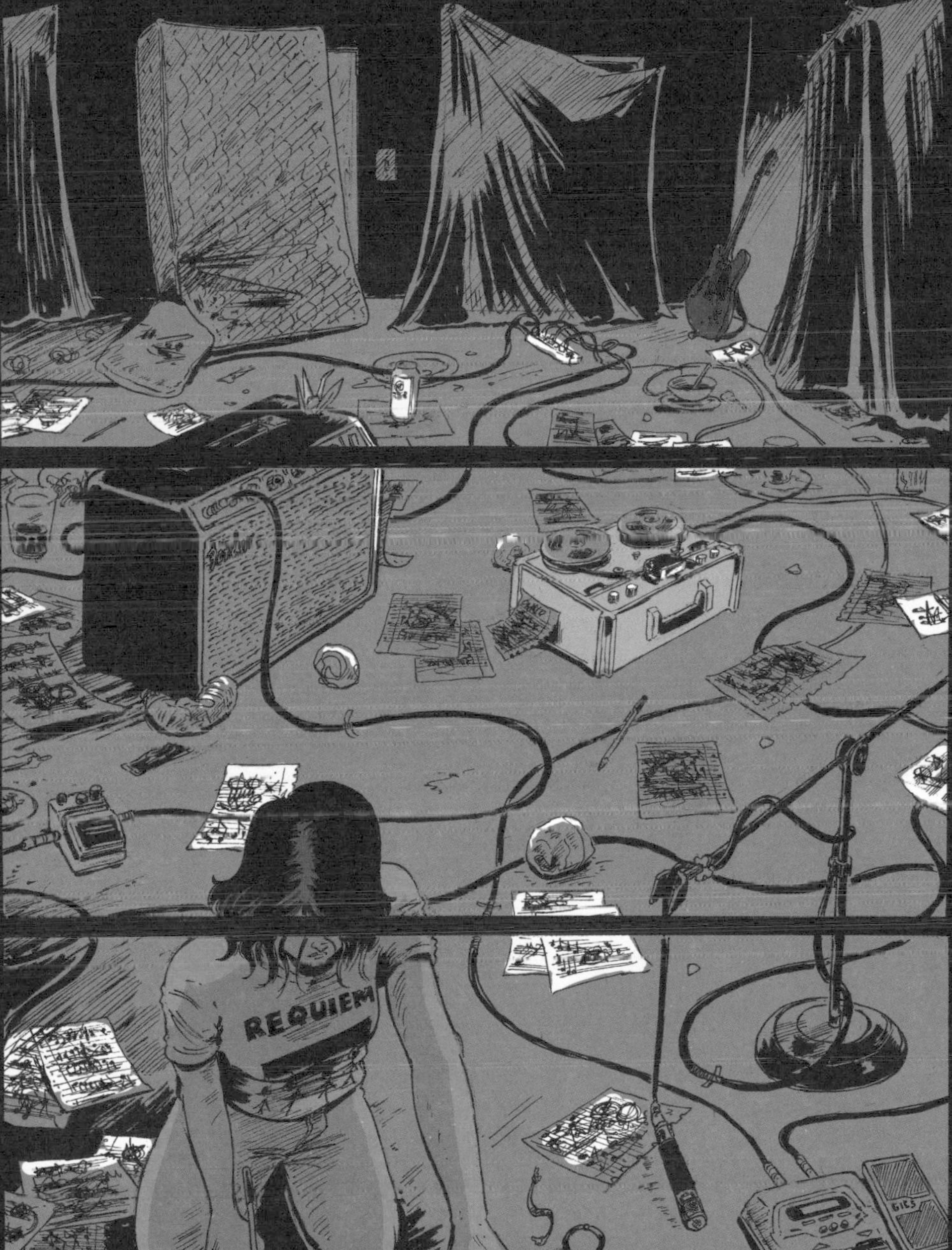
REQUIEM

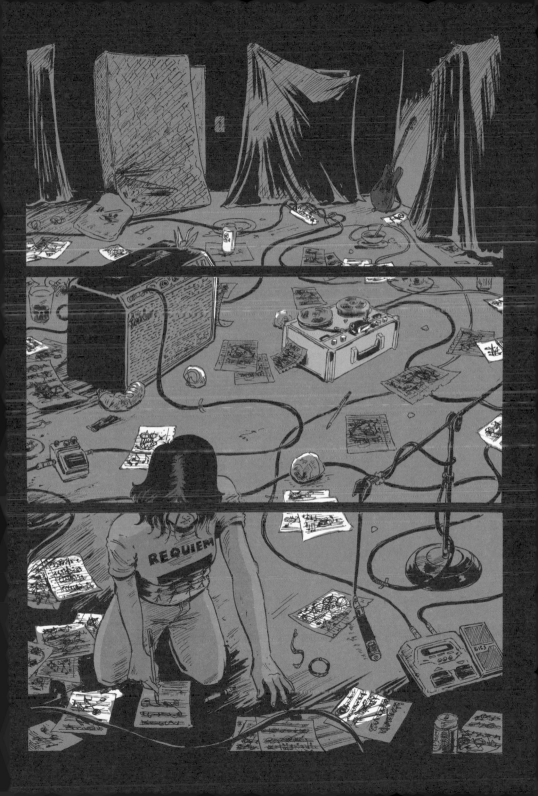

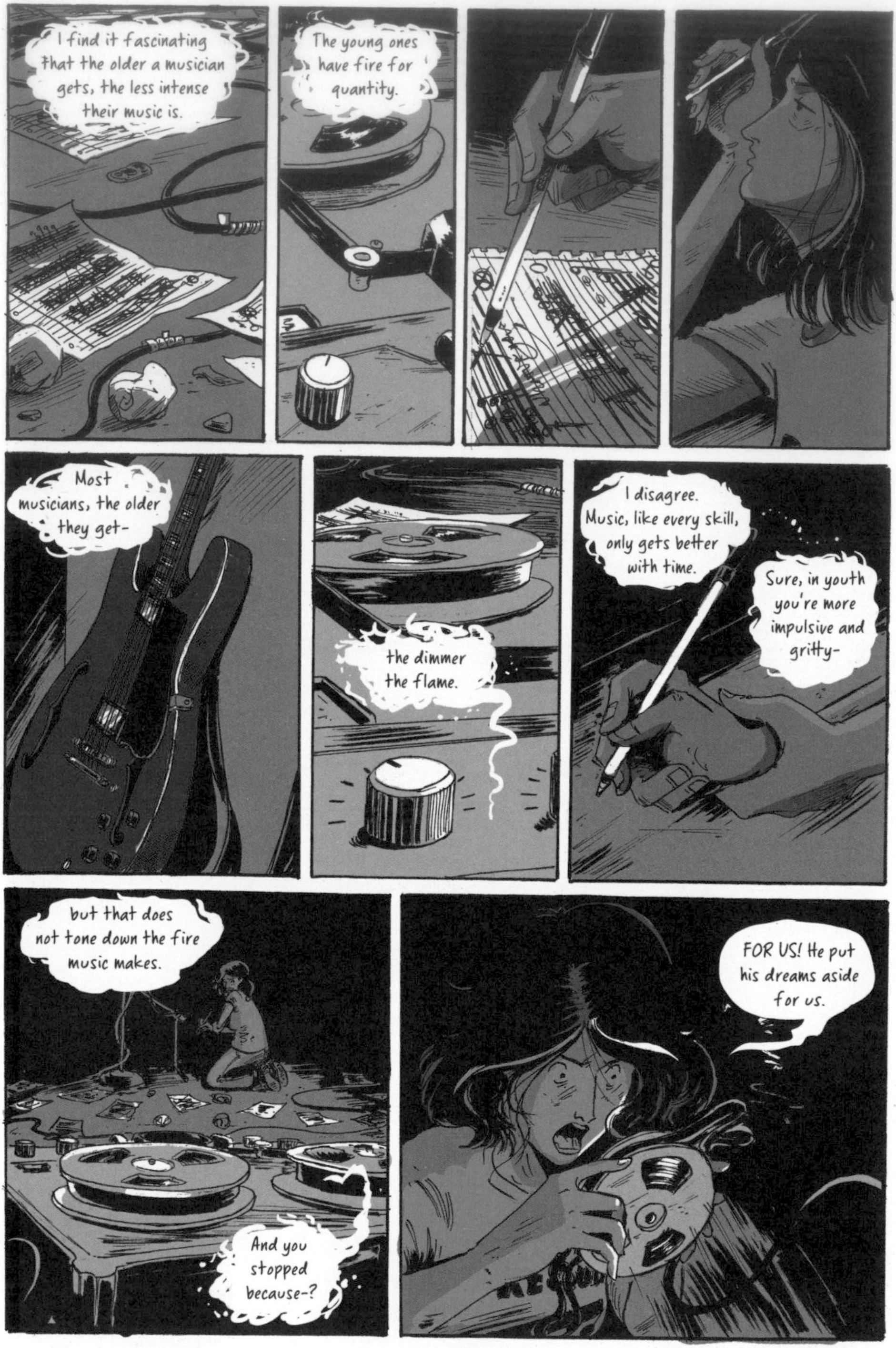
I find it fascinating that the older a musician gets, the less intense their music is.
The young ones have fire for quantity.
Most musicians, the older they get-
the dimmer the flame.
I disagree. Music, like every skill, only gets better with time.
Sure, in youth you're more impulsive and gritty-
but that does not tone down the fire music makes.
And you stopped because-?
FOR US! He put his dreams aside for us.

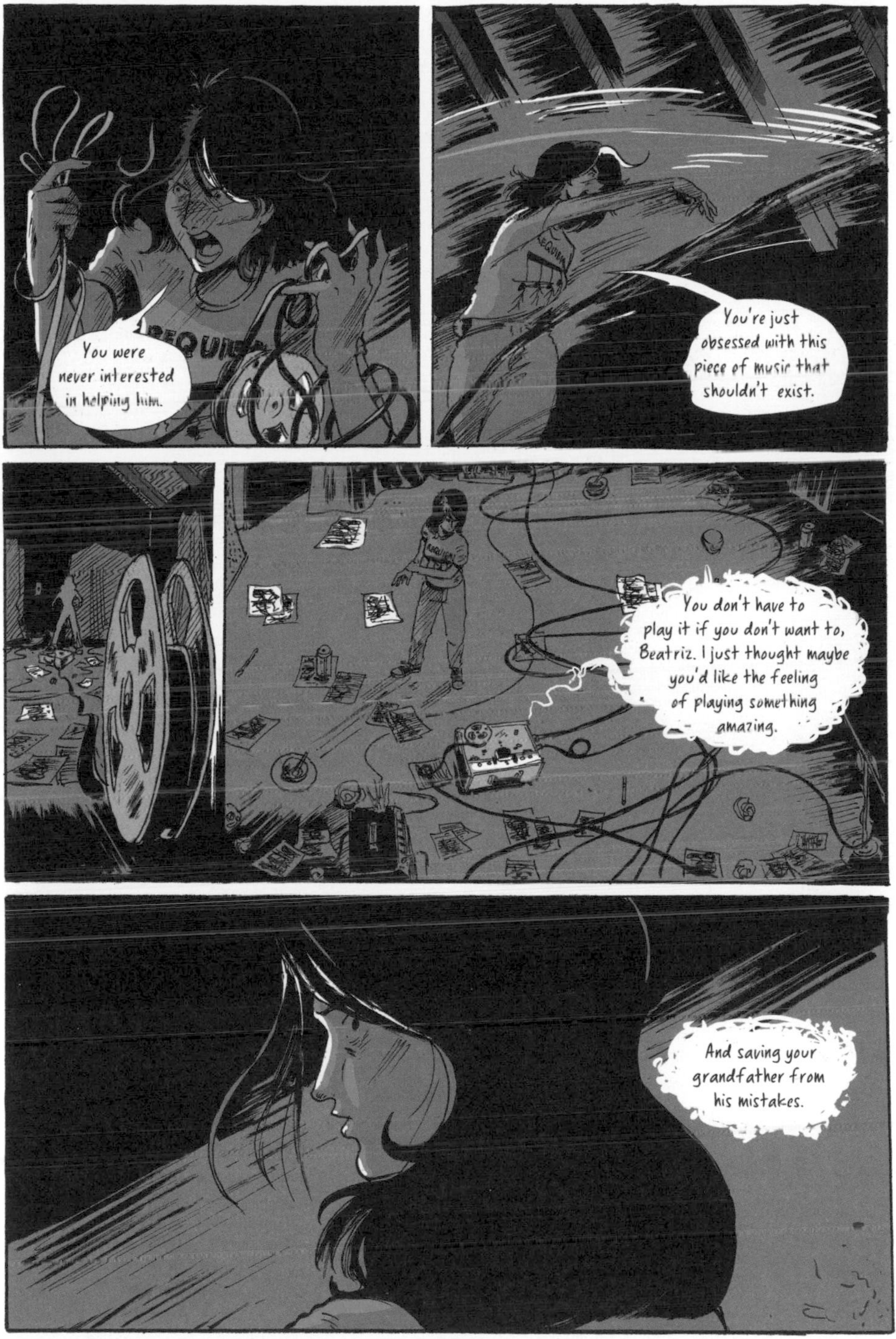
You were never interested in helping him.
You're just obsessed with this piece of music that shouldn't exist.
You don't have to play it if you don't want to, Beatriz. I just thought maybe you'd like the feeling of playing something amazing.
And saving your grandfather from his mistakes.

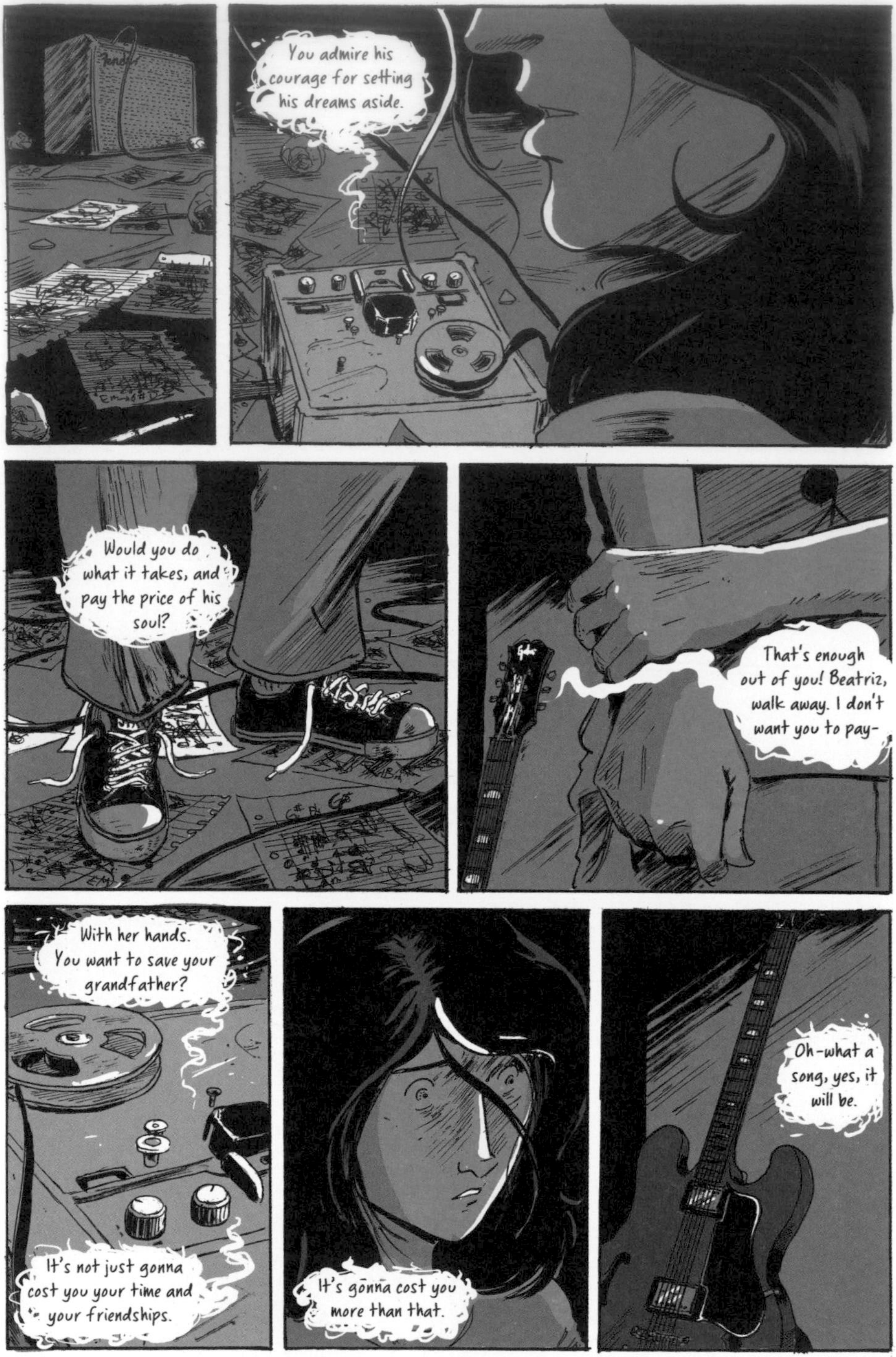
You admire his courage for setting his dreams aside.
Would you do what it takes, and pay the price of his soul?
That's enough out of you! Beatriz, walk away. I don't want you to pay-
With her hands. You want to save your grandfather?
It's not just gonna cost you your time and your friendships.
It's gonna cost you more than that.
Oh-what a song, yes, it will be.

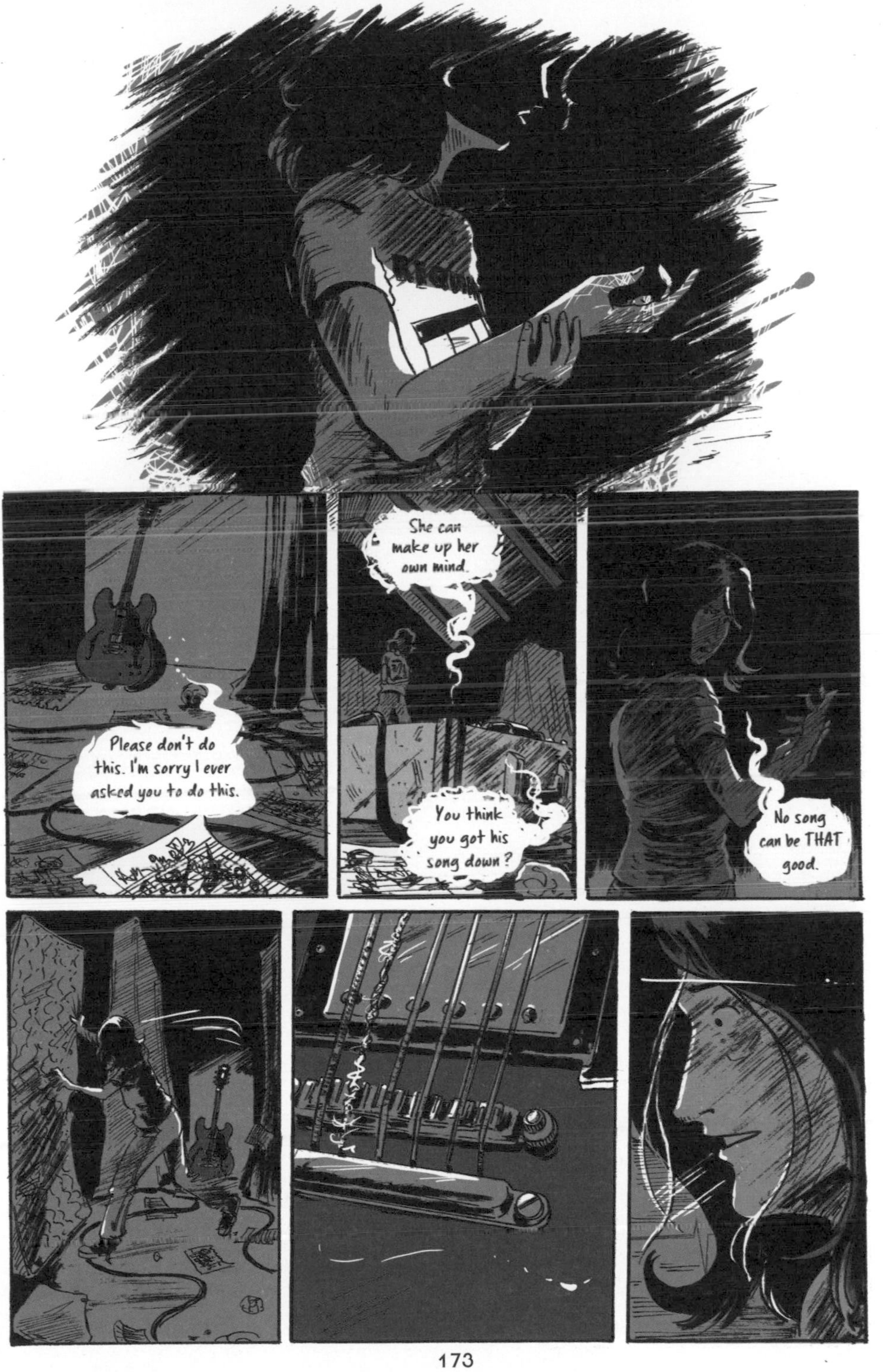
Please don't do this. I'm sorry I ever asked you to do this.
She can make up her own mind.
You think you got his song down?
No song can be THAT good.

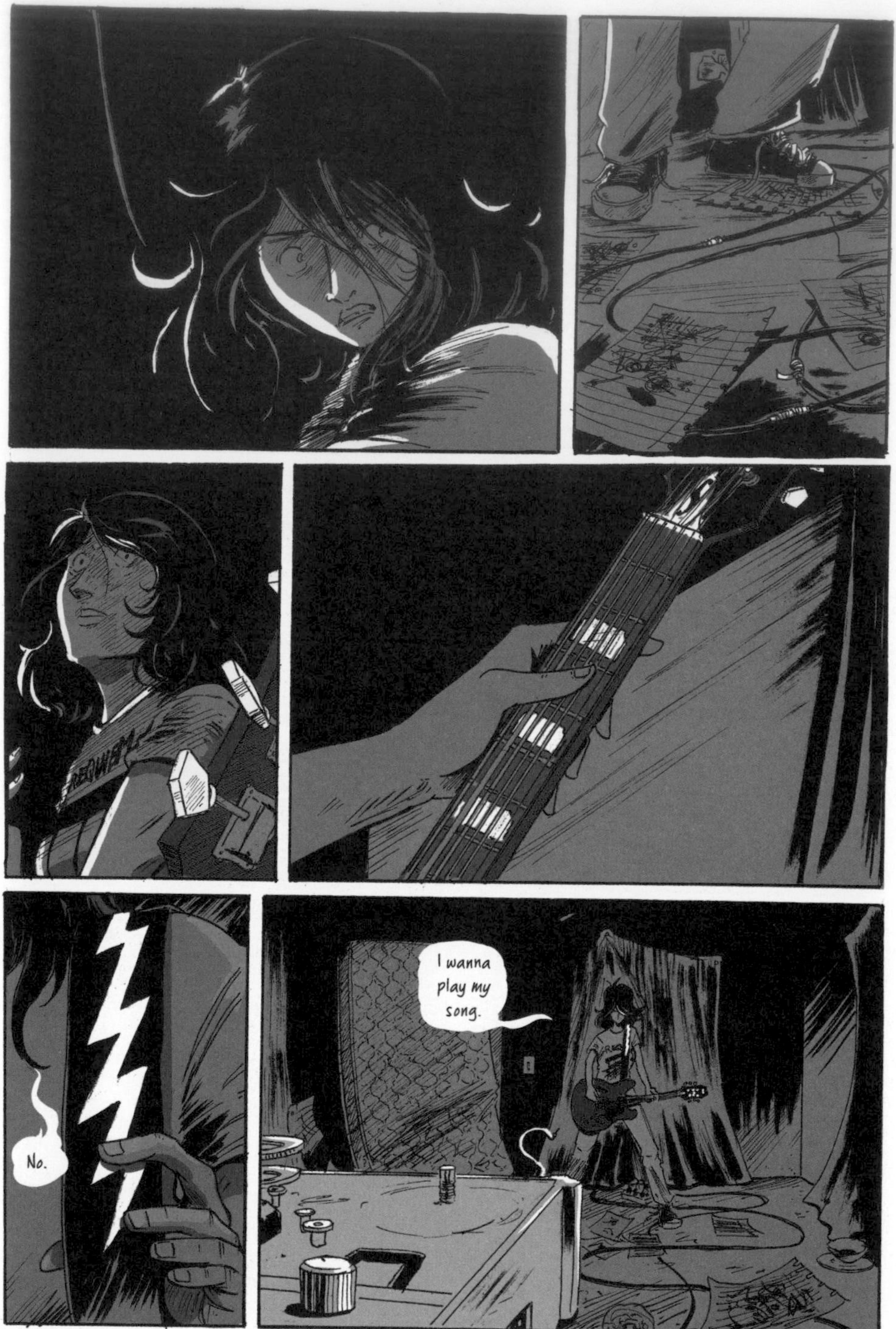
No.
I wanna play my song.

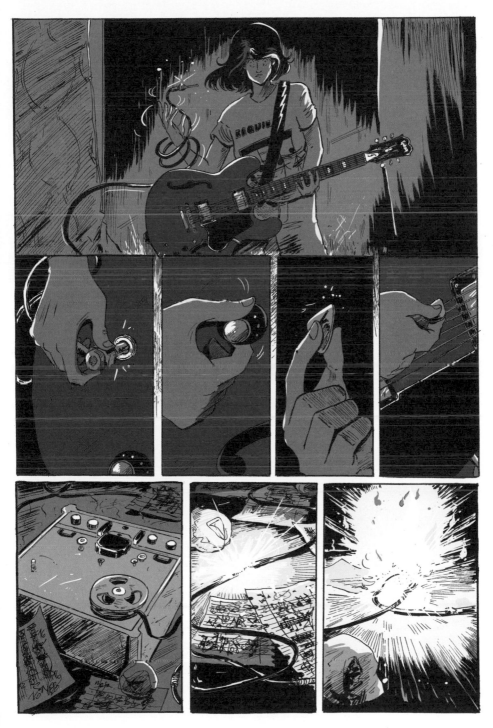

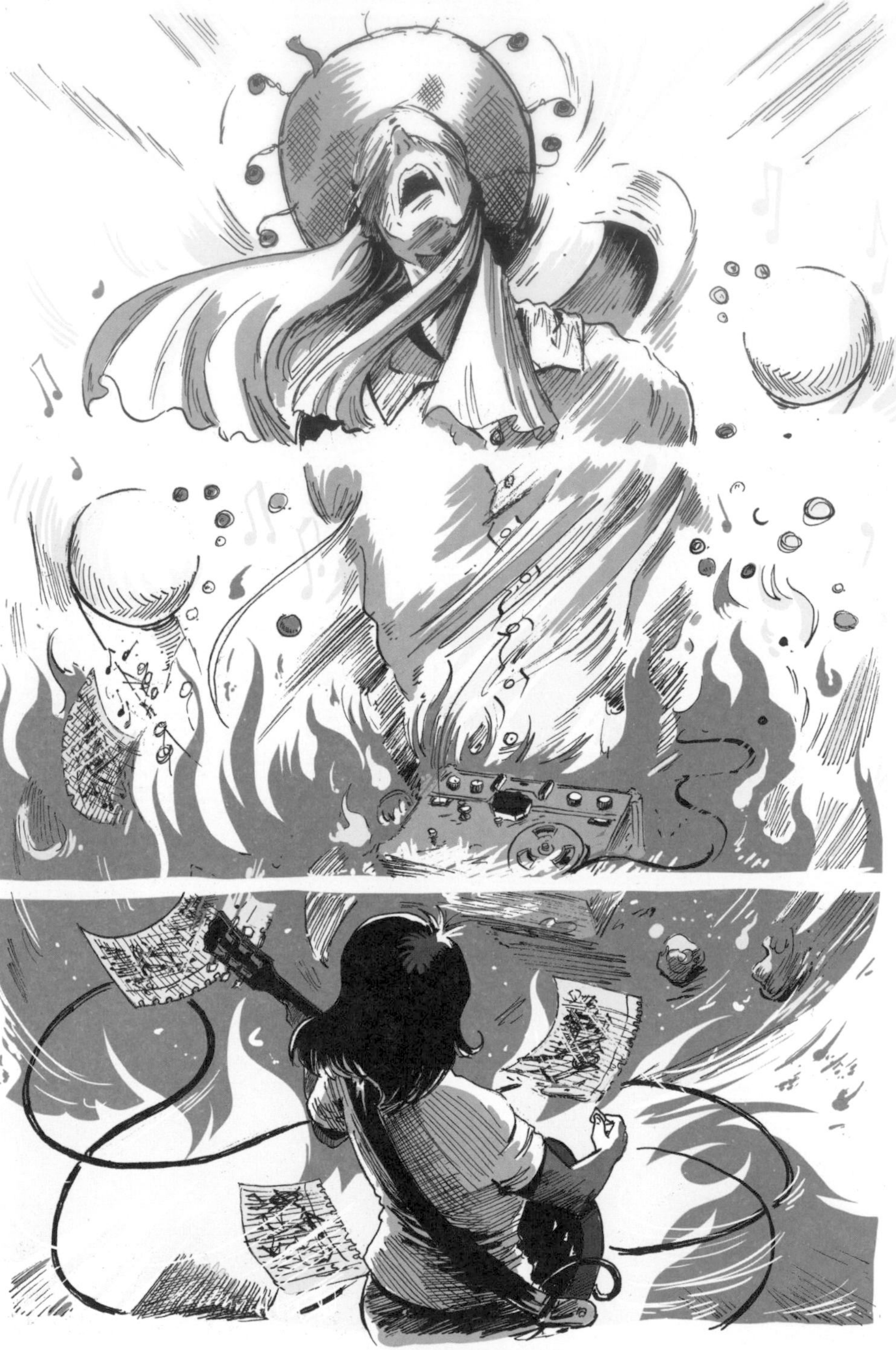

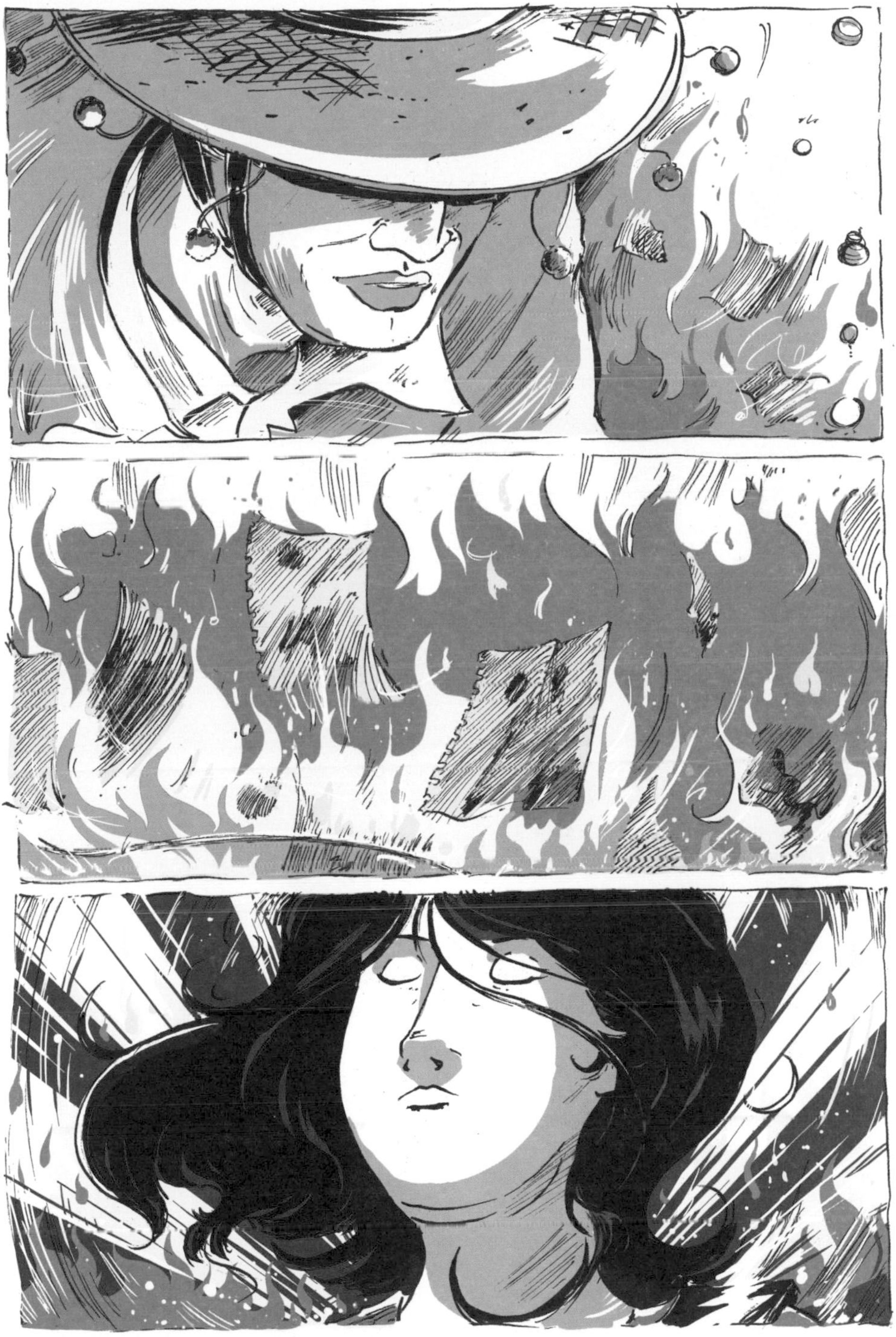

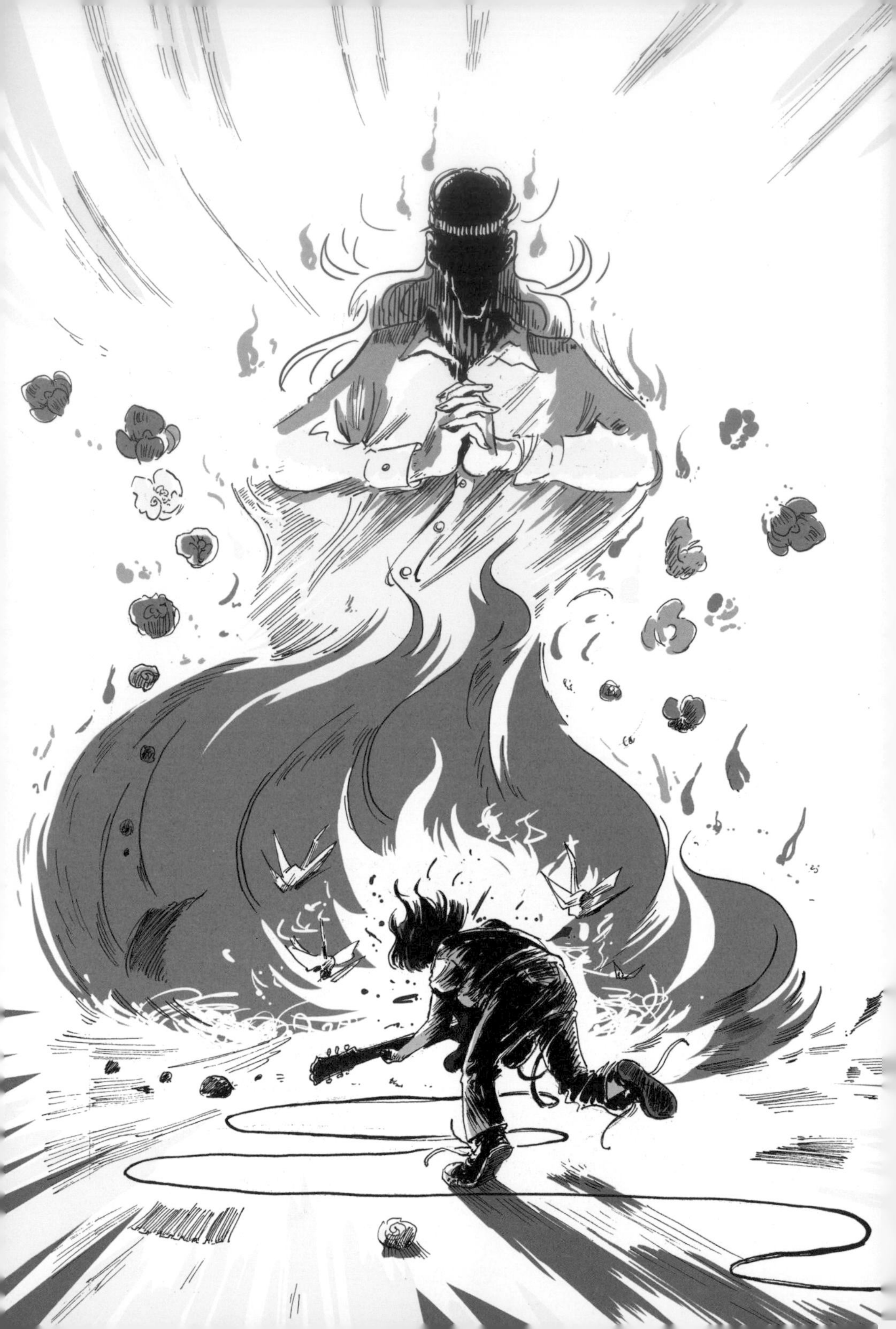

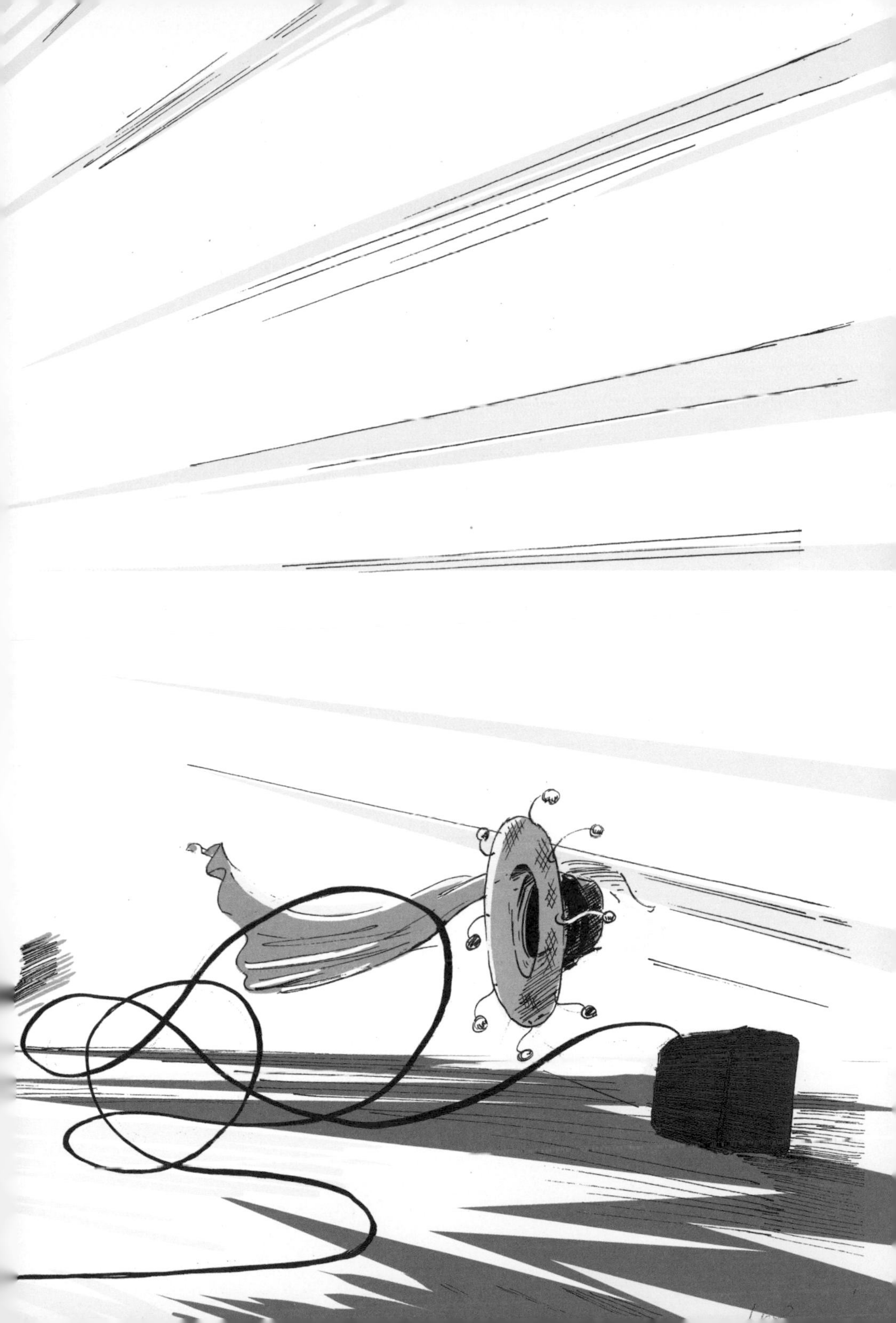

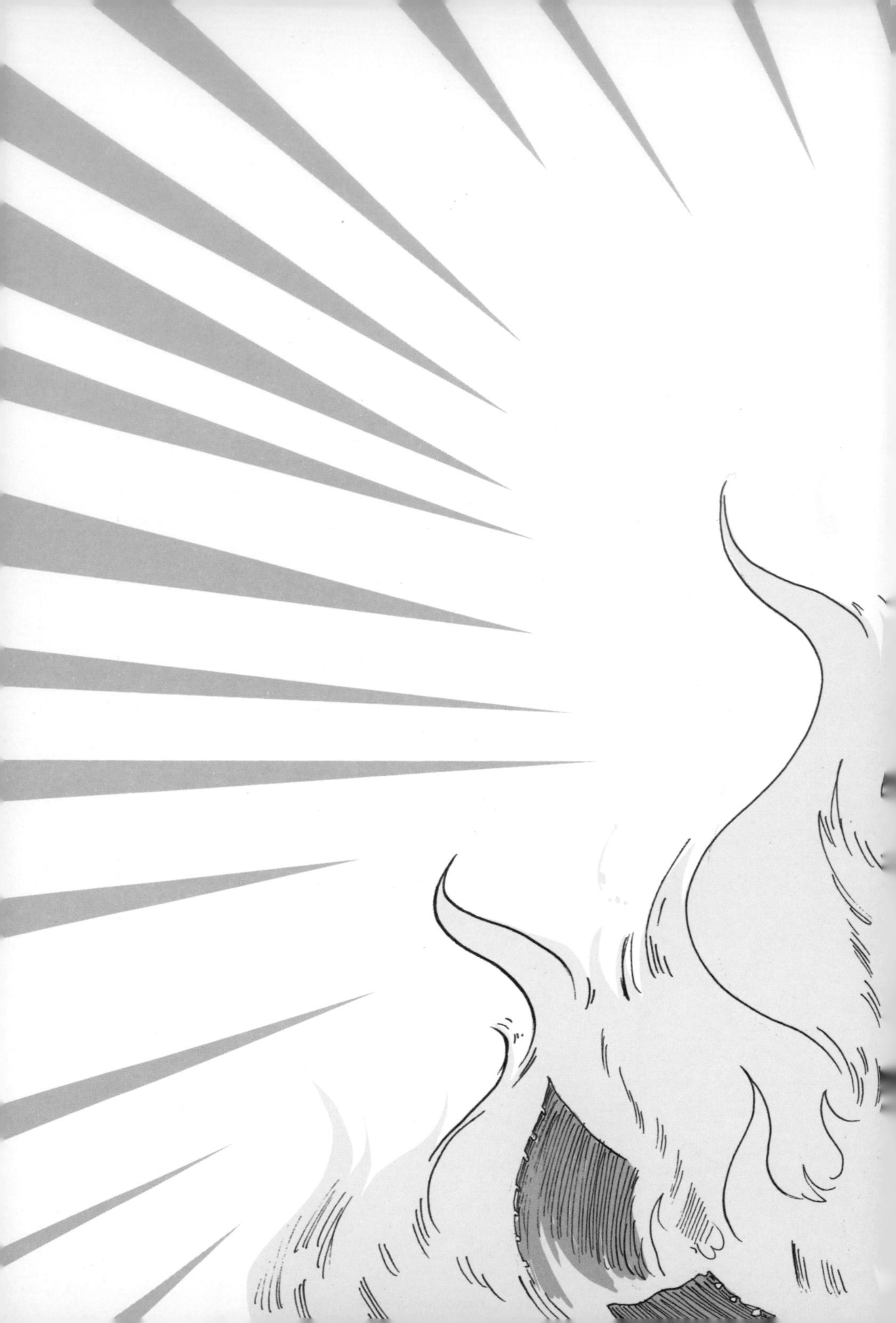

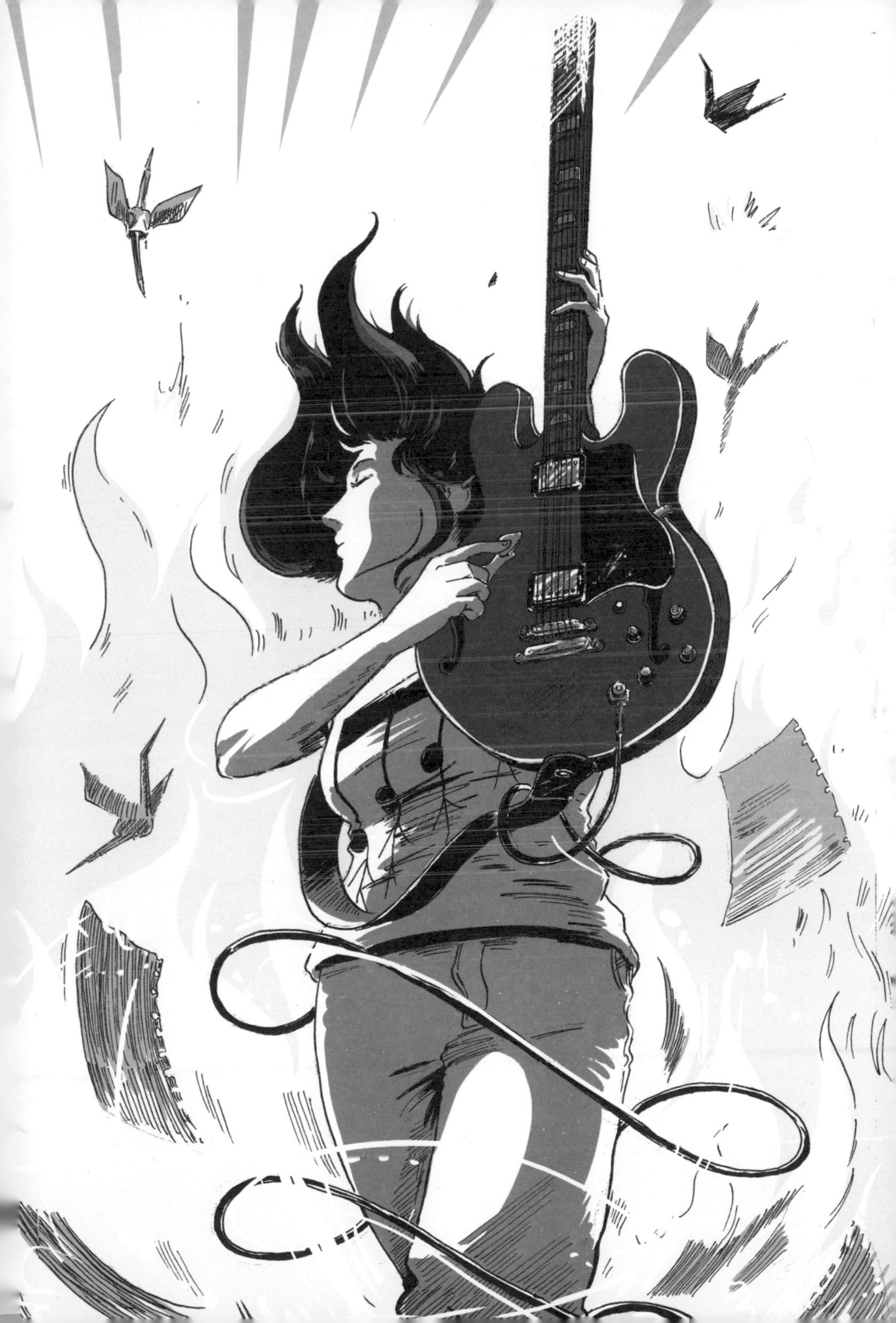

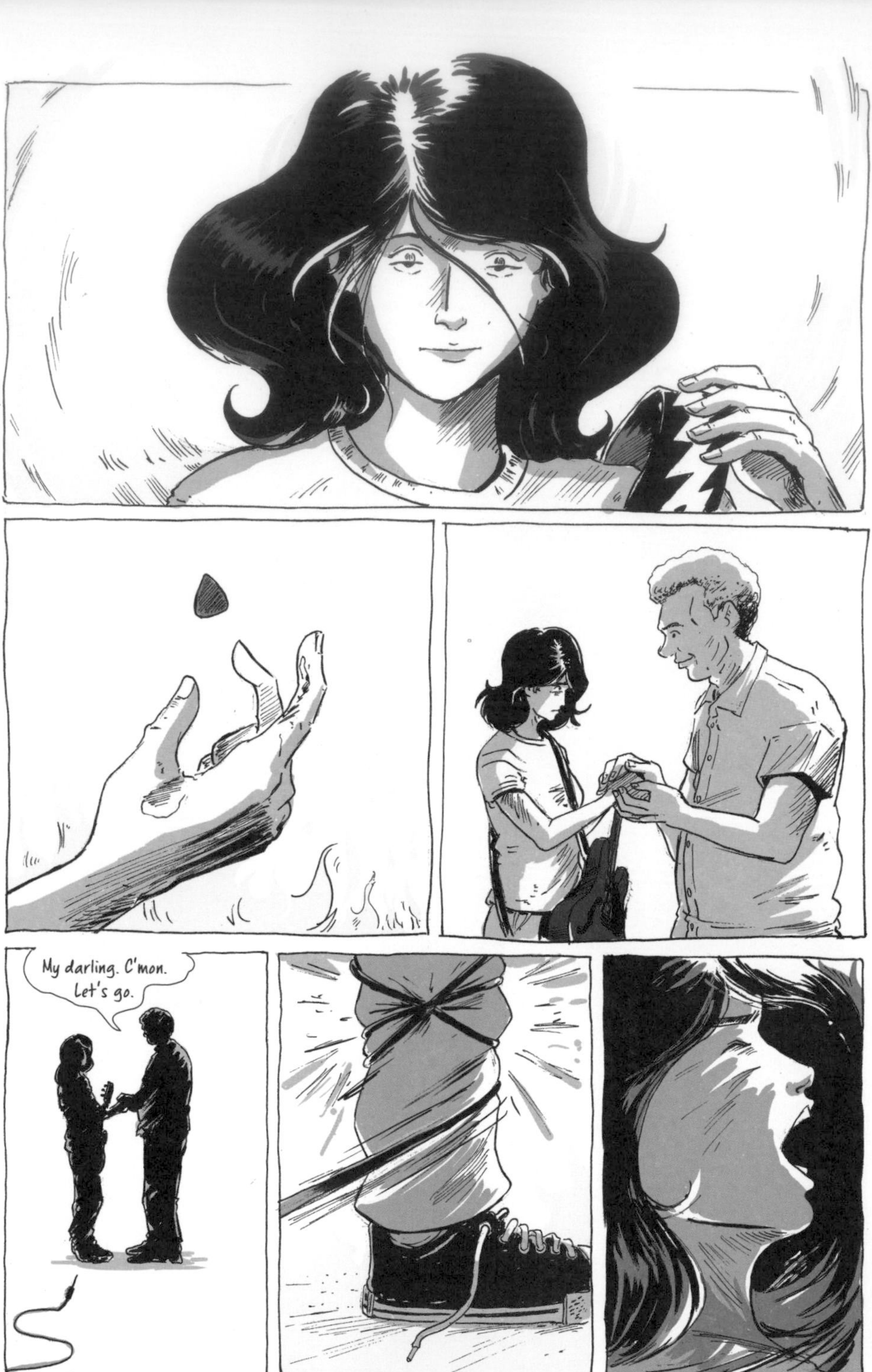
My darling. C'mon. Let's go.

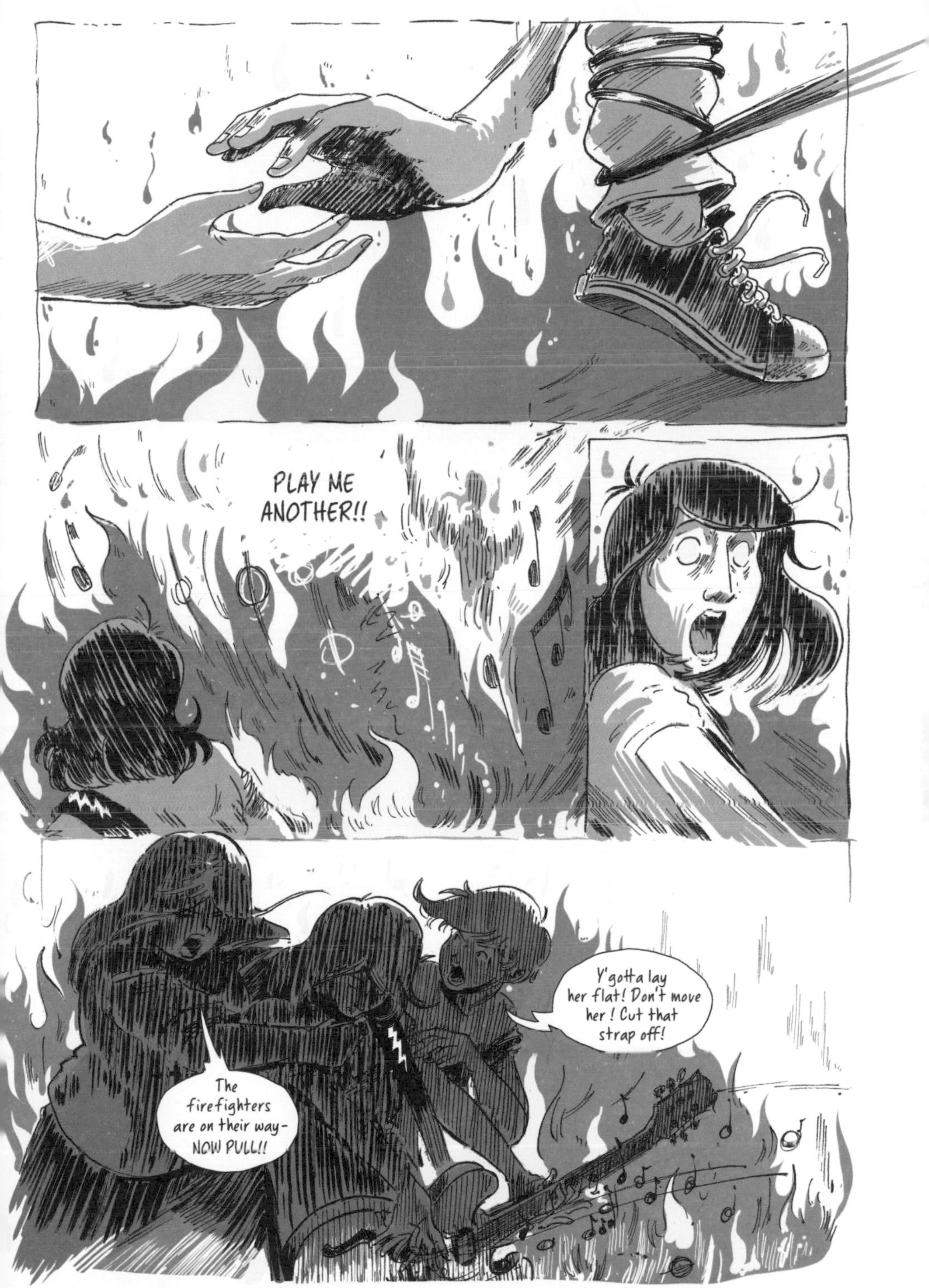
PLAY ME ANOTHER!!
Y'gotta lay her flat! Don't move her! Cut that strap off!
The firefighters are on their way- NOW PULL!!

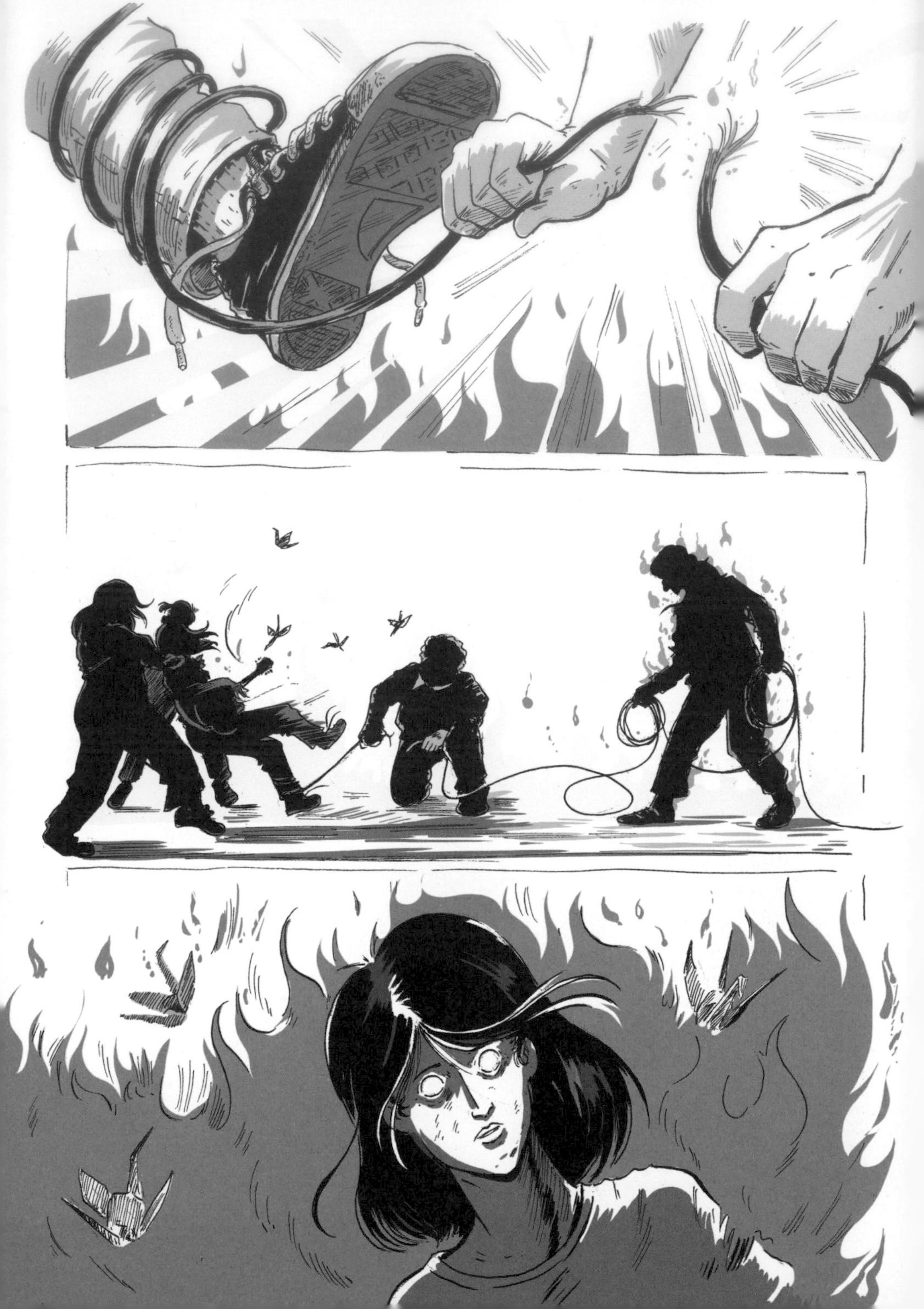

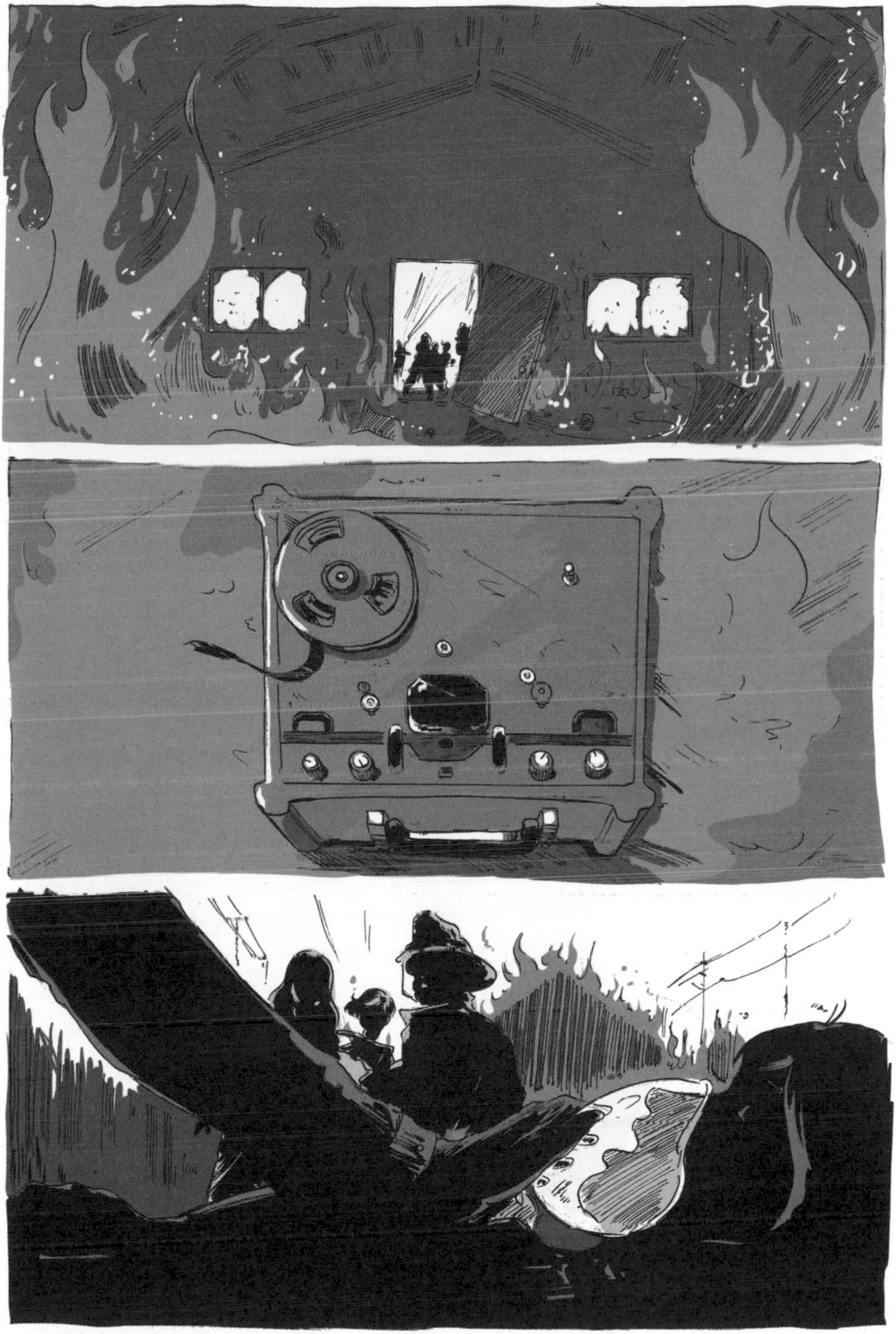

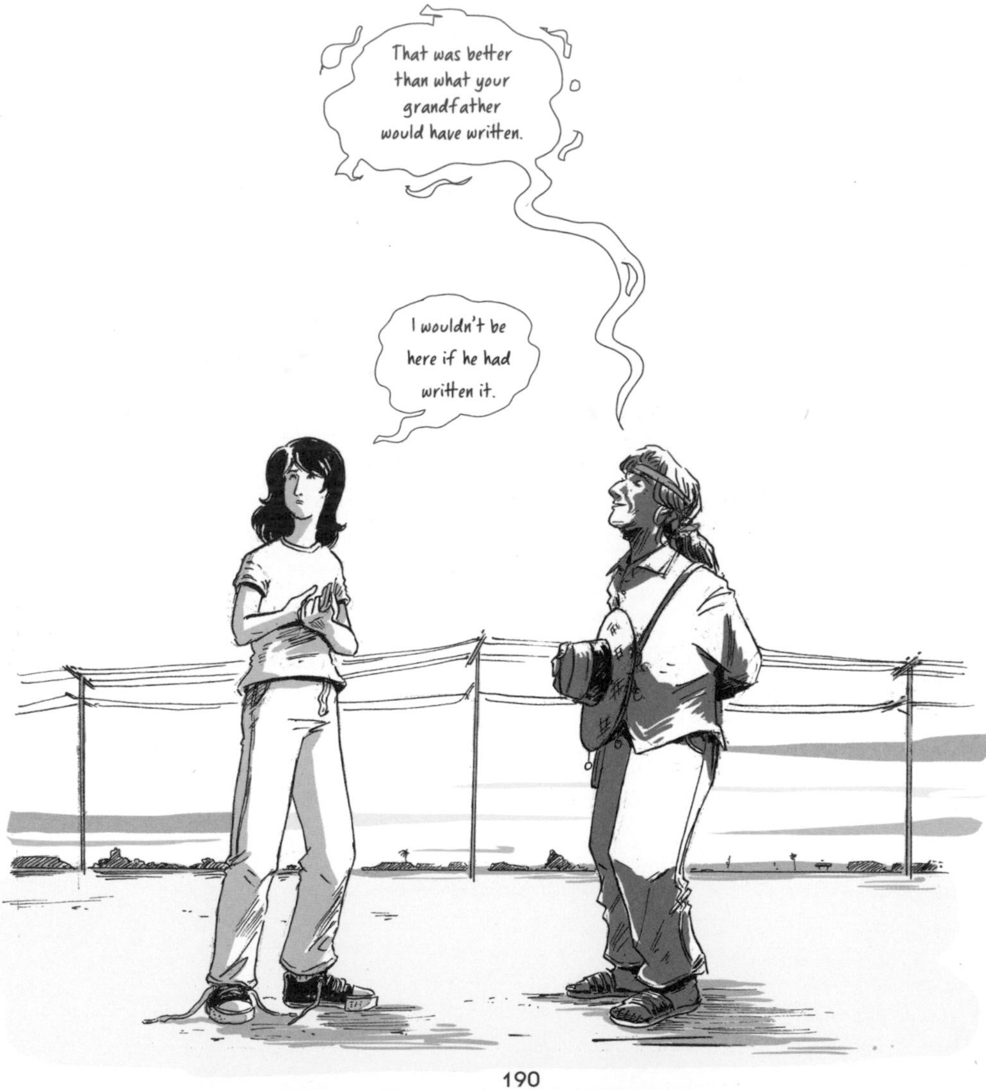
That was better than what your grandfather would have written.
I wouldn't be here if he had written it.

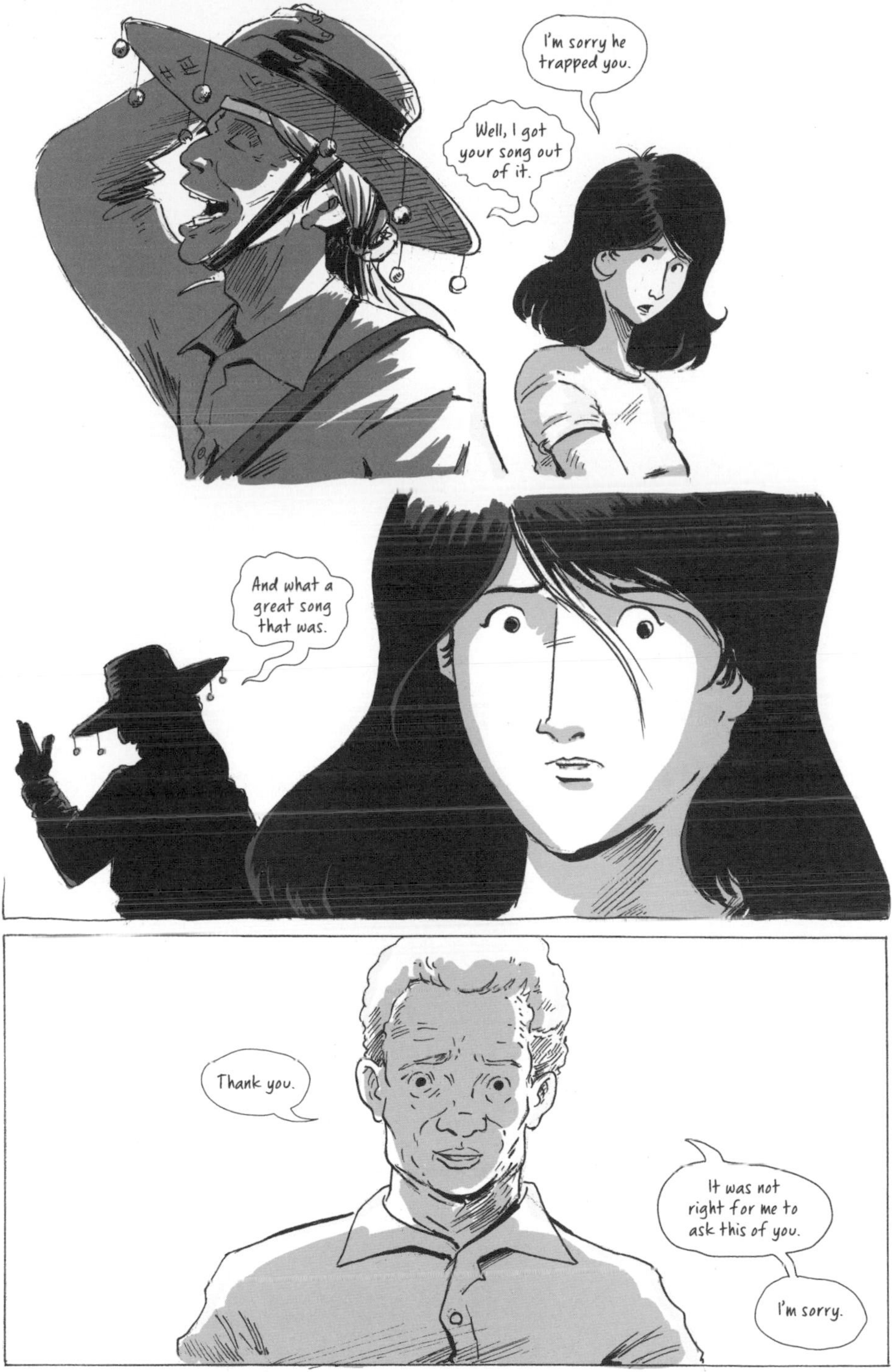
I'm sorry he trapped you.
Well, I got your song out of it.
And what a great song that was.
Thank you.
It was not right for me to ask this of you.
I'm sorry.

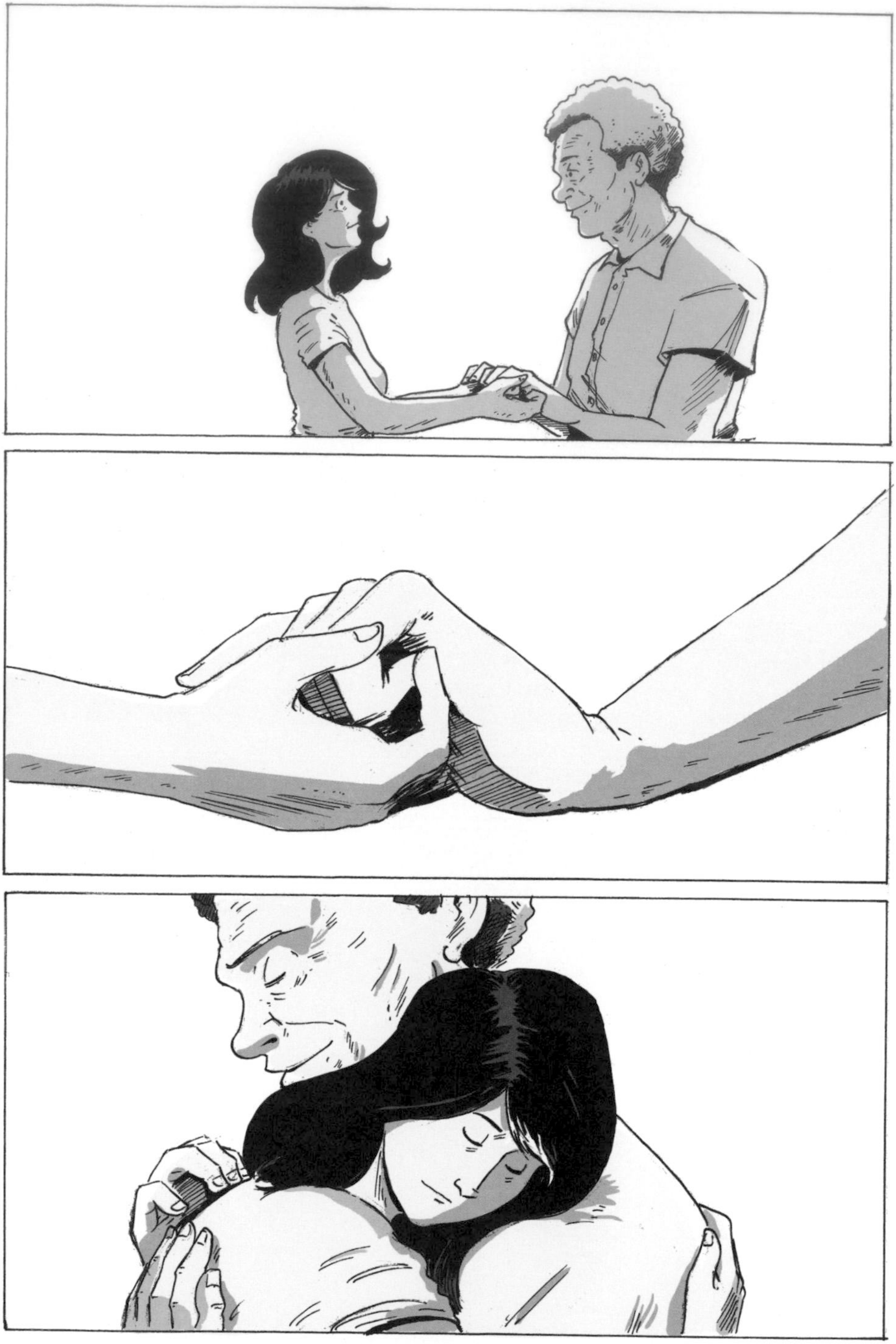

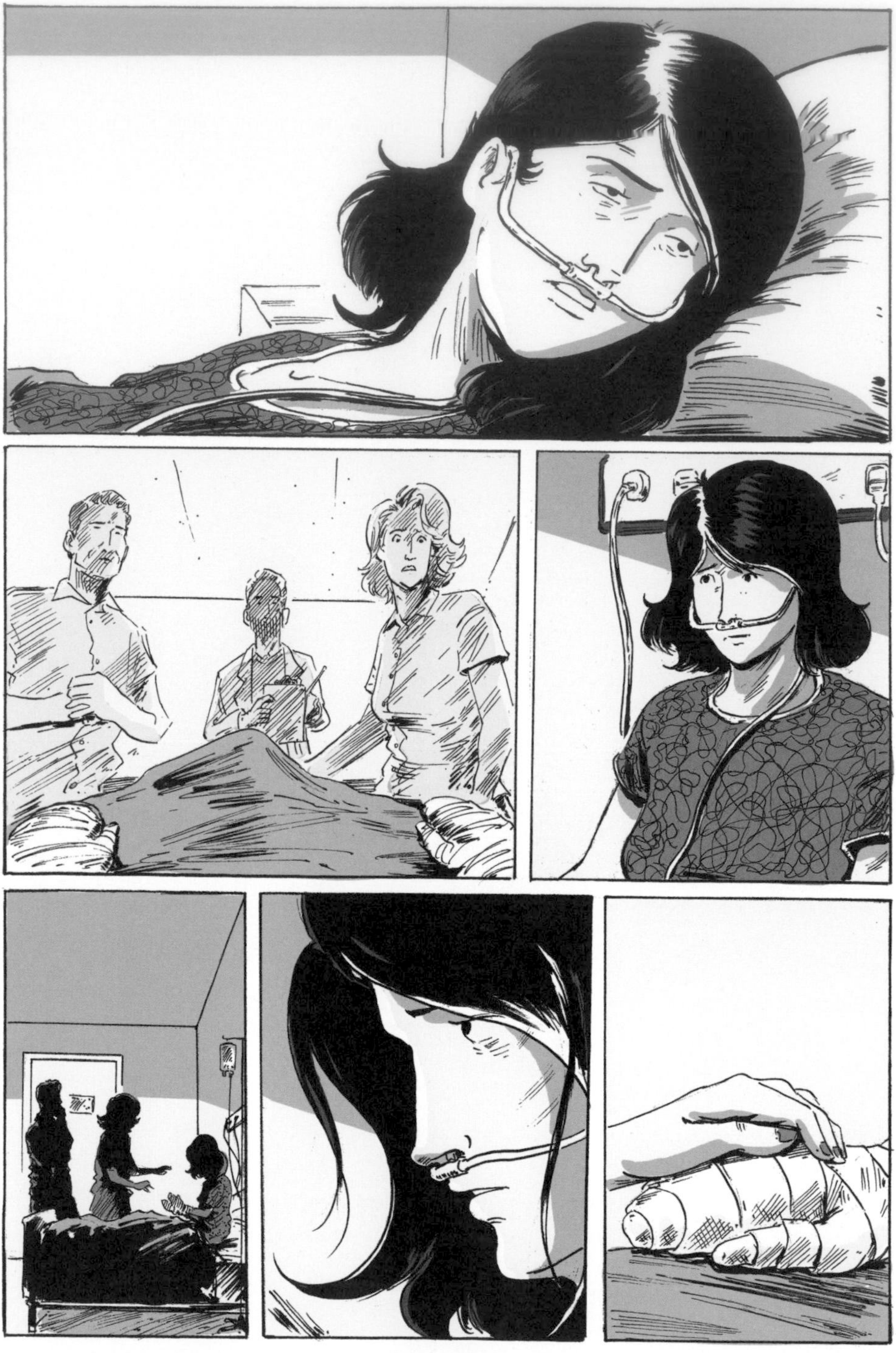

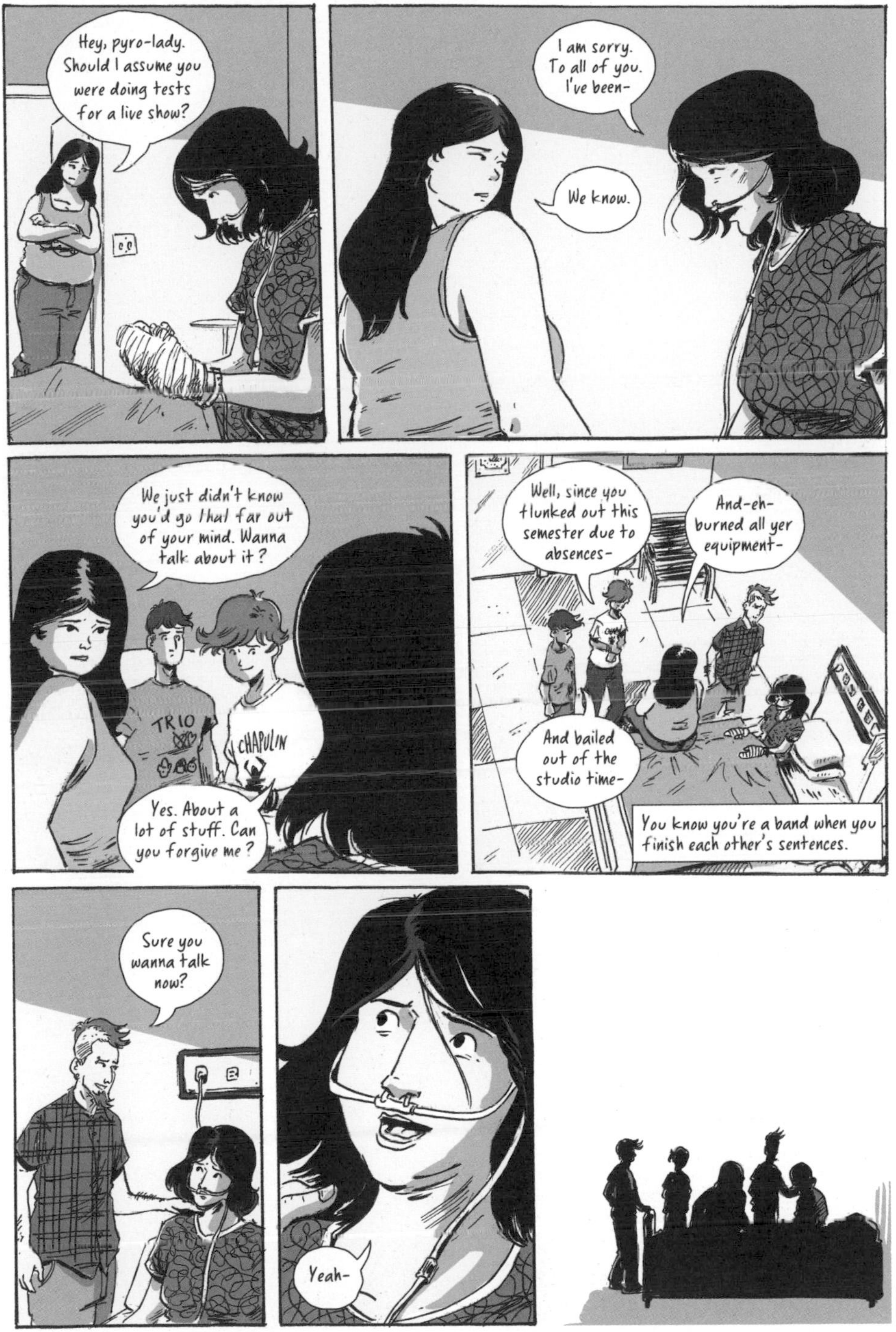
Hey, pyro-lady. Should I assume you were doing tests for a live show?
I am sorry. To all of you. I've been-
We know.
We just didn't know you'd go that far out of your mind. Wanna talk about it?
TRIO
CHAPULIN
Yes. About a lot of stuff. Can you forgive me?
Well, since you flunked out this semester due to absences-
And-eh- burned all yer equipment-
And bailed out of the studio time-
You know you're a band when you finish each other's sentences.
Sure you wanna talk now?
Yeah-

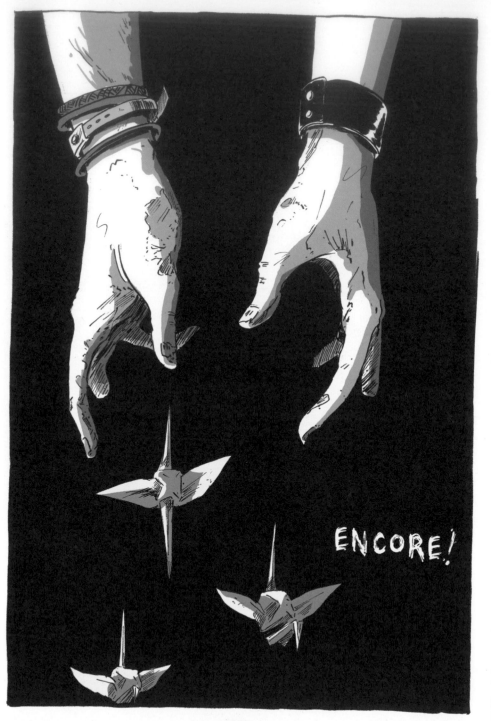

ENCORE!

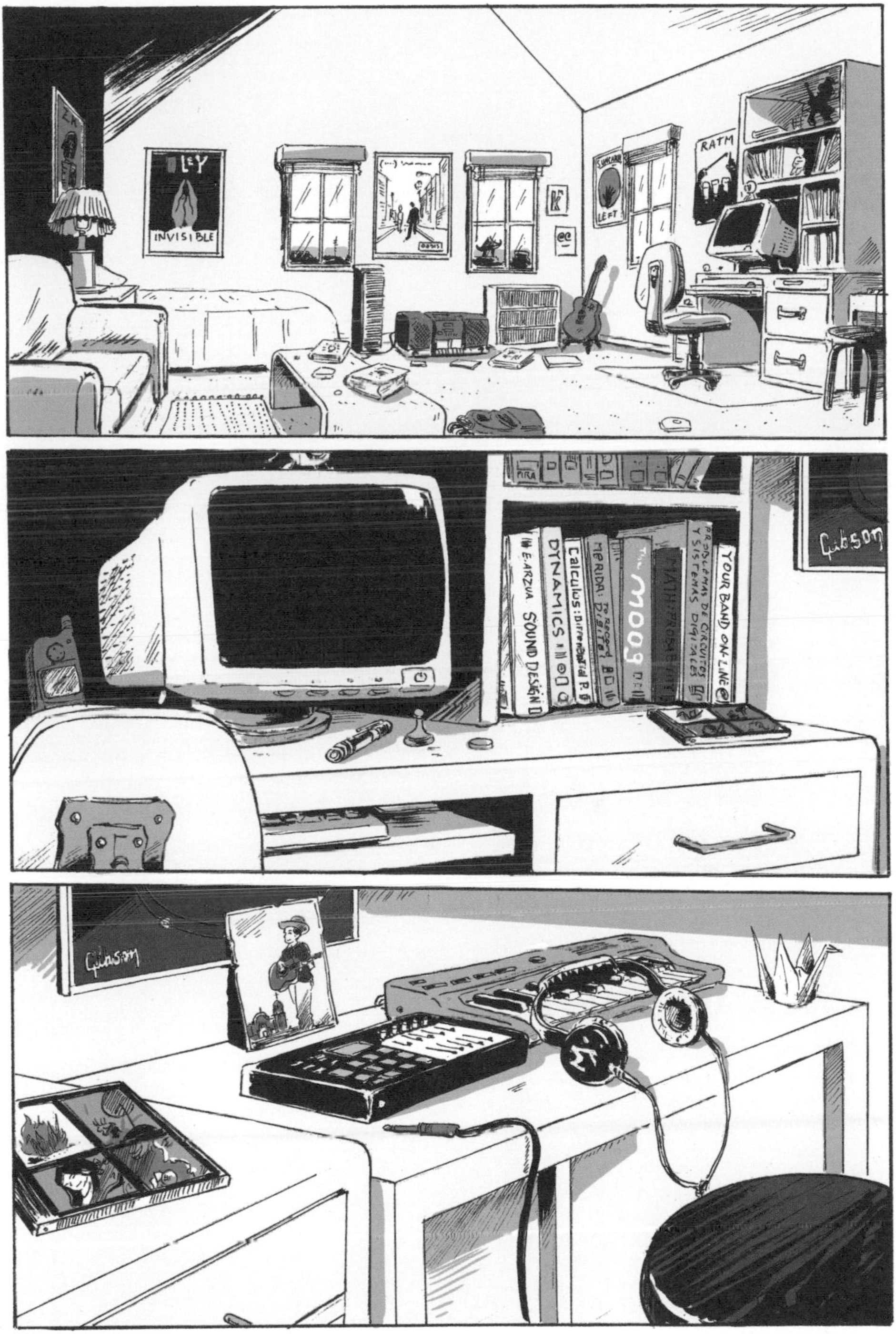
LEY
INVISIBLE
RATM
LEFT
E-ARZUA SOUND DESIGN
DYNAMICS
MERIDA: To Record Digital
Moog
PROBLEMAS DE CIRCUITOS Y SISTEMAS DIGITALES
YOUR BAND ON-LINE
Gibson
Gibson

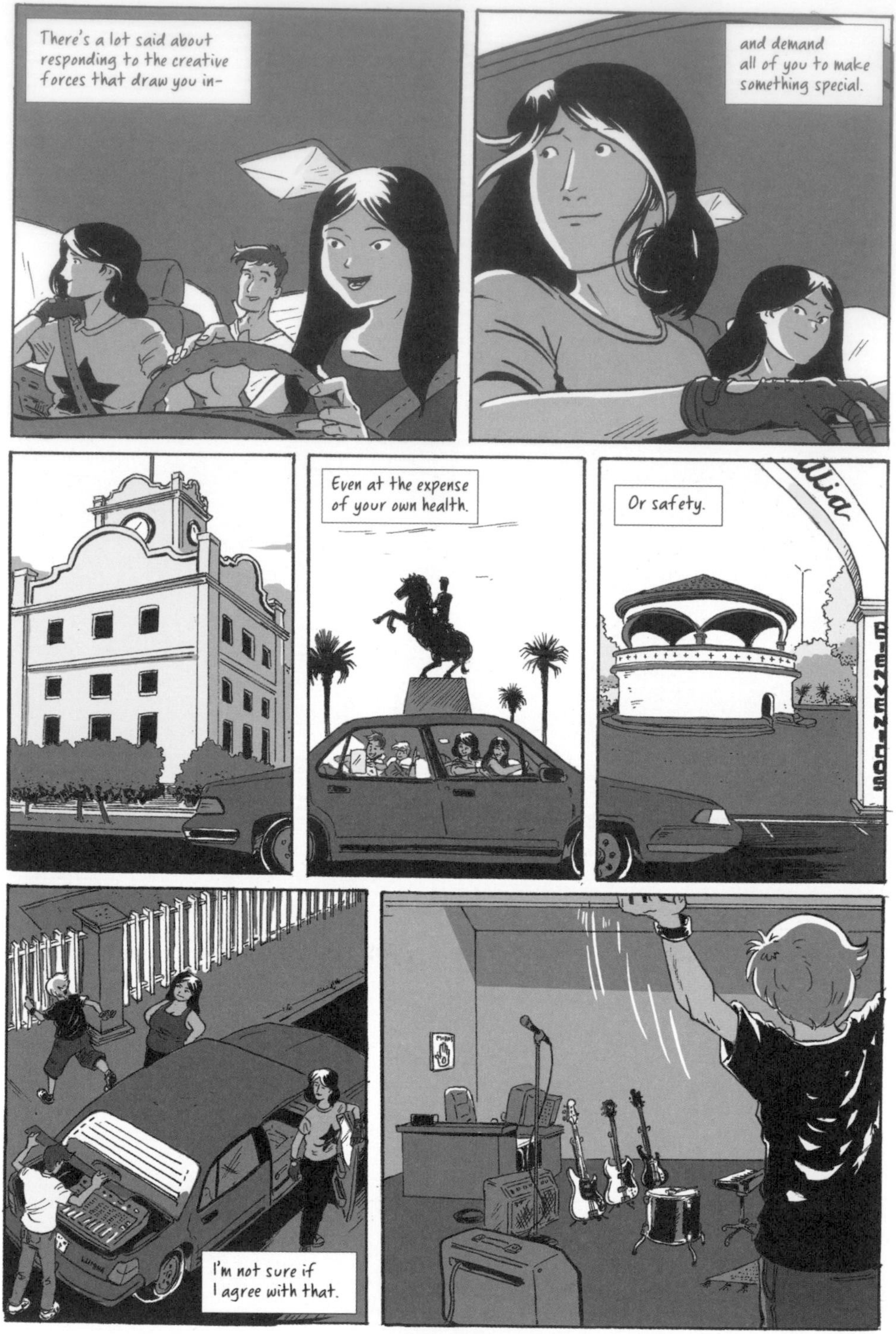
There's a lot said about responding to the creative forces that draw you in-
and demand all of you to make something special.
Even at the expense of your own health.
Or safety.
I'm not sure if I agree with that.

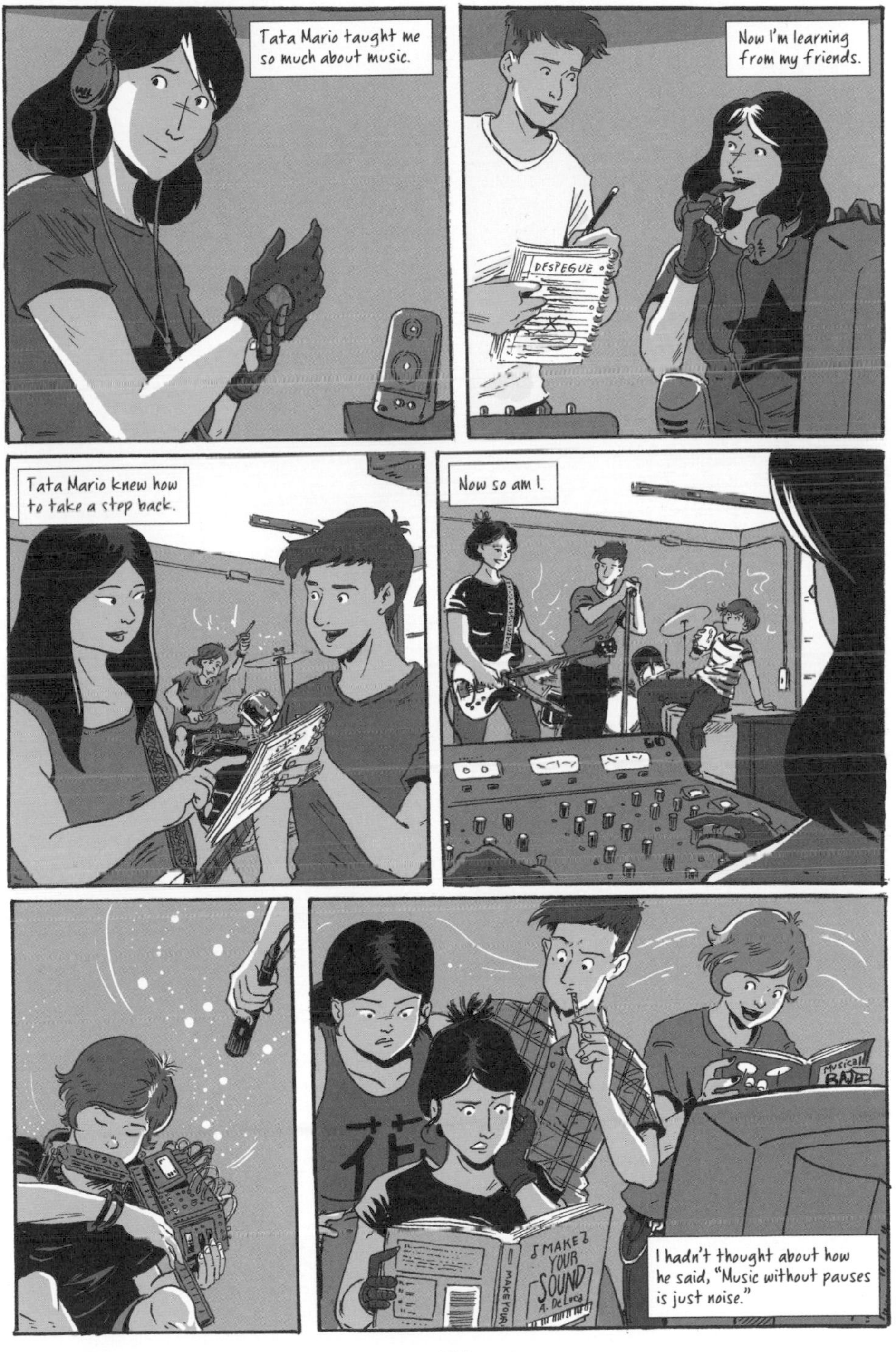

Tata Mario taught me so much about music.
Now I'm learning from my friends.
DESPEGUE
Tata Mario knew how to take a step back.
Now so am I.
MAKE YOUR SOUND
A. De Luca
Musical
I hadn't thought about how he said, "Music without pauses is just noise."

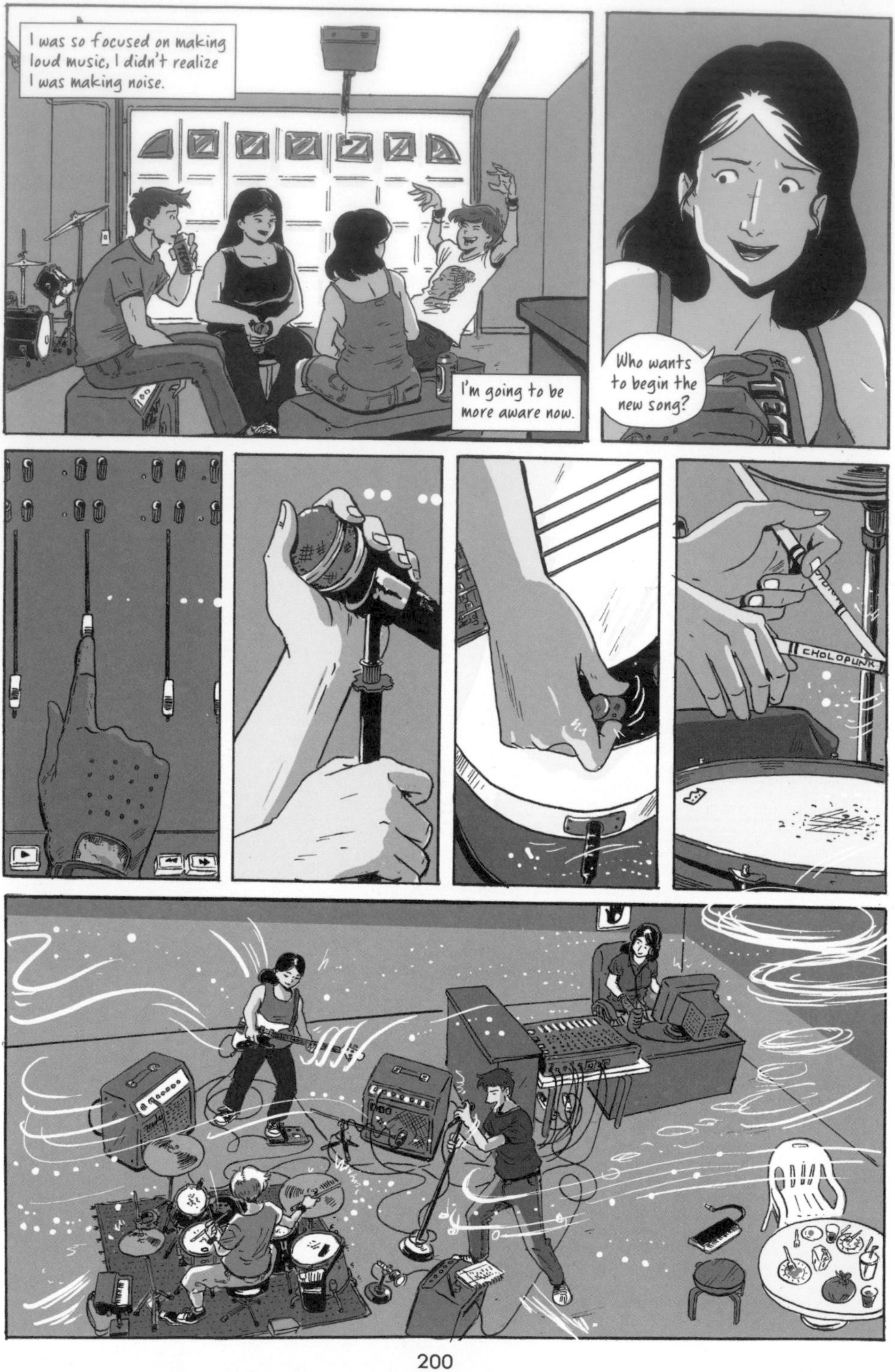
I was so focused on making loud music, I didn't realize I was making noise.
I'm going to be more aware now.
Who wants to begin the new song?
CHOLOPUNK

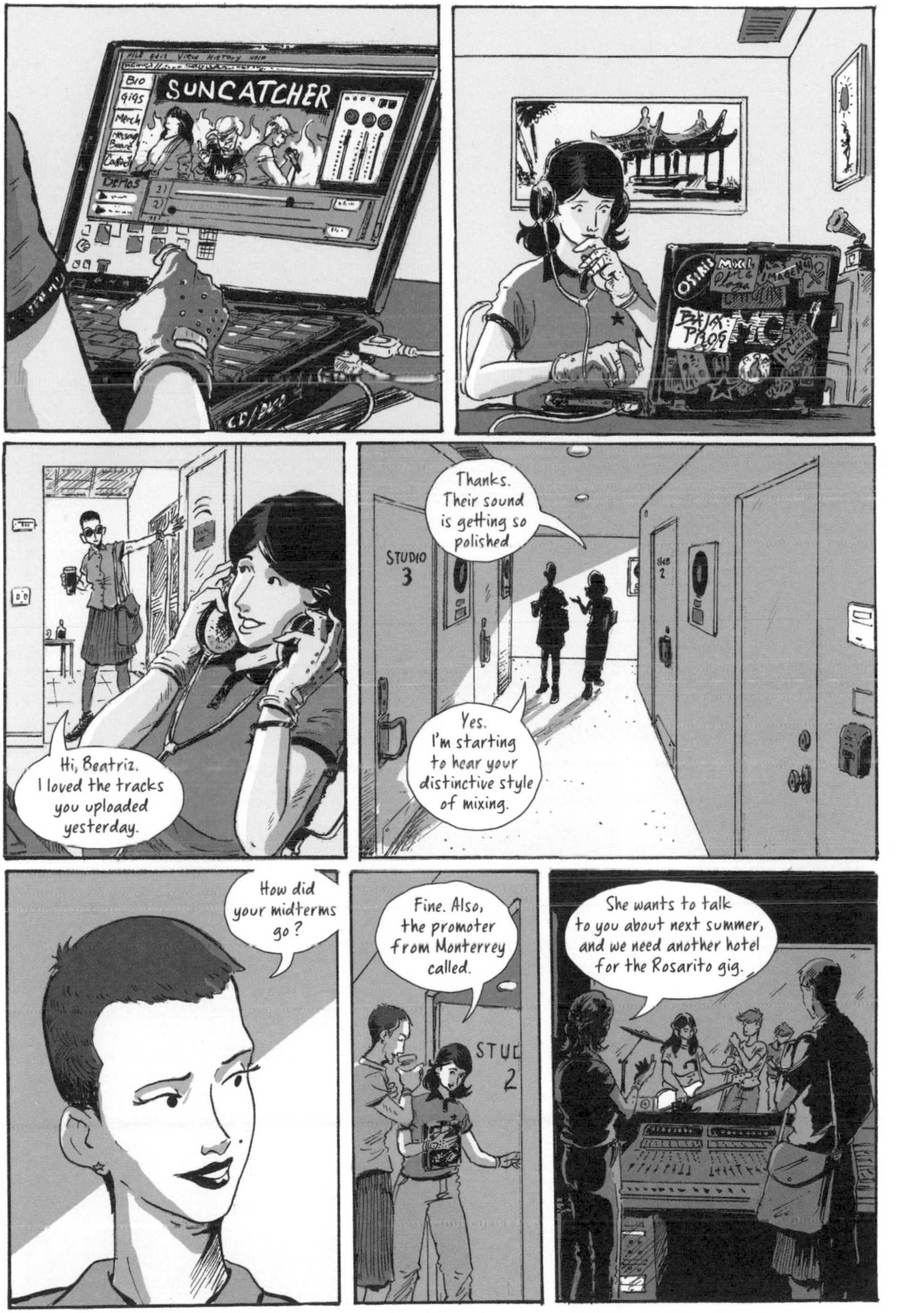
SUNCATCHER
Bio
gigs
Merch
DEMOS
OSIRIS
STUDIO 3
Thanks. Their sound is getting so polished
Yes. I'm starting to hear your distinctive style of mixing.
Hi, Beatriz. I loved the tracks you uploaded yesterday.
How did your midterms go?
Fine. Also, the promoter from Monterrey called.
She wants to talk to you about next summer, and we need another hotel for the Rosarito gig.

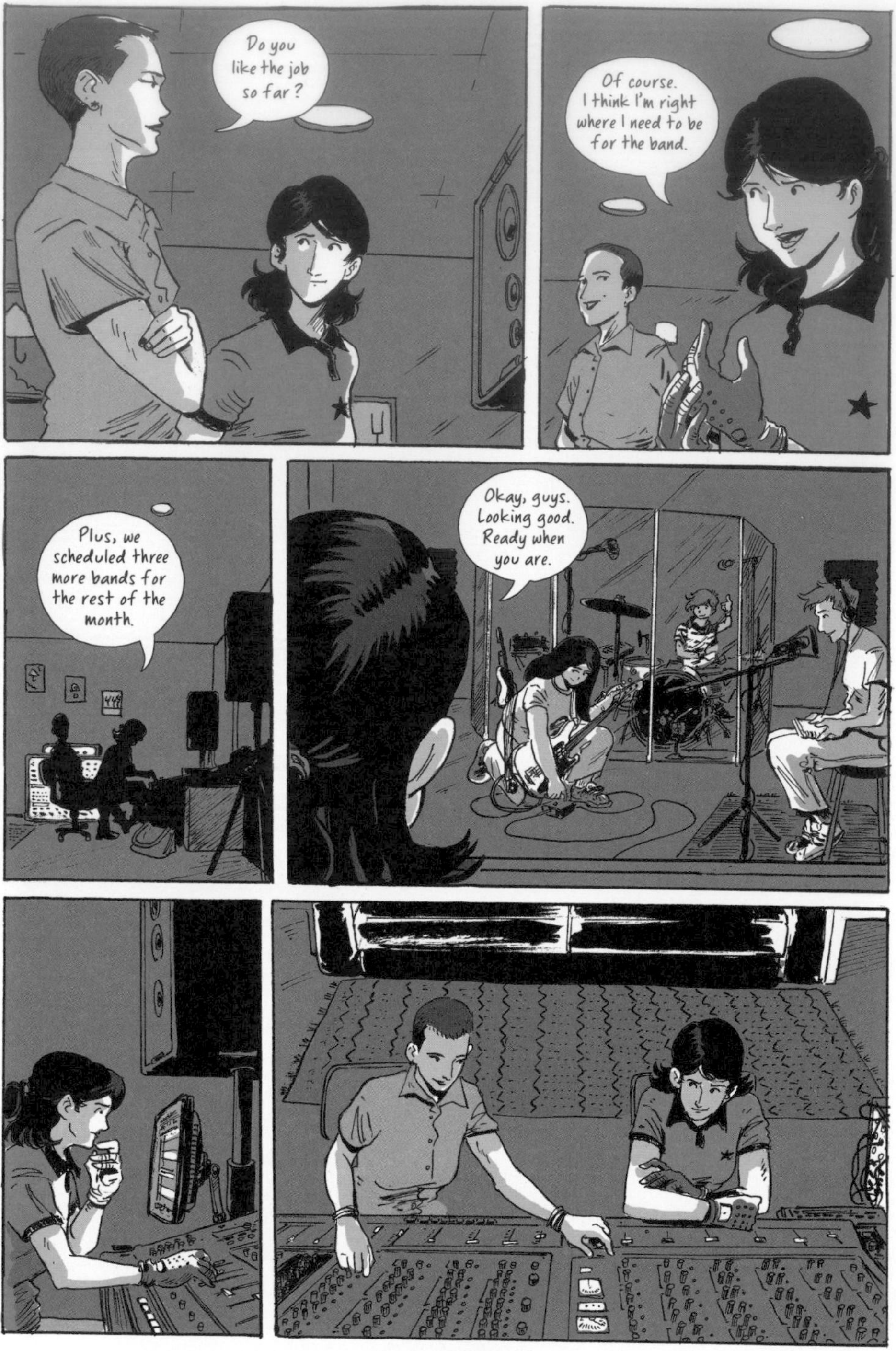
Do you like the job so far?
Of course. I think I'm right where I need to be for the band.
Plus, we scheduled three more bands for the rest of the month.
Okay, guys. Looking good. Ready when you are.

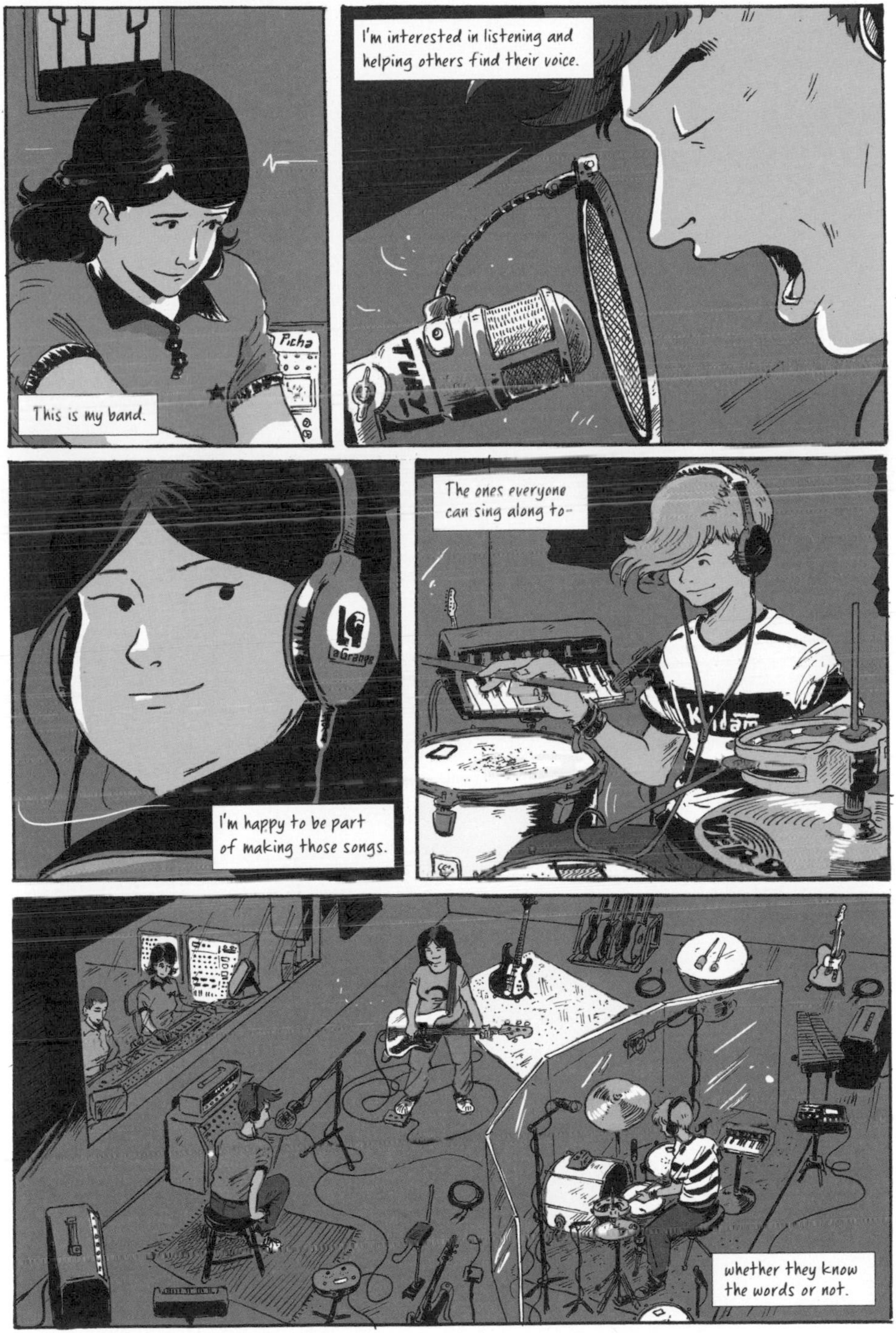
This is my band.
I'm interested in listening and helping others find their voice.
I'm happy to be part of making those songs.
The ones everyone can sing along to-
whether they know the words or not.

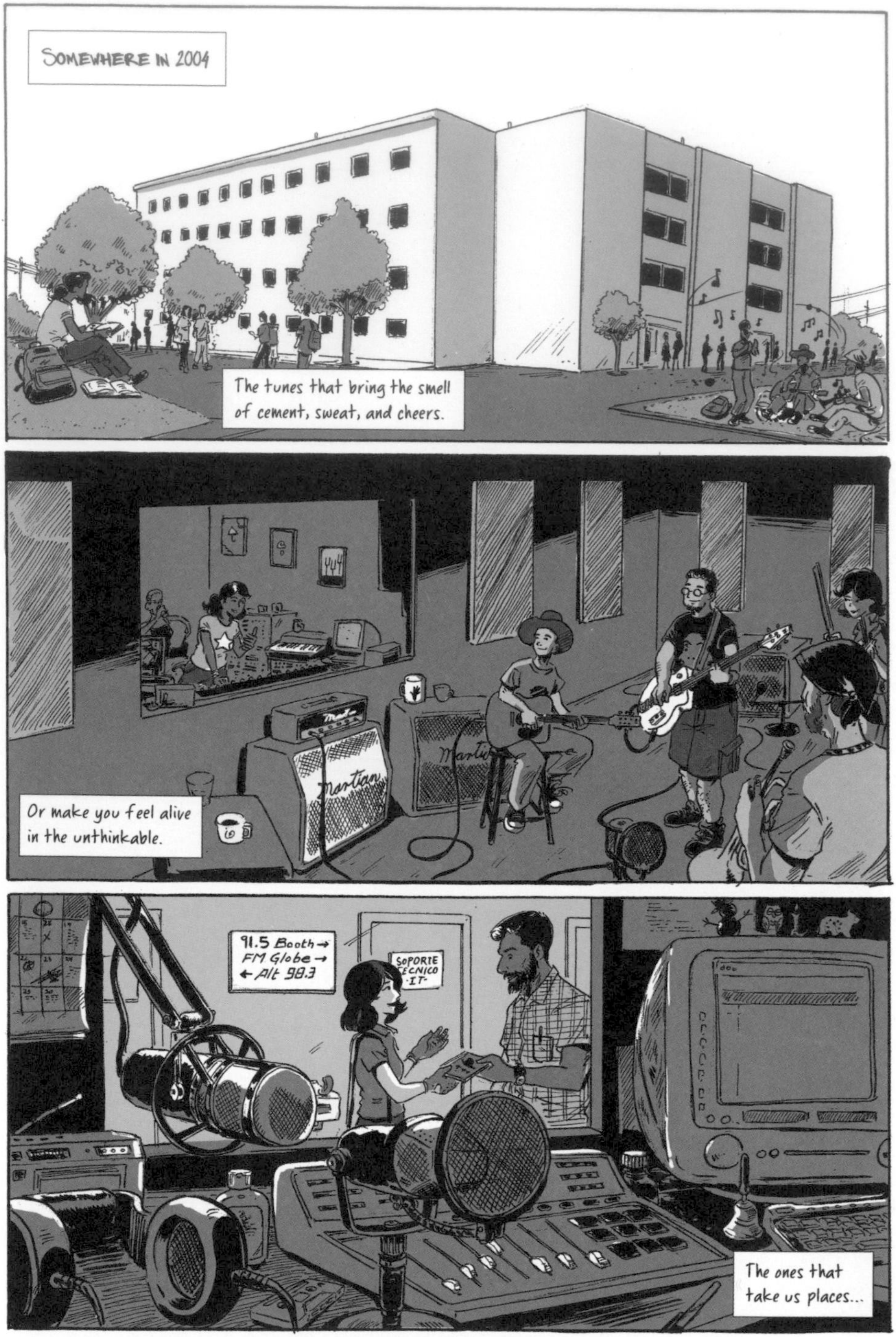
SOMEWHERE IN 2004
The tunes that bring the smell of cement, sweat, and cheers.
Or make you feel alive in the unthinkable.
91.5 Booth →
FM Globe →
← Alt 98.3
SOPORTE
The ones that take us places...

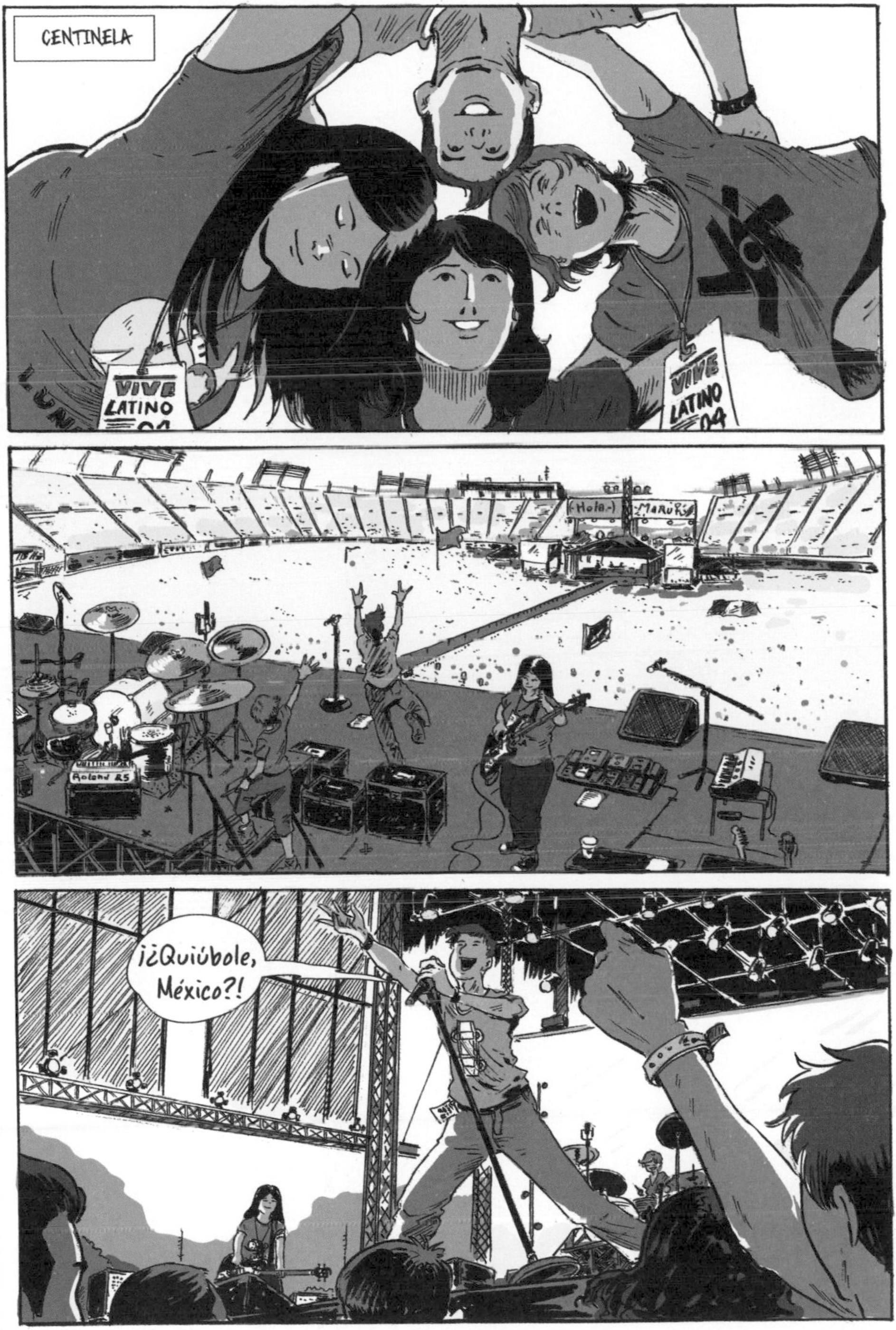
CENTINELA
VIVE LATINO
VIVE LATINO 04
Hola
Roland
¡¿Quiúbole, México?!

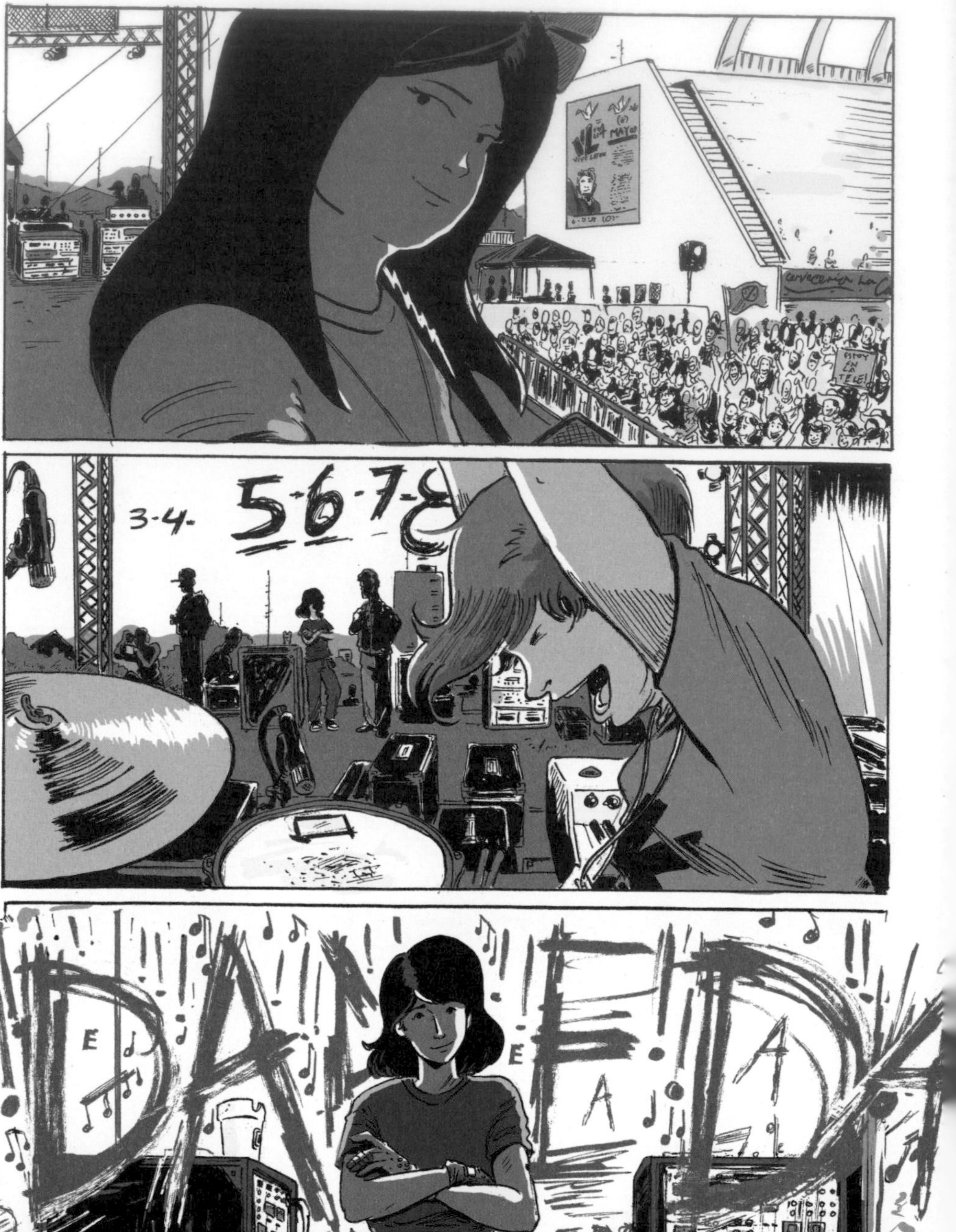
3-4-
5-6-7-8

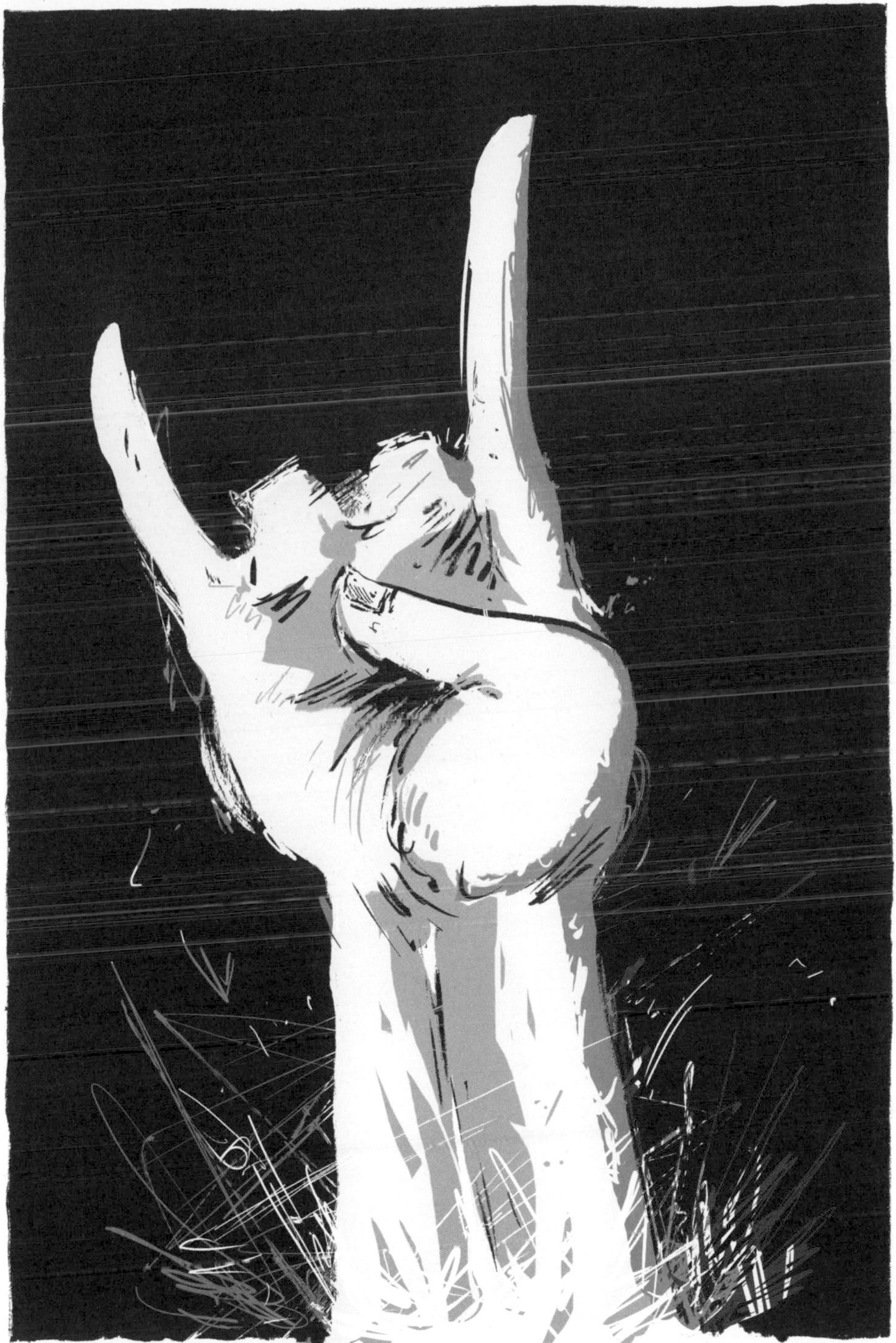

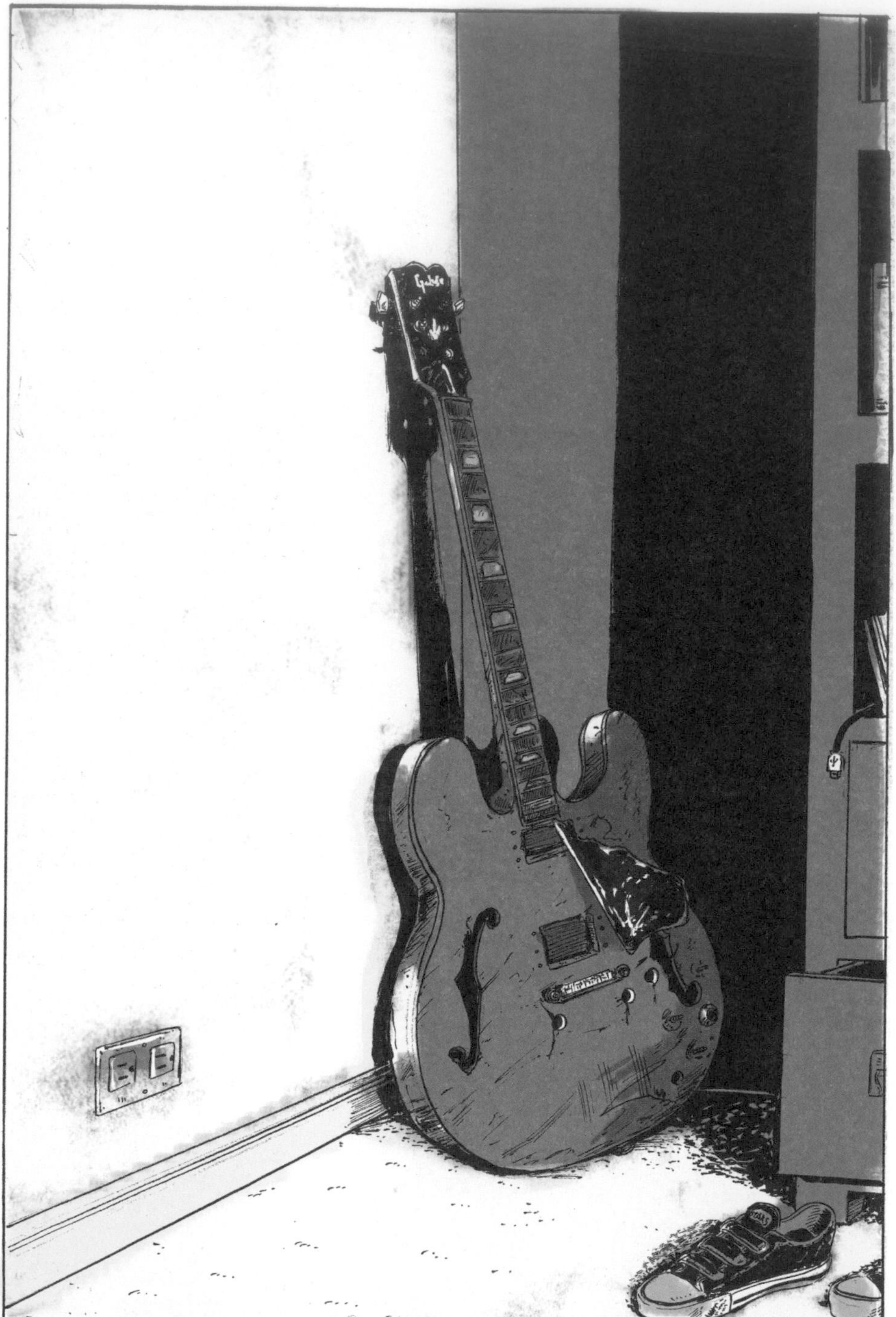

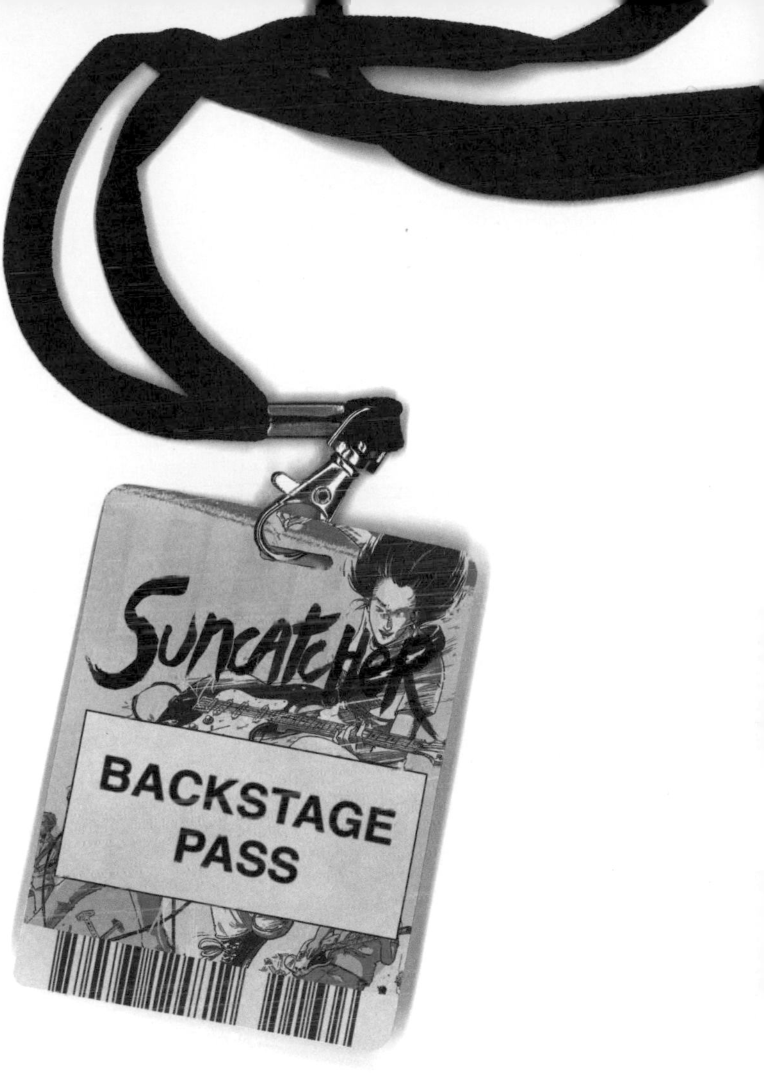
Suncatcher
BACKSTAGE PASS

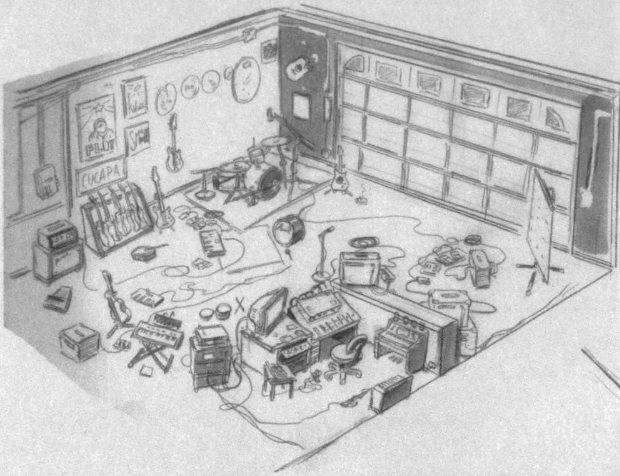

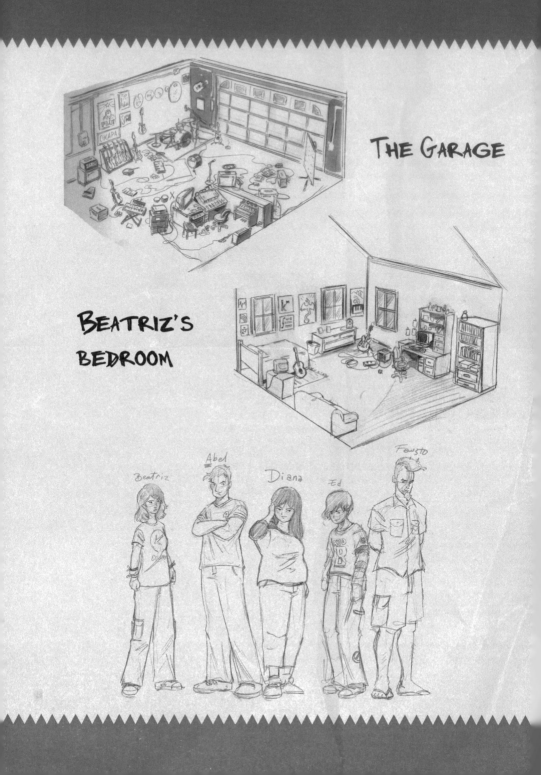

THE GARAGE

BEATRIZ'S BEDROOM

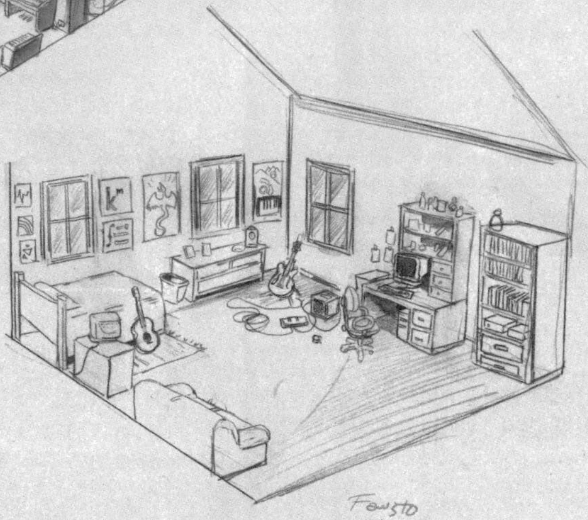

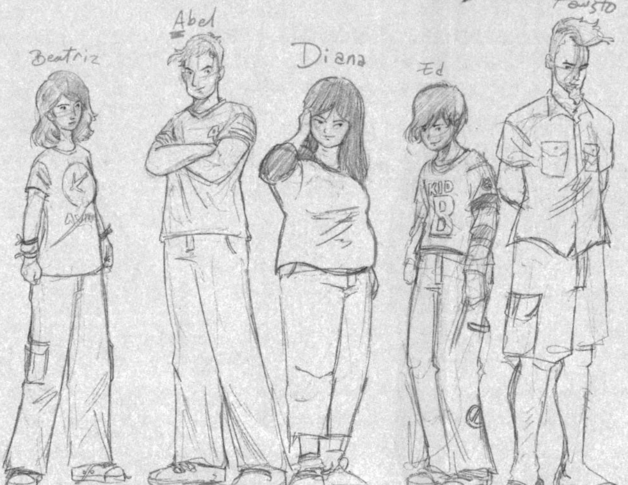
Beatriz
Abel
Diana
Ed
Fausto

AUTHOR'S NOTE

Suncatcher started simple: I wanted to make a comic about music, and I wanted a reason to draw instruments. Mostly guitars.

In the beginning of 2008, I didn't have a story. I had a few plot elements, but nothing specific. During a road trip, I committed to the idea of an enchanted guitar and the musician who would break that spell. I thought I could build something from that. I filled pages with concepts and themes rather than a story arc. It was an incoherent start, but eventually I had a beginning, middle, and end.

The script developed little by little until I found the story I wanted to tell. By talking to musicians and enthusiasts, the story was set in my hometown, Mexicali, during the music scene of the early 2000s. It turned into a story about songwriting, professional aspirations, and personal responsibilities. *Suncatcher* became about Beatriz and her relationships with other musicians.

It took more than seven years to discover all the characters. By 2015, I used my notes and interviews to put together a story that felt sincere. As I continued to show friends what I had, I listened to their advice. Every time I would get stuck, I'd turn to them, and sure enough, they would either reaffirm my choices or help me make better ones. Much like an album, this comic wouldn't have come together without the contributions of several talented artists.

I spent the last months of 2017 and the first half of 2018 producing *Suncatcher*. From pencils to digital lettering, the comic that started as an excuse to draw guitars turned into a dream project, set in a time and place where I developed my love for music. *Suncatcher* turned into my opportunity to show Mexicali to readers. It became a reminder that what makes it a wonderful place is its residents. It was my chance to talk about things I value.

Beatriz's journey is the most personal story I have written to date. I wish I could sum up *Suncatcher*'s over-a-decade-long voyage in a concise manner, but much like the process of putting this book together, I would leave a lot of things out. So I'll go with this: It has been a dream come true, and it couldn't have happened without the support and help of family, friends, and of course, Mexicali and music.

Thank you.

ACKNOWLEDGMENTS

Most special thank you to my family and friends, the whole family Pimienta and the whole family Garcia for their support and influence. Particularly my immediate family: Maria Eugenia, Fatima, Jose Mario, and Jose Maria Pimienta.

To my dearest ones: Vera, Tury, Chris, and Picha for letting me be in their band. Kristen Gish for all her support and feedback.

Mara, Chely, Carlos, David, Caro, Faister, Ana Bertha, Joss, Julie, Tony, Jessica, Colunga, Nayeli, Dany, Pamela, Rene, Chelsea, Mariana, Angelina, Andres, Argentina, Mario Vilchis, Anabel, Ema Karen, and Mare for being there during the making of this book and having a strong influence on the story I wanted to tell about the city where we grew up.

Whitney Leopard for believing in this book and helping me navigate the logistics of turning my idea into a reality. Her editorial input made all the difference. And thank you to Gina Gagliano and Patrick Crotty for helping to bring this story to life at RH Graphic.

Kel McDonald, Kara Leopard, Lisa Dosson, Francisco Guerrero, and Neleuz DG for being morally and artistically supportive. Rhiannon Rasmussen-Silverstein for all her prepress assistance and patience during the making of the Kickstarter edition of this book. Nate Peikos and Blambot for the fonts. Dan Downing for helping me with the video for the Kickstarter campaign and always being enthusiastic about making art. Tabula Rasa for lending a song to the Kickstarter campaign and for being influential musicians. El Dorado Printshop and Embroidery for their help in the Kickstarter campaign, and in particular to Beto Nes for all his art across Mexicali.

For their contribution with interviews about the Mexicali music scene, thank you to Neleuz, Rocio Chavez, Chely Mosqueda, Koko (Eduardo Rodriguez Baldas), Cholopunk Delinkuanxia (Ernesto Yañez Carrillo), Pablo Mérida, Skaren Martinez, Meggan Amos, Kristen Gish, Cecil Castellucci, Gera Montoya, and Angelina de Luca.

Some of the most inspiring local bands were Chelsea, Chapulines, Lencería, Requiem, Kinkinervia, Mexican Deal, Donnie Brasco, Uno Menos, Dulce Señor, Panic!, Madre Mostaza, In Site, Dulcinea, No Moral, Lusid, Cast, Tabula Rasa, Los Martes, Arsenal, Los García, Barra Brava, Ella Tiene Dos Androides, Letters from Readers, Todo Mal, Activistas Del Amor, Dead Stanleys, and a band my friends and I only heard once during a show that was being canceled as it was starting. They didn't introduce themselves, but as we were escorted out, we asked for their name and they just yelled "Cabeza de Monda," which we were pretty sure was fake. We never heard you again, but what we heard was *amazing*. I sincerely hope you're still making music.

Big and special thank you to my grandparents, Jose María Pimienta, Guadalupe Rendón, Mario Armando García, and Hortencia García. Their stories kept my imagination ignited.

A big thank you to all friends who contributed in one way or another, some via Kickstarter and others with a solid and encouraging cheer: Olivia, Ruth, Lulu, Tita, Martha, Diana, Nanda, Beto, Market, Raul Díaz, Hunter and Alice, Madison Carroll, Rosendo Cázares, Will, Amanda and J White, Lauren Stewart, Cari Jacobs, Guillermo Lizarraga, Luis Eduardo Oliver, Alejando Espinoza, Van Jensen, Jarrett Williams, Tom Lyle, Andrea Bell, the Hornsby family, the Seidman family, Shawn Strider, Fernanda Martinez, Lisa, Roger, Carl, Abe and everyone at Model Drawing Collective, Kaitlyn and the Rosenberg family, Brian R., Talia Ellis, Drew, Melissa, Kari, Lauren, Corrine, Marissa Mozek, RJ, Paul, and every other Kickstarter backer.

THANK YOU. THANK YOU. THANK YOU.

NOTES

THROUGHOUT THE BOOK, THERE ARE EASTER EGGS REFERRING TO MEXICALI AND PUNK ROCK CULTURE.

PAGE 1: "And for this gift I feel blessed" from "Smells Like Teen Spirit" by Nirvana.

PAGE 3: Reference to Pink Floyd's *Pulse*, The Beatles' *Abbey Road* and *Yellow Submarine*, and Nirvana, Guns N' Roses, Metallica, Queen, Sonic Youth, Café Tacvba, Enanitos Verdes, Zurdok's "Luna" music video, La Ley, and Maldita Vecindad's *El Circo*.

PAGE 4: Reference to Resorte's "Aqui no es donde."

PAGE 5: Nirvana, Loga, Axel Rose, Café Tacvba, El Circo, Caifanes, Lexington Field, El Rosario Sinaloa, La Place Calafia. April 8, 1994, is an important day for grunge fans, as it was when Kurt Cobain was found dead at his Seattle home.

PAGE 6: Reference to Radiohead's *Kid A*.

PAGE 7: Cast is a Mexicali band.

PAGE 14: Canal 66 is a Mexicali television station.

PAGE 15: October 2, 1968, is remembered for the Tlatelolco tragedy in Mexico City. October 2, 1995, is when Oasis released *(What's the Story) Morning Glory?*

PAGE 16: Mexicali's Nuestra Señora de Guadalupe Cathedral.

PAGE 17: June 16, 1997, is when Radiohead's *OK Computer* was released.

PAGE 20: "On a Friday" is a Radiohead reference. "Florecita Rockera" is a song by the Colombian band Aterciopelados. Madre Mostaza was a Mexicali punk rock band.

PAGE 21: Boulevard Benito Juárez. "Eits" is a form of "Hey." "¿Quiúbole?" is a form of "What's up?"

PAGE 29: "Gimme tha Power" is a song from Molotov's debut album.

PAGE 32: Mazatlán is a city in the state of Sinaloa. El Sinaloense music sheet by Severiano Briseño.

PAGE 34: Silverchair's "Anthem for the Year 2000." María Sabina shirt. 7500 1476 is the barcode for Cigarros delicados.

PAGE 35: Zurdok's third album, *Maquillaje*, was released on June 7, 2001. Logo on shirt is a reference to the band Jumbo.

PAGE 37: Ed wears a Pegamentos Industriales Galileo shirt. It's an industrial glue company in Mexicali.

PAGE 42: Boulevard Lázaro Cárdenas and its monument.

PAGE 43: The Fender Telecaster is similar to the one used in the 1986 film *Crossroads*. The poster references Águilas de Mexicali, a local baseball team.

PAGE 44: "En el Mero—Mero Calor" means "the very, very heavy heat." 91X radio station poster.

PAGE 46: La Abeja is a convenience store in Mexicali. Cheve is slang for beer.

PAGE 47: Arsenal, Panic, and Donnie Brasco are Mexicali bands. CBTIS is a Mexicali technical school. The Hecho en Mexico symbol is altered to say Hecho en Mexicali.

PAGE 48: Rococo Graves is a reference to Mexico City's punk rock band Panteon Rococo.

PAGE 50: Six is a convenience-store chain. DADGBE is a type of guitar tuning. La Chelsea is a Mexicali punk ska band.

PAGE 51: Lyrics to "Amor Instantáneo Ramen" by La Chelsea.

PAGE 56: Reference to Monumento de los Pioneros.

PAGE 57: "Punk rock, mi vida está bien" is the slogan of Mexicali band La Chelsea. Abel wears a Thrice *Identity Crisis* shirt. Ed wears a Weezer shirt. Diane wears a Héroes del Silencio shirt.

PAGE 59: "Corn chips gorros" is a reference to the corn chip brand Rancheritos. El Tri is a Mexican rock band.

PAGE 61: Beatriz is eating churros locos, a popular snack.

PAGE 64: Villafontana and Calafia are Mexicali neighborhoods. UABC is Baja California's state college. L. Montejano Road is a street.

PAGE 65: Diana wears a Caifanes shirt. Caifanes is a popular Mexican rock group.

PAGE 66: Beatriz and Abel's conversation is a reference to the song "The Man Who Sold the World" by David Bowie and covered by Nirvana.

PAGE 75: The posters in Beatriz's room make reference to many bands and to Mexicali's children's museum, Sol del Niño.

PAGE 78: Beatriz wears a shirt in reference to Guns N' Roses's *Appetite for Destruction* album.

PAGE 83: A view of Mexicali's civic center, movie theater, UABC Medicine's facility, Comercial Mexicana department store, Plaza Fiesta mall, and the bullfighting arena also used as a concert venue.

PAGE 85: Odisea 2002 was the name of Jumbo and Zurdok's national tour together in 2002.

PAGE 94: Ed eats carnitas rojas, which is a common dish in Mexicali Chinese food.

PAGE 96: Lenceria was a Mexicali rock band.

PAGE 110: Fiestas del Sol is the city fair.

PAGE 111: Beethoven's Ninth Symphony "Ode to Joy."

NOTES (CONTINUED)

PAGE 115: "No te dejes caer" is a song by Mexicali punk rock band Arsenal.

PAGE 122: Proconsa is a hardware store. "Morra" is slang for a girl. "Naco" is slang and a derogatory term for someone of low class or someone who behaves in an unruly manner. Beatriz wears a Felix the Cat shirt.

PAGE 135: At a Fiestas del Sol event. "Volcano's nerve" is a reference to Caifanes's album *El Nervio del Volcán.*

PAGE 146: "Wednesday (2 x 1)" is a reference to a policy in Mexicali movie theaters when tickets are half off every Wednesday.

PAGE 153: "Blistered hands" is a reference to the song "El Cachanilla." Beatriz wears a Requiem band shirt. Pemex is the name of the Mexican petrol company.

PAGE 154: Reference to Marshall Amps. A reference to Zurdok's "Luna" music video.

PAGE 157: The building number refers to Daft Punk's film *Interstella 5555.*

PAGE 195: Abel wear a Trio shirt.

PAGE 197: La Ley's album *Invisible.* Oasis's *(What's the Story) Morning Glory?* Rage Against the Machine poster.

PAGE 198: They pass by Mexicali landmarks: the old Brewery, the Vicente Guerrero monument, and Mariachi Plaza.

PAGE 201: A framed image of Mexicali's Chinesca monument, which celebrates the sisterhood between Mexicali and China.

PAGE 204: UABC's Engineering campus.

PAGE 205: El Centinela is the name of Mexicali's mountain.

PAGE 206: Vive Latino 2004 poster.

SKETCHES

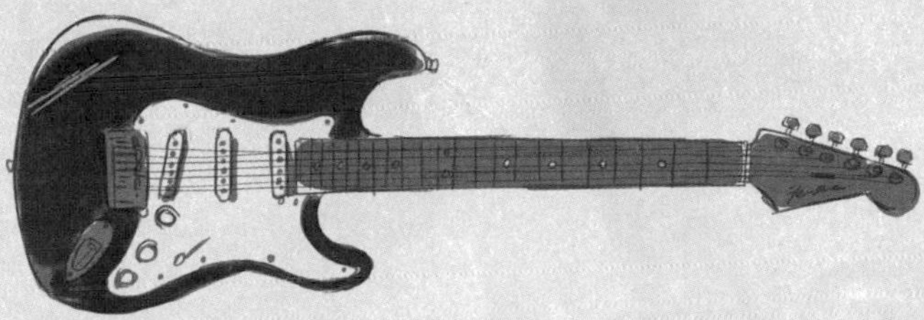

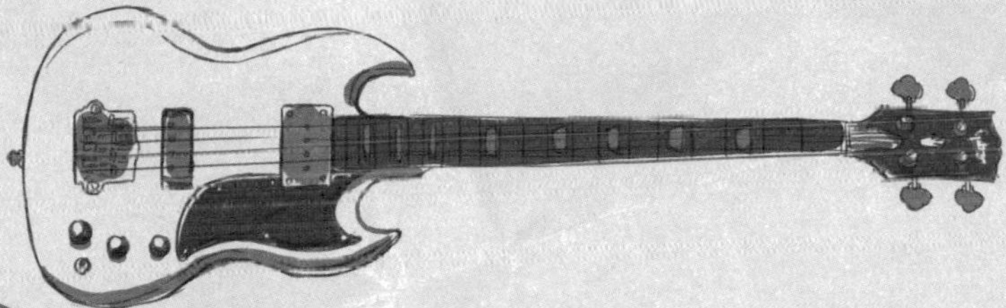

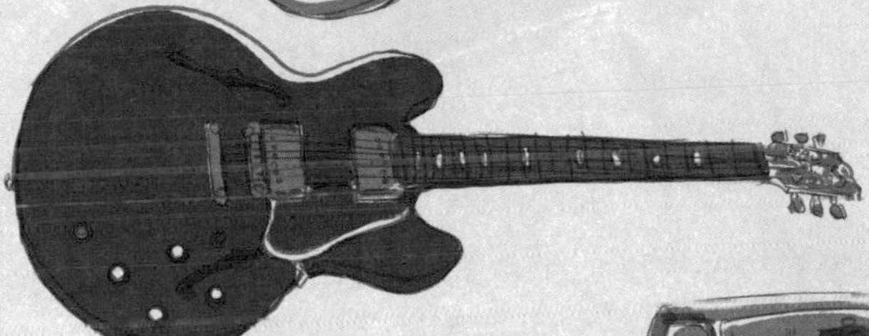

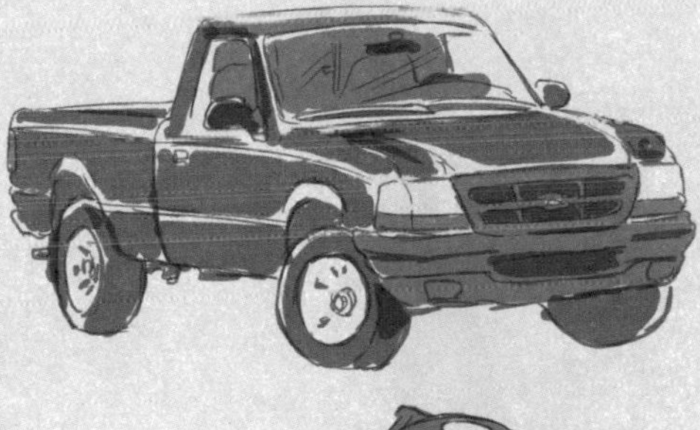

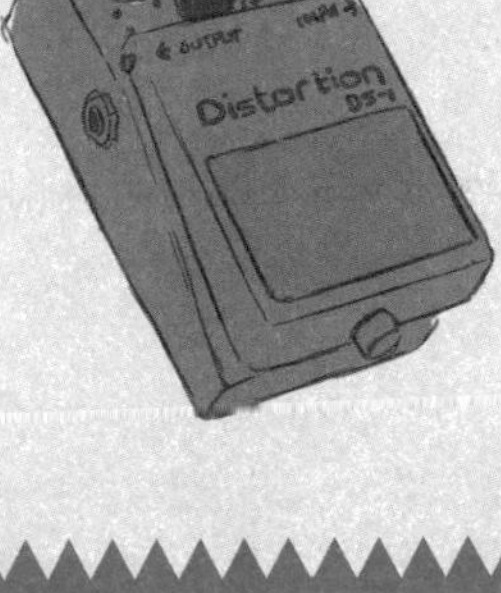
Distortion
DS-1

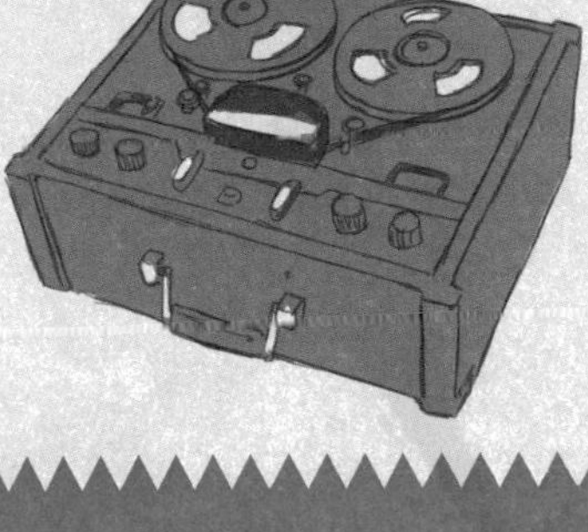

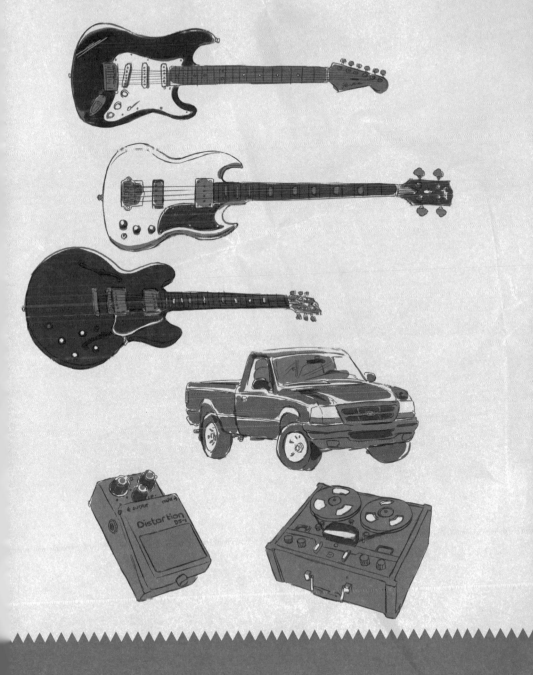

MEXICALI: CREST AND GEOGRAPHY

The Mexicali crest was designed in 1968 by Sergio Ocampo Ramirez. It was chosen by Municipal President Jose Maria Rodriguez Merida on April 9, 1968.

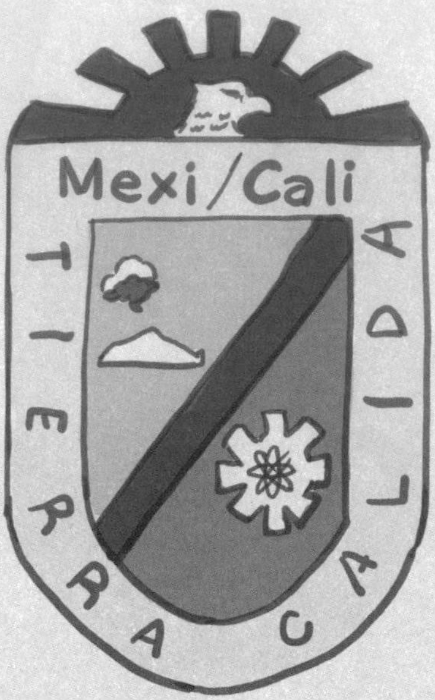
Mexi/Cali
TIERRA CALIDA

Meanings behind the crest design:

The red strip represents the Colorado River.

The blue represents the waters of the Gulf of California.

The ocher is the desert.

The cotton bud represents the fields of cotton in the valleys.

The mountain is El Centinela, a natural boundary between the United States and Mexico and a traveler's guide.

The gear with the atom represents Mexicali's science and industrial developments.

Slogan: Tierra Calida, which means Warm Land, a reference to both the region's weather and its reputation for warmhearted people.

Name: Mexi/Cali, which comes from a combination of Mexico and California.

The red sun references the region's weather.

The eagle is a reference to the Aztec eagle, symbolizing the origins of some of its population.

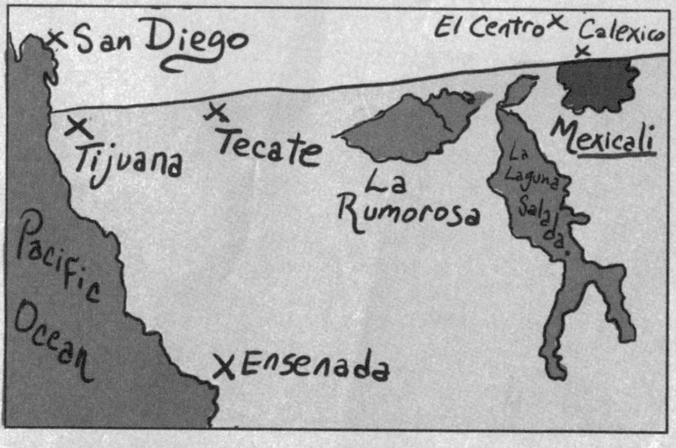
San Diego
El Centro
Calexico
Tijuana
Tecate
Mexicali
La Rumorosa
La Laguna Salada.
Pacific Ocean
Ensenada

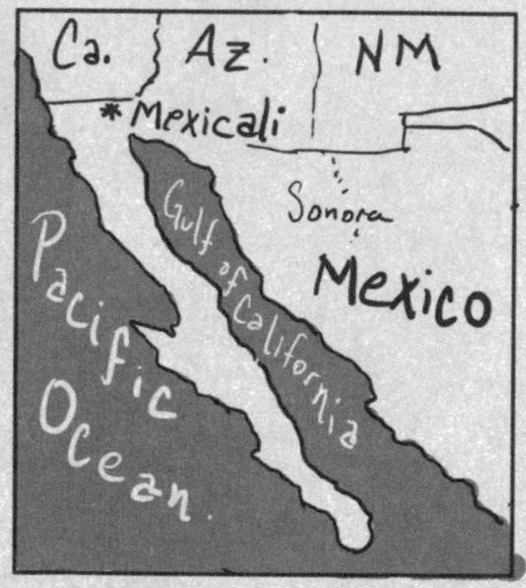
Ca.
Az.
NM
Mexicali
Sonora
Gulf of California
Mexico
Pacific Ocean.

Jose Pimienta grew up in Mexicali and studied sequential art at the Savannah College of Art and Design. He now lives in Los Angeles, making comics and storyboards. He still loves discovering music.

𝕏 @joepi
📷 @thejoepi
📘 @joepiworks
josepimienta.com

THE SUMMER 2020 LIST

CRABAPPLE TROUBLE
By Kaeti Vandorn

Life isn't easy when you're an apple.

Callaway and Thistle must figure out how to work together—with delicious and magical results.

Young Chapter Book

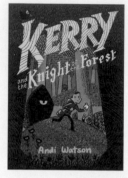

KERRY AND THE KNIGHT OF THE FOREST
By Andi Watson

Kerry needs to get home!

To get back to his parents, Kerry gets lost in a shortcut. He will have to make tough choices and figure out who to trust—or remain lost in the forest . . . forever.

Middle Grade

STEPPING STONES
By Lucy Knisley

Jen did not want to leave the city.

She did not want to move to a farm.

And Jen definitely did not want to get two new "sisters."

Middle Grade

SUNCATCHER
By Jose Pimienta

Beatriz loves music—more than her school, more than her friends—and she won't let anything stop her from achieving her dreams.

Even if it means losing everything else.

Young Adult

FIND US ONLINE AT @RHKIDSGRAPHIC AND RHKIDSGRAPHIC.COM